Diving Catch

Also by Gregory Saur

Royal Pains and Angels in the Outhouse
Otherworld: Orcish Delight (as G. D. Saur)
Stuck in the Past (with Jack Irish)
Panterror! The Epic Babysitting Adventures of Rachel Pugsley
The Pond Scum Gang
Soccer Star

Diving Catch

Gregory Saur

Saur
&
Saur

Saur & Saur

Published by Saur & Saur

Diving Catch

First Hardcover Printing

2018

Printed in the United States of America

ISBN-13 (hc): 978-0-692-80648-7

Cover Design by R.S.
Copyright © 2018 Saur & Saur
Cover images are used with permission.
Boy face: iStock.com/MShep2
Baseball player: Shutterstock.com/MW47
Baseball Silhouette: Shutterstock.com/MW47

Chapter 1

Devon watched the man approach through hooded eyes. His shoulders slouched, he stood casually on the sidewalk minding his own business while pretending to be waiting for the bus . . . but all his focus was on the man.

Inside his thin chest, Devon's heart pounded fast and furious. Each beat sounded like a baseball smacking into the mitt of glove.

Other than the man, both sides of the street were empty. Still, it felt as if there was no place to go. Devon felt trapped in plain sight. Ordinarily a guy walking his way was no big deal. Devon could just ignore him, shoot him a glare to scare him off, or even engage in a little chitchat. But this was no ordinary man. This man meant business.

Birds chirping in a small juniper tree behind Devon sang a merry tune, a soundtrack for his impending demise.

Preston Whiteside was coming his way. There was no ducking the well-known drug dealer this time.

A car screeched to a halt on the next block, causing Devon to jump. Hastily he wiped his sweaty palm on the back of his low-hanging jeans, hiding his nerves.

He risked a quick peek at Preston and quickly averted his eyes, feigning interest in the pavement.

The man kept coming straight for him.

Few kids ever dared to look Preston Whiteside in the eyes. It was best not to draw his attention. Now, just four houses away, the man decked out in a pinstriped suit acted as he was on a jaunty stroll. His hips rolled with every step and his arms swung merrily at his sides. A bright smile turned up his lips just below his pencil-thin mustache.

Never once did Preston look at Devon . . . but the boy knew. Nobody else was in sight. Preston was coming for him.

Swallowing, Devon looked again. As he did so, a feeling of dread filled his belly.

Dark, tightly curled hair hung over Preston's forehead. Thick with grease, it had sheen from the afternoon sun. More hair bounced off the back of his neck as he walked. It was shaved short on the sides and gave the effect of a poodle resting on the man's head after it had fallen into a tar pit.

Picturing that absurd image gave Devon a little courage, but not much. If he were smart, he would've taken off running by now. That would be his grandma's advice.

Thinking of his grandma brought out Devon's stubbornness. He'd just told her the other day he wasn't a baby anymore.

To prove it, Devon turned away and jammed both hands in his pockets, nearly shoving his jeans down past his waist. Quickly he yanked them back up. Shame warmed his face. Still, a bit of defiance crept in.

Devon's grandma had been riding him for days. Playing outside was too dangerous for a small boy like him, she kept telling him, especially alone. Did he want to end up like Corey Strider?

Thoughts of Corey didn't help. Corey Strider had been Devon's friend for years, since the first grade. It had all ended the month before. Corey was caught selling drugs after school one day and had been shipped off to juvie. At age twelve, he was behind bars.

Devon wasn't like Corey. Corey had always wanted to make it big—he used to brag all the time about how he was going to get rich quick and bust out of the neighborhood before high school. Devon had stopped seeing much of Corey months before the arrest. They had a falling out last summer ... shortly after Corey had gotten a visit from Preston Whiteside. After that, Corey had changed.

Still hidden in his pocket, Devon squeezed his right hand into a fist. Corey had wanted Devon to come with him to see Preston last summer. That had ended in an argument. And a few months later Corey had been shoved in the back of a police car; Devon hadn't seen him since.

Suddenly Devon turned away from Preston and started walking fast in the opposite direction. He'd been a fool. Grandma was right. Preston Whiteside was nothing but trouble. Devon had his pride, but he also had his fear. At the moment his fear overcame his pride and told him to get out of there. Fast. Devon wasn't an idiot.

"Hey, boy! You got a minute?" Like his looks, Preston's voice came out smooth and silky. It also demanded attention.

Devon swallowed as he willed his feet to keep moving. He'd been avoiding Preston and his ilk for over two years, ever since his 11th birthday. In his neighborhood, dodging drug dealers was a way of life—you either avoided them or you became one of them.

"Boy, I'm talking to you!" The smooth silky tone developed a nasty edge.

Devon ducked his head and squeezed his eyes shut in frustration. He should've stayed home and done his homework like his grandma wanted. A boy had no chance on the streets alone. He opened his eyes and turned slowly. One of the rules on the streets—you never showed fear. Even though he silently screamed in protest, his pride made him take a step back toward the man.

Preston came to a stop a few feet from Devon. His pearly white teeth sparkled.

"There you go, boy," he nearly purred. "That's some good manners you got there. For a minute I thought you were avoiding me. I mean, you just turned right around as soon as I reached you. You ain't scared of me, are you?"

Devon frowned. "Nah, I'm just late for, uh, home." He forced himself to look the taller man in the eyes. He would show no fear. It would be a mistake.

Preston's smile never wavered, but his eyes narrowed like glass marbles melting. "Is that why you were waiting at the bus stop? Now you're walking back home? That don't make a whole lot of sense, now does it?"

Devon felt his face grow hot. He'd been thinking of taking the bus to the mall . . . just to prove to himself and to his grandma that he could do it by himself. Of course the bus had been late . . . and it had been a stupid plan to begin with.

"I, uh, forgot—"

"Call me 'sir,' boy." Preston's smile vanished suddenly and he sounded dangerous.

Devon's mouth tightened as Preston loomed over him. His fear gave way to anger. Why did grownups have to pick on kids? Why did the police lock up Corey but leave Preston free? It didn't make sense and it wasn't fair.

Then the man suddenly busted out laughing.

"Good grief, boy, you should see your face! I'm only playing!" Shifting his weight, the man reached down and clapped Devon on the shoulder. "You're Devon Horner, aren't you? You're Celia's boy, right?"

Devon bit his lower lip and pulled his hands from his pockets. He wiped them on the front of his shirt. Celia was his mom, all right, at least by birth. He hadn't seen a lick of her in nearly a year, but still bore a scar on his back to remember her by. He barely gave a nod, aware of Preston's hand still resting on his shoulder. It felt like a boulder had crashed down there and threatened to crush him. Or it was a spider ready to inject him with a terrible poison . . . only it wouldn't turn him into Spiderman.

"Look, Devon, it's almost summer. You got a job yet?"

"Uh, no . . . No, sir."

Preston stepped back hearing "sir" and puffed up his chest. Removing his hand from Devon's shoulder, he wiped imaginary dirt from his left sleeve. Then he adjusted his bright red tie. "That's too bad . . . a boy like you could use some money, am I right?"

Devon tried to seem relaxed as he shrugged. It didn't take a solid "D" student to know what was coming.

"Word is, you could be good for me," Preston continued. "You see, people here talk and I listen. You've been recommended to me, boy. I could use a little guy like you."

Devon Horner had just turned thirteen but looked much younger. To a drug dealer, young boys were great tools. Nobody suspected them. His mouth grew dry. Every fiber in his body wanted to run. But it was too late now. To turn coward now would ruin his life. Preston would never let him go and would send people after him to harass and berate him until he caved. That was how it worked. You joined people like Preston, or they crushed you.

"You listening to me, boy?" Preston moved a step closer. "You want a job? Make some good money?"

The sun had risen high overhead; it beat down with little mercy. At times, early May in southeastern Virginia felt like the middle of summer. In the late afternoon, the temperature hovered in the upper eighties. Sweat beaded on Devon's forehead and his underarms were soaked.

He turned his head for a moment and that was when he saw them. Preston had not come alone.

A group of youths, some his age and some older, appeared between the two houses across the street. They had to have come from the next block and had probably been waiting for some time.

Now they sauntered toward Devon like it was all a big coincidence. Devon counted five of them. Two of them he recognized from his middle school.

"N-no, thanks," Devon muttered. He kept his eyes on Preston while keeping the approaching group in his peripheral vision.

"He good, Prest?" called one of the boys. Striding in front like he owned the world, the youth nodded coldly at Devon. This was Lou Owens, an eighth grader at Devon's school. Devon knew all about him.

At one time, back when he was in the seventh grade, Lou starred as the school's running back on the football team. Then one game he'd gotten angry after a bad play and threw his helmet toward the sideline before storming off the field. It'd just missed hitting a referee. As a sixth grader, Devon had been watching that game and would never forget the coach running Lou off the field, screaming at him. Lou had never played another game since.

Surly and quick to anger, Lou now carried the reputation of being the meanest, nastiest boy in school. Kids and even teachers were afraid of him and did their best to leave him alone. Not even grownups wanted to see him mad. Talking to him was like poking a hornets' nest.

Preston licked his lips like he tasted something sour. He crossed his arms and kept his gaze on Devon.

"You boys just wait over there a sec," he said, sounding slightly annoyed. Then he grunted. "Better yet, Lou, come on over and tell little Devon here the benefits of working for me."

Sweat practically poured down Devon's face. His feet were rooted to the sidewalk as he watched Lou eagerly trot across the empty street with a sinking feeling. They were two blocks from Devon's grandma's house.

Devon knew it was no accident that Preston had come this way—he'd been waiting for Devon to be caught by himself. Even if Devon made a break for it, he would have to get past the group on the other side of the street. They stood between him and his grandma's. Preston had planned this meeting well.

"Man, you ready to work for us, small fry?" Lou asked with a deep voice, full of pride. Even though just a year and a half older than Devon, Lou stood a foot taller and had muscles bursting from his sleeveless T-shirt. Gold earrings glinted in his ears and a heavy gold chain hung from his thick neck. Standing next to Preston, he towered over Devon.

"Lou has been a good worker for me," Preston said, sounding like a proud father. "He's done well and is ready to pass down all he knows to somebody willing to learn. You see, we have a job opening perfect for a boy like you." He wiggled his right arm to reveal a shiny gold watch from under his sleeve. "Time's running out, though, so you better make a choice before I go find someone smarter. I'm offering good money for easy work."

Devon gulped. The gold watch was meant to impress him. Lou was supposed to scare him. Both tactics were effective. He was on his own. This was the moment, he knew, that would change his life forever.

"Did Corey tell you about me?" Devon asked, looking up into Preston's cold, dark eyes. Black as midnight, they were like looking into the eyes of a cobra snake.

"Corey?" Preston asked, suddenly confused. "Who's Corey?" He never even blinked.

"You know. Corey. Corey Strider," Devon spoke with his jaw set grimly. Inside, he shivered and felt like throwing up, but he knew he had to stand up to this man. Either that, or forever be his footstool.

When he was a little kid, Devon used to talk a lot . . . and get into trouble a lot because of it. He'd since learned to curb his tongue, mostly. Silence was often the best course of action when faced with trouble. But now that trouble had cornered him, he let his tongue go. If he couldn't use his feet to run, then he would run his mouth.

"Corey was my friend. You made him get in trouble."

Lou sniffed and made to say something, but Preston cleared his throat.

"I don't know who you're talking about, boy," he snapped, clearly losing patience. "But I do know you can use some money. Look at you and how you're dressed. Don't you want money for new shoes?"

Devon licked his lips. *Why hadn't he stayed home?*

Chapter 2

Preston Whiteside had moved into Devon's neighborhood just over two years before. He'd come in a shiny black sports car with dark tinted windows and moved into a small white house at the end of the street, just a block from Devon's grandma. At first all the kids were hugely impressed with the slick-dressing, smooth-talking man with the fancy car. Rumors swirled that he was a former NFL star looking for a quiet place to live.

The older folks were less impressed and eyed him with disdain. "No sports star is coming here looking for quiet," Devon's grandma had replied with a sniff when Devon had reported the rumors. "That man is a former nothing and is looking for nothing but trouble."

At first Preston did appear to be seeking a quiet life. For days he rarely came outside except to climb in his fancy car and drive off to who knew where, but then suddenly he started walking the streets. Each evening, smiling and waving to everyone he met, he made the rounds, chatting with any willing grownup and offering candy to children. When older people gave him the stink eye and told him to move on, he only smiled wider and did as they asked. Devon's grandma was one to give him the stink eye. Preston was there, he kept saying, to help the young people out of the poverty and into hope. Still, Devon was never allowed near him or his candy.

Devon and his grandma lived in a crowded rundown area south of Williams County and, as most people put it, south of prosperity. The houses were all a single story, crowded together, and of similar build. Each had a door in the front, a door in the back, with each door flanked by windows. Most of the doors were red and Devon and Corey, when they were younger, used to laugh and say all the houses looked like faces sticking their tongues out at them.

Devon wasn't laughing now. He felt ready to wet his pants. Desperately he glanced at the houses on either side of him. The doors remained shut and really did appear like tongues sticking out at him—laughing at the jam he was in.

Devon wiggled his toes in his worn sneakers. A hole was forming near his right big toe. They were a generic brand and more gray than white. He hadn't gotten a new pair in over a year.

Lou, on the other hand, rose to his toes, showing off pristine white and gold Nike shoes that had to cost well over $200. It was no secret that in middle school, the right kind of shoes was important if you wanted to be somebody.

At the moment Devon didn't want to be anybody but somebody far from Preston Whiteside and his group of thugs. He knew what Preston wanted him to do . . . be a drug runner or maybe even seller.

The younger and smaller you were, the less the cops bothered you. Corey, roughly the same size as Devon, had been perfect for the job. Only his big mouth and reckless spending had gotten him caught.

Preston Whiteside, claiming to be true to his word, had started a lawn and garden business for the teenagers in the area. After a year, he expanded it for any young boy or girl who wanted cash for work. His business cut the grass for all the houses and didn't charge very much . . . but grew very successful regardless.

Twice police had been called on Preston, but no drugs were ever found on or near him and now he was left alone. Rumors of a secret outside source supplying the drugs to Preston were rampant, but there was no proof. In the meantime, drug use in all the surrounding middle schools and high schools had gone way up.

"I like my shoes just fine," Devon finally said, his jaw tight.

Lou busted out laughing. "No way. I mean, *what are those?*"

Preston chuckled. "Boy, Devon, look. I'm offering you good money. Just come to my place and hear me out. Lou will come too. Here, I'll tell you what." Preston made of show of fetching a large wallet from under his pinstriped jacket and started pulling out green bills.

Devon's eyes bulged, but he found himself shaking his head and inching backward.

"Prest . . ." Lou said, looking up at his boss.

Preston paused and looked down at Devon. "What's the matter?" he snapped, his voice losing all patience. "I'm offering you money right now, boy. You can put it in your pocket and have new shoes on your feet before school tomorrow. Don't you understand me, boy? This is real money!"

"I understand," Devon said, his voice rising. You didn't survive on these streets by being timid or afraid. And that meant you weren't afraid to run when you had to. "I understand you took my best friend Corey and got him in jail. Now you don't even know his name anymore! You're a fink!"

Devon turned and ran.

"Hey! You stop now, boy!" Preston shouted. He looked to be in his early thirties, but flab hung from his light brown face and his suit hid a round belly. He didn't look ready to give chase.

Lou, on the other hand, licked his lips in anticipation.

"Get him," Preston hissed. "Go on!" he shouted.

"Let's go!" Lou bellowed to his posse.

The four youths from across the street had already started walking toward them and now broke into a run. They all wore wide smiles.

Three were from the high school and they quickly pulled even with Lou. The smallest and youngest screeched for them to wait up.

"You!" bellowed Preston at the small, scrawny boy, trailing the chase. "Get down to the boy's grandma's house and keep watch! You got your cell? I want you to call me the second you see him come back, you got me?"

The boy nodded and yanked out a smartphone from his back pocket. Hurriedly, he raced back the way he'd come.

Preston pulled out a handkerchief and wiped his forehead. "That boy is going to live with regrets for a long time," he said savagely. Then, whistling, he turned on his heel and walked on.

Devon raced through people's yards, hopped over chain-link fences, and dodged more than one barking dog. One hand kept pulling up his drooping pants and he'd torn the right leg on the last fence. All the while, he couldn't escape the sounds of his pursuers. They were right on his tail.

"Watch for him cutting back!" Lou called.

"Keep him going toward the highway!" a deep voice answered. "We'll trap him there at the station!"

Devon's heart pounded and sweat poured down his face, but he kept his legs pumping. Just past the next row of houses lay a busy intersection with a Shell gas station on the corner.

As he leapt off a curb, his feet pounded the pavement. He passed a sign telling him he was on Courtney Road . . . going in the opposite direction of home. Devon never slowed.

Courtney Road led from his neighborhood to Route 13, a busy road leading to the heart of Williams County. Running two lanes in each direction, Route 13 would be the busy highway. Beyond this was what Devon's grandma called the "rich" part of town. It was a section where Devon was never allowed to go alone . . . especially by crossing the busy street.

I already broke so many of your rules, Grandma, Devon thought. *One more won't hurt.* He put his head down and used his remaining energy to keep racing. Passing the small houses, he flew into the parking lot of the Shell station and never slowed. A man at the pump stared at him but said nothing. Not even when the curses and shouts of five youths chased after him. When you were faced with trouble, silence kept you out of it.

Luckily the stoplights were on his side and Devon was able to make it across Route 13 without stopping.

Safely across, he looked back and was rewarded to see Lou and his gang forced to a sudden stop at the Shell station. The light changed to green and a line of cars rolled into action, separating Devon from his pursuers. Suddenly feeling good, Devon waved and grinned. He chest heaved and he couldn't speak, so he just waved.

The response was lost to the sound of traffic. More than one car honked its horn, thinking the finger gestures and rude language were meant for it.

Laughing and wheezing, Devon jogged up a small rise covered with mulch and flowers and cut through a thin line of trees before entering a new world of large houses with perfectly manicured lawns. *This was what it meant to be on the rich side,* he thought.

Knowing his pursuers wouldn't give up easily, Devon entered the neighborhood aware any trouble would definitely bring the police. As long as he kept moving and kept quiet he would be safe . . . maybe.

A boy with dark skin and ragged clothes had a hard time feeling safe in an upscale neighborhood, something Devon quickly learned. On his street, the houses looked silly and jumbled together, but these houses looked dangerous and carefully placed. They were mansions compared to his house. Every house had at least two stories and more windows than he had fingers. No two looked remotely alike—some even had columns spouting out from the side like castle turrets.

With every step, Devon couldn't help but feel as if he were being watched by hundreds of unfriendly eyes. His short curly hair dripped with sweat and he continued pulling up his sagging jeans.

It was a late Tuesday afternoon and few people were out. Passing between a fancy gray-stoned house and a three-story brick mansion, he smelled cigarette smoke in the wind. He couldn't see the smoker but felt eyes watching him.

Devon ducked his head and hurried past. He couldn't understand why rich people smoked. Why would someone with enough money to live in a mansion want to ruin his life by sucking down cigarettes?

All the men on Devon's street who smoked were broken and desperate. His grandma warned Devon about spending time around them—they had given up on life, she said. All their hopes, according to her, had gone up in smoke. Devon didn't doubt it. The old smokers were worn-out shells of men with bloodshot eyes and more wrinkles than the moon had craters. And the young smokers were just sad and desperate. Smoking got them through life, one puff at a time. That was sad. In order to live, they had to slowly kill themselves. Why would rich people do that? Devon had no answers and he shuddered as he quickened his step, leaving the lingering smell of smoke behind him.

A few houses down, Devon saw a woman working in a flowerbed in front of an enormous three-story brick castle. Crouched low, she didn't notice him at first. With a green blouse, tan pants, and very light skin with bright blond hair, she reminded Devon of a flower and for a moment he stood and watched her. He couldn't help but imagine what it must be like to have such a woman as a mother and to live in such a huge house.

Then the woman noticed him. She stood immediately and glared. A hand went to her hip as the other hand gripped a trowel like a weapon. It pointed toward Devon. Without speaking, she made her message loud and clear.

Gulping, Devon nearly broke into a run. His feet were sore and his clothes hung on him, soaked with sweat.

Racism was something he could never escape. In his neighborhood you had to walk in a certain way and act in a certain way—it was expected. Without a swagger or a tough front, you were dead meat. Unfortunately, acting the same way in this rich neighborhood made you into an automatic hoodlum, thug, and criminal bent on mischief.

It was all because of his brown skin, he knew. It was the same treatment he got at grocery stores, the mall, and pretty much any other place where "decent people"—people with light skin—were the norm. He hated the feeling of being judged and condemned at a glance. Slouching his shoulders, he ignored the imposing houses glaring at him . . . judging him.

Reaching the end of one block, he turned down another only to see more grand houses and carefully kept lawns. For a moment, he blinked and stared. It seemed as if people here cared more about their lawns than their kids.

There were more flowers, stone edifices, and fountains than there were playgrounds. All the grass here grew thick and green. Even scarier, there were no kids. Not a single young person was in sight. Where Devon lived, the kids trampled the yards so they were dusty and brown more than anything else.

At least Lou and the others wouldn't dare touch him here . . . or so he hoped. Thankfully he hadn't heard or seen a hair of his pursuers.

After several minutes of walking, he found himself at the edge of the vast neighborhood. A copse of tall trees provided shade on his left while the last row of majestic houses loomed on his right.

He was walking with his head bowed in exhaustion when two bicycles nearly ran him down.

"Watch it, dude!" cried a boy's voice. "Slow lane is on the grass!"

Devon gave a start and stared as two boys whizzed past, heading toward the trees. Then one slammed on the brakes and slid his bike to a stop. He turned to face Devon. The other boy jammed on his brakes and also turned.

Devon went still. Suddenly he'd rather face Lou and Preston then these two boys—at least he knew where they were coming from. Facing two pale-faced boys in a rich people neighborhood made Devon feel like a fish in a frying pan.

"Are you lost or something?" the boy who'd nearly run him down asked.

Devon flinched. His grandma always warned him about rich white people—they were nothing but trouble. Either they pretended to like you and treated you like a trophy, or they were out to hurt you in any way they could. But then he saw the boy looking at him with more mild curiosity than menace.

At least a few years younger than Devon, the boy had pale blue eyes and light hair almost the color of sunlight sticking out from under a ball cap.

"Leave him, Casey," his friend called, sounding annoyed. "We got to go!"

Both boys wore jeans and carried baseball gloves on their handlebars.

"Where are you going?" Devon asked evenly.

"The ball game!" the boy named Casey said, as if it was the easiest answer in the world. "It's the semifinals today." His eyes suddenly went big. "Hey, are you from the other team? I mean, you from Northside?"

Devon blinked and stared.

Casey didn't wait for an answer. He'd already started pedaling off. "Well, if you are," he called over his shoulder, "your team is going to get creamed! My brother is going to kick Northside in the south side!"

"Why did you ask him that?" complained Casey's friend as he started pedaling away as well.

"Because he's not from around here. Where else is he from?"

"Probably selling something," his friend said just as the two boys turned their bikes onto a hidden path in the trees.

Devon bit his lip as the bikes vanished into the woods. Then he let out his breath. His relief was short lived. As he turned to see where the boys had come from, he saw a police car cruising down the road, heading straight for him. The lights were off, but that didn't mean anything. Without stopping to think, Devon plunged into the woods where the bike riders had disappeared. Finding a well-worn path, he set off in a tired trot.

On the other side of the woods he saw a large opening and the grounds of a sprawling school. This day, he decided, was not getting any easier.

Chapter 3

"Come on, man! Coach is going to get seriously, uh, peeved if you don't hurry!"

Hearing the voice, Bobby Aaron turned with a grimace to see his best friend Chris Winter exiting the back of Hamilton Middle's gym. Chris carried his bag of bats and equipment and looked like he was on his way to the field. His mother, Mrs. Winter, followed closely behind. She smiled seeing Bobby.

"Good choice of language, Chris," she said. "I'll leave you boys here and go find somewhere to buy tickets. I know we're early, but somebody has to be around."

Bobby nodded a greeting and Mrs. Winter headed toward the baseball field. He put on a mournful face for Chris. "I gotta be here, Coach's orders," he said sourly. "Our school paper wants to do an interview with our team and I have to give it."

Chris stopped and stared at Bobby. Then he threw back his head and laughed, his knees buckling. "You serious?" he cried. "Our rag wants to do a story on *us*? We're famous!"

Bobby frowned. "Whatever, dude. Just be thankful you weren't picked for this."

Bobby and Chris attended Hamilton Middle, the home of the Fighting Bears. As eighth graders, they starred on the baseball team and this year, for the first time in over ten years, the team had made it to the county playoffs. Not only that, but for the first time in school history the team was undefeated. Today was the semifinal game against the Northside Packers, a team they'd barely beaten by a run in the regular season. The winner would move on to the coveted county championship game.

Chris whipped out his phone and checked the time. "What's the matter? Did they stand you up? Our game starts in less than an hour. Coach is waiting for us."

Shrugging, Bobby sat on the wooden rail separating the parking lot from the athletic fields. Irritably, he started kicking his baseball bag on the ground in front of him. "They're probably busy investigating if school food gives you acne. Man, I wish I could just e-mail some dumb answers," he muttered.

"Hey, at least you're in the right spot for it." Chris gestured to the large dumpster sitting at the edge of the parking lot across from them.

Bobby gave a tight smile. "The only thing more appropriate would be a toilet."

Hamilton Middle School's paper, the *Paw-fect Paper*, was a standing joke. It boasted a website that was rarely updated—and one that almost nobody visited—and put out a monthly, when they could, publication that almost nobody read . . . or read seriously. Mostly it contained "big national" news and what it meant to middle schoolers—like the latest political elections and how they were destroying the world.

What middle school kid cared about what some rich stranger did in Washington or what happened in some tiny country in Europe? Of course the paper always had some small section about student life and profiled some of the school's more popular students, but it rarely had anything about sports. And when it did, it was almost always written by some pencil-necked geek who'd only played sports with a keyboard and probably thought baseball cups were something you drank out of.

Bobby remembered the article about the football team that had run last fall. The story started with quotes from the players but then turned into a big story about football being too dangerous for middle schoolers. He remembered the offensive line using copies of the newspaper as toilet paper in protest.

"See you, dude," Chris said, smacking Bobby on the shoulder. "Just make sure you mention today's star pitcher. I always wanted to be in the Poop-fect Paper."

Bobby winced and waved his friend on. The team was supposed to be meeting for a pregame practice. Instead he was stuck waiting for the Poop-fect reporter. After the offensive line toilet paper episode, the school's athletes started calling it the "Poop-fect Paper."

"Let's hurry up and poop this one out," Bobby said softly to himself. "Then we can use the paper to wipe it."

"Huh?" asked a strange voice.

Bobby's head snapped up and he saw a dark-skinned boy about his age stepping out from behind the dumpster. Shorter and thinner than Bobby, the stranger had low hanging jeans and a faded blue T-shirt with a generic basketball picture on the front.

"What are you staring at?" Bobby demanded, once he saw the boy was alone. "You leaving your home for the game?" He nodded at the dumpster behind the boy.

The boy frowned. "At least I'm not talking about pooping my pants," he shot back.

Bobby's face went red. "You don't know what you're talking about. You don't even go to this school, do you?" He knew of only a few boys in the school with dark skin and neither one hung around dumpsters.

"I wouldn't want to go to any poopy school."

"For your information, our school is number one in baseball," Bobby said, getting irritated.

"From what I just heard, you guys should be number two," returned the boy. "Don't forget to flush."

Bobby jumped to his feet. Who was this kid? "Take it back, man."

"Or what? You're going to poop on me?" The boy started to stalk off, but suddenly his eyes grew wide and he whirled back around. Without another word, he dashed back behind the dumpster and out of sight.

"What's wrong?" Bobby called after him. "You have to go number two? Don't forget to wipe!" Thinking he'd scared the brat away, he sat back down. "Probably ran back to his rathole," he muttered to himself. "But if he comes back I'm

35

going to turn his face into poop. Then we'll see who's pooping."

"Who's what?" asked a voice behind him.

Bobby jumped as if he'd been beaned by a fastball. Whirling, he stared at the last person he expected to see conducting an interview. Suddenly, he stood up straighter and smoothed down his baseball uniform.

"Hi, uh, Melissa," he said, his voice nearly cracking. Quickly, he cleared his throat and deepened his voice. "You're, uh, here to interview me. Right?"

Melissa Streeter, tall, slender, and gorgeous, stood poised with a pen and notepad a few feet from Bobby. She wore white shorts with a buttery beige tank top that showed off smooth brown shoulders. On her tanned feet, she wore a pair of flip-flops. Silky blond hair, the color of golden honey, was pulled back from her very attractive face. Keen crystal blue eyes watched Bobby with mild amusement.

"That's the idea," she agreed. "If you don't mind, Shorty is going to take some pictures while we talk."

Bobby gulped and stared.

Shorty McCrea was a gawky redheaded boy Bobby knew from gym class. After a growth spurt in the fall, he wasn't really that short, but his name, given in elementary school, stuck.

"Just stand there just like that," Shorty said from beside Melissa. His voice, Bobby couldn't help but notice, was much deeper than his own. "You look like you saw a ghost." Shorty held up a smart phone and was clicking away.

Bobby blinked. "Oh, uh, great. Uh, I guess I'm ready." Quickly he put on a serious gaze and tried to suck in his stomach while puffing up his chest.

"Too late," Shorty said. "I'm already done with the pictures."

"I mean for the interview," Bobby said, frowning.

Shorty rolled his eyes. "I was kidding. I'm still taking pictures."

Shorty, Bobby remembered, had a strange sense of humor.

"What was the biggest challenge this year?" Melissa asked from where she sat on the rail next to Bobby.

Bobby ducked his head and swept sandy hair from his eyes. Then he licked his lips. Shorty, standing behind them, still held his phone up and Bobby kept trying to show off his right side while never taking his eyes off of Melissa.

"Oh, that's a great question," he said slowly. But what he really wanted to say was, *That's a great face.* He had to keep his focus. *Stay with the question, man!*

Melissa Streeter, besides being a reporter for the paper, also played on the softball team. This, Bobby thought, made her quite a catch, pun intended. Unfortunately, she also hung out with the high school's JV baseball team more than with her classmates. That made her out of his league. Still, a boy could dream, right?

The softball season had ended the week before with a disappointing loss for the Bears that knocked them out of the playoffs. This meant Melissa could focus on baseball and, just maybe, on Bobby Aaron.

"Uh," Melissa said, tapping her pen against her pink mouth, "the question?"

"Oh, yeah. I think our greatest challenge was, you know, believing in ourselves. I, uh, think we had some great players and, well, just needed the confidence that we could do it. Like, you know, believe in ourselves."

Melissa twisted her mouth and wrote something down.

Bobby used the moment to grab his hat from the top of his baseball bag and jam it on his head, making sure to tilt it at a slight angle.

So far he thought the interview was going well. He'd tried hard to remain humble while at the same time exuding confidence that he was the center of the team. After all, Coach picked him for the interview, right?

He cleared his throat. "Uh, just to add to that, our eighth graders really stepped up. I mean, me, and, uh, well, I try to lead by example. We created a, uh, serious tone and backed it up."

Melissa nodded absently. "So how has the team kept winning?"

Bobby threw back his shoulders and licked his lips. He had a brawny build and wanted to show it off. Even if the camera missed it, Melissa wouldn't.

"Total team effort," Bobby said. "We have a lot of young talent to support us."

At this moment, two other players had exited the school and were heading past them.

One of the boys, the taller of the two, turned their way and raised his eyebrows. "Whoa, what's this?" he asked in a deep voice. "Is Bobby interviewing for a date? Good luck with that!"

"Don't forget to tuck in your shirt!" said the other player in a high boyish voice. "Either it's hanging out, or you're really fat."

"Hey, if it's an exit interview, I'm available!" called the first player.

Turning, Bobby fought to keep his face from flushing beet red. Forcing a smile, he said, "Speaking of which, here're two of the young studs now. Hey, guys, stop for sec!"

Hopping up from the railing, he practically ran to the two seventh graders. "Stop being idiots," he hissed at them. "This is the school paper interview!"

The taller of the boys, Kevin Baker, carried a baseball bag over his right shoulder. The other boy, Henry Lee, had on a backpack on with two bats sticking up on the sides. Shorter and slimmer, Henry nearly collapsed from the weight of his pack aided by Bobby's push.

"This is Kevin, our shortstop and relief pitcher," Bobby said, clapping an arm over the taller boy's shoulder. He was hoping for a good photo opportunity, but got much more than he bargained for.

"Ow!" yelped Kevin, dropping his bag and grabbing his shoulder. "You broke my arm! You're so strong, Bobby!"

Bobby stifled a curse. The bag, carrying at least two metal bats, a water bottle, glove, and several baseballs landed on his right foot.

Henry bit his lip to keep from laughing.

"Stop being an idiot," Bobby said, not daring to look at Melissa.

Melissa, for her part, watched with a slight grin and raised eyebrows. Her pencil hadn't moved for a while.

At her side, Shorty happily started recording with his phone. "You guys are on video," he said cheerfully.

"Hi, Mom!" Henry called, mugging for the camera. He pulled on Bobby's sleeve. "Don't forget to mention my good looks," he said in a loud whisper.

"Yeah," added Kevin. "And my naturally curly hair." He patted the back of his cap where dark curls bounced lightly on his shoulders. "No extensions," he said to the camera. "It's the key to our success." Giving an exaggerated wink, he offered two thumbs up.

Bobby, his foot still throbbing, did his best to keep his temper. Barking out a laugh, he shoved the boys forward, nearly sending Henry sprawling to the sidewalk. "Go on and get out of here," he huffed. "You guys are idiots."

Henry looked back. His voice had yet to break and he still had the looks and actions of a little kid. "That's not what your sister said," he chirped.

Bobby made a face. "I don't have a sister."

Kevin raised his eyebrows and pretended to look surprised. "Oh, so that was your mom, then?"

Bobby could do nothing but feel his face grow red as the two friends laughed and high-fived each other. Then Henry gave one final look at the camera, which still rolling. "Hey, Gabby, will you go to the dance with me? Check your Facebook page!"

Bobby's shoulders sank as the two friends finally headed for the field. He looked desperately at Melissa but had no words.

Melissa tapped her pen thoughtfully on her chin. "So that was Henry Lee, right?"

Bobby nodded glumly. "His dad owns the Soup'or Subs near the mall. Why?"

Soup'or Subs was a popular sub shop featuring fresh soups and made-to-order sandwiches. Henry's dad always let his son's school and sports team host fund-raisers there. Every kid at Hamilton Middle had tasted a Soup'or Sub sub at least once.

"Oh, nothing. Just I think the whole school saw his Facebook post to Gabby. Cute kid."

Bobby sighed. It was the first time he'd actually seen Melissa interested during the interview.

Gabby Gomez was a pretty seventh grader that nobody had the guts to ask out—not after she'd turned down every boy who'd asked at the winter carnival . . . until Henry did on Facebook.

"He's a good player, too," he conceded. "Plays football and basketball too."

"Really?" Melissa asked, looking back at Bobby.

"Yeah, he's the youngest, but one of the fastest kids on our team. He plays center field and left field."

"What about the other one? What's his name, Kevin Baker?"

Bobby grunted. Why didn't she ask more about him and what *he* did? "Kevin is okay ... He plays shortstop and sometimes second base. He also plays football and lacrosse. He has a good arm. Coach likes to use him as pitcher late in games."

"What do you know about your coach?" Melissa suddenly sounded aggressive and her pen flew to her pad, ready to write.

Slightly confused, Bobby drew back. "What do you mean? He's Coach."

Melissa tightened her lips. "Well," she said, "he's the only coach in the school that doesn't work as a teacher and he only shows up for baseball activities. Otherwise he's a complete mystery."

Bobby grew guarded. He reached down and picked up his bag. "Coach Wood is a good coach," he said flatly. "If you want to know more about him, ask him. Not me. Look, I think I have to go. This interview is over."

"Wait!" cried Melissa. "What about your assistant coach? What's his name, Ted Jackson?"

Bobby paused for a moment and took a deep breath. Then he whirled to face Melissa. Shorty had stopped filming and looked a little nervous.

"I don't know what you're saying," Bobby said hotly, "but our coaches are both great. Coach Jackson works as the assistant youth pastor at my church and is the most loyal fan we have. He has our backs, okay? Too bad our school paper doesn't."

Melissa nodded evenly. "Okay, I'm sorry," she said meekly. "I know Coach Jackson is good, I was just curious about Coach Wood, that's all. Um, thanks for your time!"

Bobby Aaron didn't bother returning her wave. He stalked toward the field with a slight limp.

"Wow," Shorty breathed once Bobby had gone far enough not to overhear. "What was that all about? I thought this was supposed to be another pointless interview with a dumb jock."

"Jocks aren't dumb, Einstein," Melissa said, writing something on her pad. "Remember, I'm a jock too."

"I know and what you just did was pretty dumb. You got the best player mad right before the biggest game in school history."

"Whatever. I wanted this interview for one reason and you know it."

Shorty gave her a look. "You really think the baseball team is behind the drugs?"

"I don't know what to think. I just know somebody is passing out drugs at school and nobody knows anything about the baseball team except that they win."

"And that they have idiot seventh graders."

Melissa allowed a smile. "All seventh graders are idiots."

The walk from the school to the baseball field was a long one. Just past the parking lot was the football field, which was also used for soccer. Past the field, after a small incline, rose the outer back fence of the baseball field. Getting to the home team's dugout meant traveling along the outside of the fence to a line of trees that led to the home plate area.

Kevin and Henry were still laughing about their interview bomb when they heard a loud cough. They were walking on the outside edge of the soccer field, near a small circle of trees that provided the only shade in sight.

Leaning against one of the trees, a young teen watched them. He wore a ripped T-shirt and baggy jeans but had on shiny new sneakers. The shirt, a filthy gray, had been shorn around the middle, exposing a flat belly of dark brown skin. The boy straightened up and stepped in their direction. He looked to be around fifteen or sixteen but acted much older.

"What're you two laughing at?" drawled the teen. A gold earring glinted from his left ear.

Henry started to stop, but Kevin nudged him to keep going.

"You deaf?" the teen said louder. He hitched up his pants and sneered. "Or are you just chicken?"

Now Kevin did stop. "Look, man, I don't know who you are, but if you want to watch us play, you have to pay." He nodded toward the back of the center field fence where Mrs. Winter and another parent were setting up a desk. "Go get a ticket. If you can afford one."

"What's that supposed to mean?" demanded the youth.

"Well," Henry said, "you can't afford to buy a real shirt, so you probably can't afford to buy a ticket."

"Very funny," snarled the teen. "We'll see who's laughing later."

"Yeah, when you look in the mirror," Kevin said with a scoff. "Come, let's get out of here."

"Everyone's brave with a friend," called the teen. "But if you see a scrawny black kid you come tell me. He has no friends!"

"Whatever, dude," Kevin called back. "Go to the mall and buy a shirt that isn't half off."

The teen's eyes followed the boys as they went to their dugout. "Yeah," he muttered. "Be brave with your ugly uniforms. One day you'll be alone. You'll see." Then, quickly losing interest, he turned back to survey the schoolyard.

Devon Hill had to be around here somewhere. Lou had spotted him sprinting from the woods to this school twenty minutes earlier. He would be found . . . it was just a matter of time.

Devon slipped from the dumpster and sprinted to the thin line of trees surrounding the back boundary of the school. He'd spotted his pursuers while talking to the poop player and then spent the last several minutes listening to the awful interview. He'd at least enjoyed the part where the seventh graders barged in. Now he had to find a place to lay low for a while.

Staying just inside the tree line, he took a quick glance and didn't like what he saw. Lou prowled the parking lot and another teen stood in the trees across from the soccer field. He recognized him as Ray, a high school dropout. Devon snorted. The poop player called Bobby was striding past Ray and seemed oblivious to being watched. Ray had a very interested eye on Bobby's shoes. Devon used this moment to move through the trees toward the baseball field.

He headed down near the left field line to where the visitors' dugout sat. The visiting school had just arrived in the parking lot and players in blue and gray were piling out of a long yellow bus. Parents with younger kids were already setting up chairs near Devon. He figured he would be safe hiding out with them. Drug dealers, he thought, did not watch middle school baseball and he could get lost in the crowd.

Chapter 4

On the previous Friday, Hamilton Middle had been put through a drug search. Police dogs were brought in after an anonymous tip concerning drugs being sold in the boys' locker room. Nothing was found but a single bag of marijuana and a single bag of cocaine. Both were discovered together on the floor of a shower stall in the boys' locker room. Since then, everyone had been on edge. Only athletes ever used the showers and during May, this mostly meant baseball players.

As lead reporter for the *Paw-fect Paper*, Melissa had immediately wanted to do a story about the drugs, but as soon as she brought it up to Mrs. Warner, the principal and school paper chief advisor, she was shot down.

"We need to highlight the good qualities of our school, Melissa," Mrs. Warner had said in her office behind closed doors. "Let's face it. Every school has setbacks and hiccups. Drugs are not something we want to associate with our student body. Community members read what we write, you know? Why don't you do a story about our changing environment?"

"You mean our school environment?" Melissa had asked, already knowing the answer.

"No!" the principal had cried. "I mean our global environment! Here, I'll send you some articles. You pick one to be our lead story and follow up on it and include opinions from our students."

That was when Melissa had asked to do a story on the baseball team. If she wanted answers, she would have to get them the hard way. Luckily she had Shorty to help her.

Shorty, as he aptly put it, was the ultimate nerd. But this had its perks. Being a straight A student, he was allowed to work in the office during study hall to help sort papers. This put him right outside the principal's door during the meeting after the drug raid. He had also overheard Melissa's ill-fated meeting with Mrs. Warner. He tracked her down in the hallway right afterward.

"You want to know about the drugs, right?" he'd asked her as she was returning to class.

"Yeah, how do you know that?" she'd asked, more suspicious than scared. Shorty and she had rarely spoken before, but she could easily take down the scrawny redhead if needed.

"I listen," the boy had answered simply. "Working in the office during study hall puts me right there where, ironically, teachers have big secret meetings. You know, the ones kids aren't supposed to know about. I can tell you all sorts of stuff about our wonderful teachers. I know who's dating who and who wants to quit—"

"What about the drugs?" Melissa had demanded.

"Okay, okay. Look. I heard the police officer talking to Mrs. Warner. The bags they found are just sample bags—they're bags with tiny amounts of drugs given out by dealers for free. They're supposed to get kids hooked and begging for more. Apparently the police have been finding a lot of them in the area, but they don't know where they're coming from. They *do* know they're probably from the same source. They think there's a dealer close by getting kids to pass out drugs for him. Our school is the third one with drugs found in the last month."

Melissa had gulped. "So that would mean we have at least one dealer in our school."

"Yeah, well, probably."

Melissa had grabbed Shorty's arm. "Thanks, Shorty. Meet me after school. We have plans to make."

"Plans? What plans?"

"You're working with me now, Shorty! Together we're going to take down a drug dealer!"

"Great," Shorty had groaned as Melissa practically skipped back to class. *Being a nerd has its perks, but eavesdropping definitely doesn't.* Then his face brightened. *But I am working with Melissa.*

Melissa and Shorty now headed to the home stands shortly after the interview. They joined a steady stream of parents, students, and siblings of the players. The semifinals were proving to be a big deal.

"Hey," Shorty said, nudging Melissa in the arm. He stepped back when she stopped and stared at him. "Uh, sorry, but did you see that kid over there? He just ran into the woods."

"What kid?" Melissa asked, whirling to look at where Shorty pointed.

"He's a black kid. I saw him hide behind the dumpster before our interview. He ran out after we finished."

"So?"

"Maybe he's part of the drug thing. I mean, he could be a seller."

"Why do you say that?" Melissa demanded aggressively. "Just because he's black?"

Shorty snorted. "No, because he was hiding behind a dumpster. What kid does that in broad daylight? And why is he trying to hide now?"

Melissa frowned. She watched as the boy vanished into the woods from across the field. Even if she wanted to, she would never be able to chase him down. "Well, he does look suspicious," she admitted. "Still, that doesn't mean he's selling drugs."

"All I said was 'maybe,'" Shorty said, shrugging. He didn't sound offended. "Somebody is doing it and I doubt many parents at Hamilton Middle are into making and selling drugs to their kids."

From his vantage point hidden in the trees, Devon watched the home team gather around their coach, a tall, solidly built man with a short military haircut and a bearing to match. Standing at attention, wearing a cap pulled low, and carrying a clipboard, he had the authority of a four-star general about to make battle plans. The players knelt around him silently. All eyes were on their coach. Devon searched the players and found the two troublemaking seventh graders. The small one, number 13, and the taller one, number 4, both knelt near the front in rapt attention. There would be no playing here.

The poop player Bobby, number 1, joined the huddle and moved to the center of the team before kneeling. Another coach, clearly the assistant, moved to stand in the back. He looked like a bouncer—large beefy arms crossed his wide chest. Iron-gray hair with a tinge of black fell to his shoulders. More hair covered his chin and upper lip, making him look like a biker version of Santa Claus.

"You boys listen up," the assistant coach rumbled. "This is the most important day of your young lives. Let's not waste it!"

Devon felt a strong dislike build inside of him. A baseball game was the most important thing in their lives? He hoped the home team would get destroyed.

Devon was positive that not one kid on the Bears had ever worried about drug dealers lurking outside his door. Or had to go to bed hungry because there wasn't any food in the house. Or had a mom who loved drugs more than him. Nope. These kids were spoiled, pampered, and didn't know the first thing about real life. Kneeling behind a clump of bushes, he settled in to watch.

The Bears players and coaches wore dark black shirts with bright red sleeves. Numbers in matching red took up the back of the shirts and the words "Hamilton Middle" were splayed across the front. From a distance they looked like blood spots. All the players wore pristine, gleaming white pants. Everyone had light skin to match. Most even had the same haircuts—short and neat. Only number 4 and the burly assistant coach had hair hanging from under their caps.

I hope Northside pummels them, Devon thought grimly.

Northside had a much looser team—most of their players had uniforms wrinkled from a long bus ride and few were tucked in. They took fielding and batting practice with a relaxed air, like boys goofing off. In contrast, when the Bears took their practice, they were all business.

Devon kept his eyes on numbers 13 and 4 and had to admit to being impressed. Number 13, though one of the smaller kids, stood out with his flat-out hustle and an unhidden zeal for the game. He wore his pants tight and long, showing off skinny legs capable of blazing speed. During outfield drills, he ran down every fly ball easily, but he always made sure to catch the ball with both hands and throw it in quickly. The other outfielders were just as good, but not as fast. Not one misjudged or dropped a fly ball. In the infield, number 4 at shortstop ate up grounder after grounder and showed real chemistry with the second baseman. All their fundamentals were sound and the throws were crisp and mostly on target. The poop player, number 1, played first base and made more than one spectacular stretch to snare an occasional wild throw.

"They're like a machine," one of the Northside parents in front of Devon muttered. "I wonder if their coach programs them."

"Don't worry," another parent said. "Our boys will settle down and show them some Northside power. Just because we like to have fun don't mean we can't play ball. Come on, Eagles!"

For a while it looked as if the second parent knew what he was talking about and Devon would get his wish. The Northside Eagles, in gray and blue, jumped out with five quick runs in the first inning and looked good doing it. The Bears pitcher, a tall, strong-armed kid called Chris, had trouble settling in. He threw hard but wild. After ten pitches he'd walked two batters and recorded no outs. Then he settled on straight fastballs and the third batter laced a pitch into center field. Number 13 was there, but hesitated before charging in. Devon thought he could've dove, but the boy settled on taking the ball on a one hop before firing it in. Bases were loaded with no outs. After a wild pitch allowed a run, the pitcher, clearly frustrated, started throwing even harder. This led to another walk and another run.

"It's okay, Chris!" hollered number 4. "Just settle. We got them!"

The next pitch was cranked by the Northside batter and the ball ended up near the fence in center field. Only the center fielder's speed and quick throw to the infield prevented it from being more than a double. It still allowed three more runs to score.

The Northside parents were going crazy. Oddly, their stands were more packed than the home stands. Perhaps it was because the home stands had no shade from the trees, but the Bears' stands were only scattered with a few adults and were mostly quiet.

"Time, Blue!" barked the Bears coach to the umpire. His voice was even, but everyone could tell he was upset as he trotted from the dugout.

"Coach didn't like that pitch one bit," chortled the nearest parent to Devon. "It went right down the middle."

"Yeah," answered another, "and then ended up in the middle of the field. I think we got these boys!"

Devon, caught up in the excitement, had emerged from the trees and moved to stand next to the visitors' bleachers to get a better view. There were enough parents and kids around to keep him well hidden from Lou or any of the other thugs.

He watched as the coach met at the mound with the infielders. The coach, eyes hidden by sunglasses, had his finger out and was speaking low, but sternly. All the players stood at attention. Meanwhile, the outfielders grouped together in center field. Their voices carried to the visitor side.

"Man, I almost dove at the first one," Devon heard number 13 lament. "Probably should've."

The left fielder smacked him on the shoulder with his glove. "For that you owe us free subs at your dad's place. Right?"

"You bet," agreed the right fielder. "And the first one of us who makes a diving catch gets subs free for a week."

"Sure," replied number 13. "As long as you guys like our new wish subs."

"What're those?" asked the left fielder.

"Two slices of bread. You wish you had more."

Their laughter carried to Devon and made him angrier. Didn't they know they were being slaughtered? If he were out there, he would've made the diving catch and probably would've run down the long fly.

Devon had never played baseball on a real team or anything like that, but he'd been in plenty of pickup games. When his team was down, he got angry. These boys were in a playoff game and were cracking jokes. They deserved to lose.

"Time's up!" called the umpire.

"Hey, Henry Lee," called the right fielder as they trotted back to their positions. "Nice Facebook post. Did she say yes?"

Number 13 grinned and stared toward home.

Devon really decided to hate the Bears.

Whatever the coach said worked. The next three batters went down in order—two struck out and one grounded out to third.

Devon still watched in satisfaction as the scoreboard showed the five runs. Hamilton Middle had yet to get an electronic scoreboard so the numbers had to be put up by hand. He recognized the kids from the bikes who had nearly run him down as the ones who put up the numbers. Two hits and five runs. Not a bad start.

For a while it looked like it might hold. The Bears just couldn't get it going at the plate. The first batter popped up to second and then poop player, number 1, struck out after a long foul ball that nearly was a homer. The Bears' pitcher batted next. On a two and two count he managed a grounder that escaped into the outfield between second and third, but he was stranded on first. The next batter went down swinging. Number 13 had been on deck.

Chapter 5

The top of the second inning had the Eagles threatening to add more runs, but a slick double play started by number 4 ended the threat. That brought the home fans to life.

"Now let's get some runs!" roared one of the Bears coaches.

Devon wiped sweat from his upper lip. "Let's not," he whispered.

Number 13 led off the bottom of the second with a line drive single to left field. The head coach, coaching third, clapped hands in front of Devon. "That's the way to start! Good hit, Henry Lee! Okay, Kev, sit back and wait for your pitch! It's coming!"

Devon frowned as he watched number 4 settle into the box. Henry, at first base, took a big lead. The pitcher, perhaps too focused on the batter, didn't check the runner and Henry easily stole second as the next pitch sailed outside.

It was no secret why the Eagles pitcher got distracted. The large assistant coach stood at first, leaving the dugout free from adult supervision. Every Bear player leaned on the fence separating the dugout from the field and they were all chirping away.

"Yeah! You got this! Bad pitch!" cried a player.

"He's got nothing!" another yelled. Other players just made animal sounds. The next pitch went high and nearly to the backstop. Immediately the cries grew louder.

"Somebody needs to turn them off," huffed a parent near Devon. An older dad with a walrus mustache fingered his belt and glared at the Bears dugout. "Our boys at least have respect."

"We'll shut them down with outs," a mother told him with more hope than conviction.

Instead, number 4 drew a walk. Ball four was a wild pitch that hopped over the catcher's mitt and went to the backstop, sending Henry to third. The Bears dugout grew even rowdier and the Northside coach called for time.

"Blast it!" cried the older dad. "This isn't fair!"

The head coach took number 13, Henry Lee, aside and mumbled instructions. The coach clearly heard everything the Northside parents said, and definitely heard his own dugout, but paid no attention to that. His focus stayed on the batter and runners. Devon glared at the back of number 13, Henry Lee. The Bears player paid no attention to the parents behind him and only looked at his coach.

When the next batter dug in, Devon found himself squeezing his fists together. He didn't know why this game meant so much to him . . . but it did. After everything that happened to him that day, he just wanted to see the Bears go down.

"YEAAH!!!" cried one of the louder voices from the Bears dugout. "Here come the runs!"

Devon crept closer to the fence and tried to hear what the coach was telling Henry Lee.

"Wait for his foot to go and then you go," the coach was saying. "Got it?"

Henry Lee nodded and took his lead. His narrow waist bent low and hands stretched out in anticipation.

Devon snorted when he couldn't help but notice the red underwear bleeding through the tight white pants. He wondered if the coach was really sending his player to steal home with no outs.

It proved to be a feint. As soon as the pitcher went forward, Henry Lee raced halfway down the line and then stopped. The pitch was low for a ball.

"Get back, Henry!" cried the coach and his player quickly complied. On the next pitch the routine was repeated. This time the pitch went wide for ball two.

Devon bit his lip. He knew what was happening. The Bears coach was distracting the Northside pitcher in every way possible. The dugout provided the noise and the runner on third provided the movement. Flashing for home on each pitch had to drive the pitcher crazy.

Then on the third pitch, number 13, Kevin, took off from first going to second.

"Strike!" yelled the umpire.

The catcher shot up and fired to second. Immediately, Henry, who yet to return to third, raced home.

The umpire watching second base called Kevin out, but Henry scored easily.

"He was safe!" bellowed the coach from first base. "Are you kidding me?"

The head coach on third smacked his hands in frustration but then clapped them encouragingly. "It's okay. That's a run. Let's keep it going!"

The Bears did. Aided by their annoying dugout, they tacked on two more runs that inning. Each mistake by the Northside Eagles sent the dugout screaming with delight. When the inning finally ended, Devon glumly watched the boys add three runs to the scoreboard for the Bears. With the three runs came three errors for the Eagles.

His only consolation was that at least number 13 never added to the dugout noise. When he'd entered the dugout, he'd immediately sat on an overturned bucket and watched the action without expression. As the game went on, this became a routine. Except when he played the field or batted, number 13, Henry, sat on his bucket, keeping quiet. The Bears had one player who wasn't a complete jerk.

His friend, number 4, Kevin, Devon noted, did the opposite. He stood with his teammates and let loose some of the loudest yells at each Northside misfortune. By the fourth inning Northside clung to a 6 to 5 lead. Then in the fifth, it looked like a good ending could still happen when the Eagles added a run to push the lead to 7 to 5. It all fell apart in the bottom of the same inning.

The bottom of the fifth started well for Northside—the first two Bears batters both grounded out. Then the Eagles had to change pitchers due to a pitch count issue Devon overheard. The new pitcher was not ready for the challenge.

Bobby, number 1, greeted the first pitch with a long drive that landed beyond the outfielders for a standup long double. The next batter rifled a liner right at the leftfielder. The fielder had his glove up, but flinched and saw the ball bounce off the tip of his glove. The ball rolled all the way to the fence and the batter ended up on third. Just like that, it was a single-run game.

The following batter stared down the pitcher as the dugout kept up their antics. Of course the runner on third charged for home on every pitch before stopping and going back. The dugout worked itself into a frenzy as the pitcher worked himself into a jam by throwing three balls and one strike.

Around Devon, parents were getting more and more furious.

"Can't they keep those kids under control?" demanded a mother on Devon's left. "They're worse than my dogs at night!"

The head coach clapped his hands not two feet in front of her and told the batter to settle on the next pitch. "Crank it to the fence!" he said. "You got this!"

The next pitch went inside and grazed the batter.

Immediately the umpire signaled a hit batsman and pointed for the batter to take first.

"What?" cried the father near Devon. "He didn't even move away! He leaned into it! That should have been a strike!"

"This game is bush league!" yelled another Northside fan. Devon agreed. The Bears had no shame when it came to finding ways to win.

Of course the protests were ignored.

This brought Henry back up to the plate. So far he had two singles and had walked once. He also had two stolen bases and had scored twice. He took the first pitch and the runner on first took second.

"Get him!" cried the Northside parents as the runner broke from first. "Take him down!"

But the catcher froze. He saw the runner on third out of the corner of his eye and his arm didn't move. After a few pump fakes, he tossed the ball to the pitcher.

"There're two outs!" exploded the man with the walrus mustache. "You take him at second and the inning is over!"

The next pitch plunked the batter on the back of the thigh. The ball thrown behind him, Henry Lee could only twist his body and take the hit. He hopped from the box in discomfort, but trotted to first without a word.

His dugout cheered and waved him to first.

"If you're going to hit him, then at least throw it harder," grumbled the walrus mustache.

Devon sighed in frustration. The bases were loaded with two outs. It felt more like zero outs. When the next batter launched a towering fly to the fence, Devon turned his back and headed back to the woods. The screaming players and fans from the Bears let him know who had taken the lead.

The sun was still high, but he could see no sign of Lou or any of the other thugs. It should be safe to return home . . . if he could find it.

"Okay, boys, that's a wrap," Coach Dillon Wood boomed out. "It's time for the apologies. Coach Jackson, would you like to start?"

Immediately the boys started groaning and clapping. All of it was in jest, of course. They loved this part.

It was the end of the postgame meeting after the 11-6 comeback victory over the Northside Eagles. Gathered in right field, the team sat in a semicircle with their two coaches standing in front.

The "apologies" were a new tradition that ended every postgame meeting and were an original idea of Coach Jackson. Usually a mild-mannered man, especially in church, he had a fierce temper when coaching, especially toward umpires.

During the first game of the year he'd berated an umpire so badly he'd nearly been ejected from the game. Coming to the team shame-faced during that particular postgame meeting he'd vowed to apologize for every one of his outbursts and he'd kept his word. By the third game, Coach Wood had said the heck with it—he also needed to apologize for something every game, and so the tradition was born. After each game, both men stood in front of the team to confess at least one mistake they'd made while coaching. The players loved it and it brought the team closer. It wasn't just the players that made mistakes.

Coach Jackson, a former wrestler, gave a lopsided grin as he moved to stand before the boys. He took off his cap to scratch his unruly hair. "Well, boys," he muttered, "I got nothing to say this game. I did one heck of a standup job at first. That umpire, though . . ." This brought laughter and a few gloves tossed his way. "Seriously, boys. Every Sunday I stand as an example for you all to follow. I try to show you how a man should act. And, well, every ball game I do the exact opposite it seems."

Bobby, sitting in the front row, rolled to a knee. "That's not true, Coach," he said. "You look out for us! You have our backs!"

"Yeah," Chris added from beside him. His arm was wrapped with ice after a long day of pitching. "We can't say what you said to the ump . . . at least not if we want to play next game."

"You got that right," Coach Wood snapped without the trace of a smile. "You guys just play ball. That's your job. Let the coaches handle the bad calls. Personally, I thought Blue did a good job today. They did good."

Coach Jackson nodded. "Coach Wood is right. I appreciate what you're saying, Bobby, but it's no excuse for me losing my temper. And for that, I apologize."

"And I apologize for telling Chris he couldn't pitch his way out of paper bag," Coach Wood said gravely. "Boy, was I wrong." This caused the whole team to bust up with laughter. "Okay, that's it, boys. Now, as I understand it, there's an impromptu ice cream celebration at Cold Stone. All the parents have given the okay and vans are standing by. Forget showering. Go grab your gear from the locker room and then hop in a van and let's move out! Doesn't matter who you go with, because all your parents will be meeting us there!"

As the team gathered their gear and started chatting, Coach Wood pulled Bobby aside and asked him about the interview.

"Ah, it was okay," Bobby muttered, ducking his head.

Coach Wood frowned. "Did something go wrong? You didn't say anything to get you in trouble, I hope."

Bobby shot a glance at where Henry was readying to dump his water bottle down the back of Kevin's pants. The taller boy bent over to pack his bag and never saw it coming.

"Nah, it's just, well . . . she, the, uh, reporter, started asking questions about you, Coach."

Coach Wood frowned. "She did, did she?"

Kevin interrupted with a howl. "I'm going to kill you!" he screeched. Water soaked the back of his pants. Henry was already halfway to the center field fence.

"Hey, Kevin, get your gear!" Coach Wood barked. "Don't leave it here!" Then he turned to Bobby. "What else did she ask about?"

"Well, she wanted to know more about Coach Jackson, but mostly about you . . . like, why you only show up to baseball activities. Don't worry," Bobby added hurriedly. "I didn't say anything."

Coach Wood barely heard him. Frowning, he absently tapped the clipboard in his hands. "Well, that's interesting," he said.

Bobby caught up with Henry and Kevin as they were walking to the vans. "Way to go, guys," he huffed. "You got Coach all mad."

Kevin grunted. "Me? What did I do? I got my pants soaked by this little jerk!"

Henry just lifted his eyes and looked toward the sky.

Kevin paused in his step to deliver a swift kick to the back of Henry's pants with the outside of his cleats.

"Hey, watch it," Henry protested. "That's almost where I got hit."

"Next time it'll be your face," Kevin growled. Then he looked at Bobby. "So, uh, did you get a date with that, um, good-looking reporter?"

Bobby grunted. "No thanks to you chumps, she'll probably never look at me again."

"Don't worry," Kevin said cheerfully. "I'm sure she would have figured that part out all by herself. So that means she's available, right?"

"You guys are too much," Bobby said. "I'll see you two at the vans."

"Aren't you going to the locker room to celebrate?" Henry asked. The team liked to pump loud music and jump around after a victory.

"Nah," Bobby said, looking away. "Not today. Well, good game, both you guys."

"You too," Kevin said. "And good luck. That reporter is going to the vans too. I heard her ask my mom if she could come to work on her story. I think she said she wanted to sit by the 'baseball hunk.'"

Bobby pretended not to hear as he hurried away. His face still turned red.

As Henry and Kevin peeled off to the locker room, Bobby lugged his bag on his left, non-throwing, shoulder, cutting across the trees to the small side parking lot on the other side of the school. To avoid the rush of parents, the vans had set up in this area used mostly for buses. The Northside bus had also parked there and was already nearly loaded. The losing team didn't want to stick around. It would be a long ride home for them.

Bobby started to replay the highlights of the game in his head, especially his double. Then out of nowhere, a terrific force blasted into his back.

Suddenly he found himself face down in the dirt, the wind knocked out of him. Pain blared in his back—it felt as if a fastball had nailed him in the kidneys.

"Wha—" He tried to say something, but a shadow fell over him and another blast of pain erupted in his ribs. Somebody had just kicked him! Then a knee drove into his kidney, causing more pain. He was dimly aware of somebody kneeling on him and going through his bag. And then it was over. The shadow shot up and raced off. It took several moments, but Bobby's breath slowly returned. Groaning, he got gingerly to his knees. Next to him, his bag lay open, the contents scattered around. He saw his glove and a bat . . . but not his shoes.

"No," he said hoarsely. "No!"

His mom had bought him the newest Jordan's to celebrate making the playoffs. He had worn them before the game and planned to wear them for ice cream. Not anymore. They were gone.

"That dumpster kid," he hissed. "He did this!"

Chapter 6

Melissa and Shorty found themselves stuck in the middle row of Mrs. Winter's minivan, packed together with four loud, smelly boys bent on embarrassing themselves at every opportunity. Bobby, Melissa noted, had not chosen this van, but Kevin and Henry were right behind her. The pitcher, Chris, sat on her right and kept trying to catch her eye.

In the front seat, Mrs. Winter carried on a conversation with Coach Jackson. Both adults did their best to ignore the kids.

"What ice cream does everyone want?" Chris was saying. "Coach Jackson offered to pay, so I'm taking orders!"

"Anything with sprinkles!" yelled Gustavo Reyes, the catcher, from the back.

"Whoa, hold on!" Kevin cried out. "Ladies first. What does the star reporter of our awesome paper want?"

Melissa laughed. "Hey, I'm on business. I'm not allowed to accept perks."

Coach Jackson heard her and turned in his seat. "You're riding in a van of stinky boys. I say you earned an ice cream. Help yourself."

Melissa smiled. "In that case, I'll have a double chocolate sundae—chocolate ice cream with chocolate sauce."

"Oh, wow! Chocolate-loving girl," Kevin crowed. "Sign me up. You know, if you and Bobby don't work out, I'm, like, available."

"Sorry," Melissa said sweetly, turning to face him. "But you both strike out."

This prompted all the other boys to hoot and burst out laughing.

"That was a fail," Chris said.

"Dude!" cried Gustavo. "She brought the heater and you got burned."

"Hey," Kevin protested. "At least I went down swinging."

"So what are you writing about us?" Gustavo wanted to know. "Is it, like, about the game, or the whole season?"

"Well, I already interviewed Bobby, but it'll probably be about both," Melissa answered. Her voice was light, but careful. "I haven't really decided what to write."

At her side, Shorty rolled his eyes. He hadn't said a word since climbing into the van. He didn't look ready to break that streak.

Henry leaned over the seat and stuck his head between Shorty and Melissa. "Are you keeping the part about me asking Gabby to the dance?"

"Yeah, because that's the key to our success," Chris said dryly.

Melissa grinned. "Probably not. Sorry. Don't worry, though. I'm sure she saw your message on Facebook. That was really sweet."

Henry's eyes went wide. "Oh. You saw it too?"

Kevin grabbed the back of Henry's belt and yanked him back down to his seat. "Of course she saw it! The whole school saw it by now!"

"Really, though," Melissa said. "It's sweet. I just hope you weren't hurt during it."

"Only if Gabby says no," Kevin said, digging an elbow into Henry's side.

"Ah, leave off," Henry said, rubbing his side.

"She won't," Melissa said firmly. "If I had to date anybody here, it would be you, Henry. But you're too young for me."

That made Henry duck his head, hiding a blush.

"That's because you don't know me!" Gustavo said. A loud rumble sounded from his seat. "Uh, oops. Now you know me."

"Open a window!" cried Kevin. "We're dying back here!"

"Hold up, I got Henry's video!" Chris said. He held up his phone.

"Oh, great," groaned Henry. "Now I'm really dying."

Henry's Facebook post to Gabby, sent a week earlier, was already the stuff of legend at Hamilton Middle. It had been reposted over fifty times and had over a thousand views. It began with Henry staring into the camera while sitting on a chair in his bedroom. "This is to you, Gabby. I hope you like it," he starts out saying. Then, after clearing his throat, he starts singing, "You Are My Sunshine," in shaky boy soprano. Then, once past the first verse, he stops and wiggles his eyebrow. Suddenly a rap beat blares and he starts again, this time with a sunshine rap. His head shakes with the beat and he lays down the lyrics like he was auditioning for a music video. For the last line he changed the words and ended with,

"I go down on knee to ask, will you go to the dance with me?"

With that, he leaps from the chair and somehow manages to land back in the seat on his knees—for a second. The chair, and old wooden one, collapses and Henry, in a startled panic, vanishes with a loud bang. A few seconds go by and suddenly a red rose shoots up from the floor. "Please?" calls Henry's voice, clearly pained. There the video ends.

As they watched it in the van, the boys roared when the chair broke. Only Henry covered his face to keep from seeing. Some kids said Henry planned the whole thing, but Kevin knew better. In the gym locker, Henry had shown him the dark bruise on the back of his thigh. It had to have hurt.

Later, at Cold Stone Creamery, the remaining Bears gathered around the back booth. Everyone had made it and had their fill of ice cream, except for Coach Wood. The head coach had never shown up and had called Coach Jackson to say something important had come up at home, but he would be back for practice the next day.

The last of the parents and Coach Jackson sat at tables on the other side of the eatery, completely oblivious to what was going on with the players. They were still discussing the theft of Bobby's shoes. Bobby had arrived late and reported his attack and missing shoes. At first everyone acted horrified, but soon the players were calling Bobby another Shoeless Joe.

After a quick ice cream Bobby had left with his mom to report the incident to the police.

"Come on, Henry, do it," urged Kevin.

Henry wiggled his shoulders and hunched over his phone, busily scanning the screen. "Hold on, I'm trying to find his number." He sat in the middle of the booth surrounded by the rest of the players.

Melissa and Shorty sat in the next booth watching with open curiosity.

"What are you guys doing?" Melissa asked.

"Shh!" hissed Chris, turning and putting a finger to his lips. "You'll see. Henry is the best prank caller among us."

Shorty raised his eyebrows. "Uh, Melissa, are you sure these guys are even mature enough for your story?" he asked, finally breaking his silence.

Melissa shook her head. "Go ask Mrs. Winter when we're leaving. I think we've had enough." So far she'd gotten nowhere with her story. With Coach Wood not in attendance she'd lost the only person she cared to interview. She asked Chris, "Who's he trying to call?"

Chris looked back, his eyes dancing. "Who else? Coach!"

Melissa froze. Suddenly she didn't want to leave just yet.

"Got it!" Henry announced. "Everyone, get quiet!"

Henry pressed the button to call as his teammates leaned in to hear. Covering his mouth, Henry cleared his throat. He was about to say something when suddenly his eyes went wide and his mouth dropped open. Quickly he ended the call. "Wrong number," he said.

"Ah, come on!" Kevin cried as the others groaned. "You should have done your pizza man anyway! Remember how you called your mom and got her nearly cussing?"

"Hey, over there!" barked Coach Jackson. "I don't know what's happening, but break it up! Time to head home and get ready for tomorrow. Everyone better be at school in the morning and at practice at four. If you're late, you may sit out the championship game!"

Shorty and Melissa exchanged glances as the players got up to leave. How could Henry dial the wrong number when the number was programmed into his phone? Melissa would love to know what Henry had heard on the other line. She didn't have a chance to ask as Henry left with his mom and she and Shorty headed back to the van with Chris.

Thoroughly exhausted and disheartened, Devon finally made it to his grandma's home just after eight. He would've been there earlier but had spotted Charlie Richards hanging out by the house. Charlie was the small scrawny kid from Lou's gang. Devon recognized him from school—they actually had gym together, when Charlie bothered to dress out. After spotting Charlie, Devon had done an about-face and headed for the neighborhood park.

Located on the southernmost part of the neighborhood, the park boasted a rundown football field and a barely maintained softball field. It was just across the street from the Baptist church Devon's grandma made him attend.

Beyond the softball field was a pavement for basketball, but all the rims had been torn down and weeds grew from the cracked pavement. His grandma told him how the men in the neighborhood used to play ball games every Sunday afternoon . . . when times were safe.

Devon didn't need the stories. Corey and he used to play in those games up until their tenth birthday . . . shortly before Preston Whiteside showed up. Now only a few local teams used the field for practice. Mr. James, an old handy man who lived by the church, cut the grass every few weeks, but few people ever used it regularly.

Devon, unsurprisingly, found the park empty. Still, he'd felt drawn to the softball field. After watching the game, he'd felt the urge for baseball. Once he'd made sure nobody was looking, he'd slipped through the fence and had stood at home plate. Taking a batter's stance, he'd waved an imaginary bat and glared toward the imaginary mound. "All right, poop face," he'd said. "Give me your best."

Seeing an imaginary fastball, he'd stepped into it and delivered a mighty blast that went well over the heads of number 4. Not even number 13's speed could track it down.

"Home run!" he'd crowed as he'd started for first.

That was when Mr. James had coughed. The old man stood behind the backstop and had probably seen the whole thing.

"Nice swing," he'd commented. "But next time, drop your shoulder and tighten your stance. You're too loose. And watch your step forward. You put a hole in your swing wide enough for a truck to drive through."

Mouth open, Devon's trot had quickly turned into an embarrassed shuffle. Mumbling something about nosy old men, he'd started off the field.

Mr. James' voice called him back. "Hold on, son. I need to talk to you. You know our parish is starting that ball team, right? For the parish tournament? You interested?"

Devon's mouth had fallen open again. This time it'd been in surprise. He knew about the tournament but never thought much about it.

Williams County Little League had created a special tournament for churches across the county. The aim was to get underprivileged kids to play ball while at the same time giving some of its star players some leadership experience.

Each little league team was donating a few of its top players to a church team to act as team captains.

Devon knew his pastor had been a big part of the tournament being held. On Sundays, he was always complaining about the lack of opportunities the kids in the area had for sports.

Devon, who'd never played an organized sport in his life, had dumbly nodded. "Ain't I too old?" he'd asked.

Mr. James had frowned. "No you 'ain't.' The county set the ages for eleven to thirteen. The county don't want kids too young to throw fits or too old to start fights." Mr. James had looked Devon up and down. "I seen you play ball out here before, haven't I?"

Swallowing, Devon had nodded.

"You keeping away from them drug dealers?"

"Uh . . . yeah. Best I can," Devon had replied, ducking his head and scratching his thigh.

Nodding as if he'd understood, Mr. James had stepped up to the fence and pulled out a card from his pocket. "If you ever need me, call me. I don't care where you are, or what the situation is. You give me a call and I'll come. Got it?"

Gulping, Devon had taken the card. "I-I don't have a phone," he'd stammered.

"You find one when you need one. The Lord will provide. Now get on home before your grandma starts to worry."

Devon had scooted on back to the house and was relieved to find Charlie gone. Instead he found his grandma sitting at the kitchen table with a plate of untouched supper in front of her—cold spaghetti.

"Where were you?" she asked coldly. "I've been waiting for hours."

Devon's grandma worked the day shift as a janitor for the high school. She was always home before Devon's school let out and missed little.

"I was just out," Devon told her stiffly. He moved to sit at the table, but his grandma wouldn't have it.

"Don't you dare! This food is for a boy who minds his elders and comes home when he's supposed to. Now tell me who you were with."

"I wasn't with nobody," Devon said.

"Not with Preston Whiteside?"

Devon's face grew hot. He knew one of the busybody neighbors must've seen him stopped by Preston.

"It wasn't anything, Grandma. He just tried to talk to me. I didn't listen."

"Don't you 'Grandma' me. You call me your mama."

"My mama doesn't live here!" Devon shouted suddenly, surprised to feel tears in his eyes. "You kicked her out years ago."

"She kicked herself out and you know it! Your mama had a problem that she still hasn't gotten over. I don't want to see you go down the same road! You stay away from Preston Whiteside and you come right home after school."

Devon trembled with sudden anger. His grandma had raised him by herself since he was eight. He loved her, but lately she'd been treating him like he was still only eight. "I'm not a little kid anymore," he said stiffly.

"You sure act like one. By the way, your math teacher called today. She left a message about missing homework. Tell me you at least did your homework."

Devon bit his lip. "I hate math. She gives too much work anyway."

"Devon Horner, if you don't get to your room right now and get your homework started I'm liable to have a heart attack. And then you'll feel guilty for the rest of your life. Do you understand me?"

Devon took deep breaths. "I understand, all right. I understand you don't trust me to take care of myself. And you don't care about me being happy!"

With that, he turned and ran to his room. Once inside, he threw himself on his bed and buried his face in the quilt. He'd never known his dad and his mother had chosen drugs over him. Now he was stuck with a grandma who wanted to keep him prisoner in his own room. Life was the pits.

He must've fallen asleep because the next thing he knew, his eyes were opening and a plate with a ham sandwich lay a few inches from his head. A glass of milk sat on his makeshift desk next to the bed. The desk was really a plank of sanded wood supported by two sets of plastic boxes. That was where Devon had to do his homework. His math book sat next to the milk with a sharpened pencil on top.

Getting carefully to his feet so he didn't upset the sandwich, Devon stretched and looked at his alarm clock lying on the floor next to his bed. It said it was ten minutes before eleven. From out his window, he heard the screech of tires and loud cursing. The drug dealers were out working, he knew. Sighing, Devon picked up the sandwich and sat down to face his math.

His grandma did love him . . . just not the way Devon wanted.

Chapter 7

The next morning, Devon and his grandma acted as if the previous night had never happened. She had hot pancakes waiting on the table and a full lunch packed on the counter when Devon entered the kitchen with bleary eyes. It was just after dawn and he didn't have to be at the bus stop for another hour. The smell of fresh pancakes had gotten him up early. They were a real treat, especially on a school day.

"I have the morning off," his grandma grumbled in explanation as she ladled the last of the batter into the frying pan. "That means I have to work late tomorrow. You still better be home. I'm going to have Mrs. Kellum check on you."

Devon groaned. Mrs. Kellum was the eighty-year-old neighbor who loved to baby Devon. Still, he dug into the pancakes with real enthusiasm.

When he got off the bus at Highland Middle School, the home of the Hawks, he ran into Charlie almost immediately. The scrawny boy seemed to be waiting for him just inside the door.

"Hey, Devon," Charlie said, stepping in front of him like they were old pals. "Where'd you go yesterday?"

Devon made to ignore him but thought better of it. The dumbest thing he could do was to make enemies with Preston Whiteside. "Nowhere, really," he said. "Why?"

"Preston wants to see you. He liked the way you run. Said with your build and your speed you could make real money. Anyway, he wants you to stop by his place after school today. I'm telling you, man. It's easy money."

Devon picked up his pace as he headed for his locker. The halls were just filling with tired students getting ready for the day. Charlie kept pace.

"Look," Devon muttered, hoping nobody overhead him, "I'm busy after school. I have to go straight home."

Charlie muffled a laugh. "You serious, man? You *have* to go home? What, are you, grounded?" He laughed louder. "Man, what a baby. I told Preston you were cool, but I guess I was wrong."

Devon halted suddenly and stepped close to Charlie. "Call me a baby again and I'll—" Devon stopped and took a deep breath. Again, he didn't want to make enemies with the wrong people. "Look, man. Just tell Preston I can't do it. Okay?"

"No, it's not okay," Charlie said. "Preston wants to see you today."

Devon's voice grew hard. "Well, tell him I don't want to see him. Ever again. And if I do I might just call the police and tell them some information. And tell him Corey Strider was my friend. Is that okay, you little runt?"

With that, he pushed away and slipped into the crowd. Charlie didn't follow.

He forgot all about Charlie during his first period of history. Instead, he dreamed about baseball . . . and hitting more home runs against the Bears.

Later, during lunch, he stopped at the library to use the Internet. Looking up local middle school baseball scores he saw his school had lost to the Bears 14-1.

Devon grimaced. Highland Middle only cared about football and basketball. He couldn't even name more than two players he knew on the baseball team. Before he left the computer he saw that the Bears would be playing the championship game on Thursday . . . the next day, when his grandma would be working late.

At Hamilton Middle School, Henry plopped down next to Kevin at the lunch table.

"What's wrong?" he asked cheerfully. "Still upset Melissa won't go out with you?" He eyed his tray of beefy macaroni with trepidation. "Or are you just scared your lunch might eat you?"

"Neither," Kevin muttered. He shoved his own tray, barely touched, away. "Remember a few weeks ago when I got caught knocking down mailboxes?"

Henry grimaced and nodded. "You and Wayne Perkins, right?"

Wayne Perkins played second base for the Bears. His dad worked as a private financial advisor and was loaded. One Friday night Wayne's older brother had taken Wayne and Kevin for a ride in the back of his brand-new pickup truck. The younger boys stood with baseball bats while Wayne's brother drove through neighborhoods as close to mailboxes he could. The contest was to see which boy could knock down the most mailboxes with one swing. It ended with a cop pulling them over next to Kevin's home.

"Yeah, me and Wayne Perkins," Kevin said darkly. "He and his brother got off with a warning. I have to do twenty hours of community service *and* use all my allowance to replace mailboxes."

"Bummer," Henry said. He stabbed at his food. "When do you start?"

"This week." Kevin sighed. "You busy Saturday?"

"Hopefully," Henry said, grinning. "It's the dance, remember?"

Kevin groaned. "I forgot all about that ... Maybe community service starts next week, then."

Other members of the baseball team soon arrived and the boys fell into talking about the game against the Eagles and what would happen the next day in the championship. All their other troubles vanished.

"We're playing the Greenland Sharks," Bobby said. "They got good pitching, remember?"

"I remember you striking out," Chris said, shoving a fry in his mouth. "Me? I got two doubles that game."

Gustavo laughed so hard milk came out of his nose.

Shorty slipped into an empty seat on the end and nodded quickly before ducking his head over his plate.

At first Bobby made to say something rude but then shrugged. No embarrassing photos or videos had yet to appear from his interview and he wanted to keep it that way. Besides, Shorty at least attended a game. Most in the school couldn't say the same. The players kept up their banter and ignored Shorty.

The baseball conversation was only interrupted when Lisa Small tapped Henry on the shoulder. "Henry, Gabby wants to, well, say yes. That's all." Lisa was a small, slender seventh grader and one of Gabby's best friends. The message delivered, she whirled around and raced back to her seat next to Gabby several tables away.

For a moment there was a stunned silence. Then the boys ooed and aahed while pounding the table. Kevin slapped Henry on the back.

"You did it, man! You got Gabby to say yes to a date!"

Licking his lips, Henry staggered to his feet and took a deep breath before walking stiffly toward Gabby. Immediately half the table rose and followed.

"Somebody get a phone and record this," Kevin said excitedly. "This is the sequel to the Facebook video of the year!"

Bobby remained in his seat and stabbed at his food savagely.

"There goes the all-American boy," a voice said bitterly.

Bobby turned and saw Wayne Perkins watching Henry with a sour look.

"Yeah, I wish I could be doing the same thing with Melissa," Bobby said without thinking.

Instead of laughing, Wayne nodded. "Me too. How does Henry do it? He hasn't even hit puberty yet, but everything he does is perfect. I mean, he stars on the football team, basketball team, and in baseball. Now he gets the girl nobody else could dream of getting. He'll probably have to stand on a box if he wants to kiss her."

Bobby grunted. He had to admit that Henry did seem to have a lot going for him. "Yeah, well, he still can't hit as far as we can."

Wayne grunted and nodded absently. Then he turned his attention to Shorty, busily eating his food.

"What are you doing here, Shorty? Don't you know this table is for ballplayers only?"

Shorty swallowed and looked up. "No, I didn't know. I thought all the tables were free for students. Besides, you're here."

Wayne frowned. "What's that supposed to mean?"

"Nothing. I just know you're the nicest guy in the school and wouldn't dare pick on a student just for eating his lunch."

Wayne snorted. "Whatever, dude. I'm going to the library. See you, Bobby."

Bobby and Shorty were the only ones left at the table. Henry had taken Lisa's seat next to Gabby and a crowd had gathered to watch what would happen. Both kids—Gabby and Henry—were too embarrassed to do much else other than grin and whisper to each other.

Shorty got up and slid his tray over next to Bobby.

"What do you want?" Bobby growled.

Shorty shrugged. "Actually, I was thinking about what *you* wanted. You have a history report due, right?" He scratched at his red hair and dropped his gaze at his half-eaten lunch. "You know, I could help you with your research . . . if you want."

It never ceased to amaze the redhead. Williams County was stuck in the middle of the historic triangle of Jamestown, Williamsburg, and Yorktown—yet for some reason, its students still struggled with state history.

Bobby turned to Shorty, giving him his full attention. History was his weakest subject and he had to write about the end of the Revolutionary War and what it meant to the present day. "Okay," he said slowly. "What do you *really* want?"

"Well, um, Melissa was wondering . . . what happened with your shoes? Do you know who took them?"

Bobby bit his bottom lip. "I don't know," he finally said. "I just told the police what happened and that it was probably some black kid I saw hanging around the dumpsters."

Shorty grunted. "I, uh, saw that kid too . . . he, uh, looked a little small."

Bobby's face reddened. "Maybe he had friends. Look, I didn't see any faces, okay? Whoever it was sucker-punched me and grabbed my shoes and ran. The police said this stuff happens a lot."

In reality, Bobby was still shaken from the incident. Thankfully his injuries weren't serious and he'd only had the wind knocked out of him . . . but the thought of being attacked and robbed . . . it had kept him up most of the night.

Shorty nodded. "Okay, okay. Um, also, Melissa was, um, wondering if you know what Henry heard on the phone, um, when he called the wrong number last night."

Bobby frowned. He, of course, had heard about the failed prank call. "Don't really know," he said carefully. "Something about a woman on the other end who talked funny."

"Talked funny?"

"Look, just ask Henry, okay? I wasn't there so I don't really know. And don't even ask if it was Coach Wood's number. It wasn't. Got that?"

Bobby stood and grabbed his tray before stalking off to the trash.

Shorty watched him go thoughtfully. "I got something," he said finally. "I think."

Henry got home after school and headed straight for the kitchen. A platter of his mom's chocolate chip cookies waited for him—leftover from the weekend's farewell party for his dad. Henry's father had left for a church mission trip to Haiti and would be gone for the next two weeks. It was bad timing that he'd miss Henry's big games, but in the Lee family faith always came first.

"If that's you raiding the cookies, Henry," called his mother from upstairs, "you'd better stop. I don't want you to ruin your dinner!"

"But, Mom, I have practice at four! I need the energy!"

"Well, in that case, please leave some for your brother and sister. I promised them both cookies for dessert."

"Sure, Mom." Henry grabbed five cookies and immediately stuck one in his mouth. Cradling the other four, his hand to his chest, he used his free hand to grab the milk. His siblings could make do with the four remaining cookies.

"Oh, and Henry, you can get a ride for practice, right? Don't forget I take Anabelle to dance today." Anabelle, at six, was the youngest of Henry's siblings and she had just started ballet that year. Henry's Mom claimed she was her one escape from sports.

Henry made a noise through the cookie in his mouth and put the milk on the counter. Removing the cookie, he licked crumbs from his lip.

"I can get a ride with Kevin. What about Michael?" he asked. His ten-year-old brother Michael was in the fifth grade and another budding sports star.

"His little league coach should be picking him up early. He has a game today. Now I'm coming down, so you better have your shoes off and be using a plate . . . and a glass."

Henry quickly kicked off his sneakers and sent them sailing toward the front door. He was just in time to pile his cookies on a small plate and was in the process of taking down a glass for his milk when his mother walked in from the living room.

In her early forties, Mrs. Lee had dark auburn hair cut short and pushed back so it hung just above her shoulders. Attractive in a mom sort of way, she had a pleasant face and the trim athletic build of a former softball player.

"Henry!" she exclaimed when she saw her oldest boy. "How many cookies do you have?"

Henry, his eyes wide with innocence, gave her a slight grin. "Um, just enough?" he asked.

"I keep forgetting you're almost a teenager," his mother said with a sigh. She playfully batted his shoulder and mussed up his hair. "Good thing you're so handsome. When you finished destroying my cookies, make sure you destroy your homework."

"That would be a pleasure," Henry said as he poured his milk.

"Not what I meant! Just get it all done before baseball."

"Sure, Mom . . . maybe."

Henry had a pair of large eyes, so dark brown they were nearly black. With a small nose and a wide mouth on his thin face, he had the looks to melt any mom's heart. His hair, the color of walnut wood, was cut neat and short with sideburns extending midway past his large ears. He'd inherited his eyes and facial features from his mother—but she blamed his large ears on his father. In any case, all he needed was to give his mom his wide-eyed innocent look and he usually got his way. Unfortunately it didn't work with his baseball coach.

Before cracking open his math and history homework, Henry took his cellphone and texted Kevin, asking for a ride. Kevin replied saying no problem and would Gabby please come too? Henry texted back: *N yor Dreams.*

At three thirty, with his homework completed, Henry changed into baseball pants and his practice shirt. Gathering his gear, he sat to wait on the front steps. A few minutes later, the elementary bus rolled up and dropped off Anabelle and Michael.

A few inches shorter than Henry and skinny as a broomstick, Michael took after their dad in appearance. He had sandy blond hair and a sharp pointed chin along with his large ears. Seeing Henry sitting on the steps, he immediately swung his book bag off his shoulder and charged across the front lawn. He held his bag in front of him like a shield.

"What would you do if I was an orc attacking the house?" he shouted.

The "What Would You Do" game had been created a few months back by their dad during dinner one evening. Michael had started talking about a fight at his school and Mr. Lee had asked his boys what they would do if ever attacked by bullies. This prompted a discussion of the best ways to defend themselves, eventually leading to Mr. Lee asking, "What would you do if you were ever attacked and had to fight for your life?"

Mrs. Lee had raised her eyebrows, but when she'd tried to give her husband a warning look, Mr. Lee had put down his fork and wiped his mouth.

"Look," he'd said, "I'm all about innocent childhoods, but in this world, that's not possible. Kids all over the place, including in our own country, face terrible situations every day. Terror, drugs, shootings, and worse. We can't close our eyes and pretend they don't happen. The only way to make this world better is to recognize the bad parts and work to fix them."

"Fine," Mrs. Lee had said dryly, "if our home was attacked right now I would take my platter of chicken and throw it in the attacker's face. That way it would be of some use, because nobody is eating it."

The kids had burst out laughing, but Mr. Lee had nodded. "That wouldn't be a bad idea," he'd said.

Mrs. Lee had looked at him with feigned anger. "Is my cooking that bad?"

"No," Mr. Lee had said quickly, "but when you're fighting for your life, anything and everything near you becomes a potential weapon. You have to be creative and grab what you have at hand."

The boys had jumped in saying what they would use for weapons—from dinner knives to snot-filled napkins. When Anabelle chimed in with using her Barbie dolls to throw, Mrs. Lee begged for it all to stop.

Since then the boys had continued to play the "What Would You Do" game—one of them would create a situation where the other had to hypothetically fight for their life. The other then had to come up with a reasonable defense using whatever was on hand. Thankfully for Mrs. Lee, who'd insisted on it, the game only involved words and not actions.

Now as Michael jerked to a stop in front of the steps, his bag poised to swing like a weapon, Henry shook his head. "You'd be the smallest Orc alive," he said. "I would roll baseballs at your feet so you'd trip and fall. Then I would take a bat to you and make you even smaller."

Michael laughed. "That one was too easy. But I could just jump over the baseballs. Like this!" The smaller boy took a few running steps and leapt up past Henry to the top step of the small porch.

Henry slapped the back of his brother's pants as he landed. "I could still get you!"

Michael kicked him in the back with his heel and jumped up out of reach before Henry could retaliate.

"What about now?" Michael taunted.

"I would, but I'm waiting for Kevin. I have practice in a few minutes."

"Huh," Michael grunted. "Well, don't catch a fly in your nose!" He vanished inside the house, leaving the door open for Anabelle.

Anabelle had walked off the bus after Michael but had stopped on the driveway to watch her brothers. Before going inside, she stopped to give Henry a hug.

"I'll get Mike for you if you pay me a quarter," she told him.

Henry grinned. "Maybe later." He flicked one of her blond pigtails. She had the face of their mother but the hair color of their dad. "Mom's waiting for you."

Anabelle threw back her head and moaned. She'd much rather be a ballplayer like her brothers, but since she was the youngest and the only girl, Mrs. Lee insisted on her doing ballet for now. Softball, Mrs. Lee promised, would start next fall . . . maybe.

"I wish I could trade places," she muttered as she went inside, slamming the door.

Henry ignored her. He stared at the road and frowned. Kevin usually came early and it was getting late. Henry texted Kevin to ask where he was but never got an answer.

When Michael's little league coach stopped by several minutes later, Henry was pacing the porch. He was tempted to ask for a ride from his brother's coach, but Michael's practice was on the opposite end of the county. He watched glumly as his little brother hopped in the backseat with the coach's son and drove away.

The Bears' practice would start ten minutes. With a sinking feeling in his stomach, Henry went back in the house to find his mom. She was getting Anabelle ready for ballet.

"Hold still, Anabelle, while I pull back your hair," Mrs. Lee said from where she knelt by the bathroom. She had a comb in one hand and bottle of hairspray in the other.

In a pink tutu and tights, Anabelle stood in front of her with an unhappy look on her face. "It hurts, Mommy! Can't I play baseball instead?"

"Not on your life," Mrs. Lee said grimly. "You're a dancer!"

"But dancers wear too much yucky stuff!"

"Mom," Henry interrupted desperately. "Can I get a ride to practice?"

"What?" his mother cried, looking at him wildly. "I thought you had a ride!"

"I did, but it never showed. Please, Mom. I need to be there in five minutes!"

Mrs. Lee sighed. "Fine. Get in the car. Dance lessons will just have to wait."

"Yay!" Anabelle said, clapping her hands.

Mrs. Lee sighed again.

They never made it. Both cars in the driveway had flat tires. Sometime the night before, somebody had hammered nails into the front tires of each car. Henry ended the day sitting miserably on the steps while his mom called for roadside assistance.

Kevin finally called Henry a little before six, just when practice would have been ending.

"Dude, where are you?" Kevin demanded as soon as Henry accepted the call. *"Coach is mad as—"*

"Where were you?" Henry interrupted, fighting hard to keep his voice and emotions under control. "I thought you were giving me a ride!" He was lying on his stomach on top of his bed in his room and fighting back tears. He'd never missed a baseball practice in his life.

"I was, but I got a text from Chris saying he was taking you to practice!"

Henry sat up with a start. "What? I never spoke to Chris!"

"I know that now! When he showed up without you I nearly messed my pants! Dude, somebody stole his cell phone. He didn't have it with him and said he'd lost it in school. He said he never talked to you all day."

Henry flopped back in stunned silence. Kevin continued. He didn't sound happy.

"You still there, dude? Look, man . . . it looks like somebody played a messed-up joke on you. Chris' cell phone turned up by his bag after practice. Somebody on the team must've done it."

"What did Coach say?" Henry asked, his voice listless.

"Well, I tried to explain, but he wouldn't have it. He said every other player made it without problem and you were no exception. To tell you the truth, he came to practice kind of mad . . . I think he knows about your phone call. And he was pretty upset about how last game we

started so badly. He made us turn in all our cell phones as soon as we got to practice so we would focus better. That's why I missed your texts."

Henry squeezed his eyes shut. "So . . . what's the damage?"

"Dude. You're not playing tomorrow. You've been benched."

Chapter 8

Henry's mom, once she heard the news, was sure Coach Wood would change his mind after he understood the situation, but Henry knew better. Coach Wood had served in the army for twenty years. He lived by rules and regulations and never made exceptions. Once he made a decision, he stuck with it. For the first time ever, Henry would be sitting on the bench. And it would be for the biggest baseball game of his school career.

At three thirty on game day, an hour before the first pitch, Coach Wood and Coach Jackson stood just inside the first baseline surveying the infield. It'd been freshly raked and looked ready to go.

"So, have you changed your opinion about Henry?" Coach Jackson asked, scratching one of his beefy arms.

Coach Wood frowned and he gritted his square jaw. His pale blue eyes narrowed. "Rules are rules," he said, crossing his arms. "I have no opinion. He knew the consequences. You know that."

"Sure, I know that, but . . ."

"But what?"

The assistant coached sighed. "Sometimes you're a brick wall." Then he frowned. "Uh, does the principal know your rules? Look who decided to show up for her first game."

Coach Jackson cocked his head toward the school where a tall woman was walking their way. Long, permed hair the color of corn hung down past her shoulders; she wore a neat business jacket and matching skirt with stockings and high heels.

Coach Wood groaned. "What's her name? Shannon Worm? Warmer?"

Coach Jackson spit. "You're getting warmer. Warner, or something like that. You think she knows about Henry?"

The head coach grunted. "In this day and age? Of course. Why else would she come this early?" He and Jackson moved to the fence to meet Mrs. Warner. "Ma'am," he said in greeting, using all the false enthusiasm he could muster. "I'm glad you made it."

"Coach Jackson!" Mrs. Warner said, beaming as if she saw him every day. "It's a beautiful day for a game, isn't it? Especially for a championship game!"

"Should be," agreed the coach. "Anything I can help you with?" He crossed his arms over his chest and stared at the principal.

Mrs. Warner stopped just outside the fence. Not even the makeup covering her deeply tanned face could hide the wrinkles around her eyes, especially when she smiled. Still, she had a trim figure and had kept most of her beauty . . . even, the coach suspected, if it did require some artificial means.

Coach Wood was sure her hair was dyed and the tan came from a salon. But her blue eyes sparkled and she never stopped smiling. Coach Wood couldn't help but feel like he was looking into the eyes of a politician. He'd met many like her in the military. They were more concerned with image and rank than anything else. As long as things looked good for them, all was okay.

The principal licked her lips. "Well, maybe . . . I heard that Henry Lee may not be playing today."

Coach Wood grunted and looked down at the grass. "Well, I'm sure you heard the reason. Rules are rules."

"Yes, well, but I know his parents. You know his father owns the Soup'or Subs just down the road. They do some great fund-raising for our school."

"Yes, ma'am, I do know that." Coach Wood smiled, showing his own white teeth. "But we have rules for a purpose—I'm sure you understand that. They need to apply to everyone. If we let one rule slide, then the whole house of cards could cave in. Henry knew the consequences before he missed practice. Now he's going to learn to take responsibility. That's part of life."

Mrs. Warner licked her bottom lip and nodded seriously. Then her beaming smile returned. "Well, okay, Coach. I guess you're in charge for a reason!" She stepped back and waved at the stands where the players were just starting to gather. "Go Bears!" she called. "Bring home the trophy!"

Then she turned and headed back to the school, stopping to talk to parents as she went.

Coach Jackson moved to Coach Wood's side as they watched her leave.

"That lady wouldn't know baseball if one hit her right smack in the forehead," Coach Wood said, shaking his head.

Coach Jackson frowned. "Yeah, but I don't suppose anyone would know much of anything if that happened."

Coach Jackson grunted. "But then they would be ready to join my staff. Right, Ted?"

Coach Jackson belched. "You betcha," he said.

"Let's get these boys moving with drills. I don't want to see them sitting around. Last game we stunk in the first."

"You want everyone in on the drills?"

"Yes, Ted," sighed the head coach. "Henry is still part of this team. He does the drills. Now let's go. There's been too much clowning around lately." Clapping his hands sharply, he raised his voice, directing it to his players. "All right, boys, it's time to get going! No more clowning! Let's man up and get ready to play ball! Last game we almost blew it. It's not happening today!"

"Undefeated season!" cried Chris, hopping from his seat. "We got this!"

Henry, who'd just arrived, listlessly dumped his bag and retrieved his glove. He looked utterly defeated.

Thursday afternoon found Devon slipping out his back door with a five-dollar bill stuffed deep in his pocket. Mrs. Kellum had slipped him the money for getting his homework done early. Now she stood in the kitchen fixing up a tray of meatloaf. She wouldn't miss Devon for quite some time. And when she did, he'd be long gone.

Unfortunately, by the time Devon had finished his homework it was after four. The championship game, he knew, started at four thirty. Intent on retracing his steps to Hamilton Middle School, he never noticed Charlie watching him go.

Devon arrived at the school with the game already under way. The Bears were just leaving the field to a smattering of cheers. Not wanting to feel like a thief, Devon had taken the long way around the woods and entered the school from the parking lot. He made sure to find the desk selling tickets and reluctantly handed over the five.

Waiting for change, he asked the lady at the desk, "What's the score?"

The lady gave him an unfriendly look. "Are your parents here?" she asked frostily.

"Of course. They're over there." Devon flashed a smile and pointed in the direction of the visitor stands. "I see them!"

The lady relaxed a little but eyed him with slight distaste. "Well, ask them for the score. I just sell tickets."

"I will," Devon replied cheerfully. "You have a good evening." Instead of heading to the stands, he went behind the scoreboard, where he saw the kids with the bikes from the other day. One stood on a ladder and was putting up a number.

"Hey," he called. "Any score?"

The towheaded boy holding the ladder turned and nodded. "1-0 Sharks, but it just started. Just wait. We'll get it back." Then his eyes widened in recognition. "Hey, aren't you from Northside?"

"Not today," Devon replied as he hurried away.

"All black people look alike," he heard the other boy say with disdain.

"You're an idiot," replied his friend.

Devon had to agree. A lot of people were idiots sometimes. But not even idiots were going to ruin his night.

As he headed to the visitor side so he could sit in the shade, he tried to spot numbers 4 and 13 leaving the field. He saw number 4 right off but was vaguely disappointed not to see number 13 among the fielders.

He finally spotted him in his usual spot sitting on the upturned bucket. The boy sat slumped over with both elbows on his thighs, his chin in his hands. He never got up, or even looked up, to greet the players coming into the dugout.

Shrugging, Devon found an open spot behind a row of parents sitting in chairs next to the small metal stands. Since it was the championship game, parents and kids crowded the area and Devon easily blended in.

The Sharks had arrived from Greenland, a county located north of Williams County. It was known mostly for farmland and only supported one middle school. The players all looked as if they were from farms—they were tall and strapping and spoke with deep southern accents. Only two of their players had dark skin, but that was two more than the Bears. Devon hoped they knew how to play ball. He wanted to see the Bears get pummeled.

Much like the game against the Northside Eagles, in the beginning the visitors looked to be the stronger of the two teams. The pitcher for the Sharks was a large kid with an unruly mullet the color of dirty straw. He almost never stopped spitting and wore a sneer that intensified with every pitch he threw. From the first inning, he looked dominant. The first two Bears batters went down swinging and the third ended the inning with a soaring pop-up that never left the infield.

By the end of the fourth inning the score read 4-1 Sharks. Devon watched with pleasure as the Bears left two men on base. Their only run came from another sacrifice steal to second while the guy on third ran home. The coach of the

Bears was trying every trick he knew but couldn't get to the Sharks' pitcher.

Well, almost every trick . . . Number 13 had yet to move from his spot on the bucket. He watched the game like a kid with no money in a candy store—with no joy and a deep longing to get a taste of something he couldn't have.

Devon watched with a frown as the Bears gathered in front of the dugout for a huddle before heading out to the field for the top of the fifth. All the players leaned in to hear every word from their coach . . . all except number 13. He listlessly got to his feet and stepped toward the huddle, but never really joined it. With his head ducked low, he looked as into the game as a rapper was into folk music.

"That boy is in the doghouse," Devon whispered to himself. "Now what did he go and do?"

Then he got mad. If he'd been in the boy's shoes, he wouldn't be moping around like a sad kitten. He would at least be cheering on his teammates. Acting like he was still part of the team, helping anyway he could. Then maybe the coach would change his mind and put him in . . . the Bears could definitely use a good bat.

Instead number 13 slunk back to his bucket and sat down dejectedly. Everything about his body language said he wasn't going to play . . . and that he didn't deserve to play—it was the complete opposite of what Devon had witnessed in the last game.

"Quitter," Devon whispered.

Shaking his head, he watched the next Sharks batter step up to the plate.

The rest of the Bears certainly didn't quit. Number 1 was on the mound now. The starting pitcher had left during the last inning after giving up three consecutive singles.

"Throw it in there, Bobby," yelled the Bears coach from the dugout. He started giving code numbers along with his signs.

The numbers came out quick and precise after each pitch, sort of setting up a rhythm. At first, it worked. The first Sharks batter struck out and the second rolled a short grounder to third for another easy out.

"Keep it going!" called a woman from the Bears stands. "That's it! We'll come back!" She sounded more hopeful than convincing.

The next batter drove a fastball into the gap between third and short. The left fielder made a mistake by charging the hard-hit ball and ended up overrunning it. The ball stopped near the fence before the fielder could retrieve it. When it made it back to the infield, the Sharks had a runner on third.

All the fans around Devon were hollering. Most were on their feet and those in the stands were banging away. On the other side, the Bears' fans were very quiet.

Then the next batter, after fouling off three pitches, hit a shallow fly to center.

"It's a hit!" shouted the man behind Devon. "We got it!"

The fielder got a bad jump and the ball started dropping fast. Just as it looked to be a hit, the fielder lunged forward and made a great diving nab, just managing to get his glove under the ball as it reached the grass.

"No!" howled the man, now lunging past Devon. "He trapped it!"

The Bears crowd went wild as the fans of the Sharks protested. The out counted.

Devon shot a look at number 13, who should've been playing center. The boy still sat on his bucket, his posture just as miserable as before. It was as if he didn't care.

The play did more than end the inning for the Bears. It got the players pumped . . . and the dugout rowdy.

The Sharks players tried to act unconcerned, but Devon could tell they were a little tight. During infield warmups, he counted three errors. Then the Bears sent their first batter to the plate.

"YEEAHHH!" yelled number 4 as the first pitch went low for ball one. "We got this! Here we come, baby!"

Other players joined in.

"Please strike him out, Tommy!" yelled a Sharks parent in front of Devon. "Shut the racket off!"

Tommy, the towheaded pitcher, was tiring. His next pitch missed the target and hung over the plate. The ball was smashed up the middle and into the outfield. It went for a single.

The shouts and jeers of the Bears dugout only increased. It got worse when the next batter followed with a sharply hit grounder down the third baseline. The fielder made a diving attempt to stop it, but was too late. The ball rolled to the fence. It turned into a run-scoring double.

Devon groaned along with many Sharks fans. "Here it goes again," Devon muttered. And so it went.

The next batter drew a walk. This was followed by a shallow fly that dropped for a hit in right field, scoring another run. Runners were left on the corners.

Suddenly it was 4-3 in the fifth inning with no outs and two runners on. Devon knew what would come next. He glared at the back of the Bears coach as he calmly gave instructions to the runner on third base.

Sure enough, on the next pitch, the runner from first broke for second while the runner on third took a big lead toward home. The catcher came up firing.

"No!" yelled the parent next to Devon. "He's going home!"

Seeing the play, the Sharks shortstop jumped to intercept the throw, but by the time he got the ball from his glove into his hand it was too late. The catcher angrily caught the throw home as the runner dusted himself off at the plate. The pitcher got the ball back with the score tied and a runner safe on second. There were still no outs.

Devon shook his head. He watched the rest of the game grimly. The Sharks changed pitchers but couldn't change momentum. The Bears pounded out five more hits and four more runs before finally running out of outs. Through it all, number 13 watched sullenly.

By the seventh inning, the last in the game, it was a rout. The Bears held a 12-5 lead and were starting to celebrate. Even the head coach's severe manner seemed to be loosening. As the players huddled before hitting the field, Devon clearly heard the coach calling number 13's name.

Sounding upbeat, the coach called, "Henry! Where's Henry?"

Henry wasn't paying attention and didn't have his glove near him. He stood in the back with both hands in his back pockets looking at the ground. When the Bears took the field, number 13 remained on the bench.

Three quick outs later, it was over. The Bears had a championship.

Devon watched the team celebrate while shaking his head. As the players hugged and jumped on top of each other, number 13 watched from the fence . . . fighting back tears.

Chapter 9

Devon should have left right then and there. After all, he'd wanted the Bears to lose, right? Why would he stay around to see them hoist the trophy and pose for pictures? Because, he had to admit, he was curious. He wanted to know what happened to number 13. What would make a coach sit a good player for a championship game? Why he cared about any of that, Devon had a harder time explaining.

For some reason, though they were worlds apart and number 13 didn't even know he existed, Devon felt a bond with the kid. They were both small and were taken for granted by grownups who should know better. Devon's grandma didn't understand him, and the Bears coach clearly didn't understand number 13.

Devon watched as the Bears coach shook hands with parents and congratulated his players, but he never once looked in the direction of number 13. The boy wiped his eyes and dutifully posed for team photos, but from his stony expression, it looked as if he'd lost the championship.

After a while and what seemed like hundreds of photos from parents, the players finally gathered their gear and headed for the school parking lot.

"Ice cream celebration again at Cold Stone," called the coach as they left. "Coach Jackson is treating again!"

Devon watched the players leave. At least number 13 didn't walk alone. Number 4 went with him. Number 4 had a good day—he'd gone three for four and had scored three runs. The two players separated near the school, with number 13 going off alone to the back parking lot.

Without really thinking about what he was doing, Devon found himself following. He jogged to close the distance.

He'd nearly caught up with him when he called out, "Yo, number 13!"

The boy stopped and turned. He wore a confused look when he saw Devon. "Yeah?"

"How come you didn't play today? I mean, you looked like you were sick or something."

The boy frowned and dropped his gaze. "Don't know what you're talking about," he muttered.

Devon shrugged. "Suit yourself. But next time you shouldn't hang your head like that. I mean, it was like your dad died or something and you were at his funeral. You quit like that and no way are you going to play."

The boy just stared and then turned, walking away.

Devon shook his head, sorry he'd said anything. He'd meant to offer some sort of comfort but he'd probably done the opposite. Kids like number 13 didn't become friends with kids like him. Deciding to forget about it all, he turned to head home when he froze.

Charlie stood on the bench of the home dugout and surveyed the stream of parents and kids heading for the main parking lot on the other side of the school. Lou and two older teens stood behind him. No one had spotted him yet, but they were clearly looking.

Gulping, Devon ducked his head and jogged toward the side lot after number 13.

"Hey, man," he said, trying hard not to sound desperate. "Can I, uh, borrow your phone? I need to call for a ride."

The boy had pulled off his backpack and set it down next to a wooden railing. He looked at Devon suspiciously, but something in Devon's face must have convinced him it was okay.

"Sure," he mumbled. Reaching down, he pulled a phone from a front pocket of his pack.

"Thanks, man. You have no idea what this means to me." Devon desperately pulled the card Mr. James had given him from his pocket. Turning away from the boy, he dialed the number.

His grandma would never let him have a phone—way too expensive—but he'd borrowed phones from his cousins enough times to know how to use one.

Mr. James picked up on the second ring. Quickly Devon explained that he was stuck at Hamilton Middle and could really use a ride home . . . he would be waiting in the side parking lot away from the sports fields.

"I'll be there," Mr. James said simply. *"Hang tight."* Then he hung up.

"Thanks again," Devon said sincerely, returning the phone.

The boy nodded as he slipped the phone into his front pocket.

Clearly he wasn't interested in talking, so Devon left him to sulk. Making sure Charlie and the others weren't coming, he wandered to the front of the school to keep out of sight and wait.

Henry watched the strange kid vanish around the corner and then lost interest. At first, thinking of Bobby's stolen shoes, he'd feared the kid had meant to steal his phone or worse. He'd made sure both his bats sticking from his backpack were within easy reach.

Now that he'd been left alone, he felt more tears building. He almost wished his phone had been stolen. He hadn't counted on the game being so painful to sit through. The entire time it fell as if somebody had punched him in the gut. The feeling never let up. He'd never been benched before. And he had never played in a championship game before either.

By the time the first players reached him from the parking lot, he was in no mood for ice cream. Pulling out his phone, he texted his mom, asking for a ride home. None of the players talked to him as he kept his head bent low over his phone.

Then he felt a stream of freezing water pour down his back.

"Aiee!" he screeched, arching his back and stumbling to his feet.

Kevin roared with laughter from behind him. He held a mostly empty water bottle. Chris and Bobby, watching from ten feet away, were convulsing in laugher.

"Got your back!" Kevin cried. "Get it? Got your back? Got *your* back!"

"You're a real fruit loop," Henry said in disgust. He wiggled his back, feeling the water trickle down into his pants.

"Ah, don't be sore," Kevin said in fake sympathy. "Here, have a drink." He tossed more water from his bottle on Henry, catching him in the face.

"Hey, quit!" Henry cried.

"Sure, dude," Kevin said. "You want a ride for ice cream?"

Frowning, Henry shook his head. "My mom is already coming. Not too hungry."

"Yeah, it's hard to work up an appetite from the bench," Bobby said, instantly regretting his words. "Uh, I mean, sorry you didn't play."

Chris shrugged. "There's always eighth grade for you next year, man. Me and Bobby, though, this was it. Come on, Bob, my mom should be at the van waiting. Coming, Kev?"

Kevin nodded. "Yeah, I'll be right there."

He turned to Henry and saw the smaller boy glaring at the two eighth graders going to the van.

Kevin grunted. "You don't think either one of them had anything to do with you missing practice, do you? I mean, Chris wouldn't lie about his phone going missing and I doubt Bobby would even have the brains to pull that off."

"Don't forget about the flat tires," Henry said. Then he sighed. "No, I don't think they did it . . . but who did?"

Kevin shrugged. "There are a lot of jealous crazies out there, man. Sure you don't want to come to Cold Stone?"

"With my shirt soaked? No thanks." Henry allowed a small smile. "I'll see you tomorrow. Right?"

"Probably not." Kevin grinned. "With baseball over, Coach can't bench me for skipping school! Oh, uh, bad choice of words . . . I'll be there tomorrow."

Henry shook his head and took a kick at Kevin's knee but missed. "Don't worry. He can always bench you next year."

After Kevin left, Henry was left alone again. Slumping back against the railing, he waited for his mom.

By now almost all the Bears players were gone but not all the coaches. Henry heard Coach Jackson's familiar laughter and then Coach Wood's booming voice.

Swallowing, he decided he didn't want to face either one. Grabbing his pack, he threw it over his shoulder and walked quickly to the side entrance of the school. There he slid to a seat against the door and went still.

A green leafy bush grew next to the sidewalk and the building hiding him from sight. Through its branches he watched his coaches cross the parking lot with Wayne Perkins between them. All three were in good spirits and Coach Wood even let Wayne ride with him in his pickup.

Few players ever rode with Coach Wood—in fact, the coach only had the team over to his house once—for a cookout back in the fall for all interested baseball players. Coach lived in a secluded two-story house mostly hidden by trees. He'd warned the kids about going near the trees since they were still rampant with summer poison ivy. Instead, they were confined to a small patch of grass in the back—too small for twenty-odd boys to start a ball game or even a game of catch. None of them were allowed inside, Henry remembered. His father had respected this, saying every man was entitled to privacy, but his mom had been less than impressed. To her, the coach of a kids' team had to be open and willing to understand and be understood. Hiding behind a gruff exterior, Coach Wood was a man of mystery . . . who lived by rules he meant everyone to follow, no exceptions.

As the pickup rolled away, Coach Jackson climbed into his little green Subaru—the old green car had more miles on it than the coach had strands of dark hair.

For a moment the coach sat in his car looking at his phone and Henry felt a stab of shame for hiding. Unlike

Coach Wood, Coach Jackson was open and friendly, even with his bad temper. He always offered rides to the boys. For a moment Henry was tempted to stand up and run to ask for one, but he held back.

He didn't feel like talking and knew Coach Jackson would want to discuss the game. Chatting about a championship he hadn't played in was not very appealing. He'd messed up and had never even apologized to Coach Wood. If his father had been home, he would have expected the apology and for Henry to accept the punishment.

Thinking of his dad and the pain of watching his team win without him, Henry felt another tear trickling down his cheek. He hastily wiped it away with the back of his hand.

Usually he only cried when he lost a big game . . . but now he knew better. Being told you weren't allowed to play was even worse than losing.

As Coach Jackson drove away, Henry picked himself up and wiped dirt from his pants, ruefully pulling the back of his wet shirt away from his skin. Kevin had no mercy.

He gathered his pack and moved back to the sidewalk. Lost in self-pity, he didn't notice he wasn't alone until he heard a cough.

Looking up, he was surprised to find three youths standing there. They'd stepped over the wood rail and looked just as surprised to see him.

Then their surprise turned into something sinister.

The tallest of the bunch, standing in the back, suddenly grinned and flashed dull yellow teeth. It was not a friendly grin. His gold earring sparkled in his left ear and Henry recognized him as the guy with the "half-off" shirt from the other day. On this day he wore a long black shirt cut off at the sleeves that hung nearly to his knees. Thin ropey muscles rippled from his arms.

"Hey, there," he cooed, sounding like a snake hissing before a deadly strike. "I remember you."

Henry went still. He knew trouble when he saw it and this time he'd stepped right in the middle of it.

"You know this kid, Ray?" demanded the teenager standing in front of the others.

Though appearing to be the youngest of the lot, this one seemed the most dangerous. Thick muscles lined his chest and arms, looking ready to burst from his tight sleeveless T-shirt. A pair of gold earrings matched a heavy gold necklace hanging from his thick neck. A cold gaze of disdain leveled at Henry.

"Oh, we met," purred Ray. "Aren't you the kid who said I couldn't afford to buy anything the other day?"

Henry tried to swallow, but his mouth proved too dry. He took an involuntarily step back. Not knowing what to do, or say, he just stared.

"Not so tough without your friend, are you?" taunted Ray, smirking when he saw Henry step back. "You left here alone?"

Henry's mouth tightened. "I don't think you guys should be here," he said, doing his best to keep his voice from wavering.

Sensing fear, the group of toughs immediately moved forward to form a semicircle around him.

They carried a strong stench of cologne. Henry's eyes watered.

"What did he say?" Ray asked, looking at his companions. "Did he say we don't belong here?"

"What, because we're black?" demanded the third teen aggressively. His head was shaved on the sides just beneath short strands of dark twisted hair sticking straight up, so it looked like an explosion on top of his head. The way he sneered at Henry made him look like a human explosion ready to happen. He curled his lip when he saw Henry's eyes go wide. "What is it, white boy? You scared of us?"

Henry's hands went to his shoulder straps and he dropped his gaze. He could feel his heart pounding against his ribs a mile a minute.

Race was not something he ever really thought or cared about. Black, white, what did it matter? His father had taught him from an early age about the stupidity of judging people without knowing them ... especially by the color of their skin.

"People don't get to pick how they look or what skin color they are—I highly doubt many people's favorite color is the same shade as their bellybutton," his father liked to say. To Henry's father, people were people who made their own decisions. That was how they should be judged—only by their actions and choices, nothing else.

For Henry, this was an easy view to adopt—especially when he went to a school with almost everyone who had the same skin color as him. Most of his contact with kids of different races came through sports and that was easy to deal with.

In sports, the only thing that mattered was the color of your uniform and the name of your team. His teammates were automatically friends and opposing players were, at least for the timeframe of a game, the enemy.

If only the rest of life was so easy. Unfortunately, a lot of people wanted to make skin color a big issue.

The three guys in front of him were all older and bigger and had dark brown skin. They looked at him like he was an insect—small, disgusting, and begging to be slapped. All three looked ready and willing to do the slapping.

"No, because you guys look too old for middle school," Henry finally said, looking up. "Unless you failed a lot of grades."

He did his best to show no fear, but his eyes darted to either side, searching for any sign for help. No luck. Other than him and the three teens, the parking lot was deserted. He really wished he'd grabbed a ride with Coach Jackson.

The third teen, clearly looking for trouble, growled. "Now you calling us stupid?" he demanded, his hair bouncing wildly above him. "Who got left here all by his little self?"

"Shut it," Ray snapped at him. "We're not here for this."

Ignoring his comrades, the youngest teen grinned at Henry and crossed his arms, showing off his bulging muscles. "I'm in middle school," he said. "But you're right, I don't belong here. Maybe you got some spare cash so I can catch a bus home . . . or maybe you can spare some new shoes. You got some nice kicks on those feet."

Henry felt his fight-or-flight response start to kick in. As an older sibling, he had been in family fights before with his brother. But those were nothing major. Shoving matches with a little brother didn't count. He had never been in a real fight against somebody who really wanted to hurt him. Briefly he wondered about the likelihood of outrunning the three with his baseball pack on. Not likely . . .

"Lou," Ray said, sounding sad, "I don't think the kid understands us. Maybe you should help him out."

Lou grinned. "My pleasure." He leaned forward. Even as the youngest of the bunch, he stood several inches taller than Henry. He loomed like a cat facing a mouse, poised to pounce.

Henry met his gaze and tried not to flinch. Lou's short black hair had a jagged line buzzed from the front to the back so it resembled a lightning bolt. His eyes, the color of coal, looked about to burst into flame.

"Tell you what, *kid*," he said, making "kid" sound as if it were a nasty word. "We'll make a deal. We're looking for a runaway. If you see him, you're free to go. If not . . . well, you have to pay Ray. Cash or shoes." His hand darted out and knocked Henry's baseball cap sideways. "Got that?"

Henry licked his lips. Despite not having been in a fight, he'd witnessed his share at middle school. He knew the person who got in the first hit usually won. If it came down to it, he would have to strike first.

"Got what?" came a shout from behind him. "A hairline? Looks like you have at least five of those, Lou. Who cut your hair? A blind bat?"

Startled, the youths looked past Henry. Then their eyes lit up.

"There you are, Devon!" crowed Ray. "Charlie said he spotted you here!"

"I didn't have to spot you three," the voice shot back. "I just have to sniff the air. You guys reek! What happened? You guys steal your sisters' perfume?"

Henry shifted his body and glanced back to see the boy who had borrowed his phone earlier.

The boy, Devon, stood on the sidewalk near the front of the school. For some reason he was grinning.

Henry was about to inch away when Lou grabbed his arm and yanked him back. His other arm locked around Henry's chest and he pulled him tightly in front of him. Lou proved as strong as he looked and Henry was too startled to resist. His bulky pack pressed into Lou, but the burly boy didn't let it prevent his strong grip.

"You get over here, Devon!" cried Lou. "And we'll let this kid go."

Devon sneered back. "Why would I care if you let the kid go or not?"

"Why else did you show yourself now?" Lou asked triumphantly. He grinned. "This your friend?"

Henry had had enough. He didn't like being grabbed and definitely didn't like being used as a bargaining tool.

"No, he's not," he muttered. "And neither are you."

He raised his right foot and kicked backward, striking Lou sharply in the shin. At the same time, he twisted his shoulders. So upset after the game, he hadn't bothered to change out of his baseball cleats.

Lou's eyes bugged out and he screamed in pain, nearly collapsing to his knees.

"Hey, get him!" Ray roared.

He and the other teen lunged forward, but Henry hadn't starred as running back on the Bears football team for nothing. Throwing his weight to the left, he twisted off one grasp and juked past another, slamming his baseball pack into Ray's side in the process. The teen grunted as he staggered to the side.

Henry stomped on the third teen's foot with the heel of his cleats. Another screech and the thug went down.

"Over here!" Devon yelled at him. "Hurry, man!"

Henry complied, racing across the sidewalk as the pursuers started to organize behind him.

"I'm bleeding, man!" howled Lou. "He busted my shin!" His teeth were clenched in pain.

"We're going to pound you both, you twerps!" Ray roared.

"Over here!" Devon yelled to Henry. He led the way around the school to the main entrance. Both boys were out of breath when they reached the wall of glass doors. The doors were shut and there were no lights on the other side.

"It's locked!" Henry yelled. "There's nobody left!" He looked over his shoulder and saw the three teens on their feet and coming after them in full sprint. Lou, though hobbling, led the charge.

"Just give me a bat!" Devon shouted at him.

They stood under an overhang leading from the parking lot to the entrance. There were no teachers or parents left in the area. The boys were trapped.

Henry dropped his pack to the floor and pulled out both baseball bats, giving one to Devon. The two boys faced their aggressors.

"Put those down," Ray ordered as he reached the overhang. "And you won't get hurt."

"That's what you think," hissed Lou. He bent low and rubbed his chin. His dark eyes stared dangerously at the boys. "You, white boy, can leave now. I'll forget what you just did. But, Devon, man, you're dead meat. You get all the punishment."

Devon grinned. "Before you do anything, smile and say cheese. You boys are on camera."

Ray frowned. "What are you talking about?"

"This is a school," Devon said, grinning wider. "There're cameras everywhere, man, especially right here at the entrance. There are probably microphones, too, Ray. And Lou. You guys are all being recorded and anything you say or do will be used against you."

Just like that, the assailants turned into scared rabbits.

"Let's get out of here," Ray mumbled, backing away. "I'm not facing court again."

Lou made to protest, but then nodded. He muttered a curse. "There's always another day, Devon." Glaring, he followed Ray.

"See you, Lou," Devon said, waving the bat, still smiling.

"I'll get you," Lou called over his shoulder.

When the teenagers had gone, Devon let out a huge sigh of relief and handed the bat back to Henry. Henry took it but stared at him warily, his tongue pressed against the inside of his cheek.

"Thanks for the bat," Devon said. "Um, sorry about that . . . They were after me, if you hadn't noticed."

Henry only nodded. "No problem," he muttered. "My mom is on her way."

Devon grunted. "My ride is coming too, but we better both wait here . . . in case they're watching."

Henry stuffed the bats back in his pack. He avoided looking at Devon and didn't feel like talking. It had to be one of the worst days of his life. First he was benched for a championship game, and now he found himself in the middle of some kind of loser gang spat. He took a seat by his pack and hugged his knees.

Devon slouched against one of the doors and went just as silent. This wasn't a great day for him, either.

Chapter 10

Devon's ride showed up first, a beat-up Ford pickup. Pulling up by the curb, Mr. James honked the horn.

"That's me, man," Devon said, standing up straight and stretching. As he walked past Henry, he paused. "Hey, man, do I at least get your name? I'm Devon."

"Henry," the boy replied, almost reluctantly. It sounded more like a goodbye than a greeting.

Nodding, Devon went to meet Mr. James.

"Thanks for the ride," he muttered, opening the door and climbing in without looking at the driver.

Mr. James grunted. Then he jerked a chin toward Henry. "Who's the boy there?" he asked. "Looks like a ballplayer. One of your friends?"

Devon made a face. "Not really . . . we, uh, were just hanging out." Then he ducked his head. "His mom is coming. We can go."

Mr. James narrowed his eyes. "That right?" He raised his voice. "You there! Come over here! I don't want to leave you alone waiting. Not safe here at night."

Looking around, Henry reluctantly got to his feet and hoisted his pack onto his shoulders. He moved to the truck and nodded his thanks.

"I see you're a ballplayer," Mr. James said. "Devon, slide over and make some room. No use having him stand out there."

"Uh, no thanks," Henry said. "I better stay out here so my mom can see me."

Devon grunted. No rich kid was going to climb in an old pickup with two dark-skinned strangers, he thought. Henry, he knew, wanted nothing to do with him or Mr. James.

Mr. James nodded as if he understood perfectly. Then to Devon's horror, he proceeded to tell Henry all about the church baseball tournament. "You play little league?" he asked when he'd finished.

Henry nodded slightly.

"Good. Then you're eligible to play for our church. It's mainly for kids who want to play but don't get the chance. Somebody like you can surely help boys like that."

"If he wants," Devon muttered.

"If he wants," agreed Mr. James. "We're the Resurrection Baptist Church, not too far from here. We can have up to two little league players on our team and so far we have none. So you can bring a friend. And don't worry, all players in the tournament are eligible to be selected for County All-Stars." Mr. James winked. "The county is getting wise—some of our boys are pretty good. Here, take some forms."

Henry unenthusiastically took the offered forms. Thankfully his mom's car pulled in a moment later.

"If you decide to play, drop your forms off at our church on Sunday!" Mr. James called to him as he turned to leave.

Henry nodded and gave a small wave. Getting in his mom's car, he stuffed the forms in his back pocket. He was just happy to end the horrible day.

Henry had a tough time falling asleep that night. It was a warm night and his little brother snored in the bunk above him but that had never bothered him before.

Lying on top of his covers, he stared up in the darkness, feeling as if a dark hole had opened above him and swallowed him whole.

His team had won the championship game . . . but all he could feel was a terrible loss. Sighing, he turned on his side and tried closing his eyes . . . No sleep came. After tossing and turning for what seemed like hours, he finally rolled out of bed.

The clock on the nightstand by his bed said it was just past midnight. Standing in the middle of the room in his boxer shorts, he took deep breaths and went still. The room was strangely quiet. Then his brother's voice whispered near his head.

"What would you do if a monster came into the room right now?" he said, his voice heavy with sleep.

Henry grunted. "I would feed it my little brother and then go to sleep," he hissed.

Michael groaned and rolled over. "I would throw my shoe at it."

"What shoe? You're in bed. Now go to sleep!"

"You should be sleeping!" Michael said back to him, sitting up, now awake. "And this shoe! I always sleep with my baseball shoes before a big game."

Henry could just make out the dark shadow of his brother in the bunk above him. He knew his crazy brother held a pair of cleats. He shook his head. "So that's why Mom always says our room stinks."

"My shoes smell like victory!"

"Shh!" Henry said suddenly. "I hear something!"

"Yeah, right," Michael snorted in scorn. He started to say something more, but his voice choked off. He'd heard it too.

From just outside their room came a soft thump and then a floorboard creaked.

"What is it?" Michael hissed, rising to his knees.

"Quiet!" Henry hissed back. "Someone's there."

He crept closer to the door but crouched low and didn't move past the head of his bed. Above him, Michael had his cleats held over his head, weapons at the ready.

The boys knew monsters existed . . . not the monsters with the cheesy makeup or CGI graphics found in movies, but *real* monsters. Human monsters—the type who broke into people's homes . . . who went after kids . . . who held no value on another human's life. The scary kind.

Henry thought of the teens he'd met earlier that day. What if they'd followed him home?

Henry could feel sweat under his arms and on his forehead. Reaching down, he blindly groped around until he found his pajama pants. Anything was better than nothing.

"If the door opens, I'll rush in and wrap this around his neck," he whispered, pulling the pants tight between his hands.

"And I'll jump from above and smash his head with my cleats," Michael whispered back.

A scratching sound came from the other side of the door. And then, ever so slowly, the doorknob started to turn.

Henry's heart thudded against his chest. He could hear Michael's heavy breathing above him. The door started to open.

"Henry?" whimpered a small, tired voice. "I heard voices."

"Oh, no!" groaned Michael, sounding more disappointed than relieved. Dropping his shoes, he flopped backward on the bed.

"Hey! Ouch!" complained Henry as the shoes dropped squarely on his head.

"Anabelle," Michael wailed. "What are you doing?"

"I woke up," their little sister said simply, walking into their room. A faint light from the first floor allowed the boys to see her in her teddy bear nightie—standing in the doorway like a little lamb.

"We thought you were a monster!" Michael nearly shouted.

Anabelle coughed. Then she yawned. "I heard you guys talking . . . Henry, are you mad about baseball still?"

Henry had tried to hide his feelings at dinner that night but knew his grief had been plain to see.

"No. Come on, Anabelle," he muttered gruffly as he quickly pulled on his pajama pants. "I'll go tuck you in."

"First give me my shoes back," Michael demanded.

"Sure." Reaching down, Henry found the shoes and threw them up and over the bedrail.

"Ouch!" cried Michael. Then he leaned over. "See? I told you they would be good weapons."

Henry rolled his eyes and found his old Red Sox shirt under his pillow. Slipping it on, he led his little sister back to her room. After a quick hug, he made sure she lay back down and gave her a quick head rub.

"I'll be okay," he told her.

"Promise?" Anabelle asked sleepily. "I don't like it when you're sad . . ."

"Promise," Henry sighed as he watched his sister drift off to sleep. He didn't like being sad either. When he returned to his room, Michael's snores once again filled the air.

Very much awake, Henry quietly retreated from the room and closed the door. He followed the faint light flickering from downstairs and found his mom sitting on the couch watching a late-night talk show.

"Henry," she said looking up in surprise, blinking away tiredness. "What are you doing up so late?" Then she smiled guiltily. "Can't sleep either, huh?"

Henry nodded from where he stood just inside the living room. He leaned his head against the wall. "I just can't forget the game," he admitted.

His mom sighed. "Oh, Henry. I wish your father were here. He would have known what to do." She fingered her wedding ring wistfully. "I miss him when he's away like this, and I know you do too. Here, come sit with me. I know you're too big for my lap, but you're not too big to sit next to me, right?"

Mrs. Lee sat up and scooted to make room for her son. She wore a cream-colored bathrobe and pink fuzzy slippers— both had been Christmas gifts from Mr. Lee.

As Henry sank down on the couch next to her, she pulled him close and stroked his hair. For once, Henry didn't mind. He needed a hug right now.

His mom put her arm around his shoulders and squeezed. "I know you wanted to play so bad . . . I tried calling your coach, but he wouldn't listen to me. He kept saying he understood but couldn't do anything. It was like talking to a congressman. Some coach, huh?"

Henry grunted. "He's not easy to talk to."

"Most men aren't," his mother said dryly. "Just make sure you don't grow up to be like that. Here, since you're up, let's at least put on a baseball game. I'm sure one of the west coast games is still on." Grabbing the remote, she flipped channels until she found a game.

Henry watched, biting his lower lip. Then he glanced up at his mom's face. "Mom, what do you think about me going to a Baptist church on Sunday?"

Mrs. Lee raised her eyebrows. "I would think you better explain a little more about it."

Henry told her about the upcoming tournament.

"That would be great!" Mrs. Lee responded when he'd finished. "Your father would be very proud, I think. The only question is, is this something you really want to do?"

Henry shrugged and stared back at the TV. "I don't know . . . Maybe."

They stayed up together like this—watching the Angels play the Rangers while talking about Baptist baseball and Henry's father . . . and the next thing Henry knew, he was opening his eyes to daylight. A pillow had replaced his mom's knee and a blanket covered him.

Groaning, he blinked rapidly as he stretched out, still on the couch.

"Oh, you're awake," his mom said, coming in from the kitchen. "I didn't have the heart to wake you and definitely didn't think I could carry you. So I made waffles and sausage instead."

Henry's eyes widened. He wondered if his mom had even slept. Her eyes were puffy and she still wore her bathrobe. "What time is it?" he asked.

"Just time enough for you to go up and get ready for school and eat your breakfast before missing your bus. Wake Michael while you're up there. I'll take care of Anabelle. Oh, and if you're wondering, the Angels won in the eleventh."

Henry groaned and forced himself to stand. Walking blearily up the stairs, he stopped by the bathroom. After washing his hands, he went to his room and stepped up the small ladder to his brother's bunk. He hadn't dried his hands and they were dripping wet.

Michael lay curled in a ball with his baseball cleats hugged close to his chest. He snored gently and didn't look ready to get up anytime soon.

Henry grinned as he sprinkled water on his brother's face and then shook his shoulder.

"Hey, Michael," he said.

"Wh-what?" spluttered his brother, blinking from the water droplets.

"Don't you hate it when you forget to wash your hands after using the bathroom?"

Michael's eyes instantly snapped open. "What?" he cried. "Are you for real?"

Henry rubbed his hands in his brother's hair and then jumped to the floor. "See you later!" he shouted as he snatched the shorts and shirt that his mom had laid out on the dresser the day before.

"You're just joking, right?" his little brother hollered after him.

Henry still didn't know if he would play for the Baptist team, but he at least felt a little better.

At lunch that day, after nearly falling asleep in math, Henry slumped in his seat next to Kevin.

Kevin was moaning to Chris and Bobby about his community service starting that Monday. "The only good thing is," he lamented, "I get to play baseball doing it."

"What type of community service is this?" Chris asked. "I would think you *not* playing baseball would be a service to your community."

"Ah, laugh it up," Kevin said sourly. "This is for that dumb church tournament. I have to pick a church from the 'underprivileged area' and play for them. That means I have to miss a week of little league games."

Henry almost choked on a bite of pizza. Coughing, he put down his pizza slice. "What church are you picking?" he asked when he could speak again.

"I don't know," Kevin said with a sigh. "I wanted to play for Coach Wood, but he's coaching First Presbyterian. They're the host church, so they can't count as 'underprivileged.'"

"Yeah," Bobby said savagely. "Not enough black kids go there. Besides, Chris and I are already playing for them."

"You and most of the team," grunted Kevin. "I thought only two players could play on one team."

"Because we go there," Chris explained gleefully. "We don't count as little league players. We're stacked!"

"Whatever. I'm going to be the only idiot to join one of the loser churches. They probably won't even want me."

Henry took a deep breath and spoke up. "I, uh, was asked to play for a church . . ."

Kevin's eyes lit up and he turned on Henry, a French fry poised as a sword. He jabbed the fry in Henry's face. "Really? Which one?"

Henry licked his lips. "Is, uh, Resurrection Baptist on your list?"

Kevin crammed the fry in his mouth and dug a piece of paper out of his pocket. He scanned it rapidly. "Yes!" he cried, sending fry guts spitting from his mouth. "It's here, all right." He looked at Henry with unabashed pleading. "Please tell me you're doing it. Right? You have to, for me! Please!"

"Um, not really sure," Henry said doubtfully. "Maybe."

"Do it," Bobby told him. "Our team would love to pound you."

"Yeah," joked Chris. "And that way Coach can't bench you for skipping practice."

Henry sucked up milk in his straw and stopped it with his tongue. Lifting it up, he turned to Chris and blew it in his face.

It was decided. He would join the team with Kevin.

Melissa and Shorty stayed after school that day to work on their baseball story. So far all they had were some photos and no words.

"I just can't do it," Melissa said in frustration. "I mean, you saw that game. You were there."

Shorty nodded tiredly. He'd been listening to the same thing all day. "Yeah, yeah. Coach Wood turned down your interview request. We know. That doesn't make him a criminal. Besides, Coach Jackson let us ask him questions."

"And he did nothing but pick his nose and give blah, blah answers." She mimicked Coach Jackson's deep voice, "Coach Wood is great and got the team organized. Whoop-dee-doo." In her normal voice, she said, "Shorty, do you realize we know nothing about Coach Wood's personal life?"

"Uh, so what? What does that make him?"

"It makes him suspicious! I mean, it's obvious he's hiding something. And what about Henry Lee? Why wasn't he allowed to play yesterday? Because of the phone call, I bet. I bet he interrupted some sort of drug deal and—"

"Melissa, before you accuse somebody like that you'd better have proof." Shorty sighed. "Seriously. Mrs. Warner wants to see our story before the weekend. Can't we just put something down and call it a day?"

Melissa grunted. They were in the computer lab staring at a blank Word document. This would be for the last edition of the paper before summer break. She wanted to end it with a big one—something that mattered, something important. Something like solving the drug mystery at school.

So far all the other writers were turning in sappy stories about graduating eighth graders and the hardships of standardized tests. She didn't want to add to the pile with a corny baseball story.

"Fine," she snapped. "Then what do we know about Coach Wood?"

Shorty groaned. "Ah, Melissa . . ."

Melissa ignored him. "We know he coached here for three years. He's former military. He's smug, arrogant, and thinks he can do whatever he pleases."

"Yeah and we know he just won a school championship," Shorty said. "Welcome to American sports. Success means you're above the law."

"Until you're caught red-handed," Melissa said grimly. "And we're going to do it."

"We are?" Shorty asked. "Do what?"

"Find out Coach Wood's secret."

Shorty groaned. "You've got to be kidding, Melissa. What if he's innocent? Just because you don't like a guy and know little about him doesn't mean he's guilty. What if the baseball team has nothing to do with the drugs?"

"They have to," Melissa said, brushing off Shorty's logic. "I got my softball friends to ask around and they're pretty sure something funny is going on with baseball. They didn't give names, but some of the boys are definitely up to something. Besides, we have no other leads. We just need to learn more about Coach Wood."

"And Coach Jackson," added Shorty. He sighed again. "Fine. Let's add to your list."

"That's all I got," Melissa said dejectedly.

Shorty grunted. "Well, I know where he lives."

Melissa perked up. "You do?"

"Yeah. Our bus goes by his place all the time. And you know what? It's the quietest house on the street. You can barely see it with all the trees."

"That makes it perfect—nobody would suspect him."

"That's because nobody is ever there! I've only seen him a couple of times and that's when he mows the lawn. Melissa, give it a rest. It's Friday! We need a story for Mrs. Warner that doesn't accuse our baseball coach of something illegal."

Melissa made a face and her shoulders slumped. "I guess," she allowed. "But this isn't over. You keep your ears open in the office."

"Will do," Shorty said tiredly. "Um, speaking of which, they were discussing the dance today. You know it's tomorrow, right?"

Melissa frowned at him. "What does that have to do with anything?"

Shorty gulped. "Uh, well, are you going?" He cleared his throat as her face twisted in disgust. "I, uh, mean, most of the baseball team will be there, and, uh, well, a dance is a good place to pass out, you know, drugs . . ." he trailed off feebly.

For a moment Melissa frowned. Then her expression turned thoughtful. Finally she grinned. "Shorty! You're a genius! Meet me at my house at six tomorrow. My mom will drive us. Now get out of here and leave me alone. I'll type Mrs. Warner's story, but then I'll type my own later!"

Clearly relieved, Shorty staggered to his feet and nodded. He stopped at the door. "So . . . is it a date?" he wondered aloud.

Melissa, her hands flying furiously over the keyboard, didn't seem to hear.

Chapter 11

When Shorty McCrea knocked on Melissa's door the next evening, he did a nervous sniff test for each armpit. Letting out a deep breath, he quickly combed back his slicked-up hair with his fingers.

"Coming!" he heard Melissa call from behind the door.

Instantly he went rigid and gulped. Then, licking his lips, he told himself, "It's going to be fine. You're smooth as silk."

And then Melissa ruined it all by opening the door.

"Come in, Shorty," she said, stepping aside. "My mom's getting her keys. She loses them all the time. It may take a while."

Shorty just stared. He was slightly aware that his jaw was hanging open.

"What?" Melissa asked, frowning. "Are you okay? Do you need the bathroom?"

"Uh, what? Uh, no, no," Shorty said quickly, shaking his head. "It's just . . . you look great."

Melissa snorted. "In this stupid thing? Please, it's not like anybody is going to see my dress. I just put on the first thing I found."

Gulping, Shorty entered Melissa's foyer and tried hard not to stare at the beautiful girl in front on him. "What do you mean nobody is going to see your dress? Aren't we . . . you know, going to the dance?"

Shorty certainly hoped so. He'd spent the last hour showering, ironing, and pulling on the nicest clothes he owned. He wore dark slacks and a velvet green button-down shirt that matched his eyes. His mom, when hearing about the dance "date," had helped and even had him stick a red rose in his front pocket. Thinking of his flower caused Shorty to blush. He'd forgotten the bouquet for Melissa in the backseat of his dad's car.

Melissa laughed at his expression. She had on a dark blue dress with straps over each shoulder. The dress hugged her form perfectly and ended just above her knees. Her long, golden legs practically glowed. "Shorty, have you ever been to a school dance before?"

"Uh, now that you mention it . . . no."

"Get ready, then," Melissa said wiggling her eyebrows. "You're in for a real experience."

Shortly after, Shorty began the experience. He could feel the music before he could hear it. As soon as he stepped out the back of Melissa's mom's car onto the sidewalk in front of Hamilton Middle, he felt the ground tremble beneath him.

"Do you feel that?" he asked, his voice nearly breaking. "Or is it just me?"

Melissa laughed as she got out of the front passenger seat. "Pick up us at eleven, Mom," she said through the window. "Hopefully we'll survive until then. Come on, Shorty. We haven't even begun the fun yet."

"Oh, er, I think the fun already ended," Shorty said, tugging at his collar.

They'd arrived twenty minutes after the dance had begun, but still groups of kids were heading toward the gym. A few couples were standing on the sidewalk whispering. Some were dressed up like Shorty, but many wore plain T-shirts and jeans. Each step closer to the gym brought them closer to the reverberating bass. Shorty's ears were beginning to ring and his head had started to develop a dull ache.

He nervously fingered the ten-dollar bill his mom had made him take. He was supposed to pay for both tickets, but right now all he had the urge to do was to turn and run home.

"Two tickets, please," Melissa said when they reached the outside door of the gym.

Mrs. Lewis, the eighth grade science teacher, manned the ticket desk. She had the stance of a bouncer ready to pounce on the first hint of trouble.

"Are you two both students here?" she demanded. Then she blinked. "Oh, Melissa! And is that you, Mr. McCrea?" She sounded surprised. "Are you two coming in together?"

"That's the idea," Melissa said sweetly. She already had ten dollars extended. "I'll see you Monday!"

"Hold on," Mrs. Lewis called. "Do you want stamps to get back in just in case you leave?"

Melissa arched her eyebrows. "Who would ever want to leave a Hamilton Middle dance?" she asked in feigned shock.

The real question, Shorty quickly realized, was who would ever want to *enter* a Hamilton Middle dance?

He at least had the wherewithal to run and open the door for Melissa. Doing so, he stuffed his ten-dollar bill deep in his pocket in disgust. Then he entered his worst living nightmare. The noise hit him upside the head like a high and inside fastball. He never recovered.

A middle school dance could be described as akin to the mind going mad at eighty miles an hour in every direction. It just didn't make sense. Or, better yet, a zombie invasion at night in the middle of a war zone. Screams, explosive music, and mindless wandering seemed to be the norm. Already half the dance population seemed to have lost their brains.

Shorty tried to take it all in while remaining on his feet.

Hip-hop blared from about a dozen speakers placed along the far wall. Lined up facing inward, they acted as a mechanical firing squad that drove everyone away. The floor in front of the speakers was almost completely empty. All the students were crowded together on the edges of the gym screaming at each other to be heard over the music. Mostly the boys were on the right side and the girls gathered on the left. In the center of the speakers, two tables had been put together to form a V. There, a hired DJ played with his huge radio synthesizer that emitted the deafening music. Shorty couldn't tell if the music was any good or what the lyrics even were. He just knew it felt as if the music was like a drill boring into his head from every angle.

Decorations of balloons and palm trees made out of paper had been set up around the gym, but they mostly became hazards as people tried to walk around them. With the main lights off, nobody could see much of anything. The DJ had a strobe light at his table which kept swinging back and forth, but that only caused more havoc. Melissa had been right. Nobody would see her dress.

"Come on!" Melissa shouted in his ear. "We need to get out there and start looking around!"

"What?" Shorty shouted.

"The Plan!"

"Fan?" Shorty replied, screaming in Melissa's face. "Where? It is hot in here!"

"You need air, already?"

Thankfully the obnoxiously loud song chose this moment to end and a refreshing quiet descended.

"Good evening, Hamilton Middle!" boomed the DJ into a mic shoved near his face. "Welcome to the last dance of the year! Summer is coming and so is the hottest music on this side of the border! Grab a partner and hit the floor!"

"Quick," Melissa said, grabbing Shorty's arm. "Let's go!"

"You want to dance?" Shorty asked, his voice definitely cracking this time.

"No! We have to split up to cover the whole floor. You go to the boy side and I'll take the girl side. Keep an eye out for anything suspicious and report back to me."

"How?"

"Just yell really loud. We'll meet at the refreshment table!"

Then the music started again—really loud, drowning out any protest Shorty made. This time, more of the students congregated on the floor and the "dancing" began. Shorty headed in that direction, but quickly changed his mind. The bumping and swaying before him, along with screeching music, reminded him of banshees from a horror movie. He hurried to the wall where most of the boys still stood. It was unbearably hot and sweat already soaked his shirt. This was not what he'd expected . . .

Henry arrived at Gabby's place just after seven thirty. Unfortunately, his mom couldn't find a babysitter for the twenty-minute drive to the dance and back, so Michael and Anabelle shared the backseat with him. The front seat was reserved for Gabby.

"Go get in there, Sport," his mom said as she switched off the engine. "Don't forget the flowers. We'll be waiting here."

Henry rolled his eyes, looking miserable. "Mom . . . really?"

"No kissing," Michael said, puckering his lips. "I'll be watching!"

Annabelle giggled.

"Shut it, twerp," Henry growled as he exited the car. He slammed the door behind him. He couldn't wait for another four years when he could get his driver's license.

After making sure his tie was straight, he trotted up the steps to Gabby's front door. She lived in an elegant two-story brick house with dark blue shutters and a perfectly kept lawn. He hoped she wouldn't mind the extra company waiting in the car.

"Gabby, your boyfriend is here!" yelled a slim teenager standing just inside the front door. He viewed Henry's choice of a starched white button-down shirt, red tie, and black slacks with a critical eye. Henry hadn't even had a chance to ring the doorbell.

"You leave him alone, Eric!" he heard Gabby yell. "Hurry up, Mom! I'm going to be late!"

"Late and beautiful," huffed a woman's voice, slightly accented. "Now stand still."

"You can come in," Eric told Henry, leaning lazily against the doorframe. The main door was open, but a screen door blocked the way. "But first you have to say the password." Eric looked to be about fifteen or sixteen. He acted about eight.

Henry raised his eyebrows. "Uh, please?"

"Nope. Not it." Eric yawned. "So, I hear you play baseball, football, basketball, and can hold your breath for two hours."

"Three hours," growled Henry. "I hear you play the flute and collect Barbies."

Eric blinked and laughed. "That's it. That's the password. You can come in now." He swept open the screen door and bowed low.

Henry frowned and made sure to brush the bouquet of flowers across Eric's face as he entered.

"Nice," Eric said twitching his nose. Straightening, he mussed up Henry's neatly combed hair. "You can take a seat if you want. We can probably hook up a video game and play a few levels before my sister is ready."

"Uh, no, thanks," Henry said. The inside of the house proved just as nice as the outside. He kept looking at the flight of stairs to the right of door.

"Are you sure? I have a computer set up right over here." Eric headed into the room to the right, where a desktop computer was set up near the far wall. On the screen, Henry saw, was his Facebook post to Gabby—paused right before his big fall.

Henry felt his face grow hot. "I'll wait here," he said stiffly.

Disappointed, Eric sat on the back edge of the sofa. "Sure. Hey, I hear you dad owns Soup'or Subs. Is that right?"

Henry turned to Eric and smirked. He was ready for this. He'd visited Gabby's Facebook page enough times to know she had an older brother who loved to eat. Reaching in his pocket, he pulled out a yellow gift card and tossed it to Eric. "Here. That should last you the week."

Eric's eyes bugged out. "Thirty dollar gift card? Oh, man, I hope she marries you quick!"

"What was that?" Gabby called down. "That better not be what I heard you say, Eric! I'm coming down!"

"Be dainty, Gabriella," Gabby's mom called. "Don't mess up your hair!"

Henry's eyes grew wide as Gabby descended the stairs. To him, it was as if wings of an angel carried her.

Even Eric whistled appreciatively. "Nice going, sis," he said.

"Shut it, Eric," she snapped, but couldn't hide a pleased smile.

She wore a sparkling sky-blue dress that flowed from her shoulders like a shimmering waterfall. Her hair, put up in a twist, had a curl hanging just above her right eyebrow. With just the right amount of makeup and mascara, she looked like a model going to a high-class photo shoot.

"I hope we're not too late," Gabby's mom said worriedly, following her daughter.

"Uh, the wait," Henry assured her, "was well worth it."

Thankfully Michael was too stunned by Gabby's beauty to dare open his mouth. He kept silent the entire drive to the dance. Anabelle kept asking Gabby if she was a princess from a movie.

Henry apologized, but Gabby only laughed, clearly pleased with the attention. "I'm not in any movie, but who knows? Maybe tonight will be a fairy tale, right?" To Mrs. Lee, she said, "You know, I've never been to a school dance before. My mother never let me until she saw Henry's video. After that, she couldn't say no."

"And neither could you, huh?" Mrs. Lee said with a chuckle.

"Nope. Not me, either."

"My son has that effect on girls. Make sure he earns it, though."

Henry's face burned and he tugged on his tie. He went as speechless as Michael.

Inside the gym, the room pulsed with a new hit song and girls dragged their boyfriends to the center of the floor for an awkward mosh pit.

Henry turned to look at Gabby. "Should we?" he shouted.

Her eyes gleamed back at him. "Let's!"

They entered the dance fray and quickly cleared a space. Both proved to be excellent dancers. Gabby had taken lessons since she was three and Henry had watched enough YouTube videos and practiced with Dance Revolution to be more than competent on a dance floor. To him, dance moves could easily be transferred into football moves when playing running back. Other couples gave way and many just stopped to watch them.

"Oh, yeah!" whooped an eighth-grade girl. "Nice stuff, you two!"

Three dances later, both were dripping with sweat. Their hair no longer looked so perfect, but their faces were flushed with excitement and happiness. A slow song started to play and Henry grinned sheepishly. "Should we get, uh, refreshments?"

"Yes, let's," Gabby agreed. "I think I can use a break. Oh, my goodness, this is so fun!"

Henry led the way to the back tables where punch and cookies were being served. Just before he got there, a line of boys blocked his way. His baseball teammates had found him.

"There he is!" cried Bobby. "It's about time you showed up! Where's your hot girlfriend, lover boy?"

"Yeah," added Wayne, pushing his way to the front. "How come you're heading this way? Isn't that your song? This is the moment, Henry. Get some tongue action going!"

Other boys hooted and made rude noises.

Frowning, Henry tried to shove past Wayne. "Lay off," he said, clearly embarrassed.

"Not so fast, dude," Chris said, grabbing his collar. "We've been waiting for this moment ever since your video. Get back out there and dance with the honey." He held up his camera. "We want a sequel to the hit video of the year!"

"YEAH!" cried Kevin. Others joined in.

"Grab her, Henry!" yelled a rude voice.

Flustered and more than embarrassed, Henry turned to Gabby and froze. She stood watching him, trembling. In the dim light from the lamps set up along the back wall, he saw tears in her eyes.

"Gabby," he began, but all at once, she turned and fled. "Wait!" he cried.

Rushing after her, he lost her in the crowd of dancers. Desperately searching, he caught sight of her slipping out the back door behind the DJ. Dodging swaying bodies and nearly running over more than one student, he slipped between two speakers and made it out the door. "Gabby?" he called.

The sun had completely sunk below the horizon and the only light came from the lamps in the parking lot. Against this light he spotted a lone silhouette sitting on a bench by the flagpole.

"Gabby?" he asked hesitantly as he approached.

"Go away," Gabby answered him, muffled by sobs. "Just leave me alone."

"I . . . I'm sorry," Henry mumbled, not really sure what he was apologizing for. He hadn't told his teammates to act like goons. "What's wrong?"

Gabby lifted her head and whirled to look at him. "I thought you were the real thing, Henry. I didn't come here to be . . . to be your trophy!"

Henry stopped, stunned. "I . . ."

"I've never been so shamed in my entire life! Just go back to them and enjoy the dance."

"Not without you."

"Tough. I already texted my brother. He's on his way now. And if he sees you here, he'll probably beat you up, so you better leave!" She buried her head in her hands and wouldn't look at him.

Crushed, Henry stumbled back. Not knowing what to do, he walked back to a row of bushes that had been planted in front of the school. From there, hidden in the shadows, he watched his first date cry alone until her brother pulled up. She got in his car and they roared off.

Henry wiped his own tears away. He didn't turn when he felt a presence behind him.

"I'm so sorry, man," Kevin said, sounding like he meant it. "I-I think we got carried away back there . . . It was Wayne's idea, but . . . still . . . I'm sorry."

Henry resisted the urge to turn and belt his friend in the eye. Instead he took a deep breath and slunk off to the bench.

"Where are you going?" Kevin called to him.

"Home. I'm calling my mom."

"What about tomorrow? You still going to the Baptist church for baseball?"

Henry threw up a hand in disgust, but then stopped. "Yeah," he said finally. Baseball was something he needed now more than ever. "You going with me?"

"No. My mom turned in my form to my little league coach earlier today. I'm already set. Uh, see you, Henry."

"Can't wait," Henry said in reply, stalking off in a huff.

Melissa and Shorty never made it to eleven. It wasn't even half past ten when Melissa found Shorty curled in a ball near the exit door with his hands pressed over his ears.

"There you are!" she shouted. "What are you doing?"

"Surviving!" Shorty shouted back. He got to his feet. "Do you know how many wedgies I got tonight?"

"Let's just go," Melissa said, dragging him to the door. Outside the fresh quiet air hit like a comforting plunge in cool water on a hot day.

"Finally," breathed Shorty. "I feel alive again."

Melissa snorted. "Well," she said, "that was a waste of time. I didn't find anything but a bunch of grabby jerks." She rubbed a bruised knuckle on her right hand and grinned. "I gave one a black eye and the rest backed off. How about you?"

"You mean besides finding my underwear yanked up to my ears?" Shorty asked sourly. Then he grinned. "Actually, I did overhear some of the baseball team. They ganged up on Henry Lee and his date—sent her off crying."

Melissa stopped in the middle of the sidewalk and stared at Shorty. She grabbed him by the front of the shirt. "You mean Henry and Gabby? Did Henry make Gabby cry?"

Surprised by Melissa's sudden fierceness, Shorty gulped and shook his head. "N-no, it wasn't like that. I heard some guys talking. They wanted to shame them both . . . something about a seventh grader thinking himself too good for the rest of them."

"Who?" Melissa demanded. "What were their names?"

"I-I don't know. It was too dark and way too loud. Definitely eighth graders, though. I was coming from the bathroom and they were talking just inside the gym. There were two of them. Afterward they got the rest of the team together and they went after Henry and Gabby. They started calling names, and well, Gabby ran off. I saw Henry chase her, but neither one came back."

Melissa dropped Shorty's shirt and bit her lip. "Boys are creeps," she said savagely.

"What's wrong?" Shorty wanted to know. "What does that have to do with the drugs?"

"Probably nothing," Melissa snarled, "but I like Henry and after that Facebook video things should've gone better for him, that's all. Let's get out of this dump. I hate school dances."

"Finally," muttered Shorty as he smoothed down his rumpled shirt. "We agree on something."

Chapter 12

Devon opened his eyes on Sunday morning to the sound of pleasant humming. Frowning, he rolled to his side and saw his grandma seated at his desk with an open Bible in front of her.

"Grandma?" he asked, sounding as puzzled as he felt. After returning home on Thursday he'd gotten in a big row with her and had been grounded for the entire weekend. She hadn't said but twenty words to him since—and then only to say stuff like, "Vacuum the house and take out the trash."

Now she turned to him and smiled wide. Almost immediately after, she frowned.

"It's about time you woke up," she snapped.

"What are you doing in my room?" Devon asked blearily, sitting up in bed. It had been another hot night and he wore only boxer shorts. He quickly pulled up his sheet to cover himself.

"What does it look like? I'm reading the Good Book and waiting for my lazy grandson to get off his duff. I got a call from Pastor Thomas early this morning. He's been talking to Mr. James. Do you know what we spoke about?"

Swallowing, Devon shook his head.

"Something about you meeting a boy who plays baseball." She swung her wide hips so that she faced Devon and peered down at him with her dark green eyes. It felt as if he were being x-rayed. "Who is this boy?" she demanded.

Devon frowned. "He's nobody. Just some kid I met while . . ." he trailed off.

"While you were sneaking out of my house disobeying my orders, is that it?" snapped his grandma. She sighed. "Well, Pastor says he's going to play baseball with you. For the church."

Devon made a face. "Ah, probably not. I doubt he'll come."

"He's coming today. His momma called the pastor just yesterday. It's all set up."

"What?" Devon cried dropping the sheet. "He's coming here?"

"No! To church! He's signing up for some baseball team that you're on. But that's a good idea. Tell you what, after church, you bring him home to me. He can join us for lunch."

Devon's eyes bugged. "You mean, bring him *here*?"

"Yes, of course I mean here! I already invited your uncles and cousins. We haven't had a good family Sunday dinner since Easter. It's about time we had another. Besides," she said mischievously, "I think the pastor and Mr. James have something special planned for this afternoon. Now you go and get ready. Mr. James will be picking you up in an hour."

Devon cocked his head, deep in thought. "What about you?" he finally asked. "Aren't you coming?"

"Nope. I'm staying here and getting dinner ready." She rose stiffly to her feet. "Now get up before I find my wood spoon and make you jump."

Devon snorted. "You had this planned already!" he said accusingly. "You knew that boy was coming here for dinner!"

"What if I did? Pastor Thomas suggested it. Now hurry!"

The Lees were strictly Protestant and had never attended another church that Henry could remember.

On this day he'd rather not attend *any* church. Last night had been an utter disaster and he'd barely slept since. He started nodding off in the front seat when his mom's voice brought him abruptly to wakefulness. "We should be almost there, but I don't see the Philly Cheese Steak House. The directions said to turn right there."

"We should have taken the GPS, Mom," Michael called from the back. "I told you!"

"Oh, you hush," Mrs. Lee said in fake rebuke. "I never get lost." In the past three years, she'd gotten three GPS units for gifts. It was a running joke that she needed directions to get around the house. To prove everyone wrong, she took to avoiding using any GPS as much as possible. This led to some adventures when driving to new places.

Henry blinked and his eyes went wide. "Uh, Mom, I think I see the Cheese Shop place. It's a house . . . or was one." He pointed at an old decrepit-looking building at the intersection they'd stopped at for a red light.

Unpainted and looking ready to collapse, the building was no bigger than a garage. A tiny gravel lot overgrown with weeds sat in front. A hand-painted sign on the front window proclaimed it to be "Danny's Famous Philly Cheese Steak House—Home of the best cheese steaks south of Philly."

"Oh," said Mrs. Lee. "I guess that's it. And, no. We're not stopping there on the way back. Or ever."

A few minutes later, after driving through blocks of tiny single-story houses, they found the church.

Resurrection Baptist Church stood as a monument to all that was good in the poor area. While many surrounding houses looked sick and old, the church radiated health with brand-new shiny red bricks and spotless glass doors. Though it was only a single building, it was roughly was the size of two gyms. A small tower rose from its sloped roof and from this, a large cross, painted white, rose toward the sky.

Men, women, and children, all dressed in their finest, were massing at the front door. It looked as though every man and boy wore a full suit and tie. The women all had on bright dresses and hats decorated with flowers.

Now wide awake, Henry looked down at his rather tame blue polo shirt and tan slacks. He glanced up at his mom. "Are you sure you aren't coming in?" he asked without much hope.

Mrs. Lee smiled and shook her head. "Sorry, Sport. It's almost summer. Today is the last day of Sunday school and Michael has a solo in the children's choir."

"Trust me, Mom, I'm fine with missing it," Michael said with feeling. "Even for this."

Mrs. Lee shook her head. "Not happening, kid. After all those lessons, there's no backing out now." She turned to Henry and patted his knee. "You'll be fine. I talked to the pastor yesterday and he seems really nice. He'll look after you. Call when you're ready to be picked up." She winked and nodded toward the softball field across the street from the church. "I believe you might be staying for the afternoon. I heard something about baseball being on the schedule."

Henry nodded sullenly. His parents always taught him and his siblings to embrace new experiences. Differences were always good and they were never allowed to judge anything or anybody too harshly. He knew his dad would want him to do this. Muttering, he opened the door and stepped out.

"Love you, sweetie," his mom said. "Oh, grab your bag from the back. I packed some extra clothes . . . you know, just in case."

Henry complied, tired. Anabelle snored in her booster seat next to Michael.

"Good luck," his younger brother told him as he pulled out his pack, bulging with clothes, his glove, and a bat. "I wish our church had baseball," Michael mumbled. "All we have is a stupid choir."

Henry grinned wryly and flicked Michael's nose. "Maybe next year." Shutting the back door, he waved his goodbyes.

He watched his mom's car turn around and leave the church parking lot . . . going the wrong way. Then, alone, he hefted his bag and turned toward the church. A few passing families eyed him curiously, but nobody spoke to him. Everyone else had dark skin. This, he knew, would be an experience.

An usher took his bag at the entrance, promising to hold it until after service. "You must be the baseball boy," he'd said. Gesturing Henry in, the usher directed Henry past a small lobby and into the large sanctuary.

At first it seemed very similar to his Protestant church. Pews were divided by a center aisle and faced a large stage with a pulpit in the middle. That was when everything changed.

On the stage, a heavyset man played an electronic organ, sending jazzy notes soaring over the congregation. A younger man was setting up a drum set next to the organ while an elderly lady took her place at a large piano. A choir dressed in dark purple robes assembled in the back.

Henry couldn't stop staring. He'd heard gospel music but had never seen it live before inside a church.

Someone pulled on his sleeve and jerked him to one of the back pews.

"Sit down, man," hissed a familiar voice. "You already look out of place enough!"

Startled, Henry turned and saw the boy from the school, Devon. He plunked down next to him and tried hard to look discreet.

"Why'd you come?" the boy hissed. "I thought you were smarter, man."

Henry shrugged. "Wanted to see the band," he whispered back.

The boy grunted. "You're a funny dude. I'm Devon, in case you'd forgotten."

"Henry." The boys exchanged brief nods and the music started in earnest.

Henry nearly jumped. The drum started rolling and the organ and piano went at it like it was a battle to see which could outdo the other. Then the choir stood and launched into a rousing version of "Amazing Grace"—like nothing Henry had ever heard before.

"That's our cue to stand," Devon said, slapping Henry on the shoulder. "Hope you like it."

Henry took in the entire service with wide eyes. The music crackled with energy and the pastor, a young man with a shaved head and a goatee, lit into a rousing sermon that had nearly everyone on their feet yelling "Amen!" and "Alleluia!"

Dizzy and exhausted, Henry didn't follow everything, but he definitely wasn't bored. Several songs later, the service ended and he collapsed in the pew feeling faint.

"Like it?" Devon asked, cracking a smile.

"Uh, yeah," Henry replied, sounding dazed. "Much more exciting than my church," he admitted.

"Good, because they like you." Devon gestured to the pew behind them.

Henry turned and saw a row of five young girls in snow-white dresses staring at him. Immediately they started giggling and covered their faces. They looked to be between the ages of six and ten.

"Who are they?" Henry mumbled, sliding down in his seat.

"Most are my cousins. They'll be eating lunch with us. Come on, I think the pastor wants to meet you." Devon got up before Henry had a chance to ask him about the lunch thing.

The pews were emptying as the congregation flocked to the exits. The boys waited patiently until they were the only ones left. Henry stuck close to Devon's side looking like a lost sheep as men and women eyed him with curiosity. Some came up to welcome him and shake his hand, but most just stared.

As they left the church, the young pastor approached them. Close up, he appeared older than Henry had first thought. Lines creased his forehead and his eyes crinkled when he smiled.

"Pastor Thomas," he said in greeting, extending a wiry hand to Henry. He had a strong grip that spoke of sincerity and warmth. "So you're here to play baseball with us, is that right?"

"Uh, yes, sir," Henry mumbled. He reached for his back pocket and pulled out his crumpled formed signed by his mom. "I think my friend is playing too."

"All right, that's good," the pastor said. "That's good. I believe I got your friend's slip yesterday. I'll be your coach with Brother James. I believe Brother Devon here will be looking for you until our first practice. I understand you brought your gear, Henry?"

Henry nodded. "Uh, are we playing today?"

"If the Lord wills it, it shall be done," the pastor replied mysteriously. "But not until later. Why don't you boys go out there and play a game of catch. I have a few more church duties to take care of before baseball duties can take over. Grab your stuff, Henry."

All in all, it had been a good experience for Henry. Still, as he left the church with Devon he heard a lady behind him hiss, "What's that boy doing here?"

"Didn't you hear?" answered a man next to her sarcastically. "He's here to teach our boys how to play baseball. Like we never played the game before."

All of Henry's fears, his tiredness, and his frustration from the night before melted away as soon as the ball smacked into his glove. To Henry, the game of catch was like medicine to the soul. Any trouble he had always vanished when he took up the ball and put on his glove.

"Nice throw," he called to Devon, meaning it. Devon had a good arm.

Devon grunted in response but seemed pleased as he caught Henry's return toss.

The two stood in the grass in front of the church, oblivious to the people around them. For a brief moment the boys were free to be themselves—two souls who loved a game. Skin color and money differences were the last things on their mind.

Then after a few minutes, Devon wiped his forehead and lowered his glove. Sweat soaked the underarms of his white shirt and his tie hung loose around his neck. "So, I don't know if you know this," he said slowly, "but you're supposed to come home with me. To eat lunch. Is that okay?"

Henry shrugged. "Yeah, I guess."

"Good, because I think my cousins will be there."

Henry gulped. "Uh, okay . . ."

Not thirty minutes later, Henry found himself crammed between two white-dressed cousins at a card table in the middle of Devon's grandma's kitchen. It turned out Devon had nine cousins and two sets of uncles and aunts. At least that was what he said . . . there were so many screaming kids running around, there could've easily been twenty of them.

He and Devon had walked from the church—to, as Devon explained, postpone meeting his cousins for as long as possible.

"Trust me, man," he'd told Henry as they'd started walking, "they're all crazy. Not like me at all."

The boys had spent the time trying to talk baseball. Devon didn't have any of Henry's experience with travel teams, little league teams, or all-star teams, so they'd settled on discussing the major leagues. Henry followed the Nationals with a passion, while Devon favored the Atlanta Braves. However, not having cable TV, Devon rarely watched the games, so after a while they'd just walked in awkward silence.

The streets were pretty much empty, lined with row after row of small houses with almost no yards. Devon had kept throwing glances at Henry, his lips pursed. Henry had gotten the feeling that Devon was a little nervous . . . and perhaps embarrassed about him being there. As the silence between them had grown, it had started to feel awkward. Henry begun to wish he'd never come. Then, finally, they'd stopped in front of a low chain-linked fence surrounding a mostly bare yard. The house on the other side of the fence was much like the rest—single story, white siding, and few windows.

"Sure you want to do this, man?" Devon mumbled.

Henry never had the chance to reply.

The door had burst open and kids started pouring out, followed by a sturdy older woman wearing a stained apron and waving a wooden spoon. "Devon Horner, you get over here right this minute," the woman cried. "What do you mean walking that poor boy to death?"

Devon's family had swept Henry right in—like he was a long lost cousin. The uncles had offered crushing handshakes and hard back slaps while the aunts called him "cutie-pie" and delivered bone-squeezing hugs. At first the cousins had stared at him in awe, but then one of the boys had taken a small plastic bat and delivered a swift whack to Henry's backside before crying, "You're it!" That had sent most of the boys off screaming and running out of the house. The girls, all in frilly white dresses, had just giggled and watched him.

Devon had saved Henry by pushing him into the kitchen and seating him at the card table. The white dresses had quickly followed. So Henry had Sunday dinner with Devon's family. To Henry, it felt like eating in the middle of a circus, with him as the main attraction.

Chapter 13

The grownups took the main table in the dining room while the kids were forced to crowd around three card tables scattered throughout the house. One of Devon's uncles had brought enough chairs for everyone to sit, but most of the kids stood anyway. The little boy who'd whacked Henry with the bat stood across the table from Henry, next to Devon.

"You any good at baseball?" the little boy asked. "I play football."

"You should try baseball," Henry said ruefully. "You have a good swing."

"You bet I do," the boy said proudly. He looked to be about six. "I'm Micah. Who are you?"

Henry told him his name and then made the mistake of asking the names of the girls in white dresses.

The girls started speaking at once and the other two kids at the table, both boys a little older than Micah, joined in—all fighting to talk first.

Henry just stared with his mouth half-open, not sure what to do next. Devon was no help—he got up and mumbled something about drinks.

Left alone, Henry decided to do what a baseball coach would do.

"All right, hold on!" he said waving his hands in surrender. The little kids stopped and stared. "That's better. We'll make a lineup for who speaks first. The last kid who speaks is the cleanup talker. That means you get to talk the most. Now listen up . . ."

"So, how is the boy doing?" Devon's grandma asked worriedly. She stood at his shoulder wiping her hands on her apron.

Devon shrugged as he closed the cooler by the front door, cradling two dripping cans of Coke. "Just great," he mumbled. "Probably thinks he's visiting a zoo."

"Oh, Devon, don't you dare think that! And what are you doing here, leaving him alone with all those kids? Bring him to the couch and you two sit there. Do you realize this is the first friend you brought over since Corey?"

"He's not my friend," Devon said, frowning. "We only just met."

"Well, if he's not your friend, that's your fault! You take care of him, Devon. If not, my wooden spoon is going to take care of you! You hear?"

Rolling his eyes, Devon returned to the crowded kitchen to find Henry being pelted with bad jokes.

"What did the man tell his pet alligator when he left?" asked Marcus, Micah's older brother. "I see you, gator!"

"Yeah, and what did the cousins say when I walked in the room?" Devon said quickly. "Goodbye to their guest. Come on, man," he said to Henry. "We're changing seats."

"It's not your turn to speak!" Micah protested. "You're not part of the lineup!"

Thankfully his Aunt Jenny stepped in and demanded the little kids be quiet and get ready for the blessing and the food. Henry made his escape and followed Devon to the worn couch in the living room.

"Thanks," Henry muttered.

Devon grunted. "Yeah, my cousins can be a handful, man. You ready to eat?"

Henry had no choice. After Devon's Uncle Bernie boomed out the blessing from the other room, his Aunt Jenny came out of the kitchen and practically pushed Henry and Devon to the front of the food line, shoving plates in their hands. "Get it now, boys, there probably won't be any left later," she told them.

That was debatable. The kitchen counter had pretty much disappeared from all the food sitting on top. In minutes, both boys' plates were overflowing with ham, baked chicken, green beans, mashed potatoes, macaroni and cheese, and a sweet cornbread muffin.

Back on the couch, Devon offered Henry a can of Coke and the boys fell to eating. Henry ate like he'd never seen food before.

Devon shook his head and started eating, apparently just as ravenous. His nervousness slowly eased and he settled in to enjoy the best food he'd had since Easter. He'd been sure Henry would be having a miserable time but things seemed to be going all right.

"Good, huh?" Devon asked, his mouth full of ham and potatoes.

Henry could only nod. Minutes later, plate empty beside him, Henry settled back in the couch and sighed with pleasure. "I feel like I can never move again," he said.

Devon grinned. "Just wait for the chocolate cake for dessert. My grandma makes the best."

Henry groaned. "Not yet I hope . . ."

Just then Devon's grandma called from the kitchen. "Devon, come in here! I have your coach on the line. He wants to talk to you!"

"Coach?" Devon said, frowning. "Who is that?"

It turned out to be Mr. James. "Devon," he said crisply, "you bring Henry down to the church in two hours, got that? We have a game set. Just like old times."

Devon gulped. "Two hours?" he protested. "What am I going to do with him before that?"

"You figure that out," Mr. James snapped. "Some of the boys can't make it until then and we still have lots of work to do."

"Great. I doubt I'll make it until then either," grumbled Devon.

In the end, he did make it. Killing two hours proved to be no problem at all. When Devon hung up the phone and returned to the living room couch, he found Henry fast asleep. Mary, one of the cousins, tried to climb up next to him, but Devon shooed her away.

"Nobody wakes him for two hours," he said.

"You guys do this every Sunday?" Henry asked Devon, his eyes gleaming with excitement.

"Used to," Devon said, grunting, but clearly proud. "But maybe we'll start again. Come on, I'll introduce you."

Twenty minutes earlier, Henry had awakened to find Devon kneeling above him with a finger to his lips. Three girls had fallen asleep on the floor; all were curled up next to the couch. Silently, the boys had tiptoed from the room, going down a small hall to Devon's bedroom where Henry's pack had been stored. Soon after, the boys went out the back door ready for ball.

They had both changed into old jeans and T-shirts and each carried a glove and bat. Henry wore his Bears cap while Devon had on an old, faded Atlanta Braves hat.

The walk back to the church had revived Henry, especially when he saw what lay on the other end.

The softball field across the street had been transformed into one fit for baseball. An artificial mound had been brought in, white lines had been painted, and bases were all set. A group of players gathered at home plate.

As they made their way across the football field, Henry counted fifteen kids about his age or older. With Devon and him, it was almost enough for two full teams.

"Sure you want to do this?" Devon mumbled next to him. He kept his head low and wouldn't look at Henry.

Henry swallowed. "Uh, yeah. Why?" Then he looked up at the players again and saw what Devon meant. None of the faces looked very happy and they were all looking at him. "Um, is it too late to turn around?"

"Probably," Devon said. "You agreed to this and we're here."

"Right," Henry mumbled. "I'm an idiot."

"There you are!" cried Mr. James loudly, appearing from behind his beat-up pickup. He'd parked on the grass just outside the fence down near first base. The elderly man walked with a spring in his step as he strode to meet them. "How do you like our pitcher's mound? A friend of mine donated it from the high school." He looked straight at Devon and winked. "It pays having inside help. Took just about all of us to carry it to and from my truck, but it promises to be regulation."

Devon gulped. He knew who the inside help had been . . . his grandma had connections with the athletic director of the high school. Perhaps she didn't always understand him, but she did look out for him.

Mr. James' eyes twinkled. "So you boys ready to play ball?"

Chapter 14

The boys waiting at home plate watched Henry approach coolly. Some looked openly hostile. One of them, a taller boy, spit in his direction and tried to stare down the light-skinned boy.

"So the prodigal child arrives," a heavy-set boy muttered sarcastically. "We're saved."

Henry bit his bottom lip and stared past the kids at the backstop. Stopping to stand behind Devon, he put a hand on his hip and dangled his glove at his side. He refused to look down or look intimidated.

Devon, for his part, cleared his throat and toed the dirt nervously. He never looked up.

Thankfully, Mr. James stepped forward and rubbed his hands together. "Okay, boys, I'm glad you all made it," he said. "It's been a long time since we played ball out here."

"Longer since we played with a cracker," drawled the tall boy.

Mr. James shot him an angry look. "Jack, you best watch your mouth!" The boy, Jack, glared back but then ducked his head.

Mr. James drew himself up to his full height and looked ten feet taller. Nobody dared look him in the eye. Glaring, he spoke loud and clear. "Now let's get one thing straight. We're here for baseball and that's all! If you can't accept that, then get off the field now, because I won't have it!" Mr. James turned and pointed to the church. "Everyone look over there and look real good. Because in that building skin color don't matter and neither does it matter on the baseball field! What matters is that we do our parts to make each other better! Got that?"

Jack finally raised his head and nodded. "Just let's play," he muttered.

"Yes," barked Mr. James. "That's what we're here for."

"Everything okay, Brother James?" called Pastor Thomas, walking in from the football field. He'd exchanged his black suit for sweatpants and a T-shirt. A baseball glove was tucked under his arm.

"Peachy, Pastor Thomas," answered Mr. James, still glaring at the boys in front of him. "Now let's introduce ourselves and make up teams."

Henry couldn't keep track of all the names. The tall kid was Jack and the hefty kid introduced himself as Larry . . . then there was DeAndre, Jesse, Caleb, and a host of others. He was just happy to be allowed to play, even if he was picked last.

It was the first time he could remember that he'd been selected last for a sport. Instead of making him angry, it actually felt good.

They made a mistake, he thought as he trotted onto the field. *Time to prove it.* Playing baseball on a Sunday afternoon with no pressure to win . . . how could he be upset?

Devon, who ended up on his team, nudged his arm as they went to their positions. "Sorry," he muttered.

Henry shrugged. "I never played pickup baseball before," he confessed. "Not with full teams like this."

Devon grunted. "Yeah, I know. I saw you play. You're all fundamentals with no jazz." He grinned. "Now get ready for all jazz and no fundamentals. Oh, and by the way, you're in right field."

Henry quickly saw what Devon meant. The boys from Resurrection Baptists weren't bad athletes. On the contrary, some were very good. It was just that they had little to no coaching . . . except from television and YouTube.

From his position in right, he watched what Coach Wood would call "flash-ball." Flash-ball was when players tried to be flashy, showing off rather than going for the easy, safe play.

It started with the first batter. On the second pitch, he knocked a routine ground ball right to Jack at shortstop. Instead of waiting for it, Jack charged the ball, swooping in from the side. He waited until the last possible second so he had to dive to snare the ball with his glove. Getting to his knees, he fired wildly to first, missing the first baseman high and wide by several feet.

The ball clanked against the fence and the runner, who should've been out by a mile, scooted to second. He would have gone farther if Henry hadn't charged from his position to back up the play. He grabbed the ball and whipped it to third.

One of the players on the other team whistled in appreciation. "Nice toss, dude. Hey, Jack, he's got a better arm than you, man!"

A lot of guys hooted and heckled Jack's error. Furious, Jack just kicked the dirt.

The next batter popped up to second. Yawning, the second baseman stood idly by until the last possible moment when he suddenly whipped up his glove, snatching the ball from midair. That became the norm. Routine, easy plays were made as hard as possible while errors were jeered with little mercy.

By the middle of the second inning, Henry's team was down four runs to two. In that span, not a single ball had made it even close to right field. Trotting in to the dugout, he took a seat at the very end. He doubted he would hit anytime soon.

"Yo, kid," Jack said, surprising him. "You're on deck. Don't strike out." He held up a scratched batting helmet.

"That's you, man," Devon said from the other side of the fence. He'd gotten a solid single last inning and had scored one of the two runs. This inning he stood in as the first base coach. "It's time to show us what you got. If you got anything."

Licking his dry lips, Henry put down his glove and picked up his bat. Accepting the offered helmet, he moved from the fenced-in dugout to the on-deck area. The helmet was too big and kept slipping down, but it was manageable.

Jack snorted behind him. "I bet he goes down in five pitches," he said loud enough for Henry to hear.

Henry ignored him as he focused solely on the pitcher.

The kid on the mound looked to be slightly older than Henry and was certainly taller. He threw downhill, his pitches dropping sharply. At the release, the ball looked high, but it came in at the knees or lower by the time it reached the plate. Mostly he fired fastballs, but he did have a curve that he tried now and then.

Henry watched as the leadoff batter struggled to pick up the pitches and went down swinging on four pitches.

"All right, here comes the prodigal son," Larry called from first base. He tried to leer at Henry but got no response from the smaller player.

"Larry, you should stick your tongue back in your mouth before flies land on it," Devon said to him. "I'll bet you a dollar this kid reaches first."

Larry glared over at Devon. "You support this cracker? You're on!"

"Mow him down, Johnny," called the shortstop.

Henry let the first pitch go by.

"Strike!" Mr. James, wearing only a mask, served as the lone umpire. Pastor Thomas evened the teams out and stood in left field with his glove.

Henry stepped back and twisted his hands on his bat. He didn't have his batting gloves and the too-big helmet kept slipping into his eyes.

"Don't be scared, kid!" yelled Jack from the bench. "Just wait two more pitches and you can come right back here!"

"Great teammate you have," the catcher told Henry.

Mr. James had also managed to scrounge up two sets of catching gear, as well as a few batting helmets. But, he warned the players, no athletic supporters. They were at their own risk there.

Henry ignored the catcher. He didn't need any more distractions.

The next pitch came in low but was called for another strike.

"Hey, that bat isn't a decoration!" Jack shouted. "Use it!"

"Maybe he will when he comes back to see you," Devon shot back.

The catcher chuckled as he threw the ball back to the pitcher. "You know, you can always join our team. Just strike out and you'll be helping us a bunch."

Henry allowed a slight grin. All the infielders were standing around more focused on the banter than the batter. None of them even crouched to a ready position on the third pitch. Henry saw it zoom down toward his knees heading for the outside of the plate.

He'd guessed fastball and had guessed right. Swinging for the bottom of the ball, like he'd been taught for low pitches, he felt sharp contact and immediately took off for first.

With a metallic crack, the ball shot between the surprised third baseman and shortstop. Pastor Thomas scooped it from the grass and tossed it in to second. "Let's look alive in there," he hollered. "You infielders fall asleep during my sermons too!"

After taking a wide turn toward second, Henry returned to first, his face blank. Still he let out a deep breath.

Devon greeted him with a smack on the arm. "There you go," he said with a nod. "Now it's time you really show them."

"Lucky hit," Larry said. He stepped toward the pitcher. "What was that last one? A granny throw?"

Jack had gone silent from the dugout, but some of the boys were razzing him. They seemed more amused at Jack's expense than impressed with Henry's hit.

"What is this, Jack? Opposite day?" one boy said. "You said that kid would be out!"

The next batter was a tall, quiet boy who already had the beginnings of a mustache. He waved his bat dangerously and stared toward center field.

"Time!" called the catcher, getting to his feet. "I've seen this kid hit at school. He can crush it."

Devon pulled Henry close to him as the infield gathered on the mound with the catcher to discuss strategy.

"I mean it," he whispered. "You got to show them something here. This is your chance."

Henry looked at him with a grimace. "Like what?" he asked. "I just got a hit."

"Look, man, don't you get it? These guys don't care about simple hitting and fielding. They want to see some real play. You know, like Jackie Robinson. I heard stories how he used to drive pitchers crazy when he was on base. You need to do the same! I've seen your speed. They don't expect you to be nobody. Prove them wrong, man. That's the only way you're going to be part of this team."

Henry's mouth twisted as he considered Devon's words. "Okay . . . just tell me what to do."

Devon smacked the side of Henry's jeans. "Run. Watch the pitcher and take off when you can. Go!" He shoved him toward second. "No small leads."

"Let's play ball," Mr. James called. "The sun ain't going to wait!"

It was near three on another hot sunny afternoon, but a breeze from the north brought some relief. To Henry, it was perfect baseball weather.

Watching the pitcher, Henry took three large steps toward second and crouched low. His fingers twitched and his toes started to tingle. At any moment he needed to dive back to first or take off for second. The pitcher gave him a disdainful glance and then turned to the batter. Henry heard Devon snort behind him. It would be off to second.

Johnny, the pitcher, had barely started his windup when Larry yelled, "He's stealing!"

Caught by surprise, Johnny flinched in midpitch and ended up throwing a weak wobbler. The ball fluttered halfway to the plate before bouncing in the dirt and rolling to the catcher. Henry made it to second standing up.

Henry's dugout went wild with laughter. "What type of pitch was that?" cried one of the boys. "My grannie can throw better! Man, she drops her teeth better than that throw!"

"Mr. James," called another, "I think we need to move the mound closer!"

Scowling, Johnny caught the toss back from the catcher. He glared at Henry before turning back to the batter. As soon as he did, Henry took a lead toward third. His toes dancing in the dirt.

"Watch the runner!" called the third baseman. "He's leaning this way!"

Whirling, Johnny threw to second, but Henry saw it coming. He dove back and reached the base easily.

"He's quick!" the second baseman said, returning the ball to Johnny.

"He's an out waiting to happen," the clearly frustrated pitcher growled.

Again, when Johnny turned to the batter, Henry danced for third and then retreated to second. He watched the ball like a hawk.

"Throw the ball already," Jack hollered from the dugout. "Let's go!"

The next pitch came from the stretch. Johnny had learned to avoid windups with Henry on base. Henry broke for third anyway.

"Get him!" cried Larry.

The batter swung wildly and then jumped out of the way as the catcher leapt to his feet, ball in hand. His mask flew off as he hurled the ball to third.

Henry dove under the tag and ended up lying on top of the base choking on dust and groaning.

"Safe!" cried Mr. James.

The third baseman still smacked Henry's backside with his glove. "Nice steal, man," he said, sounding as though he meant it.

"You okay, son?" Mr. James called as Henry got gingerly to his knees.

Wincing, Henry nodded and grinned sheepishly. "Yeah . . . next time I'm bringing my cup."

Johnny choked with laughter and threw down his glove. Most of the boys joined in.

"All right, now we got a ball game!" cried Jack. "Let's get this run in!"

"Watch for the steal at home!" Larry roared.

"I can't," Johnny complained. "He's camouflaged. With his orange clothes and white skin he looks like part of the field."

Henry grinned and beat some of the dust from the back of his jeans. His entire front and back were covered in orange dirt from the infield.

The kid standing as the third base coach offered Henry a hand for a high five. "I'm DeAndre. Nice running. You ready to take home?"

Henry slapped the offered hand and shrugged. "As long as you let me."

On the next pitch, he did what he'd learned on the Bears. As soon as the pitcher started the pitch, he started for home. He jerked to stop when it went wide for a ball. However, everyone else thought he meant to steal.

"Get him!" cried Johnny.

The catcher jumped to block the plate. Seeing Henry going back to third, he threw without thinking. The only problem was that Henry stood in the base path so the throw went wide. The third baseman wasn't expecting it. The ball ended up in left field and Henry had an easy trot home.

His entire team, including Jack, greeted them at home plate and pounded him on the head and back.

When he finally made it to the dugout bench he was met by Devon carrying an old paint bucket.

"Here you go," Devon said, turning the bucket over next to the bench. He grinned. "Your seat. I told you I watched you play on the Bears."

Henry took the seat, shaking his head ruefully. "Uh, thanks," he muttered, slightly embarrassed.

"What's that?" Jack asked, eyeing the bucket. "A white boy seat?"

After that, the game settled and became fun. The next inning, Henry was told to play center. Though the razzing continued, it was all done good-naturedly. The boys just enjoyed the game. It went on this way until the fifth inning. Nobody really knew the score at that point, but it was pretty even.

That was when Charlie and Lou walked in from across the football field.

"What's this? The field of dreams?" Lou called out loudly, his voice dripping with sarcasm. "Only this is where dreams come to die."

Charlie cackled at his side.

Henry's team had just gotten up to bat, but all the players had stopped to watch the two boys saunter toward them.

"Afternoon, boys," Pastor Thomas greeted them coolly. "You here to play?"

Lou and Charlie stopped just outside the left field fence.

"Nah," Lou said, grinning. "Just watch." His eyes met Devon's and he nodded a greeting.

"Who are they?" Henry whispered to Devon.

"Trouble," Devon replied flatly. "I'm sure you recognize the taller one."

Henry nodded. "Yeah . . . and I'm sure he recognizes me." He shuddered slightly.

"Just stay away from them," Devon told him. "They won't start anything."

Staying away soon proved hard to do.

"Sorry, boys," Pastor Thomas was saying, "but if you don't want to play I'm going to ask you to move along."

"It's a free country," Lou said, shrugging.

The pastor crossed his arms. "And you can freely move along in it."

"And if we play?" Lou asked aggressively.

The pastor sighed. "Then you're more than welcome, just as long as you don't start any trouble."

Lou and Charlie joined the game. After that, the tension started to build. All of a sudden the good-natured ribbing stopped and the fancy play vanished. Charlie joined Henry's team, while Lou took Pastor Thomas' spot in left field. The pastor moved to umpire first base.

After three uneventful outs, the teams swapped. Lou came up to bat to lead off the inning.

Jack stood on the mound.

"Why don't you have the new boy pitch?" Lou asked, grinning as he swaggered to the plate. "Yeah, I see you, new boy!" he called. "Your skin is blinding my eyes!"

"His name is Henry," Jack said, frowning.

"Is that a fact?" said Lou. "Hey, Henry. How do you like it here? Find any Oreos yet? Black on the outside but white on the inside."

"Okay, boys," Mr. James growled from behind the plate. "Enough chatter. Let's go."

Lou laughed. "Just trying to break the ice. It's so quiet, man."

"Too bad you hit as well as you talk," Devon called from where he was playing shortstop. "Like trash in the gutter!"

Lou glared and started to say something back but saw Pastor Thomas staring at him. Swallowing, he put on a big smile. "This next pitch is for you."

The next pitch went down the middle. His eyes opened wide, Lou stepped into it and smashed it toward center.

Henry saw it coming and quickly turned. Breaking to his right, he tracked the ball on the run, but only watched helplessly as it sailed overhead, bouncing to the wall.

Devon groaned. "Should've dove," he said. Then he looked over his shoulder and waved his hands wildly. "Throw it in! Quick! We got him!"

Lou had dropped the bat and stopped to admire his hit. Now seeing Henry's speed to the ball, he took off for first. He'd turned for second without slowing, ignoring the calls from his team to stop at first. The ball from Henry came to the cutoff man before Lou had even made it halfway to second.

Devon raced to cover the base. He took the throw just as Lou started his slide. Crouching low, he turned to deliver the tag when Lou plowed into him, headfirst. The batting helmet nailed him between the legs and Devon went down in agony. The ball rolled free.

"Safe," Pastor Thomas said, not sounding like he meant it. "Clear the way, give him room!"

Lou got to his feet grinning. He turned to where Devon rolled in pain and toed him in the back. "Sorry, man, but you can't stop a train. And it's a-coming."

Devon only moaned in response.

Chapter 15

Matters were made worse when a minivan rolled to a stop in front of the church.

Kevin Baker hopped out and waved.

"Yo, Henry!" he called. "You guys started without me!"

Devon had just gotten to his feet and was starting to breath normally again. The players had used the moment to grab water and were milling around in the infield.

"Who is that?" Lou said, squinting. "Looks like a saltine cracker."

Mr. James sighed. "That, I believe, is the last member of our team. Kevin Baker. Henry, you'd better go meet him."

Henry had mixed feelings when he sprinted across the outfield and hopped the fence. One part of him wanted to keep playing, but another part of him had the urge to get Kevin and go home.

"What are you doing here?" Henry said by way of greeting. "How did you even find this place?"

Kevin smacked the front bill of Henry's cap. "Your mom, you idiot. I called looking for you, but she said you were playing baseball here. She gave directions to my mom and said we could drive you home."

"My mom gave you directions and you still found it? That's impressive."

"We used our GPS." Kevin gestured to the players watching them. "So, is this the team?"

Henry bit his lower lip. "Mostly, I think. Um, you better be careful. Some of them are rough."

Kevin raised his eyebrows. "Are you kidding? I'm always careful. Besides, you haven't seen rough until you've seen me."

"What's up, guys?" Kevin called, raising a hand in greeting as he reached the infield with Henry. "Sorry I'm late. We still playing? I hope I didn't bring my glove for nothing."

For a moment nobody spoke. Then Mr. James nodded at Pastor Thomas.

"Yeah," he said. "We're still playing. Lou, you're safe on second. Kevin, go to shortstop. I think Devon could use a break."

"Hold on," Lou said, looking at Devon. "Let Charlie pinch run for me. I could use a break too."

Devon slumped to a seat in the front row of the rickety wood bleachers set up behind third base. He held a cold water bottle between his legs. Lou eased down next to him.

"Sorry about the slide, man," he said, grinning. "Didn't know where I'd land."

"No problem," Devon grunted. "Guess that makes us even."

Lou laughed. "Maybe. But Preston still wants to see you."

"And I still don't want to see him," Devon shot back.

Lou nodded and chuckled. "Yeah, I figured that. Don't worry, he didn't send us here today for you."

Devon frowned. "Then why are you here?"

"Why else? To play ball. I heard about some rich kids coming to teach us poor boys how to play baseball." He nodded toward Henry. "Looks like it's true."

Sighing, Devon turned to look at Lou. "Look, man. Henry is all right. He spent most of the day with me. He's not what you think."

"Yeah? Is that so?"

"Yeah."

"You're a fool, man. Rich people don't help poor people unless they have a reason. Those boys aren't here for you. They're doing it for themselves and then they'll be out of here and they'll never come back. You'll see."

Devon shook his head stubbornly. "They're okay."

Lou grunted and jerked his head toward the field. "Sure about that? Then what's happening out there?"

Devon looked to where Lou gestured and frowned. Out on the field, the new kid, Kevin, wasn't making friends.

"Come on, pitcher!" Kevin yelled after ball two was called. "Put one over the plate. We got your back!" Looking to his right and left, he pounded his glove. "Hey, guys, if you're going to play defense, get ready! Put your glove to the ground and bend your knees! Come on! Look alive!"

His teammates never looked his way, but they were clearly not happy. Many had gritted teeth.

The next pitch turned into a grounder toward third. Kevin, glove at the ready, swooped in front of the third baseman to snap up the ball. He did a quick turn to third, but nobody covered the base. Charlie had run on contact and would have been out easily. Instead, grunting, Kevin pivoted on his back foot and delivered a long, accurate throw to first to get the batter by a step.

"That's one!" he called. "Should've been at third, but that's okay." He nodded at the third baseman. "Next time the guy runs from second, cover third, okay?"

"What are you doing, man?" Jack exploded from the mound. "You cut him off! He had that play!"

Kevin stepped back, caught off guard. "What are you talking about?"

Jack threw down his glove. "I'm talking about you stealing the ball from DeAndre! He was going to get the ball, tag out Charlie, and throw to first for a double play!"

Kevin frowned and laughed. "Are you serious, man? He was just standing there!"

Jack lost it. Rushing at Kevin, he started yelling, "You think you know everything, do you? Just because you're a cracker and your mom drives a rich van you think you can come here and tell us how to play? You crazy?"

217

"Whoa, stop that!" Pastor Thomas said. "Break it up!"

Jack and Kevin were nose to nose now. Neither one was ready to listen.

"You're the one crazy!" Kevin shouted. "I made the right play!"

Jack shoved Kevin in the chest and Pastor Thomas stepped between them. "Enough!" he shouted. He turned to Jack and put a hand on his chest. "Don't you dare put your hands on another person, you hear?"

"He started it!" Larry protested, rushing on the field. "Him and Henry! Why do we have sorry rich kids coming here to begin with?"

"Because," spat Jack. "They're white."

"Ha . . . ha . . . ha," Mr. James' voice boomed mockingly. He clapped his hands as he walked toward them from home plate. Everyone went silent and turned to him. "Congratulations, boys," he said sarcastically, "you sound like whiny four-year-olds." Then his voice grew hard. "This is life. Don't you get it? Over there is church. At the end of life you're going to be judged by *your actions*, not by the color of your skin. Remember that! It's not the color of your skin that matters, it's what you do *in your skin* that matters. I don't know how many times we have to say it, but it's true. All the garbage about rich people, poor people, black people, banana people has to stop! There is nothing so pathetic, juvenile, and stupid as judging a person by something as trivial as skin color. How shallow can you be? If others do it, then shame on them, but you will *not* do it here. Do I make myself clear?"

Nobody looked him in the eye, but Jack nodded sullenly.

"Good. Jack, you and Kevin shake hands. Then let's wrap this thing up. If you want to play in next week's tournament, show up here with a glove tomorrow at four. And leave your attitudes at home or that's where you'll be by four thirty! Now get on home!"

Lou grunted as he stood beside Devon next to the bleachers. They watched the other boys gathering their gloves and bats. Henry and Kevin stood by themselves laughing about something.

"So," asked Lou, "is that what you're going to do? Show up tomorrow with your two rich friends to be told how to play ball? I remember you and Corey being pretty good without them."

Devon clenched his hands and looked hard at Lou. "Corey is in jail for working for Preston."

Lou stared right back. "That's because he didn't listen. So maybe you should start." Then he grinned. "If you change your mind, find me. Because I'm won't be looking for you again. Next time it might be the others."

"What's that supposed to mean?" Devon asked.

Lou only smiled. "You'll see."

"You ready to roll?" Kevin asked Henry as Devon walked up to them. "My mom is waiting at the church."

Henry shook his head. "I'll be there in a few minutes. I have some stuff at, uh, Devon's house."

Kevin grabbed Henry's bat and glove. "All right, I'll be waiting in the van. Come quick, I don't want to be here when night falls."

"What's that supposed to mean?" Devon asked, standing between Kevin and Henry.

Kevin wrinkled his nose and scratched the back of his head. "Nothing, man. I just need to leave soon. I'm guessing you're Devon."

"And I'm guessing you're leaving," Devon said.

"Sure, whatever." Shrugging, Kevin turned and headed toward his mom's van. "We'll be waiting, Henry!"

Henry looked at Devon, his eyes narrowing. "Uh, should I go too?" he asked.

"First get your stuff," Devon growled. "Come on."

Sighing, Henry followed Devon back to his grandma's house. The boys walked the entire way in brooding silence.

"Wait here," Devon said when they'd reached the fence in front of his grandma's house. "I'll get your stuff."

Henry nodded and jammed his hands in his back pockets. What had started as an interesting day had turned great and had ended horribly. Life sometimes threw more curves than a major league pitcher.

Devon returned and held out Henry's backpack. "It's all there. You don't have to check."

"Sure . . . Thanks, I think."

"Don't mention it. Need me to walk you back?"

Henry shook his head. "I know the way now."

"Suit yourself. Make sure you get there before dark."

Henry hefted his pack onto his back and sucked in his breath. "Uh, Devon . . ."

Devon had already turned back to his house. He stopped, but didn't face Henry. "Yeah?"

"Are you going to practice tomorrow?"

Devon let the question hang for a few seconds. Then he shrugged. "Maybe."

Henry walked briskly back toward the church. All the houses looked the same, but he'd memorized the street names and knew where he was going.

It had been a long day and he was sorry it had ended so poorly. Kevin might have been wrong to say what he'd said on the field, but it wasn't like he'd done it on purpose. He'd only wanted to help. Maybe Bobby was right about the whole thing. Once in history class during a discussion Bobby had said that different races were like water and oil—they mixed occasionally, but eventually they always separated out. He'd meant to be funny, but now it just seemed sad.

The sun was just starting to set as he turned from the block to Devon's house. He walked past several houses when he heard a noise behind him. Turning, he saw two older kids trailing him. Both of them were strangers. The one in front, wearing a dark blue beanie cap, saw his face and immediately put out a hand.

"Yo, dude!" he called. "You got any change on you? We're trying to get a bus home."

Henry licked his lips and shook his head. "I don't have any money," he said. "Sorry."

"What happened to you?" said the other kid as they drew closer. He wore a black T-shirt and tan pants covered in paint spots. He and his friend looked to be high school age or older. "Looks like you rolled around in something, man."

"Sure you got no money?" asked the one in the blue cap, eyeing the backpack.

Henry kept moving in a steady walk. "Uh, no. I just finished playing baseball."

The one in spotted pants nodded. "Cool, man. I remember when we used to play ball here. That was years ago."

"Yeah," said the one in the blue cap. "I remember striking you out."

Laughing, the two passed by Henry, turning down the next street.

Exhaling in relief, Henry continued on. As he neared the church, he turned down a narrow street with overgrown grass on both sides. The houses here were abandoned and boarded up. Devon had said something about a fire in one that had caused smoke damage. Just before Henry reached the end of the street where he needed to turn left before seeing the church, he saw something move on his right.

Just as he turned to look, a crushing blow fell on the back of his neck and somebody grabbed his shoulders. Before he could react, another blow came from above. Blackness followed as he felt his knees collapse under him.

"You what?" screeched Devon's grandma. "You let that boy walk back to the church by himself?"

"He wanted to!" Devon protested. "I asked him and he said he knew how to get there!"

"I don't care! You know these streets! He's an innocent as a lamb! Drug dealers walk these streets!"

Devon started to roll his eyes, but his grandma grabbed him by the arm and yanked him off the couch. "You go back out there and make sure he gets where he's going safely. Do you hear? Don't you come back until you do it!"

"Grandma—"

"Don't you 'Grandma' me! You better get out there right this minute!"

His uncles and aunts had already left so he was on his own. Grumbling, Devon stormed out of the house and started after Henry.

He's probably already in the van driving away, he thought. He remembered what Lou had said about rich people—that they wouldn't stick around a moment longer than necessary.

Devon suddenly jerked to a stop. Lou had also mentioned that he wasn't at the field for him—he was there because the rich boys were coming . . .

Devon broke into a run. Charlie and Lou served as scouts for Preston Whiteside. Lou had warned him about some others. If they weren't after Devon . . . who were they after?

Chapter 16

"Nice hit, Shawn, you knocked him cold on the first try," congratulated the lone female of the bunch.

"Just grab his pack," Shawn snapped. He ran a hand through his oily hair and made sure no unwanted eyes were watching. His other hand supported the kid's unconscious body.

It had gone perfectly to plan so far. Once the kid had been spotted walking alone, he had his team set up the ambush.

Hiding in the tall grass, they'd let the kid pass before swooping down. A couple of well-aimed blows knocked the boy out like a light. Now they just needed a few minutes longer.

"Quick!" he urged.

The third member of the party helped the girl pull off the boy's backpack. Then he tossed it into the tall grass.

"Shouldn't we get him out of sight too?" asked the girl. She never could be silent for long . . . or smart.

"Brilliant idea," the third member muttered.

"Shut it, you two," Shawn hissed. He grabbed the boy's dead weight with both arms and dragged him into the grass before dropping him with a thump. "Lexi, go through his bag. Mark, take the shoes. Don't forget, we have to make this look like a robbery. Let's move! Do this fast! We can't be here, remember." Bending down, he rolled the boy onto his stomach and started rummaging through his pockets.

"Hey!" shouted a voice from behind them. "The police are coming!"

Devon was just turning the corner when he heard the voices. Crouching down, he peered over the grass and saw three teenagers—one of them holding Henry's limp form. He watched in horror as the tallest one dragged the body into the grass. He knew this was one of the classic knock-him-down-rob-him hits. Only this one was completely different. Something funny was going on. The teens didn't look very interested in stealing anything . . .

Devon grunted and got a bad feeling. Having seen enough, he cupped his hands around his mouth and yelled that the police were coming.

Immediately the teens dropped everything and broke into a run. They fled through the tall grass, disappearing behind one of the decrepit houses.

Yelling, Devon gave chase but stopped at the house. Beyond it was a thin line of trees that ended at the road to the church. He didn't want the teenagers to find out that it was only a kid pursuing them.

Moments later he heard a car roar to life and the screech of tires. Through the trees he caught a glimpse of a dark green lowrider shoot by. Then everything went quiet. His knees shaking slightly, Devon turned to go back to Henry. Rushing to his side, Devon dropped to his knees and felt for a pulse. He breathed a sigh of relief when he found one.

Henry opened his eyes to find himself lying on his side surrounded by green, scratchy grass. The back of his head ached like it had been used for batting practice. Groaning, he forced himself to a sitting position and blinked. Devon knelt three feet away, his back to Henry, going through his book bag. Henry's shoes lay beside the bag.

"What are you doing?" Henry asked groggily. "What happened?"

Devon gave a start and quickly closed the bag. Turning to Henry, he licked his lips. "Ah, man, you're awake," he said, sounding relieved. Still, he kept his eyes averted. "I, uh, was making sure they didn't take anything. Good news, they dropped your cell phone." Devon reached into his pocket and produced Henry's phone. When Henry made no move to take it, Devon tossed it to him. "I don't think they got anything. I stopped them in time."

Henry just stared. "Who were they?" he finally asked, rubbing the back of his neck. He did not sound thankful.

Devon looked Henry in the eye. "No idea. I promise. I've never seen them before, but there were three of them. Two guys and a girl. They looked like they were in high school. Look, man, I don't know what you're thinking, but I promise they're not from around here."

Stretching his head back, Henry winced and tried to clear his thoughts. He remembered the blow but nothing after. Taking deep breaths, he tried to control his anger. "Get away from my bag," he said, struggling to keep his voice in check.

Devon got to his feet and backed away. "I'm serious, man! Those people were whiter than chalk. They're not from here! Their clothes were nice too, and they didn't even look like criminals." Devon suddenly sounded scared. "Look, you don't think I did this, do you?"

Henry closed his eyes and put his head between his knees. "I don't know what to think," he muttered miserably.

Just then they heard Kevin's voice. "Hey, Henry! Henry, is that you? Are you coming?"

Devon's eyes grew wide. "You're not going to tell him, are you?"

Henry looked up, his chin resting on his knees. "Tell him what?"

Devon gulped. "Look, man, I promise, I came up to find three white people going through your stuff. I scared them off and they drove away. That's it. But if you tell anybody else, they're going to think I did it. You know it and I know it!"

Henry rose stiffly to his feet and stood for a moment while his head cleared. "Just give me my stuff," he muttered.

"You won't tell?"

"I won't come back here ever again, that's for sure."

"Henry!" cried Kevin. He came into view jogging from the opposite end of the street. "What are you doing, man?"

"Putting my shoes on," Henry said stiffly. "I, uh, fell and sort of spilled everything."

"How did your shoes come off?" Kevin asked dubiously. Then he saw Devon. "Is everything all right?"

Devon turned away and stood with his head bowed and arms crossed.

"Yeah, I just got rocks in my shoes," Henry replied.

"You have no idea what you had," Devon muttered. With that, he walked away without looking back.

Henry never did tell anyone what really happened. He made it to the van with his head ringing and spent the ride home feeling heartsick and exhausted. Kevin thought Henry was mad about the whole Gabby incident, so he didn't push for conversation. Instead, he talked to his mom about the Baptist team and how it was going to take a lot of work to get them in playing shape.

"They have no discipline," he said, shaking his head. "They could use a good coach like Coach Wood."

At home, Henry tried going straight to his room, but he was intercepted by his mother at the door.

"Young man," she said when she saw him, "you better strip right where you stand and head straight for the shower. Michael and Anabelle are at friends' houses, so hurry up! I'll be in the laundry room getting some industrial stain removal ready."

Too tired to protest, Henry complied.

Once showered and changed into his pajamas, Henry sank into his bed and covered his face with his arms. He knew his dad would be calling like he did every Sunday night when he was away, but he couldn't talk to him just now. He wouldn't know what to say ... One thing was for certain, he was certainly *not* going to see Devon again. That was the last thing he remembered before darkness took over.

Sometime around midnight his phone buzzed by his bed signaling a text. At the first buzz, Henry's eyes snapped open and he went still. He'd been dreaming of a faceless monster chasing him down the street and demanding his shoes. His phone buzzed again, reminding him it had only been a dream.

Rolling over, Henry saw that it was from Kevin asking if he needed a ride to practice tomorrow. Sighing, he grabbed his phone and texted back: NOT GOING. Then he switched off his phone. Lying back, he fell into a dreamless sleep.

The following morning, on Monday, Hamilton Middle went into full lockdown mode and the drug dogs returned. It lasted several hours and every single backpack in the school was searched. When it finally ended, not one student was called in for questioning.

Melissa found Shorty at lunch and took the seat across from him. "Okay, Shorty," she said bluntly, "tell me the scoop. What was that all about?"

Startled, Shorty looked up and accidently shoved his meatball sub into his chin. "Oh, ah, scoop?" he asked, hastily wiping away the tomato sauce with a napkin. "About what?"

Melissa looked at him incredulously. "The lockdown!" she exploded. "What else?"

"Oh, uh, that." Shorty held his sub in both hands and went in for a bite, but sauce dribbled out of the back end and splattered on his pants. "Ah, man!"

"Shorty!" Melissa cried. "What happened?"

Shorty sighed and put down his sub in disgust. "This is all I know: Somebody called the school and reported that a student had drugs on him. It was definitely supposed to be a boy. But the thing is, nothing was found. So the police think it was a false tip from a troublemaker. But, and this part you'll like, the dogs did find traces of drugs . . . in the boys' locker room. There. Is that what you wanted? Can I get back to decorating myself with meatballs?"

"Thanks, Shorty. I knew I could count on you." Melissa pushed aside her untouched lunch and started tapping her fingers on the table. "I wonder what it all means." Then she looked up. "Wait, you said there's something else?"

"No, I didn't, but yes, there is." Shorty looked up from where he'd been trying to wipe the meatballs from his pants with a napkin. "Look around the cafeteria and tell me what's wrong."

Melissa lifted her eyebrows and frowned. Then she sighed and scanned the noisy cafeteria. "Let's see ... the sixth graders are throwing food ... half the eighth graders are out of their seats ..."

Shorty snorted. "That's all normal. No, I mean what's different. Give up? Where's Henry Lee sitting today?"

Melissa look confused. "Uh, I don't know ... with the baseball team, I guess."

"Nope. Turns out Henry isn't sitting anywhere that I know of."

Melissa hunched down in her seat and looked sad. "Oh, is this about Gabby? I hear she didn't show up today."

"Possibly," Shorty said. "But—" He raised a finger dramatically. "I overheard Kevin during the lockdown. He said something about a baseball game yesterday. Something happened there and now Henry won't talk to Kevin, or play baseball again."

Melissa made a face. "But baseball is over. The team won the championship last Thursday."

Shorty shrugged. "I just know what I overheard. I think it was something about a Baptist team. Now if you'll excuse me, I need to find some wipes for my pants." Getting up, he stalked away, leaving Melissa sitting alone with a perplexed look on her face.

"Baptist baseball team?" she asked aloud.

Earlier that morning, in another school, Devon had found Charlie *and* Lou waiting for him at the entrance to Highland Middle.

"Get away," he growled, trying to push past them. "Not in the mood right now."

Lou blocked his way and shook his head. "Too bad, because we are in the mood. We're in the mood to pound you if you don't talk. What happened yesterday after baseball?"

Devon stepped back. He stared Lou in the face, trying to read his eyes.

Charlie snorted. "You'd better tell us, man. Preston is seriously mad at you."

"Shut your face, Charlie," Lou growled. He didn't look away from Devon.

Devon smiled slowly. "I'll tell you what happened. Nothing. Absolutely nothing happened. Tell that to your Preston Whiteside . . . and just maybe nothing will."

234

Then he deftly stepped past before either Lou or Charlie could react and walked on without looking back.

Lou didn't move for a long moment. "This isn't good," he said at last. "Preston was right about Devon. He's going to flip." He sounded a little scared.

Chapter 17

Henry stepped off the bus to find a familiar beat-up pickup parked in the driveway. Mr. James sat on his front step with a glass of lemonade. Seeing Henry, he lifted a hand and waved.

"Hey, there, Henry," he said. "I've been waiting for you. Your mom said it was all right if we talked, if that's okay with you."

Henry swallowed. He'd spent the entire day avoiding everything about baseball. He'd spent the lockdown reading a football novel and ate his lunch in the library looking up basketball highlights. During math class, he'd actually completed his review work for the standardized tests scheduled for the following week. Kevin, who sat behind him, had kept pestering him to talk, but Henry had ignored him entirely. Now he had no choice unless he ran away from home. Baseball wouldn't leave him alone.

Sighing, he walked toward his porch.

"Come sit beside me, Henry," Mr. James said. "I'm too old and tired to get up too many times."

Henry dropped his backpack near the steps and took a seat next to the older man. "Is this about baseball?" he asked listlessly, not making eye contact.

"No, son. It's about you. Devon told me what happened. I wanted to make sure you were all right. Your head feel good?"

Henry blinked. He didn't think Devon would be the first to tell about the attack . . . unless he wanted to establish his side of the story first. Henry still couldn't make up his mind about what had actually happened. All he could think about was waking up to see Devon going through his bag.

Would Devon sneak up on him, conk him in the head, and try to steal his—what? Cell phone and shoes? What else did he have worth taking? It didn't make sense . . . but he had seen Devon going through his stuff and he had been acting guilty of something. And why would three teenagers from a nice neighborhood rob him in a bad neighborhood? Thinking about it all made his head hurt.

"Uh, yeah, I'm fine," Henry muttered, wiping his nose.

Mr. James put an arm around Henry's shoulders. "I've been robbed before, son. It's a horrible feeling. Have you told your mom about this?"

"They didn't take anything," he managed to say. "I can't prove anything."

Mr. James sighed and looked up at the clear sky. "That doesn't change the horrible feeling, does it? I'm just glad you're okay. Now. I want to know the truth. I heard his side. Do you think Devon had anything to do with this?"

Henry bit his lower lip and then shook his head slowly. "I don't know him very well . . . but unless he's a real idiot, probably not."

This made Mr. James chuckle. "Well, he can be an idiot, but I don't know about a *real* idiot." Sobering, he took his arm from around Henry's shoulder. Resting both arms on his legs, he put his fingertips together. "Devon is a good kid. He lives in a bad spot, though. You probably noticed he lives with his grandma. Did he tell you why?"

Henry shook his head.

"He won't like this," Mr. James said, "but I'll tell you. I'll tell it straight. It's because his dad left before his first birthday and his mom is a flat-out drug addict. He spent the first years of his life with a woman who cared more about sticking needles in herself than she did about taking care of her own kid. His grandma saved him from that life. It hasn't been easy for him, but he's making it. And he's never been involved in any robbery that I know of."

Mr. James leaned back and raised an eyebrow at Henry. "So now we come down to it. He's scared right now, Henry. That's another reason why I'm here."

"Scared of what?" Henry asked with a frown. "That I'm going to say that he tried to rob me?"

"Oh, it's more than that. He's scared that he lost a new friend ... that you won't be coming to baseball practice today. And I'm scared too. Because if you don't show, then he probably won't show. And then I'll be in a spot of trouble. I'm sure you noticed yesterday, but we need all the talent we can get." Mr. James got to his feet and laid a gentle hand on Henry's shoulder. "I buried my only son. Now I look out for other boys and I sure don't want to bury any more. For some of these boys, baseball could be a chance to make it. To keep out of trouble until they're old enough to escape." He paused and looked at Henry thoughtfully. "That's all I had to say. I'm glad you're okay and I hope to see you again, Henry. You have a good day, now."

Henry stood and nodded. He watched thoughtfully as Mr. James climbed into his pickup and drove off.

"Now what was that all about?" his mom asked, poking her head out the door. "He said he wanted to talk to you about something, but never said what."

"Uh, I'll tell you later, Mom. I need to do something!" Henry slipped past her and raced up to his room, pulling his cell phone out of his shorts pocket. Kevin answered on the second ring.

"That you, Henry?" Kevin asked warily. "You still mad?"

"I just have one question, Kevin. Think. Right before you found me yesterday putting on my shoes, did you hear a car drive off?"

"Uh, yeah . . . it was really loud. That's when my mom sent me to look for you. She was afraid you'd get run over or something."

Henry let out a deep breath and flopped back on his bed.

"Henry? Henry? You still there? What about the car?"

"Nothing, Kevin. I'll tell you later. I got one more question. Can you still give me a ride to baseball today?"

When Henry slid open the door to Kevin's mom's van later that day and saw what was inside, he slammed it shut immediately.

Kevin knelt on the other side with two letters decorated with hearts. "Hey!" he cried. "Come back!"

Kevin's mom, Mrs. Baker, burst out laughing. "I told you that would be a fail!" she said from behind the wheel. A younger mom with dark curly hair, she enjoyed teasing her son.

Henry slid the door open slowly. "What are you doing?" he asked warily.

"Helping you, man! These are for Gabby."

Henry responded by tossing his baseball bag into Kevin's outstretched arms, knocking the boy into his seat.

"I'm serious," grunted Kevin, pushing the pack aside. "I started a plan to get her back for you! Look, I wrote poems you can use."

Henry groaned as he climbed in next to Kevin. "I think I'd rather walk." He snatched the nearest poem and crumpled it into a ball. "Think fast," he said, tossing the paper at Kevin's nose.

Soon the boys were engaged in a game of catch of the crumpled poems as Mrs. Baker drove. The love poetry never saw the light of day.

After Sunday's pick-up debacle, only ten players showed up for Monday's practice. Two of them, Charlie and Lou, left soon after Kevin arrived with Henry. When Devon spotted Henry, his eyes went big and he sprinted across the football field to meet the two boys. All past animosity with Kevin seemed to have vanished . . . for the time being.

"I thought you weren't coming," he said to Henry by way of greeting.

Henry shrugged. "Uh, yeah, but then Coach called to say we each get to throw a beanball at Kevin."

"Ha!" Kevin scoffed. "Very funny. If it came from you, I'm perfectly safe. Here. Take your pack." He'd just finished stuffing it with the rest of his poetry for Gabby.

The first day of practice for the Baptist baseball team was all about the basics. First, to the embarrassment of many, the equipment rules were reviewed and each player had to confirm that he had "athletic support." Nobody wanted a repeat of Devon's experience. Devon cringed just thinking about it. Then it was on to fundamentals.

To get things started, the boys partnered up for a game of catch. Devon had looked to pair up with Henry, but Henry and Kevin were already tossing a ball. Devon ended up throwing with Jack. Neither Devon nor Jack had nice things to say about the two outsiders.

After several minutes of catch led by Mr. James and assisted by Pastor Thomas, the boys broke into groups to work on fielding. Half did infield drills while the other half practiced in the outfield. All the drills were quick, lively, and turned into games. Pastor Thomas even brought out an old boom box and put on old gospel music.

As the first notes of an electric organ rang out, Kevin and Henry stared at each other. It was quite different from practicing with the Bears, but soon both boys found it more fun ... more free. Each of them easily had the best fundamentals, but some of the other players showed flashes of brilliance.

During breaks, Henry and Kevin used the time to size up the other players. Jack had a strong arm and a slick glove, when he was in position to use either one properly. Larry definitely established himself as the best first baseman. Some of the other players, DeAndre, Jesse, and Caleb clearly knew what to do in the field. And the talkative catcher named Tashaun had returned. He was solid behind the plate.

The rest, though, were a work in progress. Percy, a short burly boy, just wanted to hit. He barely moved when fielding. Lucas and Rodney, brothers who had dreams of being pro wrestlers, were always looking for an excuse to be on the ground, wrestling each other. They had to be separated multiple times.

When practice finally ended, the tired team gathered around a water cooler on the dugout bench. Everyone grabbed cups of water or water bottles.

"Nice practice, boys," Mr. James said, clapping his hands. "We showed real potential out there."

"That's code for 'we stunk,'" Tashaun said, squirting water into his face. "Lots of room to grow comes next."

"Just means we have a lot to improve on," Kevin said, wiping his brow.

"Yeah, that's what I said," muttered Jack. "Some of us . . ." he trailed off when he saw Mr. James staring at him. "Some of us need a shower," he finished lamely, squirting the back of Kevin's head.

"Hey!" Kevin cried. Turning, he flung the contents of his cup at Jack.

"Water fight!" cried Larry, grabbing his water bottle.

"Hey, now!" Mr. James said, but his words were lost as a sea of boys started tossing water at each other.

Standing in the back, Devon shook his head as the others engaged in a water fight. "Come on, man! Really?"

Huffing, he sat on the end of the bench farthest away from the water. "You guys act like a bunch of kids!"

"We are kids!" Larry shouted as he gleefully emptied his water bottle on Jack's back.

Devon rolled his eyes, missing the moment as Henry snuck up behind him and dumped a full bottle on the front of his pants.

Devon shot to his feet, shrieking. "Hey!" he shouted, his eyes going wild. "That's freezing!"

"You sound like a girl, man," teased Tashaun. Water dripped down his face. "You should join the choir for soprano!"

"You'll be singing soprano in a moment," Devon growled through gritted teeth. He took a step and sucked in his lips, his eyes squeezed tight. "You had ice in that!"

Henry was far out of reach by then. He hastily grabbed his glove and bag. "See you guys tomorrow!" he sang and ran off.

Kevin had left the water melee quickly after being doused with at least two water bottles. He waved at Henry to hurry up.

"Wait! Hold on!" Devon begged. "I can't walk home like this!"

"Like what?" Tashaun asked. He flung a cupful of water at Devon's face.

Kevin and Henry returned to Mrs. Baker's van dripping wet with Devon between them.

"Hi, Mom," Kevin said guiltily. "Do you, uh, mind giving, uh, Devon a ride? He's not far, but he's, uh, a little wet."

Mrs. Baker looked up from a romance novel and covered her mouth in dismay. "I thought this was baseball practice, not swimming practice!" she cried.

Then she saw Devon and her mouth dropped open and her eyes widened.

"Oh, uh, of course. Not a problem," she said, quickly composing herself and offering a wide smile.

Devon and Henry exchanged glances. They both wondered if it was the water or something else that had caused her to hesitate.

Kevin and Henry both wore old baseball pants, generic T-shirts, and their Bears ball caps. They looked like ballplayers. Devon had on baggy gray sweatpants, now soaked in the front, and a blue T-shirt with both sleeves cut off. He had his glove tucked under his arm while he fidgeted with his faded Atlanta Braves hat. He thought that to Mrs. Baker, he must look like a thug.

Devon ducked his head. "Thank you, ma'am," he said.

Mrs. Baker blinked and swallowed. "You have better manners than my son. Of course, get in! This van was just cleaned and it's about time it smells like wet smelly boys!"

Henry and Kevin grinned sheepishly as they climbed in the back. Devon followed without a hint of a smile. He'd seen

Mrs. Baker's face when she'd first seen him. It was a look of fear.

The boys were far from friends, but the ride was a start. Devon sat in the back, stone-faced as he gave directions to his house. He thanked Mrs. Baker politely when he left, but barely made eye contact with Henry or Kevin. He'd yet to talk to Henry about the other day, but he did say he would see them both at the next practice.

The rest of the week flew by quickly. At Hamilton Middle, despite the teachers constant harping about standardized tests, all the talk was mostly about summer plans . . . and baseball. The Williams County First Annual Church Tournament started Saturday and every boy who played baseball was either participating or planning on going to watch.

Since it was affiliated with the Little League, the players in the tournament were eligible for all-stars—this, claimed Bobby, was for two reasons: One, the best players in the league could play and represent a church. And two, the league could scout out any hidden talent in the underprivileged areas.

Bobby bragged that all the tournament all-star selections would come from his team. It didn't hurt that Coach Wood also helped with the selections, so few people doubted him.

The Resurrection Baptist team just hoped to field enough players for a team for the first game. Their numbers had not increased as the week progressed. In fact, they dwindled further when Percy stopped coming. Thanks to an unplanned beach invitation, though, their fan base grew.

It all started at the end of Thursday's practice, just two days before the start of the tournament. Pastor Thomas was hitting pop flies to the boys in the outfield. Keeping in the tradition of the week, Tashaun made a game of it. He offered one point for a catch and two points for a diving catch. A dropped ball earned a negative point. Courtesy of Henry, the winner would get a Soup'or Subs gift card. Henry had made the mistake the day before of letting the guys know that his father owned Soup'or Subs, and ever since, every drill ended with a player winning a free sandwich.

On Henry's turn, the pastor hit a shallow fly that looked sure to drop. The boy's blazing speed, however, brought him close enough to make a decent attempt at a great dive. Instead, he slid on his knees and trapped the ball with his lap on the first bounce.

"Ah, man!" cried DeAndre. "I thought you had that one, boy!"

"Didn't want to rob me of Soup'or Subs, huh?" jeered Larry.

Devon went to meet Henry as he trotted to the back of the line. "You have a hard time with diving, don't you?"

Henry lifted his head and frowned. "No . . . I do it fine in football. With baseball, I don't know . . . I just don't want the ball to get past me," he finished lamely.

Devon sighed and put an arm on Henry's shoulder. "You always have to play it safe, huh? Man, tell you what. We're going to the beach on Saturday. You should come."

"Aren't we playing a game on Saturday?" Henry asked doubtfully.

Devon shook his head. "Our game isn't until one. We have plenty of time in the morning. My uncles and aunts will be there . . . with all my cousins. I could use you to escape."

"Be where?" demanded Larry. "Did I hear you're going to the beach?"

"Which beach?" Jack wanted to know. "When are we going?"

"Hey!" protested Devon as all the boys turned their attention to him. "Wait a minute. This is my family going!"

"I can make it," DeAndre said. "My family won't miss me."

"That's it!" Tashaun crowed. "Team beach party this Saturday morning!"

"Oh, yeah!" Kevin said, hearing the last part as he ran in from the drill. "I'm in!"

Instantly everyone froze and turned to Devon. Kevin had yet to be fully accepted by the team. During most drills, he still tried to give tips and added unwanted criticisms. Earlier, he'd confided to Henry that he was just doing his community service—he was making better ballplayers. What he was really doing was making himself unpopular . . . mostly to Devon.

"Fine," Devon muttered gruffly. "Everyone can go . . . I'll let my folks know." He sighed. "Be at the James River Park at nine."

The team cheered, completely abandoning the drill.

Chapter 18

Aside from joggers, the James River Beach Park was almost always deserted until midafternoon when shoppers would visit the nearby stores. On that Saturday morning, though, a baseball team stormed the beach.

At just past eight o'clock, Devon arrived with his Uncle Bernie and Aunt Jenny's family. They were the scouts charged with setting up a beachhead.

Mostly secluded from main roads, the small sandy beach lay beneath a tiny tourist town perched on a large hill overlooking the river. A two-story motel sat across the road that ran parallel to the beach. Next to the motel were a cluster of restaurants and gift shops, but these were mostly closed until summer.

Traveling further down the road, the beach petered out into large rocks lining the river. Here it turned into a fancy tourist area that featured expensive restaurants, wine stores, antique shops, and a parking garage, all open year round. Before the summer season, the beach area remained mostly neglected and the entire area was largely unwelcoming to anyone who wasn't a responsible adult.

Devon's Uncle Bernie ignored the parking garage, which would mean a much longer walk, and settled for parking at the motel, just across the street from the beach.

"If they try to tow us, we'll see them coming and move our car," he mumbled shutting off the engine.

Nobody was around and they parked with no trouble.

They immediately staked out a large sandy swathe of the beach by sticking in four beach umbrellas and unfurling several towels. The little kids quickly fell to making sand castles while Devon helped his uncle carry a portable grill from the car, already loaded with charcoal.

"Just watch," Devon grunted as he crossed the street with his uncle. "Nobody's going to show up."

"Just means more food for us," his uncle said through gritted teeth. "After all this work, we're going to need it! Let's get this close to the water just in case somebody has a problem with us grilling."

Devon grunted but made no comment. There were no signs posted against grilling, but it didn't take much for somebody to get offended these days. Few people in this area had dark skin. If there was a complaint, he doubted it would be about the grilling.

The James stretched over a mile wide at this point, but the water rarely grew fiercer than water in a bathtub. Flat and shallow by the shore, swimming here was perfect for small children and beginners. The only drawback was that the river fed into the Chesapeake Bay. This meant saltwater mixed with freshwater and that meant jellyfish were often carried in. The James River Park Beach was notorious for jellyfish stings.

By nine thirty, the grill, blankets, and cooler were set up near the water and Devon had been proven wrong. The entire team had arrived.

"Look!" cried Shorty, shading his eyes against the sun. "There they are!"

"Don't point!" hissed Melissa, pulling his arm down. The two of them stood on top of the stairs leading from the tourist area down to the waterfront. "We don't want to be spotted!"

"No kidding," Shorty replied sourly. "I never wanted to be here in the first place."

"You're the one who told me about this," Melissa reminded him. "You said Kevin and Henry would be here with a bunch of kids from the Baptist team. Something happened with Henry and that team last weekend. Remember? And he's the one who called Coach Wood's phone and got some funny message. I'm telling you, he's a link in this mystery."

Shorty sighed and shook his head. "I seriously doubt he's the drug dealer."

"Yes, but he might know who is. Come on. Let's get closer."

Henry stretched out his body and inhaled the salty air. Throwing his arms above his head, he yawned. This was a pregame routine he could live with.

"Nice pigeon chest," Kevin drawled lazily from where he lay on the towel beside him. He lifted up his shades. "You know, there aren't any girls to impress, so you might as well lie down."

Henry kicked sand on his friend instead. "Just toss me my glove," he muttered, hugging his chest. "Devon and I are going to play catch."

"Sure thing." Kevin turned to grab Henry's glove. Rising on his elbow, he whipped it at his friend's head.

Henry ducked just in time and the glove smacked DeAndre in the back.

"Ow!" he cried. "What was that for?"

"Sorry," Kevin said. "Just testing your reflexes!"

"You mean testing my nerves," DeAndre muttered, scowling. He stalked to the nearby umbrella and plopped down on a towel near Jack and Larry.

Kevin and Henry exchanged looks and stifled laughter.

"So much for building relationships," Henry said, snatching up his glove. "Idiot."

"Hey, that one was your fault," Kevin protested. "You said you were playing catch. You shouldn't have ducked. Speaking of relationships, have you read my poetry for Gabby yet?"

Henry kicked sand in his friend's face and went off to find Devon.

Henry found Devon just in time.

Two boys in long T-shirts, shorts, and sandals had wandered out from the hotel and crossed the street. Clearly tourists, they had the look of pampered kids with golden skin and gleaming blond hair. They had accosted Devon's little cousin Micah, who'd been playing in the sand near the sidewalk. He'd wandered away from the umbrellas and was by himself when the boys stood over him.

"What are you doing, kid? Digging for treasure?" asked the taller of the boys, grinning snidely.

Micah looked up and frowned. "I'm just digging," he said.

The other boy snorted. "Don't you know? His people love to dig. They were slaves, you know, so they've had lots of practice. It's probably all they know how to do well."

Both boys laughed. And that was when Devon found them.

Devon had been by the grill when he'd seen the boys with Micah and he knew instantly that trouble was afoot. Without a word, he ran to his cousin.

"Micah," he demanded. "Get away from the sidewalk. Now!"

"But—"

"You heard me! Your mom doesn't want you over here."

Micah went to protest, but something in Devon's voice made him grab his plastic shovel and scamper to the umbrella where his mom sat facing the water, blissfully unaware.

The two boys watched with undisguised disdain.

"That's a good little boy," the older boy said loud enough for Devon to hear. "He obeys really well. Like he's had lots of practice. You know, from his ancestors."

Devon narrowed his eyes and felt his jaw clench tight. For a moment he froze. His T-shirt fluttered against his rigid body as he glared at the boys.

The taller of the two looked to be about his age, but he was inches taller and huskier. The other boy was just as burly but at least a year younger. Each had their bright blond hair slicked back and wide mouths; they looked to be brothers. The older one wore a gleaming white golf visor sporting a small American flag on the front. Both wore sunglasses that probably cost more than all of Devon's clothes put together.

Neither boy seemed intimidated by Devon, a lone boy in a T-shirt and bathing suit.

"What did you say?" Devon asked, instantly regretting the anger in his voice. He didn't want trouble like this. Not now.

"Calm down, man," the boy in the visor said, leaning back and crossing his arms in front of him. "We just came out to enjoy the beach and found you all here. Crowding up the place."

"Yeah," added his younger brother. "Do you people even know how to swim?"

The older brother couldn't help himself. "Maybe this is how your kind takes baths," he mumbled just loud enough for Devon to hear.

Devon could feel both hands form into fists. He was about to say something ugly when he heard Henry call him.

Taking a deep breath, he answered. "Over here!"

Henry stepped out from behind an umbrella and headed over.

When they saw Henry, the brothers looked at each other and started backing away. Thin and scrawny compared to the brothers, it wasn't the size of Henry that intimidated them. It was his skin color.

"What's going on?" Henry asked as he stopped next to his friend. "You know these guys?" he asked Devon.

"I hope not," Devon said, glaring at the boys. "They were just leaving."

"Whatever," the older brother said. "We were told this river was polluted. Now we know why."

The younger brother swallowed and grabbed his brother's sleeve. "Come on," he said nervously. "Drop it."

Henry frowned. "Where're you idiots from?" he asked.

"Why do you want to know?" the older brother asked, pulling away from his younger sibling.

"He wants to know so we never go there," Devon said. "We like to stay away from polluted cesspools."

"You don't have to tell us," Henry added. "Just as long as you go back and stay there. I'm guessing it's a lot like the stomach of a fat cow. Because it sure makes a lot of—"

"Hey!" interrupted a deep voice from across the street. "You kids get over here!" A large man stuck his head out the door and glared at the brothers. "You stay away from riffraff!"

"Come on," muttered the younger brother. "Let's go."

With ugly faces, the brothers gave one last look at Devon and retreated back to the hotel.

"That's it, like good little boys," Devon said to their backs. "You two obey well."

"Maybe one day you'll learn to think too," Henry called.

Neither boy turned around as they made their way back to their angry father. The hotel door slammed shut behind them.

Henry raised his eyebrows and nudged Devon's arm. "So what was that about?"

Breathing out heavily, Devon shook his head angrily. "That," he said, "was life." He turned and saw Henry's glove. "You ready for a game of catch? I really need one right now."

Henry didn't know what to say, so he said nothing. People who say there's no more racism, he thought, were people like him, the people who never had to face it.

Soon Henry and Devon were engrossed in a game of catch by the water. The rude brothers weren't mentioned again. The sun had just started warming the day and both boys had stripped to their swim trunks. It felt good—feeling warm sun on their backs and hearing the pop of the ball slapping into their leather gloves. A nice breeze blew in from the river, slowly easing away the tension.

Still, Henry couldn't shake the sight of Devon facing the two racist boys. The jerks. He hoped he'd never acted like those idiots and vowed that he never would. Playing on the Baptist team wasn't any different than playing on any other team. The kids here just wanted to play ball and be accepted. He sighed. So then why did if feel like the team wasn't really a team yet? They just hadn't gelled.

The rest of the team lounged in the sun or under umbrellas. Some listened to music, while others, like Kevin, caught up on sleep. There was no togetherness.

Devon's uncles manned the grill and the smell of cooking sausage filled the air. Nobody else had seen what had happened with the boys.

Only Micah was aware of the confrontation and he was busy with the rest of Devon's little cousins, building sandcastles and trying to bury Tashaun's feet while he slept.

"You ready for some diving catches?" Devon called to Henry, shaking him from his thoughts. "This is the place to do it!"

Henry gave a half-hearted shrug. "Sure."

Devon grinned, looking relaxed. It would be like old times. He and Corey used to go to this beach all the time. One of their favorite things to do had been diving catches. They would take turns—one would throw the ball near the other, but would intentionally throw it either too far or too short, and the other would have to make a spectacular grab for a point. It was more fun in the water, but with the water still cold from the winter, the sand would work just fine.

"The thing with diving," Devon explained, "is to not worry about what happens next. It's just you and the ball. Everything else goes poof. You just put all you got into making the play. If you fail, too bad. But if you make it, man, it's the best feeling in the world."

"Just bring it!" Henry said, squatting low, smacking his glove.

The first throw went well wide to his right and he sprawled awkwardly, missing the catch by several feet.

"Great!" called Devon. "That's how *not* to do it! Come on, man! Loosen up!"

Henry got to his knees, frowning. "I couldn't get that one if I had a six-foot fishnet!" Getting to his feet, he retrieved the ball from the sand and tossed a lazy lob several feet in front of Devon.

Devon snorted with disdain at the throw and didn't move at first. Then, all at once, he sprang forward, leaning low. Just when it looked as if the ball would plop into the sand, he dove forward, leaving his feet and stretching out his glove. The ball thudded into the leather inches from the sand.

Devon stuck up his glove arm in triumph as he shot to his knees. "That's how you do it, boy!" he crowed.

Henry rolled his eyes, but couldn't help shaking his head in admiration. "Lucky," he muttered.

"Lucky, nothing," Devon responded. "Man, your problem is that you're too tight. Everything about you is too tight."

"What are you talking about?" Henry asked, taking offense.

"Man, when I first saw you playing ball for your Bears team, your white pants were so tight I saw your red undies. I still don't know how you move in those things. No wonder you're skinny like a Popsicle stick."

Henry frowned and sheepishly scratched the side of his bathing suit. "Yeah, well, it's better than when I first saw you. You wore your jeans so loose I thought you'd trip and fall every time you took a step! At least I don't wear my undies above my pants like you."

Devon narrowed his eyes and curled his lip. Then he broke into a wide smile and laughed. "You got me there! I hate those jeans, man. Now catch this!"

He threw the ball well over Henry's head and went to his knees in mirth when Henry fell on his skinny backside trying to make the catch. It was just like old times . . .

Soon both boys were laughing in delight or frustration as the ball either fell short or landed in their gloves.

"That's it!" Devon cried a short time later, after Henry went full out on a dive but missed. He spitted sand while the ball rolled behind him. "Sometimes you have to risk everything and hope for the best!"

"I just hope sand is good for you," Henry muttered, spitting and wiping his mouth. "Gross!"

Devon laughed. "No problem, man. But save some room for later. We're having real sandwiches."

"Ha-ha." Henry got up to retrieve the ball only to find Devon's little cousin Micah holding it while carrying his red plastic bat. He gulped.

Seeing Henry looking at him, Micah held up the ball and stuck out his bottom lip. "Pitch to me," he demanded.

"Wrong ball, bighead!" Devon shouted. "Give it back to us and go find the plastic ball."

Micah shook his head stubbornly. "Nobody will play with me."

"I'll play with you later," Henry promised, eyeing the bat warily. "I promise. Just give me the ball."

"No!" Micah cried. "Now!"

"No?" Devon yelled. He threw down his glove and ran at his little cousin. "Don't say no to me, you little twerp!"

Micah dropped the ball and fled to his mother, crying as he went.

"Great," Devon muttered, stopping next to Henry. "Now I'm going to get in trouble and be forced to babysit the brat."

Henry picked up the ball and tossed it to him. "At least we got the ball back. Maybe no more diving catches until it's clear."

Hearing Micah's cries, Jack and Larry looked over and soon joined Henry and Devon with their gloves. Quickly, a four-way game of catch ensued.

Henry was just getting into the rhythm of it all when he felt a sharp pain against the back of his bathing suit.

"Play with me now!" yelled Micah, readying his bat for another swing. "Poopy head!"

"Hey!" Henry yelped, dancing away while grabbing his sore spot. "Watch it!"

"Crazy kid with a bat!" yelled Larry. "Look out!"

"Get out of here!" Devon shouted at his cousin.

"Devon, you leave your cousin alone!" Micah's mom called from under an umbrella.

"Tell him to leave us alone!" Devon cried back. "We're acting in self-defense here!"

"Take him to the water and get him wet!" his aunt shouted back. "That's what he really wants."

"Oh, yeah?" Devon asked, his eyes narrowing. "Is that what you really want, Micah?"

Micah gulped and shook his head vigorously. As he dropped the bat, his eyes went wide. Suddenly he noticed all the big kids facing him.

"Too bad!" Devon said with an evil grin. "Grab him!"

Screeching, Micah took off running, with Devon, Jack, and Larry giving chase.

Henry stuck his glove on his head and watched the chase in bemusement. It looked as if the game of catch was over for a while. Yawning, he drifted toward the umbrellas. By the time he returned to Kevin, he heard Micah's wild screams turn into shrieks followed by a big splash.

"There!" cried Devon's voice. "How do you like it?"

"More!" cried the boy's voice, sputtering. "Do it again!"

"How did it go?" Kevin said, yawning. "Sounds like they're sacrificing some kid to the river."

Henry frowned and dropped to the sand near the towel. "I don't know," he said after a moment. "This sure is different from the Bears."

Kevin rolled onto his side and brushed sand off his leg. "What do you mean?" he asked. "This team isn't as good for sure, but we're decent."

Henry sighed. "Yeah, I know . . . it's just, you know, not everyone gets along. We're too . . . different."

Kevin pushed himself up to a sitting position. "Well, we didn't always get along with the Bears, either. We just had Coach Wood to unite us. He always found something to bring us together."

Henry rested his arms on his knees and nodded. "That's what we need," he said glumly. "Something to unite us."

"We'll find something," Kevin said, not sounding very confident.

Just then piercing shrieks of pain split the air.

The boys shot to their feet and joined a mad dash to the river, where the screams had originated. Henry's first thought was of the brothers at the hotel. Had they come back and started something?

Even Devon's grandma, who wore a long dress and carried a cane, came hurrying out of her chair. She and the boys joined the crowd gathered around Micah, who stood dripping wet and bawling.

"It was a jellyfish," explained Devon sounding scared. "He ran right into it and got stung on the leg."

"Oh, my poor baby," exclaimed Micah's mom, rushing to swoop the boy up in her arms. "No jellyfish is going to hurt my boy and get away with it!"

"I see it!" cried Marcus, Micah's older brother. "There it is!" Though he stood only ankle deep in the water, the little boy jumped back as if threatened by a shark. He pointed excitedly a few feet from shore. "It's a big one, Mamma."

"You stay away from it!" cried Devon's grandma. "Those things are vicious!"

Most of the boys on the baseball team ran to get a look. Nobody, though, dared enter the water.

Kevin and Henry remained in the background. They looked at Micah, now whimpering, and looked at each other.

"We need something to unite us, right?" Kevin asked, his eyes gleaming.

Henry's eyes widened. "No. You're not serious," he said.

"Oh, yeah, I am," Kevin said. "Let's do this! Come on!"

Henry groaned, but dutifully followed. "I hate you," he muttered.

"First one stung wins," Kevin cried back in delight. He raced to the water. "Where's that monster that picks on little kids? Where's he at?"

From the arms of his mother, Micah stopped crying to watch.

"Right there," Jack said pointing. "It's a big one all right."

"Not for long!" yelled Kevin. "Charge!" Screaming, he ran full tilt into the water and dove headfirst where Jack had pointed.

Yelling, Henry followed right after. He stretched out in a dive next to his friend and landed right on the stupid thing. Severe pain raked across his stomach and his ribs and he shot out of the water gasping in pain.

"It got me!" screeched Kevin, thrashing next to him.

"Me too!" cried Henry. "Watch it, you're pushing me—" He fell back on the jellyfish.

Henry came up howling, grabbing at his back.

Devon watched in shock at the stupidity before him, but then he tightened his jaw. "Come on, guys. Let's help them!"

"You serious, dude?" Tashaun asked in a hushed tone.

Screaming, Devon charged into the fray. With a moment's hesitation, the entire team followed. Nine boys were soon dancing and thrashing in the river yelling threats and mild curses at the jellyfish.

"Cut it out!" screeched Henry. "I think it's in my suit!"

The young cousins all gathered at the water's edge and watched in frightened wonder. Micah rubbed the welt forming just over his knee and sniffed. A smile slowly spread across his face.

The adults watched too but more in dismay and disgust.

"Those boys have gone plumb crazy," Micah's mom said, shaking her head. "What's this world coming to?"

"Don't know," mumbled Devon's Uncle Bernie. "But that poor jellyfish got it coming. Now it's just plain jelly."

Chapter 19

Melissa and Shorty watched the boys attack the jellyfish in horrified fascination. They leaned against the front of the motel and took it in, their mouths gaping open.

"Why are boys so stupid?" Melissa finally asked.

"I plead the fifth," Shorty answered, shaking his head. He looked at Melissa. "You don't suppose . . . that they're all on drugs, do you?"

Melissa snorted. "They probably need to be."

Watching from across the road, through a gap in the umbrellas, they saw the boys stagger from the water, most of them overcome with hysterical laughter. Many collapsed on the sand and rolled around in mirth.

Kevin left the water last. "I think we got it!" he crowed.

"More like it got us," groaned Henry, falling to a knee. "I have jellyfish guts all over me. Ow!" he yelped as he pulled stinging goop off his belly.

Melissa was just about to suggest they leave when Shorty pulled on her sleeve. "Hey, Melissa," he hissed. "I don't think we're the only ones watching them. Look."

Melissa turned and saw a small green car low to the ground. Parked facing the beach, three figures were crammed in the front. One of the figures held a set of binoculars trained on the boys at the beach.

"Now that's interesting," she said. Her eyes narrowed. "I think I recognize that car ... Shawn Graham from the baseball team drives one like it."

"Um, maybe you shouldn't get too close," Shorty told her as she started moving toward the car.

"I just want to make sure it's Shawn."

Suddenly someone in the car turned and saw her. Instantly all the figures swiveled toward Melissa and then ducked low. The car roared to life.

"Look out!" Shorty yelled.

Running toward Melissa, he pulled her back as the car shot in reverse, narrowly missing her legs. Then it jolted forward, turning with screeching tires as it exited the parking lot as if it had been launched from a catapult. In seconds in vanished from sight.

"What was that all about?" Shorty asked when his breath returned.

Melissa straightened her shirt and smoothed down her shorts. "That," she said, "was definitely Shawn. I even recognized his stupid girlfriend, Lexi. Something strange is definitely going on."

Shorty gulped and nodded. "I'll say," he said. "You nearly got killed and don't seem to care."

"Meat tenderizer, boys," Devon's grandma said, "That's the best thing for jellyfish stings."

Devon's Uncle Bernie snorted. "Actually, I know another way, but it's not fit for, well, let's just say the girls wouldn't like it."

"Meat tenderizer," repeated Devon's grandma firmly. "You boys take turns and pass it around. You'll find it in the cooler. Then you'd better pack up. You all have a game in a few hours."

The entire team was soon gathered around the cooler by the grill. Devon's uncles were taking the last of the sausages from the fire while his grandma sat back in her chair under an umbrella.

"At least now we have a name for our team," Tashaun said gravely as he watched Devon fish out the bottle of tenderizer.

"What? The Stupids?" Jack asked with a snort. He rubbed rising welts on his left arm.

"No, the Jellyfish, duh," Larry said.

Kevin laughed. "Yeah, that's us! We're the jellyfish! Jellyfish in the house!"

Nobody could protest or argue. And nobody gave Kevin a dirty look.

Most of the boys had superficial stings, but Henry and Kevin had received the worst. Waiting until last, they took the bottle of tenderizer to the public restrooms just off the beach. Devon followed unhappily. His grandma had made it clear that he wasn't allowed to leave Henry's side. Somehow she'd heard of the attack the previous week.

Devon slumped on a bench inside the bathroom as the two boys took separate stalls. Laughing and joking they tossed the bottle back and forth over the top as Devon listened.

"I don't think I'm going to sit still for a week," Henry said. "This stings!"

"Yeah, that's the point," Kevin said. "You should've seen your face! I never saw anything funnier in my life! What were you thinking?"

"That my best friend is an idiot!" retorted Henry. "It was your idea, idiot!" Then he sucked in his breath. "Pass me the tenderizer stuff. I don't think I'm sliding headfirst today."

Devon gritted his teeth and got to his feet. It was like he didn't even exist. Like he didn't matter. He thought back to the two jerks from the hotel and for a moment he saw Henry as one of them.

Henry had a best friend all right. Devon had nearly forgotten. Henry just hung around for baseball. After the tournament he would be gone. He would go back to the world where picking on little kids was okay, just as long as they had the wrong skin color.

Leaving the bathroom, he leaned against the brick wall and stared at the river. For a moment he wondered how things would be if he had light skin and lived in a fancy house like Henry and Kevin. Or like the two brothers at the hotel. Was that all it took to have a happy life?

"Hey, man!" Kevin said, interrupting Devon's thoughts as he stepped out of the bathroom. "What are you doing here? Do you still need the tenderizer? I hope not, because it's pretty much gone and . . . I don't know how clean it was in the end."

"I don't need anything," Devon said gruffly. "Come on. We have a game to play."

Mr. James and Pastor Thomas arrived for the scheduled one o'clock game an hour early and spent the next half hour wondering where their players were.

"I told them to be here early," Mr. James grumbled for the fifth time. He looked down at his feet and the heavy bags holding batting helmets, bats, and balls. "They were supposed to carry the equipment."

"Patience, Brother James," soothed the pastor. "We still have time. Boys are boys."

"Patience doesn't get them here," Mr. James said with a frown. "And we're not going to have enough time for batting practice if they don't hurry." He kicked the grass. "How can the whole team be late?"

They were at the field at Hamilton Middle, the closest field to First Presbyterian, the host church. With eight teams competing, it was a single-elimination tournament over three days. The winners of round one moved to the semifinals the following day. The championship would be held on Monday afternoon.

Earlier that morning, First Presbyterian had already moved on, winning their opening game against Holy Baptist by a score of 12–1. Holy Baptist proved to have a holey defense, as they had more errors than hits. In the next game, which ended right at noon, Lutheran Trinity took down St. Jerome's Catholic Church by a single run. Now Saint Christopher's Catholic Church had already taken the field and was busy with warm-ups and drills. The visitor side sat empty.

"You have a team coming, right?" the head umpire asked Mr. James, approaching from home plate.

Mr. James grunted. He leaned against the chain-link fence separating the dugout from the field. "We're praying on it."

"The Lord will provide," Pastor Thomas added. "We hope."

"Well," the ump said, looking at his watch, "we start in a little over twenty minutes. We have another game after this and can't fall behind schedule."

"We understand," Pastor Thomas said. "Believe me. The Baptists like to show up late."

Mr. James cleared his throat. "Speaking of the—erm, of the boys. Here they come."

In the parking lot, a mini convoy of minivans and station wagons pulled up and started offloading the Resurrection Baptist players. Some of them were still buckling their pants and straightening their new baseball jerseys or adjusting their hats.

The hats, pants, and jerseys were courtesy of an anonymous donor but had arrived during Friday's practice in Soup'or Subs boxes. Mrs. Lee had asked Coach Jackson to send the boys' sizes by e-mail and had spent an afternoon at various used sports stores, buying out every pair of gray youth baseball pants she could find. The jerseys had been specially ordered and were a dark purple with "Resurrection Baptist" freshly ironed on the front with numbers on the back. The lettering and numbering were done in yellow. The hats, ordered with the jerseys so the colors matched, had a simple RB on the front.

"Well," the ump said, hitching up his pants as he watched. "If you all lose, you'll at least look good doing it."

"Amen to that," Pastor Thomas said. "And then have a beach party in right field."

A stream of children and grown-ups followed the players, all dressed in beachwear and carrying beach umbrellas and towels. Devon's Uncle Bernie pulled the cooler loaded with sausages and drinks. They hadn't had time to eat at the beach.

His cheeks puffing out like a blowfish, Mr. James jogged to meet his team. "What in the h—" he started to yell before remembering where he was. Taking a deep breath, he started again. "What have you boys been doing?"

"Don't worry, Coach," Tashaun said, grinning. "We got us a new name."

"Yeah!" crowed DeAndre. "We're the Jellyfish now!"

"The what?" Mr. James said, frowning. The boys had extra pep in their step as they came toward him.

Something had changed and it wasn't just the uniforms. They actually resembled a real team. Kevin even walked between Lucas and Rodney, two boys he'd never acknowledged before except when criticizing their fielding. Now he was talking to them like they were best friends.

Mr. James scratched his head. His anger had drained away and been replaced by confusion.

"We were just, you know, bonding," Jack explained, lifting up a dark arm covered in ugly welts. "We're all jellyfish brothers!"

"Oh, yeah!" Larry said. He lifted up his jersey to show off a round belly crisscrossed with similar welts.

Wincing, Mr. James gestured for Larry to pull down his shirt. "Never mind," he said. "Just get to the dugout and get ready to play."

The Jellyfish Brothers, as they called themselves, were ready to play. Picked as the visitors, they batted first and wasted no time in demonstrating that batting practice was overrated.

St. Christopher's Catholic Church had its own private school and was the only church with a year-round baseball team. This made them cofavorites with First Presbyterian to win the tournament. Their pitcher, a burly eighth grader, made no secret of what he thought of the Baptist team.

"If this was basketball, I'd be worried," he said loudly while throwing his warm-up pitches. "Only two players we have to worry about and I bet nobody can guess which ones."

The kid from second base chimed in. "Where did these guys come from anyway? Their fans look like beach bums!"

Their fans consisted of Devon's family, who were setting up a picnic behind third base. Devon's grandma was busy stuffing sausages into rolls and passing them through the fence to the hungry players inside the Baptist dugout. Larry took two and Jack wolfed one down in three bites.

"Just play ball, boys!" called their coach. In a blue and white jacket with school colors, the coach from St. Christopher's had a ruddy face and a serious mouth that rarely smiled. "Take care of business and we celebrate at Soup'or Subs!"

Hearing them in the dugout, Henry scowled. "Not if I can help it," he muttered.

Devon batted leadoff. He swung at the first pitch and delivered a smoker that sizzled between the shortstop and the surprised third baseman. By the time the ball returned to the infield, Devon easily stood on first.

Jack followed with a shallow fly to center that barely dropped for a hit. Not sure if the ball would land or be caught, Devon held up and remained on second.

That brought up Henry.

"He's not one to worry about!" Kevin cried out. "You already faced the dangerous hitters! Trust me!"

The pitcher nervously wiped away sweat and glared toward the visitor dugout. He knew about Henry from little league. Suddenly he blinked rapidly. Half the players in the dugout were eating sausage rolls. His next three pitches didn't come near the plate. Then, in desperation, he threw a carefully aimed pitch right down the middle. Henry swung away and fired a sizzling line drive into the gap between center and left field. Two runs scored and Henry pulled up at third.

"Time!" yelled the home coach. His face red, he ran to the mound.

Henry used the moment to trot over to Mr. James, coaching third, and pass him his batting gloves.

"I don't know where you boys were," Mr. James told him, sounding befuddled, "but this jellyfish thing sure is working."

"Hey, show him yours," Larry called from the dugout. "Pull up your shirt, Henry. Show Coach James your jellyfish power!"

Henry made a face and shook his head. "We're in the middle of a game," he protested.

"So?" Jack cried. "We're jellyfish brothers, we can do anything!"

Mr. James turned with a frown and his mouth dropped open. "Hey! Are you boys eating in there? Are you all crazy!"

"Jellyfish crazy!" answered Larry, biting into another roll.

"Sorry, but these boys are hungry," Devon's grandma said from the other side of the fence. "You can get one too if you want!"

Mr. James swallowed and turned back to the game. "I don't believe this," he muttered. Then he turned his gaze up to the sky, as if imploring for mercy.

All the mound meeting did in the end was prolong the misery—both for Mr. James and St. Christopher's. Kevin, batting next, worked the count to 2 and 1 before cracking a single up the middle to score Henry. As Henry entered the dugout, Devon had an overturned bucket waiting for him.

"The jellyfish throne," Devon said solemnly. He'd added the words to the bucket in sloppy handwriting with a Sharpie.

Henry rolled his eyes as he sat down and turned his focus to the game.

When the top of the first finally ended, the score was 8–0, visitors. The Jellyfish had stung first.

St. Christopher's never recovered. The game finally ended with a score of 15–6. The Baptist team moved on.

St. Christopher's still didn't know what had happened.

Chapter 20

That night, Melissa woke up to a terrifying crash on her window. Shooting to a sitting position, she went still. She strained her ears but heard nothing. Then from just outside her house, she heard a car speed away, the tires squealing.

Her heart beating fast, she waited several seconds before sliding out of her bed. She knew she hadn't been dreaming when her younger brother Benjamin appeared from his room next to hers, wiping his eyes.

"What was that?" he asked blearily. "It sounded like something hitting the house."

"You wait here," Melissa said to him grimly. "If I'm not back in ten minutes, wake up Mom and Dad."

She hurried downstairs and stopped in the garage to pick up a softball bat. Slipping into sneakers, she went outside and investigated the ground under her window. It took a few moments for her eyes to adjust to the darkness, but she spotted a dark bundle in the grass. She picked it up with trembling hands and saw it was a rock with a note tied to it.

Racing back inside, she told her brother it was nothing to worry about and sent him back to bed. Then she got in her bed and turned on the lamp by her pillow.

Her heart thudded as she unfolded the note. Then it stopped altogether. For a moment she couldn't breathe. The words were typed in boldface. They meant business.

STOP ASKING QUESTIONS. YOU'VE BEEN WARNED.

There was no signature.

After a long moment, Melissa's breath returned. She reread the note five more times. With the paper still held in a trembling hand, she fumbled for her cell phone and dialed Shorty's number.

After the third round of ringing, Shorty answered. "Hello?"

"Shorty!" Melissa nearly screamed, dropping the note at the sound of voice. "Has anything strange happened to you tonight?"

Shorty sighed on the other end. "You mean besides you calling me at two in the morning . . . ? No."

"Good. Call me if anything does." She hung up and sank back onto her pillow, her heart and mind racing a mile a minute.

The rock terrified her, but at the same time, it thrilled her. Finally, she'd gotten a breakthrough. After all her investigating, she'd actually found a legitimate clue . . . but what was it? What had caused some twisted jerk to throw a rock at her window with a warning?

Then she sat up with a start. Shawn's car and the Baptist team. Somehow it all tied together with the drugs at school.

Grabbing her cell phone, she texted Shorty. She asked him to meet her at the church baseball tournament later that day. Earlier she'd learned the scores from a softball friend who attended First Presbyterian, so she knew Coach Wood's team and the Baptist team would be there. She was getting close. Excitement slowly eclipsed her fear.

A bolt of lightning flashed in the distance, followed by a peal of thunder.

The fear returned.

Henry woke up early to the patter of raindrops outside his window. Groaning, he rolled out of bed and pulled on his pajama pants. Checking the window, he saw dark ominous clouds stretching over the sky like a large black eye. The rain was more like a drizzle, but in Virginia the weather could change in an instant.

Careful not to wake his brother, he stopped by the bathroom before heading downstairs with his cell phone. Rain or not, he knew he had a job to do . . . something he'd been avoiding all week.

Gabby had returned to school the past Tuesday but had yet to speak to him since the dance. She kept herself surrounded by her friends and they always gave him the evil eye whenever he tried to approach.

Flopping on the couch, he called her house number. He sat up straight when Mrs. Gomez answered on the fourth ring.

"Mrs. Gomez?" he asked. "This is, uh, Henry from Gabby's school . . . I have a huge favor to ask you."

He knew it was early, but thanks to Facebook, he knew the Gomez family went to an early Catholic service on Sundays. At first Mrs. Gomez sounded annoyed, but then she softened after hearing Henry out. In the end, she promised to help with his plans . . . but didn't promise anything about them working.

"Gabby," she told him solemnly before hanging up, "is not happy with you. Neither is Eric. You'll need a lot of luck."

Good luck seemed to favor Henry that day. By the time he'd changed for church and gotten Michael out of bed, the sun had broken through and the clouds gave way to mostly blue skies.

Mrs. Lee had heard Henry's plan the night before and had more than supported it. She'd suggested a few extra touches that had caused Henry to blush and Michael to fall to the floor laughing while singing about Henry and Gabby sitting in a tree.

The last week he'd attended his first Baptist service. This week, he'd go to his first Catholic Mass.

His mom groaned when he knocked on her door, reminding her of the early service time.

"Get your sister," she said tiredly. "Put her in the car as she is and I'll sort it all out when I get back home." The Protestant church they usually attended didn't start until eleven thirty. Gabby's service was at eight.

Henry, wearing the same clothes he'd worn to the dance, slipped into St. Jerome's Catholic Church just over ten minutes late. Nervously, he pulled at his tie as he entered a surprisingly crowded sanctuary and searched for Gabby. So intent in his search, he never noticed the usher frowning at him . . . or the tall teenager standing in the back.

Shawn Graham was *not* a regular at the church, but his boss wanted him to go occasionally to blend in with the community

. . . and find new clients. It was all Preston's Whiteside's idea. Nobody suspected nice light-skinned boys who attended church to be common drug dealers. Shawn had chosen the morning service to get it over with, but he'd hit the jackpot. He gulped when he saw Henry enter and walk past. Nudging Mark next to him, he gestured at Henry.

"What's he doing here?" Mark hissed. Then he grabbed Shawn's sleeve. "Do you think he'll recognize us?"

"Not a chance," Shawn whispered. "But just in case, go out back and call Preston. I'll keep an eye on him. If he does recognize me . . . then we have trouble."

Henry, wide-eyed and looking lost, started slowly down the aisle. St. Jerome's had a large altar table elevated in the back of the sanctuary with two sections of pews divided by a center aisle. Most of the attendees, he noted, were Hispanic, but none were Gabby.

Then he spotted her near the front row, right on the end like Mrs. Gomez had promised. She'd been hidden by a large man in a dark suit.

Gulping, Henry wiped his sweaty palms on his pants legs and walked swiftly the rest of the way before sliding into the pew beside her. Gabby Gomez looked as lovely as ever in a simple black dress. Feeling his presence, she turned with annoyance and gasped in shock.

"What are you doing?" she hissed. "Are you crazy?"

Henry pursued his lips and swallowed. He made sure he kept his attention focused on the altar, where the priest had started reading prayers in Latin.

"I wanted to apologize," he mumbled.

"If you don't accept it, I'll still pound him," Eric said, leaning across his sister. "It was Mom's idea to let him come."

Gabby grew rigid and didn't say another word.

Thankfully, the priest had chosen a sermon about the importance of forgiveness and as the service continued, Gabby took pity on Henry. He had no idea when to kneel, when to stand, or what to do with his hands. She actually giggled when he tried to sit, kneel, and stand all at once.

When the service ended, she grabbed Henry's arm and smiled. "Okay, I forgive you," she said. "But I won't go to any more dances with you."

Henry wiped a trace of sweat from his brow. "Uh, how about Soup'or Subs, then?" he asked. "Eric can drive," he said hastily.

"Go," Mrs. Gomez said before Gabby could answer. "My daughter deserves a handsome boy like that!"

"Mom," Gabby said. Then to Henry she said, "I'll go just to get away from her."

"And I'll go if I get free food," Eric added.

"And I'll go if you all will move," a man next to the Gomezes said irritably. He pointed to the aisle where parishioners were lining up to greet the priest in front.

Henry found himself pushed into the line. "What do I do?" he whispered at Gabby, sounding near panic.

"Treat me like a princess," she said simply. "Then everything will be fine."

Eric frowned as he parked in front of Soup'or Subs and turned off his engine.

"Uh, Henry, I think it's closed. The lights are off and nobody's here." They were in an empty lot facing a strip of stores across from Super K-Mart. The supercenter looked to be the only store open this early on a Sunday.

Henry, feeling much more relaxed now that he stood on familiar ground, licked his lips and stepped from the car. From his pocket, he pulled out a pair of keys and grinned.

"For you two, it's open." Moving to the front passenger side, he opened the door for Gabby and bowed low. "Come on!"

"Okay ..." Gabby said, stepping out hesitantly. "This is interesting."

"What about my door?" Eric called. "Isn't anyone going to open it for me?"

Henry slammed the door in response. He ran ahead and quickly unlocked the door. Waving Gabby through, he ignored Eric's frantic calls for them to wait for him.

As Gabby entered, she gasped. "Oh, my . . ."

Henry actually had read some of Kevin's poetry . . . and then had promptly flushed it down the toilet. Instead, with his mom's help, he'd settled on balloons and flowers. The back booth had been decorated with a pink tablecloth and a tall vase bursting with flowers, four helium balloons tied to its base.

"Do you, uh, like it?" Henry asked, following Gabby inside. The door slammed shut behind him. "There aren't any crowds here," he explained. "I thought you'd like the quiet."

Gabby stood, her eyes shining, and put a hand to her face, unable to contain a smile. "What can I say?" she said, sounding close to tears. "It's . . . amazing."

Then Eric ruined the moment by banging on the door. "Hey!" he shouted. "Let me in!"

Henry turned with a frown. "What's the password?" he asked.

Eric made a face and then a fist. "I drive you home in one piece."

Henry sighed. "That works," he muttered and clicked open the lock.

After Henry gave a quick tour of the restaurant, he pulled out a huge platter of meats, bread, and vegetables from the walk-in fridge and brought it to the front counter so they could make their own subs.

"Now you're talking!" Eric said when he saw the food. His eyes lit up.

"That's right," Henry agreed, placing the platter on the counter. "We're talking, but you'll have to find your own table. Our table is reserved for two."

Eric made a face to protest, but looked back at the food. "Fine. But I get two subs."

"Deal."

As they fell into making their own sandwiches, the boys trying to outdo each other with the most ridiculous combination they could think of, they were interrupted only once.

A sharp knocking at the door brought Henry around the counter to see a tall, sandy-haired teen peering in. When Henry pointed to the closed sign, the teen nodded and grinned. Giving Henry a thumbs-up, he left without a word.

"Who was that?" Gabby asked him.

"Somebody obviously looking for my jalapeño, turkey, ham, olive, pepper, onion, lettuce, avocado, cheddar cheese, walnut, and pickle sandwich, no doubt," Eric said, holding up a large sub dripping with ingredients.

Much later, when Eric and Gabby dropped Henry off at home, they both promised to make his baseball game later that day. "That is," Eric groaned, holding his stomach, "if I can walk by then."

The blowup didn't happen until the fourth inning. In the first of two semifinal games, the Resurrection Baptist Jellyfish Brothers played United Trinity, a Methodist church from the other side of the county. It started off well for the Jellyfish—all the boys had shown up early and eager to play.

Henry had spotted Gabby and Eric right off, which was a good thing. His mom hadn't made it, as Michael had been invited to a birthday party with a bounce house at the same time. He'd gotten a ride with Kevin instead. When Kevin had spotted Henry watching Gabby, he'd grinned, punching Henry's arm. "So you finally used my poetry, huh?"

"Yeah," Henry had shot back. "For toilet paper."

The stands were packed on both sides, but most of the fans were there for United Trinity. They served as the home team and seemed to have brought their entire church with them. The Jellyfish, besides Gabby and Eric, had only Devon's uncles and cousins and Mrs. Baker cheering them on. A lot of the Methodist fans went over to the Jellyfish stands to "help out" with the cheering.

"Although," Mrs. Baker confided to Kevin and Henry before the game, "I suspect they just want our shade."

In the first inning the Jellyfish jumped out to a 2–0 lead, courtesy of hits from Devon, Henry, and Kevin.

The lead didn't hold, though, when United Trinity jumped all over Jack's pitching and banged out four runs.

"Don't worry, boys, we got this!" Kevin cried, coming off the field. "It's jellyfish power time!"

"Actually," Larry said sourly, "all my stings faded away last night."

"Mine too," DeAndre said, sounding disappointed.

In the second, the Jellyfish got a base runner, but failed to score. The Methodist team added another run in their turn at bat.

The tide had turned and it didn't bode well for the Jellyfish. If they weren't careful, their chance for victory would easily be swept out to sea.

Chapter 21

Devon angrily took a seat on the bench. His error at third had led to the run.

"It's okay, dude," Kevin said, slapping his shoulder as he went by. "Next time, just keep your glove down. We'll get it back—"

Devon flinched away from Kevin and glared. "Get off me, man," he said rudely. "I don't need your advice and sure don't want it!" Angrily, he shot to his feet and snatched up a bat and helmet and headed to the on-deck circle.

The other players looked away, their heads down. Both Mr. James and Pastor Thomas were coaching bases, so they missed the exchange.

Kevin moved to where Henry was chewing sunflower seeds from his seat on his bucket.

"What's his problem?" Kevin asked, frowning.

Henry shrugged and spit out shells. Lately Devon had been acting moody—ever since the beach, he'd barely spoken ten words to Henry.

His fingers absently tapped the bucket just above where Devon had written "Jellyfish Throne." After yesterday's game, Devon had gone off with his family without even saying goodbye.

Meanwhile, Lucas, batting ninth, managed to draw a walk, which brought up Devon. He struck out on four pitches.

Slamming the bat into the ground, he stalked away from home plate, fury written all over his face.

"Calm down, son," the umpire warned him. "We don't act like that here."

"Come on, chin up!" Mr. James hollered from third.

Devon ignored them both. Reaching the dugout, he ignored Tashaun's offered hand and dropped his helmet on the ground before stomping to the far end of the bench.

Nobody spoke as they turned their attention to the field. Henry, grabbing his bat to head to the on-deck circle started to say something, but shrugged instead. The mood in the dugout grew darker when Jack lined sharply to first. The baseman leapt up to snag the ball out of midair and then quickly tagged the surprised Lucas for a double play.

The crowd roared their appreciation.

"Jellyfish power time," muttered Larry, grabbing his glove.

"Shut up about that," Jack growled, dropping his bat as he angrily entered the dugout. "Where's my glove?"

"Hey, man, it was good contact," Kevin started to say, but Jack ignored him.

"Let it go, man," Tashaun told him. "We don't want 'good contact' in our dugout." To Jack, he added, "Don't worry, we got your back."

Jack only snorted as he snatched up his glove.

Henry kept his seat and watched the team file out to take the field, his face blank. All the joy and excitement from the other day had vanished. It was still early in the game and they were only down 5–2, but from the body language of the players, the Jellyfish looked done ... like somebody had buried their spirit in the sand.

Jack threw angrily from the mound for his warm-up and the infield went about their fielding drill with little enthusiasm and without talking.

Taking off his helmet and trading his bat for his glove, Henry trotted to center field but made a detour to third, where Devon still glowered.

"Hey," he joked, "if I make a diving catch, will that make you feel better?"

Devon turned to glare, but his mouth twitched. "Uh . . . maybe," he finally said.

"Next catch, I'm going down," Henry promised. "Just watch me."

"As long as we don't go down after," Devon muttered, turning to receive a roller from Larry at first. But his shoulders visibly relaxed and he even surprised Kevin by tossing the ball his way.

Henry never made a diving catch that inning, but the Jellyfish got around two walks by Jack with slick fielding from the infield. A well-hit grounder toward center was smoothly cut off by a sliding Kevin. Rising to his feet, he threw to Caleb at second for an out. Caleb transferred the ball from glove to hand as he pivoted quickly. He fired a heater to first, beating the batter by a step. It left a runner on third but put up two outs.

The next batter hit a slow roller to first.

At first it looked like trouble, but Larry, moving quicker than his girth would seem to allow, charged the ball and bare-handed it while sliding to his knee. Twisting, he threw a laser to first without waiting, or aiming. Jack, hustling from the mound, caught the ball on the dead run just as his foot hit the bag, three steps in front of the batter.

"Great plays!" cried Mr. James, clapping his hands. "Now get on in here and make some more with your bats!"

"Amen!" intoned Pastor Thomas.

The two men came out of the dugout and offered high fives to their suddenly jubilant players.

"Come on, boys!" Kevin cried, as he slapped their hands. "This is our inning! Let the Jellyfish rally begin!"

"Yeah, we got this," Tashaun added, grinning madly as he followed after him.

Larry, buoyant from his great play, smacked Tashaun in the back with his glove. "What you talking about? You did nothing but watch that whole inning!"

"Ow, man!" Tashaun cried. "What was that for?"

"Just wanted to get you back," Larry said, pushing his way past.

"Well, watch it," Tashaun muttered. "I'll get you back."

Slowly but surely the great defense gave some life to the Jellyfish. Now they needed offense.

Henry led off the inning. As he rubbed some dirt on his hands, pinching the bat to his side with his right elbow, he looked to Mr. James at third for signs.

The Jellyfish signs were very basic. Basically, it was swing away, bunt, or try your best. Few kids on the team even remembered to check when hitting.

Mr. James patted his thighs and made fists, giving the sign for a bunt.

On his first at bat, Henry had smoked a liner over the shortstop's head and the infielders were playing him deep. Stepping into the box, Henry gave a few practice swings and settled in.

"YEAAHH!" cried Kevin from the on-deck spot. "This is it!"

For a moment, it was as if the two were on the Bears again—so many times the Bears had been in a hole, only to come out of it with one big inning.

A thrill rushed through Henry as the pitcher went into his windup. As soon as he saw the ball heading for the plate, he dropped the bat from his shoulder and squared to bunt. As he made contact, he shifted the tip of the bat slightly toward third and took off for first.

It wasn't the best bunt as the ball shot off toward the mound, but it caught the defense off guard. The pitcher hesitated before charging the ball and Henry's speed got him to first just ahead of the throw.

"Oh, yeah!" Kevin said, giving one last practice swing. "We got this, boys!"

In the dugout, Devon sat back and crossed his arms. All the other Jellyfish players were on their feet, pressed against the fence.

"Well, well," hissed a voice behind him. "Looks like I was right. The rich white boys are teaching you baseball and they're saving the day."

Tensing for a moment, Devon breathed out slowly, but refused to turn.

He'd spotted Lou and Charlie during warm-ups before the game. They'd mixed in with the United Methodist crowd, but had made sure to wave to Devon. It had not been a friendly wave. He'd also seen Ray walking near the old football field . . . and Preston Whiteside. Preston had never left the parking lot, but Devon could recognize that pinstriped suit anywhere.

"What are you doing here?" Devon muttered out the side of his mouth.

Lou chuckled. "Funny. That's my question to you. What are *you* doing here?"

"Ignoring you."

"You keep doing that," Lou purred behind him. "I told you I wouldn't come to you again. Remember? Well, take this as a friendly warning. Preston wants his stuff back."

"I don't have it," Devon said. "Tell him I never took anything."

"You tell him that. But first . . . enjoy the game."

Angry, Devon turned, but Lou had slipped away. Devon sighed and rubbed his brow under his cap. He knew he'd just been threatened. And it was getting hot.

"What's going on?" Jack asked, turning from the fence. "What did Lou want?"

"Same thing I want," Devon muttered, pulling his cap low. "For this game to end."

Jack gave him a hard look but said nothing.

In the meantime, out on the field, the pitcher kept staring over at first and rubbing his hat. So far he'd thrown two balls to Kevin and no strikes. Henry kept taking big leads toward second and dancing with his feet. Already the pitcher had thrown to first three times. His throws did nothing but encourage the speedy runner.

Sighing, the pitcher kicked the mound and threw from the stretch. Henry took off a second behind him.

It was a fastball inside, but Kevin swung anyway, missing on purpose but hoping to distract the catcher. He jumped back and watched as Henry easily slid safely in for a stolen base. The catcher's throw had bounced twice.

"That's it!" called Tashaun. "We got it going!"

The Jellyfish fans, especially Micah, the first of the Jellyfish Brothers, screamed their approval. But aside from Tashaun, most of the Jellyfish dugout was quiet.

Then on the next pitch, Henry broke for third. This time the pitch went well wide and Kevin lay off it. The catcher had to backhand it and didn't bother throwing to third.

"No panic!" called the United Trinity coach. "Don't worry about the guy on third. We got insurance runs! Just focus on the three outs!"

At third, Mr. James patted Henry on the shoulder as the boy wiped dirt from the back of his pants. Henry's eyes gleamed with excitement.

"Nice job, kid," Mr. James said. "Now keep doing your thing. The pitcher can't help but worry about you. If he throws anything past the catcher, you go, you hear?" Henry nodded and Mr. James rewarded him with a sharp smack to the pants. "That's it! Get a run!"

Henry took his lead, squatting low. He stared at the pitcher.

Swallowing hard, the pitcher, clearly bothered, looked over at him and then at the catcher to read the sign. Then he looked at Henry again. As he started his windup, Henry broke for home.

"Look out!" screamed a fan. "He's stealing home!"

The pitcher panicked and the ball sailed wild, ending up over the catcher's head, where it banged off the backstop. Henry never slowed and scored easily.

Crossing the plate, he ran straight to his bucket after slapping elbows with Kevin. DeAndre smacked his arm from the on-deck area as he passed.

"Nice running, man," he said. "My turn is coming!"

In the dugout, the boys perked up, but cautiously. They were still losing. It wasn't until after Kevin walked and DeAndre slapped a single into right that they started to make some real noise.

Kevin stopped at third, leaving runners on the corners. Caleb entered the batter's box next. He'd struck out last time and looked ready to make amends. He let the first pitch go for a strike.

The pitcher, feeling more confident, shook out his arm and looked for a sign. That was when DeAndre, who'd quietly walked into a big lead, broke for second.

"He's running!" cried the first baseman, caught totally unaware.

Confused, the pitcher hesitated and then whirled to second. He had to wait for the second baseman to cover before throwing. As he did, Kevin immediately broke for home.

"He's running!" yelled the catcher, snatching off his mask.

The second baseman snatched the throw and stepped toward home yelling for the pitcher to duck. His throw bounced once and the catcher had to move to his right to grab it. By the time he turned for the tag, Kevin was already sliding in safely.

"He's running again!" screamed the second baseman. Safe at second, DeAndre took off for third when the third baseman had run in to back up the throw home. Nobody else covered the bag at third. The pitcher had been caught watching.

The catcher slammed the ball into the ground in frustration. Just like that, it was a one-run game. The Jellyfish had no outs and a man on third.

Kevin screamed with joy as he entered the dugout. "Oh, yes!" he cried. "Let's keep this up!"

His teammates mostly ignored him, but were impressed.

After a time out by United Trinity to calm things down, Caleb settled back in the box.

The pitcher, breathing hard, threw the next pitch low.

"Yeeahh!" called Kevin. "Come on, Jellyfish Brothers, pick it up! Make some noise!"

Tashaun complied by clapping his hands and yelling, but the other boys gave half-hearted cheers. Henry, used to Kevin's antics, didn't notice anything amiss as he chewed seeds.

Devon, though, got to his feet and moved to stand next to Kevin. "Man, tone it down," he said. "I know you do this junk with the Bears, but we don't do it here."

Kevin turned to him, looking confused. "Huh? What are you talking about?"

"You cheering every little mistake from the other team," Devon said, almost bitterly. "That's what I'm talking about. Grow up and let the game play out."

Kevin brushed him off. "Whatever, man," he said. "I'm just cheering on my team. Our team." Louder he said, "Come on, Jellyfish Brothers!"

"I'm not your brother," Devon snarled.

Kevin turned, now angry. "What's your problem, man?"

"Hey!" Tashaun yelled, jumping between them. "You guys chill!"

"Tell him that!" Kevin said bitterly. "He's been riding me all week!"

"That's because you talk too much," Devon spat. "You talk and talk, but don't say anything."

Losing it, Kevin tried to shove Devon, but Larry grabbed him around the shoulders and pulled him back.

"Cool it, man, it ain't worth it," Larry said. "You're good. I got your back. Just don't do anything stupid."

Surprisingly, Jack stood up next to Kevin and faced Devon. His eyes smoldered. "That's enough. Kevin is one of us. I know he has a big mouth, but he's one of us now. We're a team. If you don't like it, you get out."

The rest of the players stood and pressed in close but seemed to support Jack. Henry remained on his bucket and spit out a shell. He'd glanced toward Mr. James, but hoped adult intervention wouldn't be necessary. A bench-clearing brawl with one team fighting itself would look pretty bad and would probably cost them the game.

Poor Jesse, in the on-deck area, turned to the dugout. "Uh, guys?" he asked. "Are we playing or are we fighting?"

"Playing," Jack said, glaring at Devon. "Right?"

Ducking his head, Devon sat down. "Whatever," he muttered.

Slowly, the tension lifted. Kevin moved to stand in the corner. "Get a hit, Caleb!" he called, but not as loud as before. He kept his eyes off Devon.

Caleb delivered with a long drive that rolled all the way to the fence. DeAndre walked in to tie the score.

The dugout had cooled off considerably and so had the Jellyfish hitting. The next three batters went down with a pop-up, a strikeout, and a groundout.

"Yeah," grunted Kevin as he turned to get his glove. "Back to business."

Nobody responded or even glanced his way.

Pastor Thomas had seen the blowup but had chosen to let the boys handle it. As he trotted in from third, he asked

Devon to keep his seat. "When you're ready to talk," the pastor said, "let me know. Then I'll put you back in."

Devon never left the bench until the final out, being replaced by Rodney.

The game ended with the Jellyfish eking out a 7–6 win. As soon as the teams got up to shake hands, Devon grabbed his glove and took off for the parking lot.

"Hey!" called Mr. James. He started to go after him, but Pastor Thomas held up a hand.

"Not yet, Brother James," he said, sighing. "Let him cool off for a bit. He's probably upset because I benched him."

"That's too bad," Mr. James said, his eyes going hard. "Because he's asking to be benched for tomorrow's game."

Henry, lining up last in the handshake line, overheard them and came to a stop. "What if I bring him back?" he asked, turning to his coaches. "He can play tomorrow if he comes back, right?"

Mr. James sighed and clicked his tongue. "Go get him, kid," he said finally. "Good luck."

Henry ran to the front of the line and exchanged quick fist bumps with the United Trinity team before sprinting for the parking lot.

"Hey!" called Kevin from behind him, stuck in line. "What about all your gear?"

"Pack it up for me!" Henry yelled back. "Thanks!"

Kevin grumbled as he went through the line and headed for the dugout.

He pulled to a stop when he saw Gabby waiting on the outside of the fence.

"Where'd Henry go?" she asked.

"I bet I know," Eric said ruefully, standing behind her, rubbing his belly. "He probably has to go really bad . . . those hot peppers were a major mistake."

Ignoring him, Kevin had to swallow a few times to get his tongue working. He stared dumbly at Gabby. He'd never admit it, but his love poems to Gabby had come from his heart.

"I, uh, I, he's coming right back," he managed to stammer. "I'm meeting him at my van, if you want to come."

Gabby looked disappointed. "That's okay . . . just tell him I'll . . . I'll see him tomorrow."

Kevin nodded dumbly and watched her and her brother turn away. He sighed. Then he felt a mighty slap across his back.

"Come on, lover boy," growled Jack. "Pack up the gear. The next team is waiting."

One of the next teams schedule to play was First Presbyterian. Bobby was unloading his gear from his mom's trunk when he saw Henry racing from the field.

"What's wrong?" he called. "You guys lose so bad you have to retreat?"

Henry stumbled to a stop. "Bobby," he gasped. "Have you seen one of our players here?"

"Nah, but I just got here. How badly did you lose?"

Henry scanned the parking lot, searching for a purple jersey among the crowd of parents and players. "Uh, not too bad. We won by a run."

"Really?" Bobby said, sounding elated. "That's awesome! Now we can whip you in tomorrow's championship game!"

"Bobby!" barked a heavy voice. "Let's get your gear and let's go!"

Both Bobby and Henry turned. They knew Coach Wood's voice anywhere.

"Guess I'd better go," Bobby said, heaving his bag onto his shoulder.

Henry turned and saw his Bears coach standing in the grass just off the parking lot staring in his direction. If Coach Wood saw Henry through his sunglasses, he gave no sign of it. Henry bit his bottom lip. He still hadn't spoken to his middle school coach since being benched for the championship game. Seeing him now brought back a flood of bad feelings. He turned to Bobby and muttered, "See you, man."

"You bet," grunted Bobby. "Tomorrow for the championship." Then he laughed. "At least this time you get to play!"

Immediately, Henry remembered why he'd run in the first place. He needed Devon to play too—no way he could let his friend sit out the big game . . . He knew how much it would hurt.

As he searched the parking lot in earnest, he realized it was the first time he'd referred to Devon as his friend. And he realized that he meant it.

Chapter 22

Shoulders hunched, hands stuffed in his pockets, Devon walked away from the main parking lot on the sidewalk in front of Hamilton Middle School. He'd told his uncles that he'd walk home and they shouldn't wait for him. After taking turns giving him speeches about not sulking and telling him to "man up," his uncles had packed up his cousins and left in the sixth inning.

If they only understood . . . Manning up wasn't so simple for him. As a van rolled by, Devon kicked a stone with his cleat and nearly slipped on the hard concrete.

"Graceful," said a pompous, mocking voice from behind him. "Very graceful."

Devon turned. A shiny black sports car rolled to a stop next to him. The passenger side window was open, revealing Preston Whiteside at the wheel.

"I think we need to talk, Devon," he said. "Climb in."

Devon felt all his frustration and anger boil up again. "Not happening, grease man," he said rudely.

"What did you say, boy?" Preston snapped. A hand swept a hank of greasy hair from his temple.

Devon scowled. "You have more grease than a fried burger. Leave me alone." He picked up his pace, but the car kept rolling beside him.

"Wrong answer, son," Preston said.

Just ahead, around the corner of the school, was the small side parking lot where Devon had first met Henry. He figured once he made it there, he could make a dash back to the baseball field. Preston wouldn't touch him with a crowd of people watching.

Then he closed his eyes in surrender. The van that had rolled by sat parked ahead of him. The side door rolled open and Ray stepped out. On his face, he wore a wide grin. In his hand was a small-caliber pistol. It pointed right at Devon.

"Sorry, Dev boy," Ray said, sounding almost sincere. "I suggest you step this way to avoid one messy scene."

Henry was just about to give up and return to the team when he noticed the car and van parked in front of the school. A flash of purple caught his eye. His eyes narrowed.

"Devon?" he asked himself. Devon stood talking with two men—one of them well dressed. Trotting their way, he didn't see Lou slip behind him and follow.

"You have something I need," Preston said calmly, blowing on his nails. He leaned against the back of the van and never looked at Devon, who stood frozen on the sidewalk. Ray stayed a few feet away, the pistol hidden in his pocket. "I tried to take you in and help you. Then I even tried to leave you alone. But unfortunately, you stepped in where you didn't belong. So this is your fault."

Ray's eyes suddenly widened. "Oh, man. Speaking of not belonging, here comes a kid."

Devon tried to turn, but Preston moved too quickly. Pushing off the van, he grabbed Devon's arm with a pincerlike grip. "Get in the van," he hissed, his voice ruthless and cold, "or that boy is coming too."

Devon froze. His urge was to resist, but he nodded, squeezing his eyes shut.

"Good decision," grunted Preston. "Move."

Devon let himself be led to the open door and then stepped inside.

"Devon!" he heard Henry call, sounding alarmed. "Wait!"

"Get back!" Devon yelled. But then somebody inside the van grabbed him by the neck and yanked him into a seat. A strong forearm wrapped around his neck, cutting off his air.

Henry, running full tilt, had just reached the van when he recognized Ray. He tried to stop, but his spikes slipped on the concrete and he ended up slipping and sliding onto his backside, landing right in front of the teen who'd tried to attack him and Devon the week before. For a moment, he was too shocked to speak.

The well-dressed man stopped trying to close the van door and turned to face him, his face a mask of cold fury.

"Wrong move, boy," he hissed. His dark beady eyes swept the area for anybody watching. He looked calculating and devious. Then he stomped casually on Henry's midsection, knocking the breath out of him.

"Grab him and put him in the van," the man said simply. "The plan goes on."

Ray quickly complied. Grabbing Henry by the shoulders, he yanked him up and shoved him in the van. The door slid shut and clicked behind him. It was a plain, unmarked white van—the county had a whole fleet of similar ones for their maintenance workers. Nobody would think anything was odd about it sitting in front of the school.

"Now what do we do?" Ray asked. "Shawn said that kid never recognized him. He wasn't supposed to be touched."

"Well," Preston drawled, "I'm willing to bet he can recognize you and me. Especially right now. The buffoon said he wanted the kid to pay and, well, now he'll pay. This time it'll be more final."

He turned to Lou, who stood licking his lips by the sports car. "Stick around and make sure nobody saw what happened," he said. "If anybody says anything suspicious call me. Got it?"

Lou, looking sullen, nodded.

Preston turned to Ray. "Take my car. Go get a Molotov cocktail ready and bring it to me. We'll be at the barn."

Ray's eyes went wide. "Are you serious?"

"Yes, I'm serious!" Preston's said savagely. "I'm serious about protecting us! I'll text the boss man about the new developments. Don't worry. I have a plan he's going to like. Now move!"

Henry sat on the floor of the van clutching his stomach. He huddled against the edge of the seat.

Above him, Devon sat stiffly on the seat, held captive by a large youth, his arms covered in tattoos.

Henry had never felt more scared in his life. He looked up at Devon with trembling eyes, but his friend wouldn't make eye contact. His face had gone hard as stone and his eyes were just as blank.

The van had started moving shortly after the well-dressed man climbed into the passenger seat.

"To the barn," he snapped to the driver.

Besides Henry, the driver was the only other person with light skin. He looked like he was still in high school and he didn't look very happy.

"This is my dad's work van," he muttered. "I'm not supposed to be carrying passengers."

"Kidnapping doesn't count," the man in the passenger seat snapped. "Just do as you're told and you'll be well paid."

"No problem," the driver muttered. "I could use the cash." He sounded as if he was trying to reassure himself.

The well-dressed man turned to face the boys.

"This was not how it was supposed to be," he said, annoyed. "Fortunately, I have a happy ending planned." He looked at Henry and sniffed. "I don't suppose you know what's going on, do you? Your stupid friend here made things a little rough, I'm afraid. You'll have to share in the consequences."

"Where are you taking us?" Henry asked, struggling to keep his voice steady.

The man sniffed. "To a happier place. For me. How's your stomach? If it still hurts, I have the perfect cure."

"Leave him alone, Preston," Devon said suddenly. "He didn't do anything."

The man's face twisted in anger and then relaxed. "And you didn't do anything either, as I recall. I asked for my stuff back, but you wouldn't give it."

"What's he talking about?" Henry asked Devon sounding worried.

Devon closed his eyes and sighed. "Remember those guys who knocked you out? They weren't trying to rob you. They were trying to set you up. I found bags of drugs next to you and more in your backpack . . . . I took them all and dumped them down a gutter."

Henry's eyes went wide and his mouth opened in shock. "But why?" he asked incredulously. "Why would they set me up?"

Devon snorted. "Ask the driver. He was one of the punks."

The van swerved slightly as the driver's hands tightened on the wheel.

Preston sneered at him. "Keep driving and keep your eyes on the road. We're almost there." To Henry he said, "Somebody doesn't like you, boy. Somebody thinks you're an all-American kid who needs to be taught an all-American lesson. Now he'll get his wish. And more."

The way he said "and more" made Henry's heart jump. He shuddered.

Preston turned back to the driver. "Pull over here and wait. Ray should be here in a few minutes."

There were no windows on the sides of the van, but through the windshield Henry and Devon saw they were on a lonely narrow road lined with thick trees on both sides. Henry blinked rapidly. He knew where they were—an old abandoned side street called Dixon Road.

Years ago there had been houses here, but they'd been torn down by the government back in the 1940s to make the area more "colonial" and "touristy." He'd done a report on it in the sixth grade for his local history project. Since then, it'd become a place of legend and ghost stories. Many kids and even some adults swore to have seen ghosts roaming the road at night and more than one violent crime had occurred in the vicinity over the years. Few dared to drive down the road after dark.

Ironically, it was only a few miles from Henry's own neighborhood. If they could somehow escape, he knew where to go.

Unfortunately, escape seemed unlikely. Besides the guy holding Devon, another one sat in the backseat. This guy had face tattoos and wore a set of brass knuckles—the first pair Henry had ever seen in real life. He looked more than willing to use them.

"So what happens now?" Devon asked, his voice tight. "I already told you. All the stuff I found I put down the drain."

Preston sighed. "Yes, and if that's true, you cost me a couple hundred bucks. But worse than that, you still worry the boss man."

Devon's eyes widened at hearing mention of the "boss man." It was the second time Preston had mentioned this boss. He'd always thought Preston ran the drug dealing. His eyes went down and met with Henry's. Both boys seemed to be wondering the same thing. Who was this "boss man" and why didn't he like Henry?

Oblivious to the boys' thoughts, Preston continued. "You see, you saw his guys and you can identify him. That's bad. Very bad." He shook his head. "Devon, you should've come to me when you had the chance."

"I'd rather die," Devon snarled, looking up balefully at the smug drug dealer.

Preston met his gaze and grinned. "I counted on that. But if that's your choice, you're still going down as a dealer."

"Not likely," Devon muttered, getting a very bad feeling. He didn't like the nasty glint in Preston's eyes.

Preston smacked his lips. "Oh, but you are. You see, I have it all worked out. Since we have some time to *kill* . . . just sit back and listen. It's not often I get to share my plans with others."

As if talking about a new car he'd bought, Preston gleefully shared the gruesome plan he'd cooked up. He took real enjoyment in watching Devon's face as he spoke. The teens in the back also seemed to be listening with relish. Twice Devon heard one of them grunt with pleasure at what Preston said. Only the driver looked ashamed as Preston spoke. He kept his head bowed low as his hands nervously fingered the steering wheel . . . like they wanted to correct a wrong turn but couldn't.

Henry, below Devon, listened with wide, frightened eyes. All this was new to him. Devon cringed.

The drugs, contrary to popular opinion, weren't coming from Devon's neighborhood—that was all a front. Preston and his "boss man" partner had arranged it so the poor neighborhoods took the blame while the rich neighborhoods took the drugs. Sure, there were some drugs in the poor area, but the profit came from the rich kids in the schools. As Preston said, Why sell drugs to people with no money?

"So," Preston continued, "we're going to arrange a little accident to help perpetuate this belief. You, Devon, are going to shoot up this poor white boy with some happy juice. Unfortunately, you're too young and dumb to know what you're doing. You're going to overdose your friend and kill him."

Chapter 23

Beside Devon's legs, Henry went still. Devon stared at Preston for a long moment. Then suddenly, he lunged at him, trying to grab the evil man's face.

"Hold him, Antonio!" Preston cried, cringing.

Antonio, the teen behind Devon, yanked back on the boy's throat with his forearm. His other arm wrapped around Devon's middle and wrestled him down. Devon dug his chin in Antonio's forearm and twisted wildly.

"Can't hold him!" Antonio said through gritted teeth.

"Stop it!" roared the other teen from the back. As soon as Devon attacked, he'd launched himself over the seat and had grabbed Henry by the back collar, yanking him up to the seat. He'd then wrapped a strong forearm around the surprised boy's throat, quickly putting him into a sleeper hold. Now the teen's breath blew on Henry's neck as he started choking him out. Slowly Henry's wide eyes slid shut and he went down into unconsciousness. He slumped against the seat next to Devon.

"Stop it, or he dies now!" snarled the teen with the face tattoos. He still had a forearm around Henry's thin neck.

Seeing Henry relax and go limp, Devon stopped struggling and went still. He barely felt the hard punch to his gut from Preston.

"Out of the van now!" Preston shouted, furious. "Get them to the barn." He turned to the driver, who looked shaken. "You stay put and wait for Ray."

Mark nodded miserably. "Ray's already here waiting."

Devon barely felt his body being yanked from the van by Antonio. He ended up lying on his stomach with Antonio's foot firmly planted on his back. Looking up, he watched tight lipped as Henry's limp form was dragged out by Antonio's partner. Out of the van, the other teen, aptly called Tiger, stood leering down at Devon. His face tattoos made his eyes appear dark and evil. He had his arms wrapped around Henry's chest, squeezing the unconscious boy in front of him. Henry lay limp as if already dead. Devon could do nothing but watch in stunned silence.

"Ready for the party, boy?" Tiger sneered. "Today you might just become a man."

Devon doubted it. At the moment, he felt very much like a little boy.

Devon walked stiffly through the quiet trees, his head bowed low. It was worse than walking to his own execution . . . because he was going to his friend's execution . . . and he was the executor.

Antonio kept a hand on the back of Devon's collar to keep him in line, but it wasn't necessary. Tiger had Henry draped over his shoulder just ahead of them. Henry had yet to wake up . . . perhaps it was for the best.

Henry had lost his hat in the van and his short brown hair lifted in the soft breeze. His arms dangled limply. He looked even younger and smaller than normal—much too young to die from drugs.

Ray brought up the rear, carrying a hypodermic needle inside a clear plastic bag. He hadn't looked thrilled to join the party and now kept his eyes glued to the ground. Preston led the way, whistling a merry tune.

They trod a well-worn path littered with beer bottles and food wrappers. Even though it was in the middle of spring, few birds sang in the area. They'd been walking for about five minutes when they came to a small clearing with an old, rundown structure. The wood had turned gray with age and the roof sagged in front. All the windows had long since been busted, but the building still had a relatively sturdy door.

Preston pushed the door open like he was returning home. "In here, boys!" he called.

Ray came up beside Devon and grabbed his arm. "I got him from here, Antonio," he said gruffly. "Go help Preston and Tiger."

The teen looked at Ray for a moment and shrugged. "Watch him," he said. "He's a wild one."

When Antonio's big frame started for the structure, Ray leaned close to Devon's ear. "Listen, man," he hissed, sounding nervous. "I couldn't do it, okay? All I put in the needle is a sedative, all right? And it's a clean needle, brand new." He licked his lips and glanced at the old house. "I've never seen Preston like this, man, but don't worry. I'm no kid killer. I'll knock the kid out for a few hours, but nothing more. Just do what Preston says and everything will be okay, all right? After we leave, the kid will wake up good as new. I'm no murderer, man."

Standing up, he shoved Devon in the back. "Now move it!" he snarled extra loudly.

Devon had made no sign that he'd heard, but at least his heart had started beating again.

The musty building proved to be surprisingly well used. Devon found himself in a single large room with walls covered in graffiti. Empty beer bottles and trash littered the floor. A small table had been brought in and sat in the middle of the room. Underneath it was a box of candles and a pile of old pizza boxes. Overturned milk cartons were set around the table as seats. The entire place had a nauseating stench of dirt, urine, and something worse . . .

Pale putrid yellow light wafted in through the windows on either side. The windows still had glass, but they were so covered in filth that little light filtered through.

As soon as he entered, Devon covered his nose. He'd smelled this smell before . . . when he used to live with his mom. Chemicals, rotting food, urine, sweat, and a deep sense of hopelessness mixed together to create a powerful stink.

He noticed more than one used needle lying among the trash.

His insides squeezed tight and he found himself trembling.

Dimly, he was aware of Tiger still carrying the unconscious Henry over his shoulder. The teen waited just inside the door while Antonio and Preston pushed a pile of trash off the scarred table.

"Put the boy here," Preston demanded. "Hurry!"

He waited for Tiger to lay Henry across the table. Then he turned to Devon and grinned. "Welcome to the barn, boy. I'm sure you've already guessed, but this is where most of our deals happen. Lots of good times happen here. We milk filthy animals pretty much on a nightly basis. Don't we boys?"

Antonio grunted and Tiger smirked. They were like two attack dogs, both of whom loved their work a bit too much. Ray looked at Devon out of the corner of his eye and wiped sweat from his brow. He gave a slight nod.

"Okay," Preston said. "Let's do this." He pulled out a gold-plated pocketknife and opened the blade. His voice turned cold. "Devon, take the needle from Ray. Put it in the boy, you hear? Do it in one minute, or I start stabbing. If I can't stick you, I start cutting the boy here."

Ray opened the plastic bag and nodded. "Do it," he whispered. "It's your only chance."

Hands trembling, Ray found himself taking the needle. It felt heavy in his hands. This is what his mom had done . . .

Tiger and Antonio stepped back, eyeing the needle nervously.

"Don't try anything stupid, boy," Preston warned. "Ray still has a gun."

Devon ignored him. He didn't know what to do. Attack with the needle? Use it on himself? Or did he dare trust Ray and stick it in his friend?

"Get a move on, boy!" snapped Preston. "Let's go!"

Swallowing, Devon slowly approached the table. Tiger had put Henry down on his back, his arms limp at his sides. Henry had thin wiry arms and Devon could easily make out the veins.

"Sorry, man," he whispered. Then he grabbed his friend's arm and . . . froze. He knew what to do . . . he'd seen his mamma do this many times. He just needed to slide the needle into the skin and inject the contents into Henry's vein. No sweat.

But beads of perspiration dripped into his eyes, mixing with his tears.

"Do it and you can still join us!" Preston said. "It's not too late. You'll be one of us and everything will be okay. Don't do it . . ." He twisted the blade in his hand menacingly.

"Come on man," muttered Tiger. Above his face tattoos, two Chinese characters on either side of his nose, his eyes danced crazily with anticipation. He was enjoying this. "Send that dude on the one-way trip of a lifetime."

"Do it, man," Antonio's deep voice urged. "Don't be weak."

Ray, his lips pursed tight, nodded at Devon, but Devon acted as if he couldn't hear or see them. His vision blurred with sweat and tears as his hands started to tremble.

He couldn't do it. His mom had ruined her life like this. Corey ruined his life because of this. Devon had vowed to never use a needle himself or to ever touch drugs. He couldn't do it to an innocent kid . . . even if Ray was telling the truth about it being a sedative. What if Ray was lying?

A tear ran down his face, dripping off his chin. Was this how his mother had started? Someone forced her to use a needle? Or was it something she chose to do to escape a miserable life? To escape him?

"What are you doing?" Preston yelled. He took out a handkerchief to mop his sweaty brow. Grease ran from his hair onto his collar. "Use the needle! Do it!"

"I-I can't," Devon whispered. The needle still poised over his friend, he couldn't keep it still from all his shaking.

Tiger sighed loudly. "Ah, he's a little coward. He ain't got the stuff for this."

His face turning ugly, Preston readied the blade. "Okay, for the last—"

"Wait!" shouted Ray. "I got it!"

Moving forward, he grabbed the needle from Devon's shaking hand and shoved Devon out of the way. Putting the syringe on the table, he put his hands under Henry's body and flipped him onto his stomach.

Devon tried to pull him away, but Tiger and Antonio grabbed him by the arms and jerked him back.

"Little sissy," Tiger hissed in his ear. "You're nothing."

"Get off me!" Devon shouted. He thrashed wildly, but couldn't break free.

Antonio wrapped a meaty forearm around his throat and pulled him back. "Too late," growled the teen. "Keep fighting and I start squeezing." The forearm loosened slightly.

Devon still fought for a breath as he watched in terror.

Preston took it all in with an ugly sneer.

Ray, an intense look on his face, grabbed the back of Henry's shirt and the waistband of his pants, pulling the shirt up shirt to expose the small of Henry's back.

Devon blinked away tears, but couldn't stop watching. Henry looked even younger and smaller as he lay there helpless. His spine stuck up from his skinny back.

"Easier than the vein," Ray muttered, patting Henry's side, just above his waist. He never looked up. "Don't think I could see it right."

Devon watched in horror as Ray picked up the syringe and with almost no hesitation plunged the needle deep into Henry's side. The unconscious boy never stirred.

The syringe empty, Ray yanked it free and threw it on the ground. Turning to Preston, he wiped sweat from his eyes.

"Happy now?" he demanded. "It's done, all right?"

Devon slumped in the arms of Antonio and Tiger. He stared at the fallen needle and could find no words.

Preston sniffed. Clearing his throat, he calmly snapped the blade of his pocketknife shut and slid it into this pocket. Then he swaggered to the table. "I'm disappointed," he said. "I thought you'd make the right choice, Devon. You could've been one of us."

"Never," Devon whispered hoarsely. "I'll never be like you."

Ignoring him, Preston shook Henry's shoulder and slapped the back of his thigh. The boy never stirred.

"Leave him alone," Devon growled, looking up with a tear-streaked face.

"Why? He's in a good, happy place now," Preston said, turning to Devon. His voice grew hard. "Don't you weep for him. He wouldn't weep for you if the roles were switched. He's just another rich kid who don't give a flying leap for filth like you."

Devon strained to break free, but Antonio and Tiger yanked back his arms, twisting them until he cried out.

"Stupid boy," Preston spat. "You threw away your life for this nobody." The man smacked Henry's backside. "By tomorrow he won't be nothing but dust in the wind. A statistic. A reason for rich people to cry some tears and shake their heads. If it was you, they wouldn't even blink. At least this boy will get some grief." He smiled coldly. "And you'll get all the blame."

"You're sick," Devon gasped, fighting back tears and pain.

Preston's eyes tightened and his smile twisted into a sneer. "Me sick? You're the one with the muddled brain, boy. Maybe you thought you could be like him." He flicked his gaze at Henry's limp form. "Play ball with him. Be his friend." Chuckling without mirth, Preston looked at Devon. "You can't, boy. You can't be none of that. Your kind is destined for the streets, boy. Street rules, boy. Street rules. You broke them."

"I'll break you," Devon snarled back. "You're a monster."

"I'm not a monster!" Saliva flew from Preston's mouth as he glared down at Devon. "I tried to help you! I offered you a job! And when you stole from me, I offered you a second chance! And you blew it. Big time." He pointed his chin at Henry. "He got the easy way out. You ... you had your chance."

"Yeah, a real great guy you are," Devon said bitterly. "You pick on little kids and get big freaks to keep you safe."

Tiger yanked on his arm, making Devon gasp in pain.

"Call me a freak," hissed Antonio on his other side, "and I'll rip off your arm and use it to punch you in the face!"

Devon couldn't blink back the tears as his knees buckled. He watched hopelessly as Preston stepped closer to him.

Ray stood nervously behind them all, licking his lips, but making no move to intervene.

"You don't think much of me," Preston said softly. "Good. Because I don't think of you at all. Not anymore. You remember your friend Corey? Yeah, I remember him, all right. Thought he would do good for me. And he did too, until his mouth outgrew his brains. I asked him to get you to join up. Yeah, I did. Last summer it was. And you know what he said? He wouldn't do it. Told me to leave you alone. Told me you were *special*." Preston sneered the last word like it was a ball of slime. His voice grew sardonic as he continued. "So you know what I did? I made a call to some friends in high places and got him locked up." Preston bent low, right in Devon's face and grinned. "I opened a space for you. That's what I did."

Devon's eyes widened in genuine surprise. He had no idea his old friend had said or done those things. Corey had gone to bat for him and he'd struck out doing it. Fresh tears burst forth. Poor Corey. Poor Henry. Boys like them had no chance against grown men like Preston. Preston was a predator. He went after the weak, gobbling up their hope and dreams until they were nothing but breathing carcasses. To him, kids were just tools. And if they didn't work for him, they were thrown away.

"Y-you ratted on Corey?" Devon sputtered, more in despair than anger.

Preston rose to his full height, bristling. "I didn't rat! I did street justice! I sent a message that most boys would understand. You either join me, or . . . or you wish you did. Well, guess what. You *are* special. You ain't like most boys and you surely don't understand. So I'm sending another message. A message you and every other *special* kid won't soon forget." Preston glanced at Tiger and Antonio. "Put him out, boys."

Devon tried to pull free, but the two teens were ready. They never gave him a chance.

Tiger grabbed Devon around the neck from behind and started using his sleeper hold. Antonio bent low and grabbed Devon's legs to keep him from kicking.

"No!" Ray cried, finally stepping forward. "What are you doing, man?"

"Making things right," Preston said with a savage grin. He watched Devon's struggles with relish. "He has no backbone and no loyalty. I don't want him to squeal."

"B-but what are you going to do?" Ray asked dumbly, watching as Devon's struggles weakened.

"Like I said," Preston replied grimly. "You either join me, or wish you did. When we're done, he'll be dead, just like his little friend." He looked at Ray. "Once he's out, we start a little fire. This way the story reads, 'Foolish boy killed by drug overdose while his drug dealing friend dies in a fire he set to cover it up.'"

Devon tried one final attempt to break free, but the teens were too strong. Tiger's arm squeezed tight and Devon started seeing spots.

He did manage to free a leg and get a hard kick to Antonio's stomach. The spikes from his cleats dug deep and the teen collapsed in gasps of agony.

"Don't leave any marks!" Preston cried. "It has to look like an accident!"

Devon tried to step on Tiger's feet, kicking wildly, but his bucking and twisting started to weaken. Then Tiger lifted him off his feet and darkness closed in fast.

Without air to breathe, Devon felt his life and his hope flowing away. Thinking of his poor grandma, he surrendered to darkness and oblivion. His body slumped in Tiger's arms.

Kids like him had no chance. His mom had abandoned him, he never had a dad, and all his neighbors lived in the shadows of drugs. The streets took his kind and never let go.

He never felt his body hit the floor.

Ray stared down at Devon's crumpled body splayed across the filthy floorboards. He'd done some bad things with his life, but he'd never hurt kids before. Still, he did what he was told. He gathered the greasy pizza boxes in a pile and took a candle from the box.

Either you joined, or wish you had. Ray joined.

He looked on as Preston lit the candle with the lighter and set it under a folded box so the flame started licking the cardboard. Sweat ran down his forehead. The entire house was wood. The fire would soon spread and hide their crimes. Maybe then he could forget what he'd seen.

"Let's move!" Preston shouted. "We need to go before somebody sees the smoke!"

At Hamilton Middle, Melissa sat back on her bike, scanning the parking lot without really knowing what to look for.

Shorty, standing beside her on his own bike, sighed.

"Melissa," he said. "This is pointless. We're at a church baseball tournament. The only possible wrongdoing here is a bunch of hypocrites playing boring baseball. Face it. There aren't any drug dealers around!"

"Quiet," muttered Melissa. "Something isn't right."

The two were at the edge of the football field, where they'd been for the last ten minutes . . . that after spending two hours watching Resurrection Baptist squeak by in the first semifinal. They'd spent that game hiding in the woods to keep an eye on any suspicious fans and the team. Mostly they saw baseball and mosquitos. And, Shorty was sure, poison ivy.

When the fourth inning blowup happened, they'd been too far away to tell what was going on, but then they recognized the boy who'd been benched. He was the same boy they'd seen at the dumpster a week before when they'd been interviewing Bobby Aaron.

Immediately Melissa had him pegged as a prime suspect. But then, as soon as the game ended, their prime suspect ran away and couldn't be found. Worse, as they gathered their bikes, Henry Lee had also disappeared. Since then, they'd been trying to find either boy.

And this meant they weren't keeping an eye on Coach Wood, another prime suspect.

"Those guys are probably at somebody's house playing video games!" Shorty said, tossing back his head in frustration. "And that's where I should be!"

Melissa sucked on her teeth. "Or," she said, "they could be doing drugs. Come on, I see somebody who can help us."

Chapter 24

Kevin slid out of his mom's van and shut the door in frustration. He'd packed all of Henry's gear, carried it up to the van, and loaded it in, but still the kid hadn't shown up. Mr. James and Pastor Thomas were still at the field watching the second game and said they would keep an eye out for Henry and Devon. They figured the two were probably just talking somewhere, blowing off steam.

Kevin didn't know what to do—he was supposed to be Henry's ride home and his mom was getting impatient to leave. He leaned against the back of the van and crossed his arms miserably.

"Hi, Kevin!" called a friendly voice. He looked up to see Melissa coasting her bike toward him with Shorty behind her. "Is everything okay?" she asked.

Kevin stood up and dusted dirt from his hands. "Oh, uh, yeah . . . I'm, um, just looking for Henry. You haven't seen him around, have you?"

Melissa braked to a stop. "No," she said. "Why, is he missing?"

Shorty rolled his eyes and started riding in circles. He nearly crashed into a parked minivan in the process.

Kevin frowned. "Nah, he's just . . . well, he's with a friend, I think." He looked around the lot. He did a double take and started licking his lips. "Hold on. I think I know who can help." He started off in a jog. "I'll be right back!"

Melissa called for him to wait. "I'll go with you!" she cried. Kevin never slowed down.

Kevin had spotted Lou leaning on the corner of the school building facing the parking lot. When the older boy saw Kevin, he turned and started running.

"Stop!" Kevin cried, breaking into a full sprint.

Lou didn't look back, but was hampered by his sagging jeans. Kevin, having replaced his cleats with sneakers, easily made up the distance between them with his long strides.

Lou finally stopped running at the other end of the school. Whirling to face Kevin, he licked his lips nervously and refused to meet Kevin's gaze.

"Look, man," he said hoarsely. "I don't know nothing."

"Tell me where Devon and Henry are," Kevin demanded.

Lou dropped his head and said meekly. "Try Dixon Road. They probably went there." Then he jerked up his chin. "That's all I'm saying." With that, he turned and hurried around the corner.

Kevin soon saw the reason for the quick retreat. Melissa and Shorty were pedaling like mad after him.

Every boy in Hamilton Middle knew about Dixon Road. It was so close to the school that even if they hadn't been there, everyone claimed they had.

Dixon Road was an old, mostly abandoned street that went nowhere. It started and ended on the same main road, but thrill seekers still drove down it from time to time. Years before it had been a neighborhood for a poor community that had been started by former slaves after the Civil War. Then, in a decision to improve Hamilton County, the neighborhood had been torn down. All the families were forced to move to Williams County. Few boys knew this, but they all knew about the ghost stories.

"Quick!" Kevin said when Melissa and Shorty stopped their bikes. "Let me borrow a bike. I think I know where Henry went."

"Where?" Melissa asked, dutifully hopping off her bike. She rode a pink road bike built for speed.

Kevin muttered something about Dixon as he grabbed her bike and hopped on. Pushing off, he pedaled furiously back to his van.

After telling his mom to leave without him and that he was going to see Henry, he turned his bike toward the road and shot away.

Mrs. Baker watched her son ride off on the pink bike and shook her head. "Boys," she said, "should never grow up."

Shorty and Melissa watched Kevin zoom past on the road in front of school.

"Uh," Shorty said. "Now what?"

"Now," Melissa said pleasantly, "you give me your bike and I follow him."

"What?" Shorty protested. "Then how do I get home?"

"Just wait for us. It won't take long, I'm sure."

"What do I do while I'm waiting?" Shorty demanded, his face starting to turn the color of his hair.

"Watch the baseball game," Melissa said over her shoulder.

Shorty had a heavy, clunky mountain bike. She started off wobbly but soon got the hang of it. Still, she labored to keep track of Kevin's purple shirt.

Five minutes later, Kevin turned into Dixon Road and followed the mile-long street until he spotted a white van and a dark sports car parked on the side. He pulled to the side of the road and hopped off the bike. He did so just in time. Behind him, he heard the sound of a heavy engine. He ran to the woods and pushed the bike out of sight, throwing himself behind a holly tree.

A low-riding green Mazda took the corner at high speed and narrowly missed skidding into the trees across from Kevin. Correcting itself, the car accelerated to the van before skidding to a screeching stop.

A blond teenager with short hair slicked back with enough grease to make a batch of fries jumped from the driver's seat. A dark-haired girl in tight black pants and a black T-shirt climbed out of the passenger side.

"What's going on, Mark?" the teen demanded loudly, his voice carrying to Kevin. He wore athletic shorts and a Nike baseball shirt with its sleeves torn off.

The driver's side door of the van opened and a short, curly-headed teen climbed out stiffly. The shorter teen, Mark, looked scared. He grabbed his dark curls nervously and said something in a low voice while gesturing toward the woods behind the van. Whatever he said made the blond teen yell and kick the side of the van. The three settled to talking among themselves furiously.

Kevin had no idea what was going on, but he suspected Devon and Henry were in trouble. Big trouble. He slapped the pocket of his pants and groaned loudly. He'd left his cell phone in the front seat of his mom's van.

Calling himself names, he started off into the woods, heading where Mark had gestured.

By keeping Dixon Road at his back, he more or less knew he was heading in the right direction.

After a few minutes of climbing over fallen trees, walking into spiderwebs, and ducking low branches, he came on a path littered with trash. He also heard voices.

Drawing back, he ducked behind a shattered stump where a tree hadn't survived the latest hurricane.

"I'll head back to my place," an older man was saying, "and lay low. The rest of you, go out and do something that keeps you out in public. Nobody is going to trace us here, got that?"

A few mumbled murmurs of ascent answered him.

Kevin peeked out from his hiding spot and saw a burly man dripping with moisture, his hair drooping down his face and back. His pinstriped suit stuck to his pudgy body as if glued. Three tough-looking muscular youths followed him.

Kevin drew back. That's when he smelled the smoke.

Not good, he thought.

Ducking low, he headed down a path just inside the tree line. The path turned a corner and ended at an old ramshackle house . . . with smoke rising from under the door.

"Henry!" Kevin yelled. "Devon!"

Forgetting caution, he burst into the clearing and raced to the nearest window. "Hen—"

Kevin was brought up short, choking.

Even though it was covered with years' worth of dirt and grime, he could see into the window. On the other side, lying in motionless heaps, were the two Jellyfish players. Henry lay across an old table while Devon was sprawled face down on the floor. Near the wall, a pile of pizza boxes had curled into flame.

"Devon!" Kevin screamed. "Henry!"

Neither player moved.

Looking down, Kevin found an old hunk of concrete. Hefting it, he threw it as hard as he could at the window, smashing the glass.

A wave of heat rushed out.

"Wake up, guys!" he yelled as he brushed away the broken remains of the glass. He felt a stabbing pain in his left arm but ignored it.

The glass clear, he pulled himself up by the sill, ignoring the tiny bits of glass splinters stabbing his hands. Then he threw his legs into the fiery house. Smoke hit him immediately and his eyes started to water. The pizza boxes were now a raging inferno.

Devon was the closest so Kevin went to him first. He lay on his stomach with his head to the side.

"Come on, Devon! Wake up!" Kevin cried, shaking the boy.

After getting no response, he grabbed Devon by his feet and dragged him toward the window. As dead weight, Devon was much heavier than he looked.

Gasping and coughing from the smoke, Kevin hoisted him up under his arms and managed to prop him on the windowsill so his arms and head stuck out into the fresh air. He was relieved to hear the older boy groan and start to stir.

"You may not like this, but bottoms up," Kevin mumbled, grabbing the back of Devon's belt. With that, he yanked up hard, tipping the boy up and out into the moldy leaves lining the house's foundation.

Taking a final gasp of fresh air, Kevin turned back into the house to get Henry.

Smoke burned his nostrils, but Kevin never hesitated. Grabbing Henry by the waist, he pulled him to the edge of the table and yanked him to a seated position by his arms. Henry flopped like a doll as Kevin hefted him up onto his right shoulder.

Grunting, Kevin managed to move Henry into a fireman's carry, holding to the motionless boy's left arm.

"At least you're lighter," Kevin muttered, coughing. But the smoke and heat clogged his vision and nose and he could barely see where he was going.

Eyes streaming tears, Kevin staggered to the window and pitched out his friend. Then he collapsed over the sill and spent several seconds hacking and coughing.

"Kev . . . Kevin, is that you?" groaned Devon from below him. "What are you doing here?"

"Dying," wheezed Kevin. "What were you doing in there?"

"The same." Outside, Devon sat up and winced. Then he looked up in alarm. "Hey, you'd better get out of there! Where's Henry?"

"Right behind you," Kevin said. "Give me a hand and I'll be happy to join you."

Devon wobbled to his feet and grabbed Kevin's extended wrist.

Kevin propped a foot onto the sill and started to push off while Devon pulled his arm. The rotten wood on the sill chose this moment to give way and Kevin's foot slipped.

With a startled yell, Kevin's shin crashed into the sill as he flew headfirst out the window. Seconds later, all three boys were safely out of the fire.

Kevin crashed to the ground next to Devon, who fell back on his backside. Henry lay on his side just beyond them, not moving.

"I see them!" cried a voice from the path. "They're out! They're getting away!"

"I told you I heard voices!" yelled someone else. Though still far off, they were deep and unfriendly. And they were getting closer.

Kevin and Devon looked at each other and immediately started moving. Kevin leapt to his feet and helped Devon get to his. Then they went for Henry.

Kevin's shin burned with pain and his hands stung, but he had more important matters to think about. "Is he alive?" he asked Devon fearfully.

Devon gasped with relief when he saw the limp boy's chest moving. "He's just drugged," he said, tears springing to his eyes. "He'll be fine. I . . . I think—"

"Great," Kevin snapped, quickly switching from relief to action. "But we still have to move him, fast."

The voices were getting closer.

The two boys pulled Henry up and threw his arms over their shoulders. Grabbing the back of Henry's belt, they took off for the trees, away from the path.

The sounds of pounding feet were not far behind.

Once in the trees, Devon crouched in front of Henry's body, allowing the unconscious boy to fall over his back. Grabbing Henry's unresisting legs, Devon hoisted the boy up and carried him piggyback.

"Faster this way," he growled.

Kevin grunted. "I'll lead the way," he said. "I know these woods. Kind of."

Tiger, Antonio, and Ray didn't know the woods very well. They'd been to the barn but had never ventured into the trees . . . especially alone. Perhaps some of the ghost stories were made up, but maybe not all of them were.

Once they'd heard voices and spotted the boys escaping, they'd run back to the burning barn only to lose the boys in the trees. They'd grouped together instead of spreading out. After ten minutes of timid searching, they saw no sign of the boys. In another hour the sun would be setting. None of them wanted to call Preston Whiteside with the news. Not only were the boys alive, but they were free.

Now the three hurried back to the road away from the smoking barn. "What do we do now?" Tiger asked, rubbing a hand nervously on one of his tattoos.

"We keep looking," Ray said grimly. He was actually relieved that the boys had escaped. At the same time, if they told anyone, a lot of trouble promised to follow. "One of you guys text Shawn what happened. Tell him to cruise the road with his car. Mark can take the van and do the same thing. We'll find them. And when we do . . ." He sighed. "It's over for them."

Chapter 25

Melissa lost track of Kevin quickly, but there weren't many turnoffs, so she kept pedaling down the main road in hopes of finding a clue. Cars whizzed past and twice she nearly fell. Her efforts were rewarded as she reached the turnoff for Dixon Road.

"Aha!" she said, sliding Shorty's bike to a stop. "*That's* what he was saying back there."

Turning onto Dixon Road, she pedaled slowly, craning her neck to see what lay ahead. She was so focused on what was in front of her, she never saw what hit her.

She was just rounding a slight bend when a dark shape rose from her right.

Panicking, she lost control of the pedals and started to scream when a crushing blow fell from above and she suddenly found herself knocked into the tall grass, breathless.

"That's a girl," hissed a scared voice. "I can't hit a girl."

"I can," snarled a female voice.

Melissa was just remembering whose voice it was when another blow fell and she saw stars.

In her last thoughts before darkness, she heard the female laugh bitterly and say, "She'll wake up and think she ran into a ghost. Come on. Shawn's waiting."

After nearly an hour of walking, Devon fell to his knees and let Henry drop and roll free. They had taken turns carrying him and now both he and Kevin were exhausted. Soaking wet, Henry probably weighed a hundred pounds. But after all they'd been through, to Devon and Kevin he felt twice as heavy.

To make matters worse, the sun had started dropping and strange noises were emerging from the shadowy trees.

Kevin collapsed beside Devon. They were in the middle of a thin deer path on a small incline overlooking a narrow stream.

"You still know where we're at?" Devon asked, his voice raspy.

Kevin shook his head miserably, but then he frowned. "Wait a minute . . ." He peered down at the stream. Only a foot wide, it had more mud than water at some points. "Last fall we had a cookout at our coach's house. We weren't allowed inside, so we played a lot in the woods in his backyard. We found a stream like this . . ." Kevin got to his feet, excited. "I bet if we follow it we'll reach his house again."

"And if we go the wrong way?" Devon asked doubtfully.

Kevin took off his ball cap and wiped his brow. "If we go the wrong way, we'll eventually end up at the James River . . . miles away from here."

"Let's go the right way, then."

Henry still didn't stir as Kevin hoisted him up and took his turn carrying him. It was rough going and they had to stop to rest several times. Following the stream exactly took them too close to thick mud, so they kept to the high ground as much as possible. Finally, they climbed a steep hill and looked down to see the glow of bright lights shining through the trees ahead.

Darkness had almost completely descended and finding a neighborhood was like finding a gold mine.

"What now?" Devon asked, groaning. Still, relief was evident in his voice.

Kevin grabbed Henry's limp arms and lowered the sleeping boy to the ground.

"Now," he grunted, "we take a break. Then we go to my coach's house and get help." He smiled. "If there's one man who could help us now, it's Coach Wood."

"Coach Wood?" moaned Henry. His eyes opened and he sluggishly rose to a sitting position. "Where?" Then he blinked. "Okay ... what happened?" he asked groggily. "What did I miss?"

They'd been too scared and too panicked to talk much before. Now the boys sat in a small circle and shared everything about what brought them to their shared predicament. Devon spoke most of the time and apologized for his behavior ... especially toward Kevin.

Kevin waved his hand. "Ah, you're right. I am a loudmouth." Then he squirmed uncomfortably. "Besides, I need to apologize to you too ... I was sort of a racist jerk before."

Devon raised his eyebrows. "Really?" Then he chuckled. "But you did save my life. Thanks, man."

Henry muttered his thanks too.

Kevin grunted and ducked his head. He stretched out his injured shin and winced when he pulled up his baseball pants. He couldn't see much in the dim light, but it throbbed and a massive dark sport marred the area. "How about we keep going now?"

Henry stared at Kevin's leg. "You carried me on that?" he said in awe.

"Good thing you're so small," Kevin said, easing his pants leg down. "But I think you're walking on your own now."

"Agreed," Devon said, climbing stiffly to his feet. "My back feels like it's been used for second base too many times."

Resting hadn't helped their muscles and with their adrenaline ebbing, Devon and Kevin had a tough time moving. Walking in the dark woods didn't help matters.

Feeling guilty, Henry took the lead and guided them down the hill and over the stream toward the neighborhood. Kevin had been right. The stream had led them right near the back of Coach Wood's property. Across the stream they could make out the back of his house set off from the rest of the houses.

"You know what?" Kevin finally said when they'd finished crossing the stream. "This is ridiculous. Devon and I are moving like two cripples. Henry, run ahead and get help."

"But I'm not leaving you," Henry said, sounding scared.

"If you don't, then my cleat will meet your little backside," Devon growled. "I'll kick you to your coach's house."

Melissa woke up to a painful headache. She opened her eyes to see more stars . . . only these came from the night sky.

"Ooohhh," she groaned. Carefully she sat up and immediately felt waves of nausea wash over her. Twisting to her side, she vomited up her lunch.

Feeling a bit better, she staggered to her feet. It took all her effort not to pitch forward. She gingerly felt her head and found two lumps on the back of her skull. Crusty blood matted her hair.

The night sounds of crickets and frogs filled the darkness around her. She'd been lying on the side of Dixon Road for quite some time. Only the moon and starts provided her with light. She frowned when she found Shorty's bicycle . . . what was left of it. A car had run it over, bending the frame and crushing the front tire.

Sighing, she felt her pockets and was relieved to find her cell phone. Her hands trembled as she made a call.

357

"Sh-Shorty?" she said.

"Melissa, where are you?" Shorty exploded, making her grimace. "You've been gone for ages!"

"Shorty ... I need you," Melissa said, unable to stop herself from crying.

Instantly Shorty sobered. "Tell me where you are. Me and my dad will be there in a snap."

"Bring the fire department too," she said.

Henry cautiously emerged from the woods into Coach Wood's backyard. He nervously wiped the corner of his mouth. He remembered what Preston had said about somebody wanting him taken down. The only person he could think of was Coach.

As he approached the driveway he saw a car parked and visibly relaxed. Coach Jackson's car was impossible to miss. If Coach Jackson was there, he would at least have an ally.

He reached the edge of the paved driveway by the garage when suddenly the floodlight over his head snapped on.

Panicked, Henry jumped for the nearest hiding place and ended up in the shadows behind a trash can. He heard the voices of his coaches from the front of the house.

"Keep me posted," Coach Wood's voice boomed out. "I would help with the search, but I got some important personal matters to attend to."

"I completely understand," replied Coach Jackson's voice. "Hopefully this can all be sorted out before your game tomorrow."

"Won't be a game if those boys aren't found. Goodnight, Ted."

"I'll call you the minute I hear something," Coach Jackson's voice promised.

Henry heard a door close and then whistling. He remained crouched behind the garbage until Coach Jackson's large form turned the corner and crossed into the light in front of the garage.

He wore a bulky green polo shirt and baggy jeans supported by a thick black belt that sagged against his bulging belly. From his jeans he pulled a set of car keys and wiped them absently on his polo shirt, stretched to the limit by his girth.

"Coach?" Henry said tentatively. He'd never been so happy to see the friendly coach. "Coach Jackson?"

The coach froze so suddenly his car keys clattered to the pavement. "Who-who's there?" he said after a moment. His face had the startled look of a deer caught in headlights.

"It's, uh, me," Henry replied, rising from his hiding spot and stepping into the light. He held his hands in front of him and looked slightly embarrassed.

"Henry!" gasped the coach. His eyes bugged out like Henry had just stepped from the grave. "Wh-what are you doing here? I-I thought—well, you were missing!" For a moment he looked totally befuddled. "I worried something terrible had happened! Where're the others?"

Relieved to finally find an adult to help, Henry gestured toward the trees behind him. "They're on their way. I came to get help. Kevin is a little hurt."

"Kevin's with you?" Coach Jackson looked relieved. "Is that Devon boy there too?"

Henry nodded. "They're a little farther back. We need some help."

Coach Jackson moved toward him and held out an arm. "Come here, guy," he said. "I was so afraid something terrible had happened."

Grinning, he knelt in front of Henry and put two meaty hands on the boy's shoulders. "Look at you. Something terrible *did* happen." He looked Henry up and down. "Your hair is full of branches and you reek of smoke. Looks like you've been through the wash without the soap. Tell me, did you guys get a chance to call your folks?"

Henry shook his head. "None of us had a phone."

"You can use mine . . . you little brat!" All at once the coach changed. His face became a mask of hate and rage. "You're supposed to be dead." His hands closed in and grabbed Henry by the neck.

Caught completely off guard, Henry barely had time to grab the coach's wrists before his entire body was lifted off the ground and slammed into the garage door. His vision blurred and a dull ringing filled his ears. In desperation, he kicked out.

"Ow!" roared the coach as Henry's cleat caught him in the thigh. "You always ruin everything!" Releasing Henry's neck, the large coach grabbed him by the shirt and threw him into the door again.

A resounding bang shivered through the door, echoing into the night.

Henry lost his breath and his eyes glazed over as his head banged into the door.

The large coach grabbed the boy in a chokehold. Muttering curses, he put the boy out with a quick sleeper move. It was a move he'd perfected as a high school wrestler and had taught to his closest underlings. Already half unconscious, the boy went under easily, going limp in the large man's arms in mere seconds.

Breathing hard, the coach lay the boy down on the driveway and turned him onto his stomach. Then he checked Henry's pockets.

"Stupid morons can't do anything right," he muttered. Reaching back into his own pocket, he pulled out a small bag and was just stuffing it in Henry's back pocket when a noise from the trees stopped him.

"It's you!" cried an angry voice from the darkness. "Leave him alone!"

Coach Jackson lurched to his feet and faced the voice. "Come out here," he hissed, "or so help me, I'll stomp on this boy's windpipe!"

Devon ran into the light and stopped. His legs spread out and he hunched forward in a predatory manner. "You're the big drug dealer here," he spat, his words drenched with anger.

Coach Jackson sneered and took a step in the boy's direction. "And you're the little creep who keeps getting in my way."

"Why?" Devon asked him. "Why go after Henry?"

Coach Jackson spat a gob of saliva toward Devon's feet. "I'll tell you why, son. Because I hate people like him. And his father. I hate everything they stand for. That boy's father didn't think I was good enough to work for the church. He didn't want me even coaching baseball." As he spoke, the coach crept even closer to Devon. "He's a goody-goody judgmental prick. I hate people like that."

Devon responded by backing away while moving to his left, never taking his eyes from the coach's hands. That was where the attack would come from. He knew the coach was just talking to distract him. At any moment, he would pounce. All his instincts told him to get away. To save himself. That wasn't an option. He wouldn't leave Henry in the hands of this mad man. "Too bad he was right about you," he said hoarsely. "You're not good enough. You're nothing but a fake."

"What do you know?" growled the coach. As they moved in the slow, dangerous dance, the coach continued his mad tirade, still looking for an opening to strike. "He thought he had the perfect son. Used to brag about him all the time. So I wanted to ruin him. I wanted to ruin them both. And I'm still going to do it. By the time that brat's poppa comes home he's going to have a dead, drugged-out boy. And you're not going to stop me."

Devon licked his lips. "You're crazy, man," he said. "You need help."

Before Coach Jackson could respond, they heard the front door open around the corner. "Who's out there?" Coach Wood bellowed. "Ted, is that you?"

Coach Jackson looked furious and ready to explode, but he hid it behind a deep breath. Drawing himself up, he wiped his hands on the sides of his jeans.

"You better come out here," he called loudly, glaring at Devon. "We got trouble."

Coach Wood arrived at the front of his garage wearing socks and an unhappy expression. Reaching the light, he stopped, utter shock registering on his face.

"What's all this, Ted?" he asked, looking at Coach Jackson for an explanation.

"Caught a little drug dealer on your property," Coach Jackson said, nodding at Devon. "Caught him with Henry, here, going through his pockets."

Devon froze and started trembling. He knew where this was going . . . a boy like him found in a neighborhood like this? Of course he would be labeled a thug.

Coach Wood could be innocent of dealing drugs, but who was he going to believe? His assistant coach whom he'd known for years, or a strange dark-skinned boy from the poor side of town? It didn't take a genius to figure it out.

"Henry?" Coach Wood said, sounding dazed. Then he spotted the crumpled form of the boy lying at the base of his garage door. "What happened to him?" He rushed over and knelt at his side, checking for a pulse.

"I think the little punk clubbed him," Coach Jackson said. "Looks like both boys have been up to some nasty business. Henry had drugs in his pocket and this creep-o was stealing them. Like I said, I caught him in the act."

"You're lying!" Devon said, his bottom lip quivering. "You're the creep-o!"

Coach Wood looked up incredulously. "Henry Lee was using drugs?"

"Sure looks that way," Coach Jackson said, ignoring Devon. He shrugged sadly. "Probably started using with his new baseball team. I bet half those Baptist players are dealers."

"That's not true!" Devon cried. Hot tears ran down his cheeks. "You did that to Henry! You were putting drugs on him like you did last time!"

"Hold on!" Coach Wood barked from where he crouched over Henry. "Both of you! I don't care what happened. Right now we need an ambulance."

"And the police," grunted Coach Jackson. "I'm on it." Whipping out his cell phone, he quickly dialed a number and walked toward the road into the shadows. "You don't move, drug boy," he called over his shoulder.

Devon wiped away tears. All his worst fears were coming true.

"Listen," he said desperately to Coach Wood. "I don't know you, but Henry never took any drugs and I don't deal drugs! I know you don't believe me—"

Coach Wood held up his hand. "Hold up, son. I never said what I believed. We'll settle this matter in due time. Come over here."

Devon looked at the coach, feeling his knees shake. Everything he knew about the world told him to turn and run. The coach only wanted to grab him and hold him until the police came. The only thing that kept him from fleeing was his fear of what would happen to Henry if he left.

"Come on. Hurry up," Coach Wood told him as he extended an arm. "I'm not trying to hurt you."

"Watch it!" Coach Jackson demanded, coming in from the shadows. "That boy is dangerous!"

Coach Wood stood up slowly and faced his assistant coach. "Ted, tell me one thing." He sounded tired but also angry, as if he was doing everything he could to keep from screaming. "If this kid is what you say he is, and did what you say he did, then why is he still here?"

Coach Jackson went still and made no comment.

Coach Wood turned to Devon. "Son, just because I'm old doesn't make me stupid and ignorant. I believe you."

Coach Jackson growled, "Not a good call, Coach."

"Get behind me, son. Now!" Coach Wood's voice cracked like a whip.

Devon followed his orders.

"Okay, Ted," Coach Wood said, his voice low and hard. "I don't know what games you're playing, or why you did what you did, but I suggest you get off my property real slow. And never lay another finger on another boy again."

Coach Jackson's face turned ugly. "Is that right? You stupid self-righteous—" Overcome with fury, he reached into his jeans and pulled out a snub-nosed revolver. It looked big and black in the light. "Now do you want to listen to me, huh?"

Devon went still. He'd seen a real pistol before, but this was the first time he felt sure it would be used . . . against him.

"Whoa," Coach Wood said, holding both hands out in front of him. "Nobody is trying to hurt you, Ted."

"Yeah, they're just trying to ruin my life. These stupid kids really botched things up. I didn't call the cops. I called some friends and they're on their way. So why don't we all go inside and wait for them. But first . . ." Coach Jackson cleared his throat and called loudly into the dark. "Kevin! I know you're out there! You come here in two minutes, or you're losing some friends and maybe your coach!"

"I'm coming!" Kevin yelled, disgusted. Walking with a limp, he emerged from the dark and moved to stand by Devon. Coach Wood made sure to put himself between the boys and the gun.

"Always the hero," Coach Jackson sneered. "Okay, hero. Pick up your boy Henry and carry him to the house. The two little punks go first. If anything happens I don't like, then I'm shooting Coach and then Henry. Got it? Now move!"

"Do as he says, boys," Coach Wood said calmly. "We'll get through this."

He waited for Kevin and Devon to walk in front of him and then stooped low to gather Henry.

Coach Jackson snorted, keeping the revolver trained on Coach Wood.

The grim procession moved silently from the garage to Coach Wood's front door. Kevin opened the door. Devon entered, followed by Coach Wood carrying Henry's limp form in his arms. Before he could shut the door, Coach Jackson grabbed Kevin's arm and flung him inside. Kevin fell and slammed into the bottom step of a flight of stairs facing the door. He groaned in pain.

"Don't try any tricks on me," rumbled Coach Jackson. "I'm not apologizing for anything tonight!"

"Boys, don't try anything," Coach Wood said. "Nobody is going to get hurt. Just follow orders."

Coach Jackson barked an unpleasant laugh. "That's right. Do as you're told. Everyone, to the couch." He waved the pistol menacingly, directing them into a spacious living room where a large couch sat against the far wall. "Sit down!" he ordered. "Coach, you sit in the middle where I can see you."

Sweat dripped from the large man's forehead, but the gun never wavered. As Devon sat, he knew one thing for sure: it would be a long night. And he hoped he would live long enough to see it end.

Chapter 26

Henry stirred and opened his eyes to a waking nightmare. He remembered the savage face of Coach Jackson and felt the life being squeezed out of him . . .

His body jerked and he tried to get up.

"Settle," he heard Coach Wood whisper above him. "It's okay."

It wasn't okay. His brain fuzzy, Henry sat up in his coach's lap to see his assistant coach aiming a pistol at him. Blinking, he quickly took stock of the situation. Kevin and Devon were seated on either side of him, also being held prisoner.

"Welcome to Coach's home," Kevin muttered beside him. "The only way we could get in is by gunpoint."

"Hush," Coach Wood growled. "Not funny."

Coach Jackson made sure to stay several feet away so a sudden rush would be useless. Seeing that Henry was awake, Coach Jackson instructed him to slide over and sit on Devon's knees.

"That way," he said, "little dark boy won't try anything stupid. You're like his seat belt. Keep you both safe. For now."

Next he made Coach Wood get his cell phone. The coach had left it on the table in the next room. Dutifully, followed by the pistol, he got up to retrieve it and, as directed, dropped it on the floor before returning to the couch. Wearing heavy boots, Coach Jackson calmly stomped on the phone, smashing it to bits. Any hope of escape seemed to be fading fast.

"Now," the large coach said, smiling. "We wait for reinforcements."

"Can't we talk something out?" Coach Wood asked. "You don't want to do this."

"Maybe I do," Coach Jackson said, grinning. "You have no idea how much power I have right now."

"It's all going to come crashing down," Coach Wood said. "You know that."

"Maybe. But if it does, you're the first target. You don't know what it's been like for me," Coach Jackson said. "I wasn't lucky like these boys growing up." He shook the pistol at Henry and Kevin. "I had to work for a living before I could be a kid. Nobody helped me, so I helped myself."

Coach Wood shook his head. "I trusted you, Ted."

"Don't lay your failings at my feet," Coach Jackson snapped. Behind him, the doorbell rang. "That," he grinned, "would be my reinforcements."

"Sure it isn't pizza?" Kevin mumbled. "We're having a party."

Reinforcements arrived in the form of Shawn, Mark, and Lexi. They were followed shortly by Tiger, Ray, and Antonio.

"Good work, boys," Coach Jackson mocked as they filed sheepishly into the room. "You let three little brats escape and nearly bring us all down. Apparently I'm the brains and the brawn of this outfit. We got a lot of work to do, so listen up! Mark, you and Tiger watch our prisoners. Lexi, you go outside and watch the front door." Coach Jackson handed her the pistol. "Shoot anyone who steps out unless I say otherwise. The rest of you, come into the kitchen and we'll work on the plan." He turned meaningfully to Coach Wood. "I know Mrs. Wood will be returning in an hour. When she does, let's have everything ready for her."

Between Henry and Kevin, Coach Wood went tense and his face turned beet red. Henry exchanged a quick look with Kevin. They didn't know Coach Wood was married.

Henry felt Devon squirm under him.

"He's going to kill us," Devon whispered.

Coach Wood made no sign that he'd heard. Then he slowly moved his hand to Henry's leg and tapped it once.

Henry licked his lips and went rigid. His coach was sending him signs.

Mark, his face pouting, took a seat in an easy chair facing the couch from other side of the room.

"You're supposed to be watching them," Tiger growled, standing with his arms crossed just inside the room.

"I am watching them," Mark said snidely. "From here I can see them just fine. They're not going anywhere."

As the two teens spoke, Coach Wood turned his head to Henry and whispered out the side of his mouth, "Just like when you're on third." Then he tapped the steal sign on Henry's thigh. "On my signal."

Henry's body tensed. He understood what Coach wanted. He was to fake a run for it, but then stop. Coach Wood was a master at distraction.

Mark sighed and sank his head back into the cushioned chair. "My dad's going to kill me if he finds out I still have his van."

Coach Wood grunted loudly. "You boys must be real tough to take down three little kids."

Mark and Tiger turned on the coach, glaring.

"Shut your face," Tiger said, raising his fist with the brass knuckles.

Coach nudged Henry. "Now," he said. "Go!"

Henry jumped off Devon's lap, surprising his friend, who had no idea about the signs. He took two steps toward the kitchen on the right but then quickly stopped.

"Hey!" roared Tiger. Thinking the boy was running for it, he lunged forward to cut off the escape.

That's when Coach Wood launched himself from the couch, flinging his full weight into the teen's chest. His right arm extended, he caught Tiger flush in the face, nailing him right between the tattoos.

Tiger went down in a bone-jarring heap with Coach Wood on top. The coach didn't stop there. Jumping to a sitting position, he snatched a heavy hardcover book from the coffee table and smashed it down on Tiger's head. Jackie Robinson's face grinned from the front cover as Tiger groaned from underneath, going limp.

Mark squealed like a pig from his chair and curled in a ball, covering his face.

"Move, boys, now!" roared Coach Wood, still gripping the Jackie Robinson hardcover. "Get up the stairs," he hissed. More softly he said, "Find a way to call for help!" He pushed himself off Tiger, stomping on the moaning teen's chest as he stood. "This way!"

"Hey! Stop them!" Coach Jackson snarled from the kitchen.

It was a mad scramble. Coach Wood pushed Devon and Kevin ahead of him toward the staircase. Henry reached it first but had to retreat when Ray turned the corner, coming from the other side of the kitchen. He stopped at the foot of the stairs, blocking their escape.

"Stop there," he roared, waving a sharp kitchen knife in front of him.

"Climb up the railing on the side!" Coach Wood shouted. "Come on!" Still herding Kevin and Devon, both slowed by exhaustion and injuries, he flung the hardcover at Ray, making the teen duck.

Then pushing past Kevin and Devon, he reached Henry and grabbed the boy by the back of his baseball belt. Barely slowing, he hefted him up to the railing. When Henry grabbed on to the side of the railing, Coach Wood shoved the back of his pants up and over.

"You're next, Kevin!" the Coach said, his voice both calm and urgent. "Find a door up there and lock it behind you!"

Getting a boost from his coach, Kevin shook off the pain from his leg and clamored up the side of the stairs like a monkey with his tail on fire. With a boost from Coach, Devon followed. Kevin tumbled onto the middle of the stairs and turned to help Devon over.

Ray, seeing an opening, chose this moment to charge around the stairs, aiming his knife at Coach Wood's exposed back.

He never looked up and never saw it coming.

After being dumped onto the stairs, Henry had scrambled to his feet and grabbed the closest weapons he could find. He'd slid off his cleats one at a time.

As his friends had climbed over the railing, he'd moved two steps down to give them room and he saw Ray unleash the attack. Without hesitation, he launched his cleats one at a time.

The first bounced off Ray's shoulder, causing the teen to stumble and wave his knife wildly in the air in the direction of the surprise attack. The second shoe caught him on the forehead and he went down, screaming in pain. The shoe had landed spikes down.

The three boys had made the stairs safely and Coach Wood turned to face any future attack.

By this time, the other attackers had arrived. The coach was soon locked in a wrestling match with Shawn as Coach Jackson watched, yelling advice and looking for an opening to join the fray.

Antonio, seeing the boys watching on the stairs, charged at them. He took the stairs two at a time.

"Get back!" Kevin yelled to Henry. He shoved the smaller boy to the top of the stairs. "We'll hold him! You find a place to hide!"

"Yeah, right!" Henry protested.

"Find weapons then," Devon yelled. Just beneath them, taking a page out of Henry's book, he sat on a step and raised both cleats toward Antonio's face. The teen stopped his charge and warily approached the two boys. Ray had yet to recover and Antonio respected the sharp cleats.

Down below, Tiger, his nose smashed and still wearing a dazed look, also rejoined the fight. Soon Coach Wood was backed in the corner below the stairs with three opponents trying to take him down.

Henry was alone on the top floor desperately searching for a way to help the others. The stairs led to a long hall with several rooms on both sides. Nearly slipping in his socks, he ran to the nearest room on the left and discovered a trophy room. Baseball awards and photos were everywhere. One of the items, hung on the wall, was an autographed bat.

Henry grabbed it and rushed to the stairs. "Here!" he cried, tossing it down to Kevin.

"Get more!" Kevin yelled as he caught it by the handle.

The bat in hand, Kevin stepped in front of Devon. Swinging the weapon menacingly, he backed Antonio down several steps. Then seeing his coach in trouble, he leaned over the railing and called for him to look up.

Coach Wood had just shoved Shawn into Coach Jackson and Tiger, sending the three assailants stumbling backward. Seeing Kevin, he gratefully reached up and accepted the offered bat.

"Now," he said. "Who wants to play hardball?"

Spitting mad, Coach Jackson ducked low and drove his head toward Coach Wood's knees. The head coach chopped down with the bat, nailing the large rump and sending his assistant coach crashing face-first to the floor. Tiger and Shawn both backed up cautiously after that.

In the meantime, Ray had regained his footing and wobbled to the stairs. A small gash on his forehead trickled blood.

"Don't you have a gun, man?" Antonio demanded from where he stood on the bottom step. Kevin's bat and Devon's cleats made him wary of going any further.

Ray shook his head miserably. "I left in the car . . . I never signed up for this."

Antonio grunted. "Lexi has one. Where is she?" Raising his voice, he yelled for Lexi.

By this time, Henry had had more time to explore. He returned to the stairs with another baseball bat and a hat full of baseballs.

Lexi opened the door with her pistol at the ready only to see three well-thrown baseballs coming at her.

Screeching, she threw up her hands and flinched. The pistol flew behind her, sailing back through the open door and clattering into the night. She slid down in a heap as the balls nailed the wood just above her head.

"That's it!" roared Antonio. "We're coming for you three freaks! You're dead! All of you!"

With Ray following behind him, Antonio charged up the stairs. Kevin went to meet them with a bat, but Antonio brushed him back, slamming him against the railing. Kevin lost his breath as his ribs struck the wood. Groaning, he fell to a seated position, barely avoiding a nasty spill down the stairs.

Antonio, screaming like a maniac, continued his charge, leaping past Devon and his cleats.

Devon promptly turned and jumped on Antonio's back and started gouging the back of the teen's legs with his spikes.

Antonio made it to the top of the stairs before falling to his knees, screaming in pain.

"Get to a window and call for help!" Devon yelled to Henry.

Ray paused on the stairs next to the groaning Kevin. He didn't look too enthused about going after Devon, but then he saw the smaller boy turn and run down the hall. He went to give chase, but Kevin, still dazed, managed to stick a foot out and send him sprawling.

The older boy fell hard just below Devon and Antonio, barking his shins on the stairs. He yelled a curse and pressed his head against the floor in pain.

"You're going to pay for this!" hollered Antonio, rolling to his side, away from Ray, in an attempt to throw Devon off his back.

Devon hung on for dear life, but then Antonio had him pinned to the floor and threw back an elbow that connected with Devon's middle.

The boy immediately let go and gasped in pain. He fell off Antonio, gripping his side.

The teenager loomed over him with a snarl.

"You got him?" Ray asked, lunging to his feet.

"Oh, yeah. Go get the other kid," snapped Antonio. "Hurry!" His eyes, flashing with anger, never left Devon.

Ray limped past, growling under his breath. "They're all dead," he muttered. All past feelings of mercy were gone.

Before, he had no reason to hurt a kid. Now, he had every reason to kill.

Devon groaned as he tried to catch his breath. He had little chance.

Antonio grabbed Devon's shirt with both hands and shook the boy. "You should've joined us when you had the chance, kid. Or better yet, died back in the fire."

He yanked up on Devon's shirt, lifting him off the floor, and then slammed him back down. "You don't belong with rich boys in a fancy house. You belong with us!"

"Sorry ..." gasped Devon. "But I flush stuff like you down the toilet."

Antonio's face turned even uglier. "If that's the way you feel about it, then—*oof!*"

All at once he jerked up straight and slumped to the floor beside Devon with a groan.

"Then that's how I feel about it," Kevin snarled, standing above them. He readied the baseball bat for another swing, but Antonio only whimpered.

Then suddenly the teenager's foot shot up and caught Kevin in the stomach.

"I'll kill you for that!" Antonio hollered, his pain turning into vengeful rage.

The bat clattered to the floor as Kevin collapsed to his knees.

Antonio growled like an animal as he scrambled up and launched himself at Kevin. He took the boy down hard and pressed a forearm across the younger boy's neck. "You'll die," he hissed. Only inches from Kevin, his eyes were crazed with fury and his face twisted into pure hate as his arm dug into Kevin's throat.

Flat on his back with the beast on top of him, Kevin could offer no resistance. His own eyes went wide with fear as he fought for a breath. *This is it*, he thought. *I'm dying.* He started seeing spots and knew it would soon be over.

"Not today!" Devon shouted. He rolled to his feet and unleashed a flurry of kicks into Antonio's side—his spikes causing lots of pain.

Henry found something better than a window to call for help. The upstairs didn't have a phone, but it did have wireless Internet.

In the second room on the left Henry found an open laptop sitting on a desk just inside the door, waiting for him.

With screams and roars of pain intensifying behind him, he raced to the computer and urgently scanned the screen. Coach Wood had his e-mail open.

Eyes lighting up, Henry quickly hit 'send all' and hurriedly typed a message. Just as he finished and grabbed the mouse to send, Ray loomed in the doorway.

"No you don't!" the teen roared.

Any previous sympathy had definitely vanished. His left arm hung limply at his side. Blood ran down his chin and multiple bruises covered his face. Like a true bully, seeing a smaller, weaker target, Ray didn't hesitate to attack.

Henry shifted his body so his back faced the enraged teen as he desperately tried to click send. But then Ray was on him.

Grabbing Henry by the back of his pants, the teen yanked the boy from the computer, slamming him to the floor onto his backside.

"You're so dead!" Ray hissed as Henry rolled onto his back, trying to kick free with his legs. Ray's face twisted in ferocity. He grabbed Henry's shoulders and sat on top of the boy's legs, pinning him to the floor. "I tried to save you, you stupid—!" Ray finished with a bad word.

Henry tried to twist free, but had no chance. He only infuriated Ray. Calling Henry another bad name, he tried kneeing Henry between the legs. It ended very badly.

Out in the hall, Devon's kicks struck hard and true. Antonio roared with pain and rolled away from Kevin, leaving the boy gasping for air. Antonio tried to get up to face the new threat, but when he rose to his knees Devon kicked him hard right between the legs, in a spot with no protection. The teen fell back and tripped over Kevin.

Still breathing in new life, Kevin grunted as the heavy teen fell over him, sprawling just above the stairs. He felt no pity as he used his feet to send Antonio down.

Screaming in pain and fear, Antonio couldn't stop his momentum as his body tumbled downward, starting to pick up speed. But then his right hand shot out and grabbed Kevin's leg, the same leg that he'd hurt escaping from the barn. Kevin cried out in pain and started sliding for the stairs.

Devon grabbed him by the arm and stopped his fall.

From down the hall, they heard a giant scream of pain and knew Henry was in trouble. They could do nothing but hold tight and hope.

The cry of pain had come from Ray. His knee struck a hard athletic supporter with all of his weight behind it. His body shuddered at the pain and for a moment his grip loosened.

Taking advantage, Henry twisted free. Rolling onto his stomach, he lunged to his knees, reaching for the computer.

Ray, growling like a wounded animal, snared the back of his shirt. "Not happening," he grunted, his voice wracked with pain.

Henry's eyes went to the mouse. The cursor lay just over the send button, the mouse just a few feet away. Ray was bigger and stronger. He would have only once chance at this. Ignoring the tugs behind him, he leaned forward and dove for the mouse.

Ray, caught by surprise, gasped in pain as his sore knee buckled and he lost his grip. Henry slammed into the desk and snatched the mouse. He clicked the send button just as Ray grabbed his left arm.

"I'm going to break this in two for what you did to my knee," the enraged youth roared in his ear.

Desperate, Henry used his free arm to reach for anything nearby and grabbed a coffee mug from the desk. Turning, he brought it down on Ray's face as hard as he could.

Ray's nose crumpled and he went down in a screech of pain as the cup shattered. His screeching almost drowned out the sound of sirens.

Henry staggered back and collapsed on the floor, feeling the adrenaline leave his body. His chest heaved wildly as he crawled backward away from Ray. He didn't stop until his back hit the wall. There, he jerkily got to his feet and stumbled past the crumpled form of Ray toward the doorway.

It was over.

For a short while Kevin and Devon thought it was over for them for good. They were in major trouble. Antonio had stopped his plummet down the stairs by grabbing Kevin's leg. Devon had kept Kevin from falling too, but now the large teen had them both where he wanted them.

Kevin laid halfway down the stairs and Devon knelt just above, yanking him up by the arm. Antonio was just below Kevin, his body covered in cuts and bruises. Still, he was far from done. His mouth twisted in an unpleasant smile as he slowly rose above the boys. Standing on the stairs, his face was level with Devon's.

"Game over, boys," he hissed.

Then a loud shriek arose from above and sirens sounded from outside.

Immediately Antonio's expression turned to one of fear.

"It's the police!" he roared. "The police are coming!"

Below, Coach Jackson heard the yelling and sirens. "It's not for us!" he roared. "The police were never called!" He got painfully to his feet. Both arms were covered with welts. "Finish the job! Don't leave until it's done!"

Tiger and Shawn were trying to corner Coach Jackson in the kitchen, but they couldn't get past the baseball bat.

Antonio had lost his confidence and his focus. His attack wavered as he listened to the sirens and Coach Jackson's order. When he looked back at the boys, he was just in time to see Kevin, his wrist held tight in Devon's grip, perform a short hook slide down the stairs at his ankles.

His arms waving wildly, the large teen fell back and found nothing but air until his body crashed painfully onto the stairs. This time he couldn't stop himself. Screaming as he went, he fell head over heels and finally came to a halt at the bottom of the stairs.

Groaning, he looked up with a whimper.

Devon and Kevin stood together looking down at him. Henry, limping slightly, appeared from down the hall behind them. The three boys looked exhausted but ready for a fight.

Antonio only groaned. Ray had had no better luck.

The sirens grew closer. Suddenly bright headlights shone into the house. Among the sounds of grunts and the thumps of battle, the sounds of car doors opening and slamming could be heard clearly.

Lexi, whimpering, got to her feet from where she'd been covering her face with her arms. She peered out the open front door.

"Oh . . ." She said a bad word. "Uh, guys? There are, like, a hundred cars out there."

From where he lay at the bottom of the stairs, Antonio rolled to a seated position. Hearing Lexi's voice, his face turned from pain to panic.

"I'm out of here!" he cried. Nearly falling as he pushed himself to his feet, he ran from the stairs, his right arm hanging limply by his side. Sprinting past Lexi, he shot through the open door without looking back. The girl blinked and then got to her feet and rushed out behind him.

Ray, holding his broken nose, stumbled from the hall and quickly went down the stairs after them.

The boys made no move to stop him. Devon and Kevin looked at each other and both sat down heavily on the top stair. Henry leaned against the wall behind them. He promptly slid to a weary seated position.

"I feel like a baseball after it's been used in a home run derby," Kevin muttered.

"You look it," grunted Devon.

"You don't look much better," Kevin responded. Then he coughed. "Oh, and thanks for saving me . . . again."

Devon allowed a tired grin. "Right back at you. I didn't keep score, but I think we're even."

Kevin offered up his right hand. "We're friends then?"

Devon looked at the hand and then smiled wide. He took it and shook firmly. "Friends, man."

Henry, too sore to get up, only groaned. "You guys are such losers."

Meanwhile, seeing his forces abandoning him, Coach Jackson yelled for retreat. "Get to the cars!" he bellowed as he followed Ray. Tiger and Shawn were quick to obey, but none of them made it.

A welcoming committee stood outside waiting for them . . . and it wasn't the police.

Chapter 27

As soon as Henry sent the e-mail, over fifty cell phones received the message:

HELP UNDER ATTACK MY HOME

Melissa had already reported her suspicions about Coach Wood to the police while on her way to the hospital for a concussion, but nobody really believed her until the flood of 911 calls. Each one reported Coach Wood's house to be under attack.

Many Bears parents were already out in their cars searching for Kevin and Henry and were just around the corner from Coach Wood's house. Mrs. Baker had started phoning for help when her son hadn't returned home for supper. When she'd reached Mrs. Lee and discovered Henry and Devon were also missing, panic mode had set in. In minutes, the word was out to find the missing boys.

So when the e-mail came, most of the cars went straight to the source. They beat the police there by several minutes. When the flashing blue lights did appear, they found a traffic jam of cars parked along Coach Wood's street. The police finally arrived at the scene on foot only to discover much of their job had already been done. Dads armed with baseball bats stood in a grim circle in Coach Wood's front lawn.

Trapped within the circle, Coach Jackson, Shawn, Lexi, Antonio, Ray, Tiger, and Mark all knelt with their hands in the air. Ray's nose was crooked and blood streamed down his face; more covered his shirt. Both of Tiger's facial tattoos were hidden by massive bruising around his eyes. All the others, besides Mark and Lexi, had puffy bruised faces.

Mark had been hiding behind the chair the entire time the fight had been going on but had rushed out when he saw Coach Wood come toward him with a bat. All of them were very glad to see the police. They'd much rather go to jail than face the bat-wielding fathers.

Despite the latest developments, it was just another peaceful night in one house in Williams County. Whistling a merry tune, Preston Whiteside stepped from his bathroom wrapped in a towel. His hair hung around his head like a flushed mop. He yawned as he made his way toward his bedroom when somebody knocked on his door.

The knocking started softly but grew louder.

"Not interested!" he called, annoyed. "Come back tomorrow!"

The knocking stopped and Preston belched.

"Some stupid boy trying to score cheap stuff," he muttered. "I told them not to come to me!"

After putting on a T-shirt, he went to the front room and dropped onto the sofa to watch television. So far nobody had reported the tragic news of the fire and dead boys. That would probably come in the morning. He imagined there would be some worried parents looking, but nobody would find the tragic scene until later.

All of a sudden an engine roared to life right outside his front door.

Startled, Preston leapt to his feet and nearly dropped the towel. Tires squealed and Preston cried out in alarm, his towel falling free. Then he dove for cover as a terribly loud piercing crash blasted into his door, blowing it off its hinges.

Glass shattered and the front wall caved in as the front grill of a pickup truck burst into his living room.

"Interested yet, Preston Whiteside?" roared Mr. James from the front seat of his truck. The pickup went in reverse and backed out as quickly as it had come in. A crowd of older men and women appeared in the hole it had left.

Devon's grandma stood in front.

"Preston Whiteside," she said icily. "You have a choice. You either turn yourself in to the police right this very minute . . . or that pickup is coming back. Only next time, it won't stop."

"Wh-what is this?" Preston sputtered, peering over the couch. "Are-are you crazy?"

"You're the crazy one," Devon's grandma said, glaring at him. "You ruin souls and lives. That ends tonight. You'll never mess with another boy or girl as long as you live and unless you call the police, that won't be very long. What's it going to be?"

Behind her, a lot of the men carried rifles and shotguns.

Preston swallowed. Reaching out from behind the chair, he snatched up the towel. Then, the towel clutched around him, he stood on trembling legs. "L-let me just get my phone," he said.

"Do it," Devon's grandma said. "And don't think about dialing the wrong number. I've already done called the police. You decide if they come for an arrest. Or a body."

Stumbling into the table behind him, Preston hastily dialed the police. The phone to his ear, he didn't dare look up. After swallowing, he cleared his throat. "Ah, yes . . . my name . . . my name is Preston Whiteside. I'm a drug dealer and want to turn myself in. That's right . . ."

Within hours, almost every drug dealer associated with Preston Whiteside and Ted Jackson had been locked up or was fleeing the state.

Even before Preston's unexpected visitors, Charlie and Lou had blown the whistle and were both in the custody of their parents. They both cried with relief when they heard that Devon had survived.

Thanks to Melissa and Shorty, the fire hadn't spread from the old house. The fire department had arrived just as the structure collapsed, taking its horrid history of drugs and violence with it. Melissa had to stay the night in the hospital for observation. Shorty remained with her until visiting hours ended. Exhausted and relieved, he sat by her bed and watched her drift off to a well-deserved sleep.

Back at Mr. Wood's house, things slowly died down. He used a borrowed phone to call his wife and ask her to come back a little later . . . and if she could, stop at a store on the way. It took some explaining, but she agreed.

That done, he walked into the living room where three exhausted, battered, traumatized, and stunned boys sat staring at a baseball game on the television.

All the statements to the police had been completed and a doctor had examined and subsequently treated each boy for superficial cuts and bruises.

The doctor, a father of one of the baseball players on Mr. Wood's team and loyal customer of Soup'or Subs, had worked in Mr. Wood's living room and advised against taking them to the hospital. "All you boys need," he said cheerfully, "is good rest and some time to process what just happened." He'd spent extra time with Henry, having the boy remove his shirt and lie flat on his stomach across Coach Wood's table. The doctor then had carefully inspected the puncture wound from when he'd been drugged. After questioning Ray extensively about the injection, he was relieved to say it was just a sleeping drug. Ray had dully explained what he'd used, how much he used, and how he'd had kept the needle sterilized. After, the doctor had shook his head and said sadly, "You could have been a great doctor, son. It's too bad you threw it all away." Handcuffed and between two officers, Ray had tried to shrug off the comments, but he ended up hiding his face and blinking away tears as he was led to the line of flashing police cars. Henry, the doctor had concluded, would be fine. Still, he did take a blood sample and made sure to let Henry and his mom know to monitor the site and to call if they noticed any changes.

Henry's and Ray's moms had arrived as soon as they could after Coach Wood had called them with the news. Both moms were nearly in shock and a little shaky. They'd stood and watched the doctor at work with pale faces. Each of them knew they'd almost lost a son that day.

While the doctor conducted the checkups, Mr. Wood had said his goodbyes and gave his heartfelt thanks to the parents who'd come to the rescue and had cleaned up the mess, getting his house back in order, as much as possible. His college bat, autographed by his teammates, now had dents and nicks, and he'd lost a hardcover edition of a Jackie Robinson biography, but his home at least felt safe again. Now he just needed the boys to feel the same way.

He'd pulled both moms aside and spoke very plainly about helping their sons. Mrs. Lee reached Henry's father on her cell phone and put him on speaker to be part of the conversation. It took some doing, but Mr. Wood managed to convince the parents to let their boys stay at his place for the night, to help them mentally recover and, hopefully, find closure to the terrible ordeal. At first both moms refused and Mr. Lee wasn't sure, but the boys, who'd of course listened in on the conversation, had all voiced support to their staying with Mr. Wood. They weren't ready to leave each other's sides. Still, only after the good doctor, who'd just finished packing up his supplies, spoke up, saying it would be good for the boys and could help reduce mental trauma, did the parents relent.

Mr. Wood had then immediately called Pastor Thomas to ask for permission for Devon to also stay. This was allowed only after Mr. James had driven Devon's grandma to Coach Wood's place. She'd wanted to look at her grandson to make sure he was in one piece. She'd then promptly agreed to let him spend the night. "The boys need a man's presence after all this," she declared. "Besides, they proved they're old enough to decide for themselves." Then she'd promptly swooped in on Devon and hugged him tight before playing planting a kiss on his cheeks. "Don't you ever scare me like this again, young man, or you may not sit for a week," she'd said, whacking him in the thigh. "I mean it," she'd finished, blinking back tears. Devon had been too shocked to resist and had feared Henry and Kevin might get similar treatment. Thankfully his grandma had only given each of the sheepish boys a hug and sincere "thank you" before walking out and climbing in Mr. James' pickup. Oddly, the pickup had quite a bit of damage to its front bumper and huge dents in its hood. Now, finally, with the hour approaching midnight, the boys and the coach were alone.

"You boys probably have a lot of questions," Coach Wood said, moving to sit in the chair Mark had hidden behind. All the boys looked at him, suddenly alert. Coach Wood rubbed his forehead. "I can't promise to answer them all, but I'll start with my wife."

Coach Wood leaned forward in his seat and explained the mystery of Mrs. Wood. She'd gotten sick years before . . . really sick. Diagnosed with cancer, she started treatments that eventually ended with her living in a hospital for the better part of three years. A few years ago she'd been in remission and, wanting a fresh start, they'd moved to Williams County. Both had always wanted kids, but with her sickness, it wasn't possible. So he started coaching baseball and she spent much of her time volunteering at a children's hospital.

"That's where she was tonight," the coach said. "She reads bedtime stories on Sunday night in the cancer ward." The coach cleared his throat. "Last week we got a scare. A test came back from the doctor that suggested the cancer might be returning . . ." He shot Henry a look. "That was the night we won the semifinals. I had to rush home and I found my wife . . . not in a happy place."

Henry licked his lips and ducked his head as he remembered his phone call from the ice cream place. No wonder the coach had been angry with him.

The coach sat up, a twinkle in his eye. "Don't worry, she's okay now. In fact, she'll be getting home any minute. But first I asked her to do some shopping." He cleared his throat. "Now I'm not the best judge of sizes, but I think you'll find her with some bedclothes and toothbrushes. Oh, and I ordered some pizza."

Mrs. Wood arrived to the aroma of fresh pizza. The coach and the boys were practically inhaling two entire pies in front of a Braves game as she walked in the door.

"Save any for me?" she asked cheerfully.

Coach Wood jumped up from his seat and rushed to help with the bloated shopping bags. Wiping grease and sauce from their fingers, the boys followed. Introductions were made and Mrs. Wood beamed at her company.

She turned out to be a small woman with stretched skin and tired lines marking her face. She stood just a few inches taller than Kevin and, with thin arms and her head covered with a patterned scarf, had a frail look to her. But her delicate build didn't stop her bright emerald eyes from sparking with life. Instead of a handshake, she hugged each boy and called them "poor dears" and thanked them for keeping her idiot husband safe.

"Now it's time for showers and off to sleep," she said, gesturing toward the shopping bags. "Everyone look for a pair of shorts and underwear that fits and grab a T-shirt!" She'd bought a pile of each, all of various sizes. "All extras will be donated," she said cheerfully.

Sheepishly, the boys complied.

The Woods had two bathrooms with showers, so the boys took turns. Devon and Kevin went first while Henry helped Coach and Mrs. Wood lay out sleeping bags in the computer room. He made sure his sleeping spot was farthest from the door.

Even with the broken coffee mug long since cleaned up, every time he looked at the laptop he was reminded of Ray pulling him down and jumping on him.

Mrs. Wood chatted with him about his family and told Henry how his Coach—Dillon, she called him—always talked about his team. She never mentioned anything about the benching at the last game, but Coach Wood's ears turned a little red.

Less than an hour later, freshly washed boys tiredly climbed into their bags and turned out the lights.

Back on the couch, Coach Wood and his wife snuggled together.

Upstairs they heard Kevin laughing. The lights had gone out, but that didn't mean sleep came immediately.

"So," Mrs. Wood said dreamily, "this is what it's like to have three boys . . . You always wanted boys."

Coach Wood grunted. "And you always wanted girls."

"Boys are fine," Mrs. Wood said, smiling.

"Well, they certainly did a fine job tonight." The coach yawned. "They did everything right."

"So did you, dear. I'll go and wash up. I'll call when I'm ready."

Henry woke with a start. Shooting to a seated position, he gasped for air. It took a moment for him to realize where he was and that he was safe. He'd been dreaming of Tiger and Ray coming after him with baseball bats. In the dream, he couldn't move his feet. They were just reaching for him when he'd woken up.

Shuddering, he climbed out of his sleeping bag and padded around the snoring figures of Kevin and Devon to find the bathroom.

It was a warm night and he'd pulled his shirt off before bed. Looking in the mirror, he saw a tired boy peering back. Faint red lines crossed his stomach and chest, the remains of the jellyfish attack. It seemed like such a long time ago. Dark bruises formed between the lines. Those were more recent.

Suddenly he remembered—the championship game was later that day! Just thinking about it made him groan.

After using the bathroom and washing his hands, he stumbled back down the hall and gave a start when he saw a shadowy figure in the hall.

"Couldn't sleep either?" Devon asked in a low voice. "Come on. There's a light downstairs . . . Right now, I don't like the dark."

The boys quietly crept down the stairs and found Coach Wood still watching the game. Seeing them, he motioned for them to join him.

"Tough night," he said dryly. "You two take the couch. I'll have the chair." When they'd settled down, the coach scooted forward in his chair. "I don't suppose you boys want to talk about anything."

Devon cleared his throat. "Uh, I just want to say . . . thanks for believing me . . . Man, I really thought I was a goner."

Coach Wood frowned. "I still can't believe Ted turned out that way . . . I've known him for years, since he moved into the area." He looked at Henry. "How about you, Henry?"

Devon grinned and elbowed Henry. "This guy can't complain, man. He slept through most of the bad stuff!"

"You got that right," Kevin said, limping stiffly as he climbed down the stairs. The doctors had wrapped his shin and had said it was just a deep bruise. Otherwise he had a few minor cuts on his hands and some sore ribs. "And we had to carry his sorry rear end."

Henry responded by kicking Devon in the leg. "Hey," he protested, "who found those bats and baseballs?"

"Yeah," Kevin said, moving to the couch. "While we fought for our lives you got to do a scavenger hunt."

Coach Wood winced. He'd heard the story during the police interviews. "I'm just glad everyone made it out okay . . . even if my trophy collection didn't."

The coach and boys started talking about the fight and the talk eventually led to baseball.

"You know, Coach," Kevin said, "we're supposed to be playing you in a few hours."

"Yeah," Henry muttered. "Right after school."

Coach Wood chuckled. "Don't worry, boys. Our adventure tonight had some ripple effects. Bobby's dad called your principal and explained the situation. Tomorrow, not only you guys but the whole school can show up tardy or not at all with no penalty." He sighed. "Having a coach and respected youth pastor turn out to be a murderous drug dealer is not something to take lightly. I suspect there will be a lot of phone calls and absent students tomorrow."

"Not your fault, Coach," Kevin said. "We never knew either."

"My fault or not, it was my responsibility. I messed up." He rubbed his eyes and suddenly looked very tired. "I messed up quite a bit." Dropping his hands, he looked straight at Henry. "Henry, it was wrong of me to not let you play in that championship game. There are few championship moments in life and you deserved to be a part of that one."

"Don't worry, man," Devon said, as Henry looked down, clearly embarrassed, "Tomorrow is the championship game, remember? The Jellyfish will take the title!"

Coach Wood grinned. "Maybe. But I'm still going to do everything in my power to win. That's the way I'm programmed. I coach to win. We'll see what happens. Oh, by the way, speaking of that, I had Bobby's dad call a team meeting for the Bears tomorrow morning." He looked pointedly at Devon. "And I expect you to be there. So let's not stay up too late."

They settled in to watching the end of a Padres game until Kevin and Devon couldn't keep their eyes open. Henry had already fallen asleep, his knees tucked to his chest and head on the couch's armrest.

Kevin laughed when he saw him. "All he does is sleep!" he said, stumbling to his feet. "Should we leave him?"

"Nah, man," Devon said, yawning. "After this night, we three are sticking together."

"Don't worry, boys," Coach Wood said as he stood and stretched. "I'll carry him. He's had a long day."

"*He* had a long day?" Devon said. "What about us?"

"We all had a long day," Coach Wood amended. "Let's all get some sleep."

Kevin and Devon followed the coach up the stairs, muttering.

In the computer room, they turned the light on long enough to climb into their sleeping bags. Henry barely stirred.

"'Night, boys," the coach said as he shut off the light and closed the door.

As soon as he'd gone, Kevin hissed at Devon.

"Hey," he said. "How about we teach sleeping beauty here a lesson about falling asleep too early?"

"Huh?" groaned Devon. "What are you talking about?"

"Come see what I found on the desk!" Kevin held up a handful of colored markers.

Chapter 28

Early that morning, Hamilton Middle sent a robotic call to every teacher's and student's home. In light of recent circumstances, it said, students would allowed to come late without penalty, or to miss the entire school day ... counselors would be available for students who did show up and, rest assured, the staff of Hamilton Middle was committed to doing what was best for its students.

Henry woke to find Kevin and Devon already gone. He barely remembered being carried up to bed and crawling into his sleeping bag. Struggling to a sitting position, he frowned. His bag had been unzipped entirely on one side . . . and black marker covered his chest and stomach. He shot to his feet and raced for the bathroom.

"Ah, man!" he cried, staring in the mirror. "Those jerks!"

A black marker mustache had been added to his upper lip as well as a black circle under his right eye. Stick figures playing baseball covered his stomach and chest and an arrow pointed to his back. Turning, he saw somebody had written SLAP ME across his back. He was definitely going to slap somebody.

Thankfully the marker wasn't permanent. After another shower with furious scrubbing, he managed to remove most of the damage. The smell of frying bacon and fresh pancakes led him to the kitchen table, where Coach Wood, Kevin, and Devon were in the middle of breakfast.

"There he is!" Kevin said by way of greeting. "What took you so long?"

"Yeah, man," added Devon innocently, "we were down hours ago."

"Oh, you poor dear," Mrs. Wood said, setting a plate of steaming pancakes on the table. She stopped and put a hand to her mouth. "I didn't notice the black eye last night!"

That set Kevin and Devon laughing. Coach Wood lifted looked confused.

"What's the joke?" he finally said.

"Them," muttered Henry, taking an empty chair across from Kevin.

"Let's just say you need new markers," Kevin said.

"And more soap," Henry added.

Coach Wood and his wife exchanged glances. So, their looks seemed to say, this was what it meant to *really* have kids.

Later that morning, at just past eleven, the entire Bears team showed up and gathered in the coach's living room—filling the sofa and chair and finally the floor. Parents were asked to wait outside while Coach Wood spoke only to his players.

"I know we usually end meetings with this, but I want to start with apologies," the coach began by saying.

He stood in front of his team with his arms crossed and his feet spread. Every boy looked up at him with complete attention. By now they'd heard what had happened the night before. Kevin, Henry, and Devon sat in front and had already fielded dozens of questions before coach had asked for quiet.

"First," Coach Wood said gravely, "I'm sorry that I failed you. I let each one of you down. Coach Jackson was a mistake that I take full responsibility for. For those who don't know, he's now in jail and he's going to stay there for a long, long time. If any of you have something to say about him, or something to report about him, then come to me later, or tell your parents. You're all still boys. Nothing that you did can be judged as wrong as long as you own up to it. Got that?"

A few of the boys squirmed and looked away.

Coach Jackson took a deep breath. "Enough about him. I also apologize for putting winning above everything else. It's no secret that I like to win. But there're more important things in life than scoring runs on a baseball diamond. You boys are what matter. Your character, bravery, and the choices you make are what's really important. That being said, I want to do something I've never done before. You eighth graders know I always pick the team captains before the first game of the season. Well, for next year's team I have captains already selected. Kevin Baker and Devon Horner, get up here."

Devon looked stunned, but Henry smacked him on the leg and grinned. He'd been asked to be captain earlier but had told Coach Wood he had a better idea.

"Now Devon," Coach Wood said as the cheers and clapping died down, "doesn't even know this yet, but he'll be attending our school next fall." He looked at Devon and smiled. "Some anonymous donors have already put up money for your out-of-zone fee. Welcome to the Bears, captain."

Few students made it to Hamilton Middle that day, at least not until the end of school hours. By the time the church championship game rolled around, the parking lot was jam-packed. The community had taken a punch but wasn't about to go down. Students and parents flocked to the baseball field ready to support their coach. There were more people for this game than there had been for the school's championship game.

Melissa managed to make it to the game early after being cleared by doctors and begging her parents to take her. She'd had a bad knock but was more shaken than anything.

Now she walked slowly to where the First Presbyterian team had started to gather for warm-ups.

"Coach Wood?" she asked. "Remember me?"

Coach Wood looked up from a clipboard and stared at her for a moment before his eyes widened in recognition. "Oh, uh, the school reporter, right?"

Melissa nodded and grinned ruefully. "At least for another three weeks. I, um, have been talking to Kevin and so I know . . . well, I know a lot of what happened."

Coach Wood put his hands on his hips and looked up at the sky. "That boy always did have a big mouth," he said ruefully.

"Don't worry," Melissa said hastily. "I don't plan to print it in our paper. I just wanted to say . . . I'm sorry. I, um, sort of suspected *you* were behind the drugs."

Coach Wood looked at her in surprise. "Well," he said slowly, "You weren't far off in the end . . . It *was* a baseball coach." He sighed heavily. "I guess I should have given you the interview like you'd asked." He scratched his jaw. "Do you have time for one now?"

Grinning, Melissa pulled out a pad and pen from her back pocket. "Funny you should ask . . ."

Principal Warner also made an appearance before the game. Wearing a smile that looked plastered on, she greeted parents as they arrived and cheered students she recognized, reminding them of the standardized tests starting the next day.

Few kids cheered her back. As warm-ups began, she made it a point to go to the visitor dugout and find Mr. James.

"Hi!" she greeted him brightly. "You're the coach of Resurrection Baptist, right?"

Mr. James turned from watching the field and nodded slowly. "Yep. I'm the coach of the Jellyfish."

"Oh, um, the what?" the principal asked. "Jellyfish . . . is that a Baptist term?"

"No . . ." Mr. James said. "It's a stupid one." Then he grinned. "What can I do for you?"

He stood in the dugout with her on the other side of the fence.

"I just wanted to say," Mrs. Warner said with practiced sincerity, "I admire your team very much. I'm proud to have members of my students mixed in with your team. Seeing the boys together like that, you know your black boys with my . . . well, it's seeing real progress in action."

Mr. James grunted and slowly crossed his arms. His smile faded. "With all due respect," he said, "progress is when boys can play a game together without people commenting on something as shallow as skin color."

He turned back to the field. Mrs. Warner blinked several times before hurrying off. She headed back to the school. For her, it had been a long day. She just wanted it to end.

Henry, waiting his turn for batting practice, sat on his usual spot of the upturned bucket just outside the dugout. He'd heard every word. "Um, Coach," he said. "Did you know that was my principal?"

Mr. James moved to stand beside him. "Sorry, kid," he said. "You probably already know, but grown-ups don't always turn out for the best."

To help illustrate Mr. James' point, not all the parents turned out to support Hamilton Middle and its baseball coach. A few parents arrived with signs saying Coach Wood needed to be fired.

These didn't stick around for long. A pair of county sheriffs patrolled the grounds and kindly asked the two men and one woman to leave. That didn't stop a rather large contingent of support for the Baptist team. It didn't hurt that Preston Thomas arrived in an old short church bus with most of the Jellyfish parents.

"Man, look at them all," Devon said as he sat next to Kevin on the bench. "I never played in front of so many people before."

"I would give you advice on how to handle it," Kevin said, flicking back his curly hair, "but I don't want you to blow up on me."

Devon snorted in reply. Most of the Jellyfish players looked just as shaken as Devon as they trooped into the dugout. They took seats on the bench, their shoulders hunched as the crowd continued to build around them.

Both stands were already packed and portable chairs had been set up all along the left and right field fences. More chairs were being set up along the outfield fence. It seemed as if the whole county was in attendance.

"If we mess up," muttered Larry, "it'll probably be on YouTube before nightfall."

Henry spit out sunflower shells and looked at Kevin. "What do you think Coach Wood would do?" he asked.

Kevin grinned. "Embrace the situation and use it to distract us." He hopped to his feet, favoring his injured leg. "That reminds me! We need to plan for all his tactics. I know all about them, trust me."

The Jellyfish players stared up at him silently. Then Devon rose to his feet. "I agree," he said, slapping Kevin on the back. "This guy has a big mouth, so maybe we should listen once and a while."

"Yeah, thanks," Kevin said dryly. "Henry, you too. We definitely have to make a plan for Coach's base running."

"Hold on," Jack said, standing. "I agree to listen, but I'm not going to change how I play. Not for you and not for all these people watching. We play best when we're loose, right?"

"Amen to that, brother," Larry said. "Only it's hard to be loose when half the county is watching you and taking cell phone videos."

"It's like we're stars," Jesse added.

"Wait, now," Tashaun said from the end of the bench. "If these people came for a show, then we should put on a show!"

DeAndre nodded. "Yeah," he said. "My brother is here and he hasn't ever seen me play before. Neither have my parents."

Kevin cleared his throat. "So, uh, what do you guys suggest?"

Tashaun grinned. "You tell us your plan . . . and we'll tell you ours."

Chapter 29

Mr. James and Pastor Lewis didn't want to admit it, but they also suffered from nerves. As the Jellyfish had their meeting, their coaches were busy with the umpire and Coach Wood trying to piece together their lineup. They'd forgotten to bring one and Mr. James was hastily scribbling down the batting order on the back of an old envelope the pastor had found in his pocket.

After Devon's unsportsmanlike display during the last game, he'd originally been slated for the bench. However, Kevin, hobbled by his bad shin, had offered to substitute for him—he'd sit out and let Devon take his place. Besides, he'd assured the Jellyfish coaches, after the previous night, Devon was a changed kid. The coaches had agreed . . . but this meant their old lineup needed to be scrapped.

Finally, with things sorted, the game got underway.

Chris started on the mound for First Presbyterian, backed by Bobby at first. All during warm-ups they'd been strangely quiet. Bobby had even wished Kevin and Henry good luck before taking the field.

"Okay, let's go out there!" Coach Wood called from the dugout. He crouched low and started delivering signs to the catcher. True to his word, he was all business and, aside from nods to his three houseguests from the night before, he'd barely acknowledged the Jellyfish players.

Devon entered the batter's box with a mean look in his eye. After two hard practice swings, he dug in and waited.

For the first pitch, Coach Wood signaled for a changeup. Devon swung way too early—a vicious swipe that brought him to his knees.

The First Presbyterian fans cheered.

"Nice fan, kid!" yelled a student in the stands.

Coach Wood yelled for his fielders to take several steps back. He'd seen batting practice and knew Devon's power.

The next pitch was another off-speed pitch off the plate. Devon went for it anyway, only instead of swinging, he opted for a bunt. Squaring the bat, he sent a slow dribbler toward third and raced for first.

With the infield playing deep, only the catcher had a play, but he'd been caught off guard. By the time he reached the ball, it was too late. The Jellyfish had the first hit of the game.

This time it was the Resurrection Baptist fans that made noise. Their cheers increased when, on the next pitch, Devon took off for second and slid safely under the tag.

"Come on!" Coach Wood shouted at Chris on the mound. "You have to watch the runner!"

"He's too fast to watch, Coach!" yelled Devon's Aunt Jenny.

Chris kicked the mound and stared at Devon.

Returning the stare, Devon stepped off the bag and walked toward third. When Chris reacted by cocking his arm, Devon simply hopped back to the bag.

"Don't dance with him, just pitch!" hollered Coach Wood. "He's not going to take third!"

Devon went for third on the next pitch.

Jack hit a grounder foul and Devon had to return to second.

Once again, Chris kept staring at the runner.

From first, Bobby tried to yell encouragement, but it sounded half-hearted.

Devon ran on the next pitch too and the ball bounced in the dirt. Having just managed to block the ball, the catcher didn't even bother to make a throw. Devon slid easily into third for his second stolen base.

Chris exhaled and pounded his glove.

"Don't worry, he won't take home!" yelled somebody from the Jellyfish side. "Or will he?"

The other fans laughed.

Devon did feint for home, but retreated as Chris delivered a ball low.

Two pitches later, Jack took first on a walk.

"Time, Blue!" Coach Wood called, trotting to the mound. Clearly frustrated, his voice carried across the field. "What's going on out there, Chris?" he asked.

Bobby and the other infielders had joined the conference and looked just as flustered. The ball hadn't left the infield and there was no score, but it felt as if Resurrection Baptist had the game under control and was playing with them.

"I don't know, Coach," Chris said, wiping sweat from his upper lip. "They're running on every pitch!"

"What they're doing is causing distractions," Coach Wood said. He looked over at Devon. Devon grinned back. "And

419

it's working. Just worry about the batter and getting some outs. If they run, let Kyle take care of them." He patted the catcher's arm.

Henry batted next.

Chris groaned. He knew Henry could hit. Shaking his head, he circled the mound, trying to clear his mind.

"Let's go!" called the umpire. "Play ball!"

Taking a breath, Chris readied himself to pitch. Even before he began his throwing motion, Jack went for second.

"He's running!" Bobby yelled.

Chris turned and pump-faked to second before whirling to third. Devon danced toward home and then back to third. Jack slid safely into second. Chris yelled in frustration.

"That's it!" Kevin yelled from the dugout. "Here we go!"

"Let's limit the damage!" Coach Wood yelled out. "We still got this!"

Instead, Chris caused more damage by plunking Henry on the arm. Immediately Henry dropped to his knees in pain. Chris ran in to apologize.

"Sorry, man," he muttered to Henry as he rubbed his arm. "It's just you guys are driving me crazy!"

Wincing, Henry grinned at him and they exchanged fist bumps. "It's fine. We learned from the best," he said.

Pastor Thomas greeted Henry at first and checked his arm to make sure it was nothing more than a bruise. Then the pastor bent down next to Henry.

"I confess, Henry," he said, "but I don't know what you boys are doing. I didn't tell either of our boys to run. Devon and Jack, they took off on their own."

Henry shrugged, pulled off his batting gloves, and stuffed them in his back pockets. "Don't worry," he said. "We're just playing flash-ball."

The pastor stood, looking perplexed. "Then why am I worried?" he asked.

Playing first, Bobby didn't make eye contact with Henry. He edged closer to second. At least with a runner on second, Henry couldn't attempt a steal.

The bases were loaded for Rodney, Kevin's replacement. Rodney didn't look comfortable in the moment. He still preferred wrestling to baseball. He went down swinging on four pitches.

Jesse followed with a shallow pop-up to third. Suddenly there were two outs and the First Presbyterian fans were on their feet. They might just get out of the jam without allowing a run.

DeAndre strolled into the box and took a deep breath.

"Bring them home!" Kevin shouted.

He nearly came through. After a 1–1 count, he slapped a sharp liner into center. It looked like a clear hit, maybe more, but suddenly the center fielder charged forward and dove face-first, glove extended. Somehow he managed to come up with the ball.

With their fans going crazy, First Presbyterian ran off the field. They started their at bat with more relief than confidence.

As the game progressed, the confidence dwindled even further.

It started with the infield warm-ups. As DeAndre loosened on the mound, Larry threw no look grounders to the bases.

Devon playing third, Jack at shortstop, and Jesse covering second put on a show with fancy glove work and athletic throws. Each player tried to outdo the others. Jack turned his back to snatch up a slick backhand. Devon bare-handed a ball and threw it to Larry while in mid-conversation with Jack. And Jesse upped that by squatting low and bare-handing a hard roller behind his back.

On the mound, DeAndre didn't have the same arm or location as Jack, but he had his defense behind him.

After giving up a clean single to the leadoff batter, he got Bobby to ground to short. Jack met the ball smoothly and tossed it quickly to second. Jesse took it with his bare hand, stepped on the bag, and fired it to first to complete the double play. Chris, batting third, then flied out to Henry in center. Three batters and three outs. The First Presbyterian players returned to the field with their heads down.

"Come on, boys!" Coach Wood yelled as he trotted in from his third base coach position. "Look alive! We still got this!"

"Got what?" shouted Devon's aunt. "A game on your hands? Get ready for more!"

The next inning brought more of the same—flashy play, good defense, but no runs. Caleb reached first on a walk and promptly attempted to steal second with the next pitch. This time First Presbyterian was ready. Kyle, the catcher, jumped out of his stance and delivered a strong throw that had Caleb out by a foot.

Tashaun followed with a bunt that Chris misplayed. He ended up safe on first with no throw. Chris settled and got Larry on strikes. This brought the top of the order back up.

Devon faked another bunt, but this time he swung at the last possible second. He made contact, driving the ball straight into the dirt in front of home plate, sending it bouncing high in the air. It ended up over the third baseman's head and rolled into the outfield. Tashaun flew around second and went for third.

"No!" Mr. James yelled, waving his arms. "Go back!"

It was too late. The Jellyfish catcher, not the fastest runner, stumbled to a stop halfway between the bases. By this time the left fielder had gotten to the ball and had thrown it in to third. Tashaun was caught in a pickle. After a brief rundown, he was tagged out.

"Sorry," Tashaun muttered as he jogged in.

Devon, following him to the dugout, smacked him on the back of the pants with the bat he'd retrieved.

"Ah, don't worry about it, man," he said. "I get hits ruined all the time by slow catchers."

First Presbyterian had a promising start to the second inning. The first batter drew a walk and the next laid down a perfectly placed bunt between the pitcher's mound and first. But DeAndre showed off his own slick fielding. Launching himself from the mound, he pounced on the ball while twisting his body in midair. He landed facing second with the ball in his throwing hand. Shooting to a knee, he fired a strike at Jesse, who covered second. The lead runner was out by inches.

After that, the slick fielding threatened to backfire. An error by Jesse let the next batter reach first and the lead runner make it to third. Suddenly, with only one out, First Presbyterian had runners on the corners ... Coach Wood's favorite situation.

Coaching at third, Coach Wood clapped his hands. "Here it is, now!" For a while he'd looked nervous, but now he was back to full confidence.

From the dugout, just a few yards from Coach Wood, Kevin exchanged glances with Devon at third. Both boys grinned. They both knew what was coming.

Sure enough, on the next pitch, taken for a strike, the runner on first bolted for second. The runner on third watched carefully while taking a big lead toward home.

"Get ready," Coach Wood said to him.

Tashaun flung off his mask and used his whole body to throw toward second.

"Now!" cried Coach Wood. "Run!" Then he cried out in alarm. "No! Wait!"

Tashaun had his eyes and body totally focused on second, but he'd tricked everyone. He'd actually thrown the ball back to the pitcher. The ball snapped in DeAndre's glove. He calmly tossed the ball back to Tashaun. The runner, caught between third and home, just stood there until he was tagged out.

Shaking his head, Coach Wood put a hand on his hip and turned to Kevin, who stood in the opposing team's dugout behind him. "If you ever want to be the new assistant coach, call me," he said.

Kevin hid a smile as he pretended to fiddle with his glove. He made no comment

The Jellyfish broke through the next inning. Jack led off with a sharply hit liner down the third baseline. He stood on second wiping away dirt when Henry came up to bat.

"Watch the hit and run!" Coach Wood called from the dugout to his team. "Let's get this guy!" Then to Henry, who was walking to the plate, he murmured, "Good to see your black eye has faded."

Henry grinned at him and took his warm-up swings.

"This next pitch is going to be a curve," Coach Wood told him.

It was a fastball and Henry was ready for it. He made good contact and sent a scorching grounder between first and second. Jack, ignoring Mr. James' signal to hold up, tore around third and slid into home. Chris, seeing Henry's wide turn, had cut off the throw, but Henry scampered back to first before Chris could make a throw.

The Jellyfish crowd exploded and even the First Presbyterian fans gave a nice ovation. Most knew Henry from school and were aware of his role in taking down the drug dealers.

The First Presbyterian fans stopped their clapping soon after. The game was supposed to be an easy win for them. So far, it had proved to be more trial and tribulation.

Rodney, after multiple fouls, managed a slow roller to third. He was out at first but was able to advance Henry to second. Jesse followed with a single into shallow left, moving Henry to third.

Coach Wood groaned loudly when the ball went back to the pitcher. Then he got to his feet and yelled to the infield. "Get ready for him!" he shouted. "We know what's coming!"

Mr. James scratched his head. "How does he know?" he muttered. "I certainly don't!" He clapped Henry on both shoulders. "I guess you know what you're doing, kid," he growled, "but an insurance run would be mighty good."

Henry nodded. As the pitcher checked for a sign, he eased off the base and took three steps toward home. Spreading his legs wide, he bent low and watched the pitcher intently.

Chris looked over at him briefly and then went into his windup. Immediately Henry feinted for home.

It was a pitchout. Kyle, the catcher, jumped to his feet as he received the pitch at chest height. Pivoting, he fired to third, catching Henry between the bases.

Instead of panicking, Henry juked to third and then charged for home. As he did so, he watched the catcher and saw where he was positioned. Staying in the baseline, he made sure to run right at Kyle, cutting off the throwing angle from third.

Sure enough, the throw back home was high and to Henry's left. As he saw Kyle reach for it, he flung himself face-first to the right and managed to put a hand over the plate as he slid past. The tag whapped him in the thigh soon after.

"Safe!" cried the umpire.

Hopping to his feet, Henry trotted back to the dugout, heading straight for the bucket. He kept his cool and calm exterior, but inside he was jumping for joy. Stealing home was a rare feat and the feeling never got old. The Jellyfish crowd roared while the First Presbyterian fans groaned. Henry's teammates slapped his helmet and offered high fives. Then he sat down ... right on the cup of cold water Kevin had slipped under him.

Yelping, Henry leapt to his feet in a startled panic. Water soaked through to the skin and dripped down his legs.

Jack and Larry howled.

"Got you again!" Kevin cried, doubling over with laughter.

Shocked, Henry stood frozen for a long moment.

Devon shook his head. "What, man?" he asked. "Too excited? Couldn't hold your water?" Then he added to the insult by whacking the soaked area with his glove. "Looks like you need some toilet paper, man."

Henry stood frozen for another several seconds. The dirt from his sliding mixing with the water created a terrible image against his gray pants.

"Man," said Larry, "if that's what the bucket is for, you should turn it over."

"I hate you all," Henry finally muttered. Huffing, he walked stiffly to the bench and sat down.

Soon after, Rodney poured a cup of water down the back of Jack's pants.

By the time First Presbyterian got up to bat, three Jellyfish players had soaked pants. Henry had gotten revenge on Devon.

Mr. James was not amused as he saw the soaking bench and the wet players. He hollered that the next boy to waste water could waste away on the bench.

"I'm guess I'm free then," Kevin joked. He sat next to Rodney, who'd given way to Lucas to play right.

Rodney grunted. "You're the one who started it."

Pastor Thomas took a different approach. "If it were holy water," he mused, "we could get a whole lot of baptisms and converts this way."

Melissa watched it all happen from the stands in disbelief. Boys, she decided, were impossible to understand. She sat in the bottom row, just in front of Mrs. Lee and Anabelle.

"Look at Henry's pants," Anabelle said with a giggle.

Mrs. Lee groaned. "I'm trying hard not to . . ." She pretended to cover her eyes.

Fans around them chuckled, prompting Mrs. Lee to groan.

Looking back at them, Melissa grinned. "Don't worry, he's still cute," she said.

"It's a good thing he is," Mrs. Lee said ruefully. "Otherwise I'd leave him here. I just hope I can get the stains out. I know I'll never get the memory out."

She raised her voice and called sharply to a boy leaning against the fence in front of Melissa. "Michael, you get back here! I don't want you getting involved."

Michael turned and grinned. "Can I have your phone then? I want to take pictures!"

"Sure," Mrs. Lee said. "Climb up here and get it. I know your father would just love to see what he's missing. But watch where you step! I don't know why you insisted on wearing your baseball cleats."

"I told you," Michael said, sounding exasperated. "Henry said they worked as some of the best weapons around. I have them just in case somebody tries to attack us during the game."

430

Mrs. Lee rolled her eyes and leaned closer to Melissa. "You'll have to excuse my sons . . . both of them. They have this horrible game called 'What Would You Do' and I'm afraid it actually worked out last night."

Melissa's ears perked up. "Oh?"

As Michael took the phone and proudly explained how the game worked, Melissa listened attentively. She couldn't wait to get started on writing her story. It would have to be heavily edited before it was fit to print in the school paper, though.

Chapter 30

First Presbyterian couldn't get much of anything started on offense. But their fans did get a kick out of seeing Henry trot to the outfield in brown-spattered pants. Jack and Devon had managed to jump up in time to avoid a thorough soaking, but that didn't prevent the catcalls and whistles.

"What, you guys need a potty break?" Coach Wood asked Devon as he took his position at third base.

Devon couldn't hide a grin. "Not every day we beat a coach as good as you," he said. "We got excited."

"Don't get your hopes hope just yet," Coach said. "The game isn't over, you know."

Three outs later, Coach Wood shook his head. The score remained 2–0 in favor of the Jellyfish.

By the last inning, the bottom of the seventh, the score was 3–1. First Presbyterian had finally broken through after a long double by Bobby and an RBI single from Chris. Now, with no outs, in the last half inning of the game, they had the tying run at the plate.

It had been a tight game, but Resurrection Baptist had been in control almost the entire time. Now, for the first time since the first inning, it looked as if First Presbyterian had life. They were looking for a walk-off win.

Devon replaced DeAndre on the mound to start the inning, but he was already starting to labor. The past day's events had finally caught up with him. His body ached and his mind just wanted to relax.

Blinking, he got the sign from Tashaun and stood to face the batter. Taking a deep breath, he flung a fastball that went wide. Tashaun lunged for the ball but missed. The ball rolled to the backstop and Chris took second base.

The First Presbyterian players had started to make some noise in the dugout. But when they started to jeer the bad pitching, Coach Wood ran from third and made a slashing movement. "Cut it!" he said. "Cheer your team and that's it!"

The wild pitch became moot when three pitches later, Devon issued a walk.

"Time!" Mr. James called.

Devon wiped sweat from his brow as he waited for Tashaun and Mr. James to reach him.

"Sorry," he mumbled when Mr. James stepped on the mound. He gave up the ball and hung his head.

"For what?" Mr. James demanded. "For walking away from your team yesterday? Yeah, I can see you apologizing for that. But you then saved your teammate's life. That's something you never apologize for. No matter what happens on this field, at the end of the day, you still saved Henry and brought down a drug dealer."

The boys from the infield nodded and Jack smacked Devon on the back. "We got you, man," he said.

Mr. James pressed the ball back into Devon's hand. "Do you know how many other kids you saved by taking down that drug dealer?" he asked. "You don't have to apologize for anything for a long, long time, son. The only people who really need to apologize are your mother and father for walking out on you. But I promise you this: no matter what, I'm not walking out on you. And neither is this team. Got it?"

Jack and Tashaun smacked their gloves in support.

Devon licked his lips and nodded. "I got it."

Mr. James squeezed him on the shoulder. "Good. Throw what you have left and see what happens. Win or lose, we're still winners here."

Tashaun nodded at Devon. "I'll just hold my glove out. Try to hit it."

Devon grunted. "Sure, man." He didn't sound too confident.

"Okay, play ball!" called the umpire.

Digging deep, Devon put all he had into the next pitch. It flew from his hand and went straight down the middle toward Tashaun's glove. It never made it.

The batter absolutely crushed it. With a loud, solid metallic boom, the ball flew from the bat. It soared up and flew toward the fence in deep center.

"Go, go!" screamed Coach Wood, urging the runners on.

Devon leaned on his knees and dropped his head. Then he lifted it when he heard Jack gasp.

Henry, a streak of purple, charged after the ball. Still yards away as the ball descended, he flung out his glove. His eyes never left the ball as he laid out in a full dive. Player and ball crashed into grass.

The screaming crowd paused as Henry slid to a stop. Then he rolled to his knees, his glove extended displaying the secure ball. The crowd erupted as Henry hopped to his feet and hurried a throw to second.

By this time, both runners had rounded third. They stopped in confusion as their fans yelled for them to go back. They had no chance.

Devon watched in amazement as Jesse tagged second base and threw to first. It ended in a triple play.

Henry had to duck for cover as he trotted in from the outfield. The entire team ran at him and started to dog-pile. Playing in a championship was definitely better than winning a championship while on the bench. Even better? Coming up with the winning play of a championship.

When the bodies finally untangled and the teams started to line up for handshakes, Coach Wood pulled Henry to the side.

He playfully grabbed the boy's head and shook. "Look at you," he growled. "You look like a mess. Like somebody tossed you in a blender and turned it off too early. Nice catch, though."

Henry ducked and hid a grin. Dark green grass stains marred the front of his pants while dirty brown stained the back. His purple shirt, smeared with grass, looked like it had polka dots on it.

"Thanks, Coach," he muttered.

"Don't thank me," Coach Wood said, smacking his shoulder. "I yelled to the ump that you trapped it. Who taught you to dive like that, anyhow?"

"That would be me, Coach!" Devon said, slipping from the line of players to join them. He smacked the brown-stained back of Henry's pants with his glove. "That's how you do it, man! Diving catch to win the game!"

Coach Wood grinned as he shook his head, watching them. "Maybe I'm not the greatest coach after all. I still have things to learn."

After the handshakes, Bobby asked to speak privately to Kevin, Devon, and Henry.

"I need to talk to you guys," he said, sounding miserable. "It's important."

Feigning calls of nature, the four boys met in front of the school, away from the streams of fans heading to their cars.

"What is it?" Kevin asked.

Bobby sighed and dug into his hip pocket. He pulled out a rolled crumpled paper. "It's a joint," he said miserably. "From Coach Jackson." He ducked his head, ashamed. "He gave it to me after we won the championship game last week . . . said I was old enough now." He sighed miserably. "I was saving it for today . . . after we won. Man, I'm really sorry."

"But you didn't win," Devon said, looking confused.

Bobby nodded. A tear trickled from the corner of his left eye. "I know that. I, I was an idiot, okay? I went along with Coach Jackson a lot. He didn't like you, Henry. He thought you were always a goody-goody." He wiped away the tear. "I don't know who else he gave this stuff to, but I know Wayne used to brag about working for him."

Kevin grunted. "Wayne Perkins is an idiot." Then he snorted. "Still, he's the reason why I'm here. If it wasn't for him and his brother, I wouldn't have gotten my community service and I never would've joined this team."

Bobby nodded glumly. "I know, but I'm an idiot too. I thought Coach Jackson was good." He held out the crumpled joint and took a deep breath. "Here, take it."

Henry stared at in fascination. He'd never seen drugs on the street before.

Devon eyed it dubiously. "Wait . . . you want *us* to smoke it instead?"

Bobby jerked as if slapped. "No way! I just wanted to say, you know, that I'm sorry. I heard what happened last night . . ."

Devon snorted. "I was kidding, man. I wouldn't touch that thing if you paid me."

Bobby laughed sourly. "Yeah, it's hard to believe people pay money for this, right?"

"Yeah," snorted Devon. "And then stick it in their mouths and light it on fire."

"So, um, you want us to turn you over to the police?" Kevin asked.

Bobby sobered. "I don't know . . . I guess I'd deserve it if you did."

Devon frowned. "Hold on. You never smoked it, right? So, really, you haven't done anything wrong."

"Take it to Coach Wood," said Kevin. "We'll go with you and he can turn it over to the police."

Bobby sighed. "Yeah . . . thanks. I was just hoping my parents never found out."

Kevin grimaced. "Well, it's better they find out from you than from a police officer knocking on your door."

Sobered, the boys returned to the field together.

Preston Whiteside and Ted Jackson were old college roommates. After school, they'd gone their separate ways, but they had reconnected when Ted was in a bad spot. He'd lost his job and was falling into debt. In the meantime, Preston Whiteside was a prosperous businessman in search of a partner to expand his business. Ted Jackson jumped at the opportunity.

He'd always been active as a wrestling and baseball coach and had started working part time at his church. Using his connections, he rose to assistant youth pastor and soon took over the drug operation in Williams County. Preston Whiteside smuggled in the drugs while Ted Jackson directed the dealing.

It was a perfect setup. By getting to know the kids, Ted was able to handpick a select group to work under him and set up a slick operation. He and his dealers preyed on kids by being nice to them for a period of time. After a while, a kid would be singled out and offered something small, like a joint. "It's legal almost all over the country and helps relax me," Ted would have his dealers say. "You can try it, if you'd like." If the kid refused, the dealer would laugh and say he was only kidding. But if the kid took it, slowly, over time, other drugs were offered until he had a new client.

Ted rarely dealt the drugs himself but was known to be close with a select few of the Bears players. When the police searched Ted Jackson's home, they found a fortune's worth of various drugs hidden in his attic. Almost overnight, Wayne Perkins stopped hanging with the Bears players.

In the meantime, Lexi, Mark, and Shawn cooperated fully with the police and admitted to attacking Henry and throwing the stone at Melissa's window. Not even their wealthy parents could save them from a long list of charges. Tiger, Ray, and,

Antonio had all committed many previous crimes and faced serious charges. Preston Whiteside refused to speak and hired three lawyers for his defense. They had their work cut out for them.

The First Presbyterian team had scheduled a victory pool party for the following Friday. Under the circumstances, they extended an open invitation to the entire Resurrection Baptist team, as well as a select few individuals.

After a week of standardized testing, the players on both teams were ready for a party.

Melissa knocked on Shorty's door early Friday evening. The redhead had avoided her all week and never returned any of her calls.

Now he opened the door with a sigh. Sticking his head out, he asked, "What do you want?"

Melissa bit her lip. "Well, you know about the pool party tonight? Coach Wood gave me two press passes. Care to come?" She dangled up two lanyards with cards.

Shorty didn't meet her eyes. He shook his head. "No thanks. I think I had enough of working with you. Sorry."

Melissa frowned. "Who said anything about work?" She tossed the passes over her head and stepped in closer. "I'm asking you on a date." Then she leaned in and kissed the stunned boy. Stepping back, she smiled. "I haven't told you yet, but I thought you were pretty great when you came for me last Sunday."

Shorty gulped and nearly fell out the door. "You mean when you ruined my bike?" he asked, his voice cracking.

"Sorry about that. I brought mine and I thought you could ride the handlebars. The pool is only two blocks away. So is that a yes?"

Shorty looked at her. She wore a loose T-shirt and shorts over a bright red swimsuit.

"Let me, ah," he said, "let me go get changed. I'll be down in two minutes."

Melissa grinned as she waited. Earlier that week she'd turned in her article on baseball . . . a corny two-page write-up on how hard the team worked together to win the school championship . . . The real story she kept for herself. One day she planned to write a book about it . . .

Twenty minutes later, Shorty reappeared, dressed in tan slacks and a bright green polo shirt.

"Actually," he said, licking his lips nervously, "I think I had enough of baseball players for a while. I was thinking a movie would be nice."

Melissa bit her lip to keep from laughing. "Fine," she said. "But then let *me* get changed. Pick me up . . . in an hour."

"I will . . . but first . . . my name is Scotty."

Chapter 31

In the beginning, the pool party didn't look like such a good idea. First Presbyterian players congregated on one side, while the Resurrection Baptist players stayed on the other. Music blared from a radio by the pool house, but few kids were actually in the water. Kevin and Devon stood by the diving boards, not liking what they saw.

"How do we get people in the water actually talking to each other?" Kevin wondered aloud.

Devon shrugged.

Henry was no help. He sat on a pool chair making gaga eyes with Gabby. She'd arrived with her brother and immediately had Henry smitten. Some other girls from Hamilton Middle and Resurrection Baptist were coming, but not for another hour or so. Coach Wood and Mr. James wanted to give the boys a chance to bond first. They and the other adults were at the picnic area just outside the pool lighting grills and preparing hamburgers and hot dogs.

So far their experiment was a failure. The only people who seemed to be enjoying themselves, besides Henry and Gabby, were Devon's cousins. They splashed around in the baby end, keeping the lifeguards busy as they re-created the jellyfish dance.

"Toss them in, I guess," Devon answered after a moment.

Kevin and Devon looked at each other. Both boys got the same idea at the same time.

Micah grabbed Henry's arm and kept trying to pull him to the water. "Show us what you did to the jellyfish!" he urged. "We're jellyfish brothers! Remember?"

Henry sat in the middle of his chair with his knees to his chest facing Gabby, who sat cross-legged in the next chair. He looked embarrassed as he shrugged the younger boy off.

"Wait a sec, okay?"

Gabby laughed. "What is this about a jellyfish? I hear about it all the time."

Micah stopped pulling and turned to Gabby. "It stung me, but then Henry and the guys jumped on it. It got Henry in the—"

"Okay, that's enough," Henry said, hastily putting his hand over the boy's mouth. "Go find your cousin and give him some jellyfish stings with your bat."

Huffing in frustration, the little boy stomped off, dragging his bat behind him.

Gabby watched him go and sighed. "He's so cute."

"Not when you feel his bat," Henry told her. "I wonder where Devon is?" He'd just started to sit up when he found him . . . or rather, Kevin and Devon found Henry.

"Victory celebration time!" Kevin crowed.

He and Devon swooped behind Henry and grabbed him by the arms and legs, hoisting him up before he could protest. In seconds Henry found himself sitting on the shoulders of this two friends.

"Just like old times," Kevin grunted.

"Hey! Put me down!" Henry protested from his perch. He sounded more annoyed than worried.

"That's kind of the point," Devon told him. "Just be patient."

"No!" shouted Henry as he realized where this would end. "Help!"

Kevin and Devon each put a hand on the back of Henry's suit while gripping one of Henry's legs with their other arm. With a running start, they launched him up and into the pool.

Henry went headfirst into the water, his arms and legs flailing.

"That's how you dive!" Devon cried as Henry's screams were cut off by the terrific splash.

The shrill whistle from both lifeguards followed and they received loud admonishment for the roughhousing.

"Do that again and you're out of this pool!" the head guard yelled from his elevated chair. "Now help him out!"

Henry came up sputtering. After coughing up water, he paddled to the edge where Devon and Kevin waited. Both offered their hands.

"You guys are both jerks," he wheezed.

"Sorry, man," Devon said.

"Yeah," Kevin added with false sincerity. "We hoped it would bring more people in."

Henry glared as he offered up a hand. From behind Devon, he saw Micah and the two made eye contact. Jellyfish brothers stuck together.

Devon stood to grip Henry's hand and Kevin grabbed the other.

"Don't be sorry," Henry told them. "It actually worked." With that, he put both his feet on the side of the pool and kicked backward as hard as he could. Micah chose the same moment to smack the back of Devon's suit with the bat.

Two more screams ended in splashes as Kevin and Devon both went into the pool headfirst.

The head lifeguard put the whistle to his lips but then dropped it. The three boys were laughing and suddenly the other boys from their respective sides were also jumping in. Finally the pool party had started.

The group of girls arrived to a raucous game of pool baseball. Using Micah's bat and a cloth ball, the boys had set up a rough field in the shallow end using kickboards for floating bases. In the deep end, Coach Wood and the other adults were conducting swim tests and offering lessons. He'd already announced that free lessons for kids from both churches would be available in the summer . . . courtesy of an anonymous donor, of course.

Henry sighed as he collapsed back in his beach chair, a towel draped over his stomach. Gabby had left for the evening with Eric but had promised to visit Soup'or Subs the next day.

Exhausted, he rolled to his side and began to nod off. It had been a strange, scary, exhilarating, and ultimately rewarding two weeks.

He held onto two things: ultimately he'd gotten to play in a championship game and he had made new friends doing it. And the best part was that summer hadn't even started.

Tomorrow his dad would be flying in for Memorial Day weekend and practice for his travel baseball team would start. A few weeks after that would be county all-stars and summer tournaments. Then in August his thirteenth birthday would come. His best times were still ahead of him.

Yawning, he looked across the pool at Devon, who sat chatting with a girl from Hamilton. He wondered if Devon would be on the all-stars . . . but then saw Coach Wood helping a kid do the back float and he knew he would be. After all, Coach Wood helped select the all-stars. And he wanted to win.

As his eyes slid shut, Henry never saw Kevin creeping up behind him with the cup of water.

Acknowledgments

Writing is hard work, but when it comes to publishing it can often be the easiest part. Fortunately I have enough friends and helpers to make it happen. Huge and sincere thanks go to Kevin Anderson and his team of terrific editors, especially to Erin. Having their patience, insight, and skillful eyes is like having a whole team of all-stars behind me. As always, any errors found can be charged to me.

Special thanks go to Renée not only for putting up with me, but putting up with me while designing my cover . . . and for even listening to my demands (uh, I mean suggestions). Without your support I would still be in dreamland (now are you ready for my next suggestion . . . uh, I mean demand?).

And of course I cannot forget my number one test reader, my dad. I know you'd rather be reading science fiction, so thank you (and I owe you). A big, big thank you goes to both my parents, for letting me dream, for letting me go, for and letting me swing for the fences. One day I'll make it out there!

About the Author

Gregory Saur is the author of several novels for young readers including *Soccer Star* and *Royal Pains and Angels in the Outhouse*. His novel *The Pond Scum Gang* was shortlisted for the Gertrude Warner Book Award for Middle Grade Readers in 2017. A native of Virginia, he has played in multiple championship games and won many, all on diving catches, and all in his imagination. He plans to continue his remarkable baseball career . . . as a writer.

CPSIA information can be obtained
at www.ICGtesting.com
Printed in the USA
LVHW04*0218290618
582267LV00006B/16/P